MIDNIGHT ENCOUNTER

His eyes went to a little table near her, on which sat the milk and a book. He picked up the book. "Ah, *Le Morte D'Arthur*. Brushing up, are you?" he asked mockingly. "Tell me, Cousin, can you not sleep?"

Something in his tone made her answer defensively. "Why, of course I can sleep. I—I am just a bit restless, that is all."

"Here we are, both of us, restless, sleep evading us, and the answer staring us in the face. I can help you sleep, Amanda," he said silkily, very close to her now. "I can make your nights most pleasurable, you know." He softly traced the line of her jaw with his fingers.

She took a step backward. "My lord, I—" she began.

"No, Amanda, no running away. No more pretense," he commanded, grasping her by the shoulders and drawing her to him. He did not give her time to reply, for in the next moment he grabbed the long black locks behind her neck and pulled her face to his.

It was a bruising kiss, fierce and demanding. She pummeled his chest, but he crushed her body to him. He had expected her to resist; every woman did, at the beginning. Then he felt her rigid body relax, felt it begin to tremble . . . and he knew he had chosen his moment well . . .

A Whisper of Scandal

BY JANIS LADEN

ZEBRA BOOKS
KENSINGTON PUBLISHING CORP.

Also by Janis Laden:
  Sapphire Temptation
  A Noble Mistress

ZEBRA BOOKS

are published by

Kensington Publishing Corp.
475 Park Avenue South
New York, NY 10016

Copyright © 1988 by Janis Laden

First printing: July, 1988

Printed in the United States of America

For my firstborn daughter,
Tamar,
with love

"Her beauty and her wit, Her affability and bashful modesty . . ."

—William Shakespeare, *The Taming of the Shrew*

My deepest thanks to Marjorie Miller and all the Westwood writers, who nurtured this book in its infancy.

To my agent, Florence Feiler, and my editor, Wendy McCurdy, for everything, and to my typist, Mabel Mossman.

And always, to my husband, Michael, who took my regression into the early nineteenth century in stride, and has not yet demanded my return.

A whisper of scandal, a wind in the night,
Doth snatch the sweet blossoms with strangest delight,
Till petals be torn, till their beauty be crushed,
By fatal, foul winds of false voices ne'er hushed.

One stately white flower stands steadily strong,
And falters not once the cold, lonely night long,
Yet waits now and wonders, with wistful eyes bright,
If love doth deny those dark whispers of night.

—Sir Isaac Mariner

Chapter One

The Dowager Countess of Ainsley watched in great trepidation as the furrow deepened between the dark, overly abundant brows of her only son, Charles, the eighth Earl of Ainsley. His lordship at this moment appeared to be rereading, with a mixture of wrath and disbelief, the communication he had just received. He stood with his back to the gilded mirror above the fireplace in the elegant drawing room of his London house. She held her breath as she waited for the inevitable explosion, for well she knew the signs of its impending approach, her late husband having been possessed of those very same ominous brows and that very same thunderous temper.

"Damn and blast it all!" erupted Lord Ainsley, as he shook the offending missive in his right hand and banged it with his left. "The last thing in the world I want to be involved in. My own estates engage my time more than enough. And that woman—"

"Please, Charles, I cannot conceive what you are talking about. Pray tell me what is contained in that letter. That is, if you wish to, dear."

"Sorry, Mother, it's just that I cannot believe the way things have come about. The letter comes from the solicitors of—I quote—'the most recently departed and sadly lamented Viscount Millforte,'" expounded his lordship, his anger momentarily quelled by his fond parent's very reasonable request.

"Arthur's lawyers? What can they want with you, Charles?"

"It seems my dear uncle was not content with the intense discomfort into which he catapulted us in the last few years of his life, linking our family name to such scandal! Oh no, now he has further embroiled us, or rather, has embroiled *me* in his affairs. The lawyers have only been awaiting my return from abroad to inform me that I am named as co-guardian of the heir and the estates, together with—with Lady Millforte!" he said, sputtering this last, for his mother's benefit, with all the disgust his very upper class upbringing could muster.

"You—with—with—that woman?" exclaimed her ladyship, beginning to pale, and falling back against the cushions of the powder blue velvet settee upon which her ample person rested. "But what would they have you do? Certainly you are not expected to have communication with such a person?"

"I am not only expected to have communication with her, Mother, but I am requested to visit Millforte Manor as soon as is—ah—convenient," replied his lordship, his own chagrin tempered somewhat by his amusement at his very proper parent's extreme discomfort at the mere mention of her sister-in-law, the second wife of her late brother.

"Convenient? But surely you wouldn't really consider— Charles you cannot seriously entertain the notion of traveling to Shropshire?"

"Forgive me, Mother, but I truly see little choice. I cannot very well ignore such a summons. And while it is most awkward to be obliged to deal with the second Lady Millforte, still, even you will agree that in the long run it will prove advantageous to us."

"I cannot think what you mean, Charles. Association with a woman of such dubious parentage, and one whose behavior ranks only a small degree above Lady Caroline Lamb's in its depravity—well, such association will certainly not improve your consequence, my dear son," sniffed her ladyship in her most autocratic tone, desperately attempting to divert her son from what seemed to her a disastrous intention.

"Now, Mother, you are far too fond to see that my reputation is already quite sunk. Why, the brows of all the mother hens at Almack's rise in suspicion whenever I enter the hallowed portals."

"Oh, Charles, really," interjected Lady Ainsley, totally disbelieving such disclosures.

"And fear not," the Earl went on, "someday I shall contract a quite eligible alliance, current associations *not* withstanding. As it is not my intention to do so this year, you have nothing to concern yourself with on that head. As to this visit, I can assure you it is distasteful to me, but you must own that it will be to our advantage to have some influence over the management of the estates and the upbringing of the heir."

"Oh dear, the heir," moaned her ladyship, as if belatedly remembering the existence of the three-year-old Victor.

"Just so. He will, after all, inherit your ancestral lands and the title. Much as you have wanted to sever the connection with your late brother ever since his ill-fated marriage, still, I am persuaded you must retain some pride in your name."

"Of course I do, but I shudder at the thought of your becoming involved with that depraved, designing woman."

"Well, I shall stay as far away from 'Jezebel' as possible and concern myself with the facts and figures of the estates," his lordship replied with an amused glint in his eye, as he reflected that his fond mama, after his fourteen years on the Town, still managed to retain the illusion that he was quite a babe in the woods where women were concerned.

"When will you leave, Charles?" asked his mother, with obvious reluctance.

"I shall write to Lady Millforte and leave as soon as possible. I am engaged to join a small party at Ridgeway's hunting lodge in about a month's time and I should not want to have my plans interfered with."

"I see," sighed her ladyship. "And how long do you suppose you will be obliged to stay?"

"I hope not above a fortnight but I cannot really say. Unless the man-of-affairs is very conscientious, I fear the estates may be in quite some disarray. Uncle Arthur was ill for some time before his death, was he not?"

"Yes, poor Arthur."

"Well, then, it may take some doing to set all to rights. But it shall be done with as much dispatch as possible," the Earl said confidently.

"Of course, Charles, but remember there is also that woman to contend with. Surely she will not take kindly to interference in her affairs."

"I am certain you are right, Mother, but now *her* affairs are *mine,* as this letter unfortunately states. Do not trouble yourself. I assure you I shall have little difficulty in handling the young Lady Millforte." At this he smiled to himself, remembering some of the more scandalous on dits that had circulated from time to time about the lady in question. Yes, he thought, I shall have little difficulty with this woman, little difficulty, and perhaps, a great deal of amusement.

And so it was that one week later the Earl of Ainsley found himself tooling down the winding roads to the ancestral home of his mother. As he drove his elegant coach and matched grays, he watched the stark hills and dusty roads give way to the sleepy hamlets and lush greenery of Shropshire. He had sent word of his impending arrival, and he mused now that the ensuing invitation to Millforte Manor had made no mention of a nearby inn. It had rather assumed that he would be staying at Millforte. As Lady Millforte had, to his knowledge, no female relative who might be staying with her, and therefore, no chaperone, he felt this to be a marked disregard for propriety. But, of course, he reminded himself, it was for just such breeches of propriety that the second Lady Millforte was known. He had thought briefly of suggesting an inn himself, but decided it would be much more interesting this way.

Such fantasies as his mind may have pursued in that particular direction came to an abrupt halt as the carriage reined into the drive approaching Millforte Manor. He was indeed surprised by the well-manicured lawns, the precisely trimmed shrubbery, and the stately poplars lining the drive like so many foot soldiers standing at attention. But why this should seem in any way remarkable, he could not fathom. True, he had expected the business affairs of his late uncle's estates to have been sadly neglected, but there was no reason to assume that the gardens would be similarly untended. Yet somehow he did not think to see them looking quite so well cared for.

The Earl found himself approaching the front portal with alacrity. He had dressed with his usual care for the final stage of his three-day journey. His exquisitely tailored coat of navy blue superfine had nary a speck nor a crease after his travels, and his black hessians gleamed.

When the massive oak door opened, his lordship was

pleased to see that the imperious Jeffries still occupied the exalted position of butler in the household. Lord Ainsley smiled in recognition, his mind flitting back to the many scrapes from which Jeffries had extricated him when he had visited as a boy.

"Jeffries, good to see you. It's been many a year, but I see you are looking as fit as ever."

"Welcome back to Millforte, your lordship. I'm very happy to see you," smiled Jeffries warmly. Was he imagining it, or did he detect a hint of relief in Jeffries's voice? He wondered just how bad things were, but Jeffries's greeting augured well. It would not do for the servants to interfere with his plans in any way. And indeed, why should they? All of the staff would undoubtedly appreciate the fact that a capable male had finally come to bring order out of chaos, his lordship assured himself. For certainly it would not be domestic matters which occupied such a notorious femme fetale as Lady Millforte.

But the Earl had not reckoned on Mrs. Havenwick, which redoubtable lady hovered in the entry hall a few paces behind Jeffries, with folded arms which seemed to be holding up her rather enormous bosom, and a scowl that was meant only for him.

"Well, so you've come, have you? Humph! About what I'd expected," she grumbled, scrutinizing every inch of his person in a way that made him decidedly uncomfortable. "Well, don't just stand there, Lord Ainsley. Her ladyship is expecting you and you don't want to keep her waiting now, do you? Follow me up. I'll see you're settled in your room so you can make yourself presentable for her ladyship. Jeffries will see to your valet and luggage. You *did* bring your valet, did you not, your lordship?" she queried in a way that reminded the Earl of any number of schoolmasters he had been made to endure at Eton.

Only slightly daunted, he replied soberly, "My valet is following in a second coach and will arrive presently, ah, Miss, ah, Mrs.?"

"Havenwick, Mrs. Havenwick. Housekeeper, you know. Anything you want, don't scruple to ask me. No need to trouble her ladyship over trifles."

His lordship, nettled at having his needs reduced, sight unseen, to mere trifles, forsook to reply, but rather followed this stout, commanding woman up the magnificent Elizabethan wood-carved staircase that had always been a focal point of the house.

Perhaps five minutes later, Darby, his lordship's valet, appeared at his door, and in a very short time his lordship was proceeding back down the staircase. He was met in the entry hall by Mrs. Havenwick.

"Well, now, that's better, your lordship. Lady Millforte will receive you in the library." And without a hint of a smile, but merely a firm nod which caused her two chins to reverberate above her abundant bosom, she marched off to the library.

His lordship was somewhat taken aback that his first interview with the infamous Lady Millforte was to take place in the library. What was she doing in the library? That was a man's domain, a place of business and serious talk over brandy. The morning room would have been more like it. Yes, she ought to be writing gossipy letters to friends on a delicate gold-leafed escritoire in the morning room.

Nevertheless, he had no choice but to follow the formidable Mrs. Havenwick. As she held the door open, she announced in a very different tone from the one she had used with him, "My lady, the Earl of Ainsley is here."

Nothing his eager imagination could have conjured would have prepared his lordship for the sight before him. The second Lady Millforte was indeed engaged

13

upon correspondence, but the papers arrayed in front of her looked much more like legal communications and lists of figures than gossipy missives. The desk, of course, was his late uncle's carved mahogany desk, but Lady Millforte seemed disconcertingly at home ensconced behind it. At Mrs. Havenwick's announcement she had stirred not an inch, but had continued writing furiously. It was a full minute before she put the quill down and looked up.

Again his lordship's imagination was outdone by the reality. The young face he beheld was so fine and pale that it could only be likened to fine white porcelain. It was set off astonishingly by lustrous, thick black hair, caught up in ringlets. Her large eyes were the color of the sea, and so translucent as to make her seem almost vulnerable, he thought. Her chiseled nose and rosebud mouth were delicate, and they belied a very resolute chin.

"Thank you, Mrs. Havenwick. My lord, I trust you have had a pleasant enough journey," she said calmly, rising and walking toward him to extend her hand.

Lord Ainsley took a moment to study her. She moved gracefully, her figure slender and sensuous, her long white neck holding her head up with a great deal of dignity. She wore a beautifully simple gown of black muslin trimmed with delicate lace at the neck and cuffs. Her only jewels were a pair of diamond earrings and a ring, which he recognized as family heirlooms. Her exquisite neck was bare, and her only other ornament was the intricate Spanish comb in her hair. This latter brought on the unpleasant recollection that her mother had been Spanish and, though allegedly of noble parentage, a stage actress.

With this thought he forced his mind back to the incipient conversation. She had not smiled, nor, he realized, said, "Welcome to Millforte," or some such, which must certainly have been the more customary greeting. "My journey was without incident, Lady Millforte," returned his lordship coldly, taking her hand and bowing slightly. He saw her glance beyond his shoulder in what must have been a sign to Mrs. Havenwick, for the next moment that stout lady wordlessly took her leave.

In a flash his lordship realized why the invitation to stay at Millforte had been granted with impunity. Mrs. Havenwick had awaited a sign from Lady Millforte before retiring, almost as if she had to be sure that it would be safe for her to do so. She was like a huge angry mastiff jealously guarding its master, and it was obvious that she was all the chaperone Lady Millforte needed. That this insight should jar him he could not understand, but jar him it did, as had the well-kept front gardens and the sight of Lady Millforte behind this desk. Somehow he did not feel in command of the situation, and somehow the scene was not at all what he had envisioned. He shook himself out of his reverie and decided that it was time *he* took the upper hand.

"May I express to you my condolences on your recent bereavement, Lady Millforte," said his lordship smoothly, his lips curling in what would have to be regarded as somewhere between a sneer and a smile.

The hint of sarcasm did not go unnoticed by her ladyship, who echoed his tone as she countered, "And to you, my lord, the same." Seeing his eyebrows arch slightly she added, her eyes sparkling, her voice cool and silky, "He *was* your uncle, was he not?"

"Yes, yes, of course," recovered his lordship, and resolving not to be outdone, he asked, tilting his head slightly and allowing a certain glint to come into his eyes, "And shall I call you *Aunt?*"

Had the encounter been friendlier, Lady Millforte would have given way to laughter at the absurdity of such a notion, she being twenty-three and he at least thirty-five. But the enemy was engaged and so she said frostily, "I do not think that will be necessary, Lord Ainsley."

"Well, then, *Cousin,*" he retorted, determined to do away, as quickly as possible, with the formality in which she was attempting to cloak herself.

"Very well, *Cousin,*" she replied, her tone coldly emphasizing the last with thinly veiled distaste, and her eyes never wavering from his face. "I expect that you are tired from your journey and will wish to rest. We take tea at five o'clock in the Green Salon. Tomorrow I shall ride with you over the surrounding lands and we can go over the estate accounts. I have engaged Higgins, my man-of-affairs, to arrive after breakfast. I trust that will be satisfactory?"

"Most satisfactory. Ah, but, I should like to meet my ward today, Cousin," said his lordship, laughter creeping into the corner of his slate blue eyes as he decided that this lady was a marvelous actress, concealing well-justified uneasiness beneath coldness and brisk efficiency.

"Of course. Nurse will present him at tea. And now, my lord, I should like to finish my work."

Her performance notwithstanding, he found himself quite astonished at this unaccustomed dismissal and unaccountably miffed that she seemed to have left no stone unturned. Careful to keep every evidence of surprise from his countenance, he prepared to pary his final thrust, laden, he thought, with just a hint of sarcasm. "It has been a pleasure to meet you, Cousin, at long last. I have no doubt that our association will be a most—ah—entertaining one. Until tea, then." He bowed his head almost imperceptibly and favored her ladyship with a rakish grin before he turned abruptly and departed.

The moment the door had closed, Lady Amanda Millforte picked up her carved ivory letter opener and flung it across the room. "Damn you, Charles, Earl of Ainsley! Cousin, indeed!" she fulminated as she began pacing the room in quite a rage.

How dare he take such a tone with her! How dare he! The impertinence of the man! Such insufferable conceit!

She continued pacing about the magnificent oak-paneled room she had come to regard as her own in the past few months as she thought of the man who had just left. One could not call him handsome, for though his features were well proportioned, his dark hair full and wavy, his slate blue eyes deep-set and expressive, so haughty was his gaze and so intimidating his brow that surely one could not call him pleasing to look at. He was tall and broad-shouldered, but lean, giving the appearance of great strength. *Some* might have thought he cut a striking figure in his elegant coat, exquisitely tailored in the first cut of taste. But surely it was a mark of his arrogance that he dressed with such studied simplicity. Her own simplicity of dress notwithstanding, she thought that he used *his* to hold himself *above* the world of fashion, as if he did not deign to compete. He wore not a ruffle nor a jewel, save his signet ring, and his white cravat, though arranged to perfection, had few folds. There was no fussiness about his dress at all. He gave every appearance of a man who knew exactly what he wanted and would not waste any time in getting it.

And just what *did* he want? She had expected disdain, to be sure, for she had no illusions as to the contempt in which her late husband's family held her. The family had been quite chagrined when Arthur had taken a wife more than thirty years his junior, and worse, one whose mother was a Spaniard and a stage

17

actress, these latter two negating, in the eyes of the ton, any claims to noble lineage that mother or daughter might have had. Amanda had met the Dowager Countess but once, and so strained had been the interview that Arthur had not asked her to repeat it.

Yes, she had been prepared for disdain, and for calculated attempts to wrest power over the estates from her. Those she could deal with, she knew, with her usual calm efficiency. But this—this—familiarity— was insufferable! If she didn't know him by reputation for a shocking rake, that parting grin would have told her all she needed to know. Did he expect her to fall at his feet in the face of what he must believe his irresistible charm, as so many others undoubtedly had?

Well, she had no intention of succumbing to his dubious charms, nor would she be intimidated by that imposing brow and those cold slate blue eyes. She had been through a great deal in her life, and she'd meet him squarely on any battlefield he chose. This would be a visit he would not soon forget.

Chapter Two

The Earl of Ainsley had decided that his most prudent course was to ascertain as much about the household as possible *before* his meeting with the man-of-affairs on the following day. The state of the household would undoubtedly reflect the condition of the estates, and he might find it necessary to read between the lines at that interview.

To this end he lingered about the main floor just before teatime, and was rewarded by the appearance of Jeffries, alighting from the morning room. "My lord," said that fond retainer, "is there anything you require?"

"No, no, Jeffries. I am quite comfortable, I assure you," replied his lordship. "Er—how are *you,* Jeffries?"

"I go on quite well, my lord."

"I'm sorry about your master. It must have been very distressing for you."

"Yes, my lord. His lordship was a good man. We all miss him."

"Is it—" The Earl hesitated just a moment. "Is it difficult for you here now?"

"This is my home, my lord. And Lady Millforte is—is—kind, sir," said Jeffries, his tone impassive.

The Earl looked at him intently with narrowed eyes. *Kind* was not the adjective he would have chosen, but then, Jeffries was being careful. "Ah, tell me,

Jeffries," his lordship continued casually, so to put the very upright servant at his ease, "why do you suppose Lord Millforte wanted me here?"

Jeffries's eyes widened and his normally stately posture became even more stately as he said, his nose rather high in the air, "I can assure your lordship that I can have had no knowledge whatever of his lordship's intents. I have never been, you know, an—eaves-dropper."

"No." The Earl grinned. "But if memory serves me, you are a keen observer of human nature *and* an accomplished mind reader. I'm not asking what you heard, my good man, merely what you think."

"Ah, well, in that case," Jeffries began, allowing his rigid torso to relax a very little bit as he bent conspiratorially toward the Earl. "It is my considered opinion, my lord, that the late Lord Millforte was—er—worried about—about—" He paused, as if loath to go on.

"About what, Jeffries?"

"About Lady Millforte, my lord."

"Ah, I see. Why, Jeffries?" he persisted, barely suppressing the glint in his eyes and the excitement in his tone.

"Well, my lord, she—ah—she has—tendencies, you see."

"Tendencies, Jeffries?"

"Yes, my lord, she, well, her ladyship is a bit of a—er—" Jeffries coughed delicately and cleared his throat, then continued in a very low voice, "A bit of a—reformer."

"A what?" fairly shouted his lordship, at once shocked and disappointed by this disclosure.

"A—reformer, my lord. She is very kind and generous, and she has, you know, ideas, sir, and when she gets an idea she's very—well—" He hesitated, looking most uncomfortable, so that the Earl relieved him of his misery by venturing to finish his sentence for him.

"Ah—strong-willed, perhaps?"

"As you say, my lord," answered Jeffries.

"Am I to understand that Lord Millforte may have wanted me here to curb some of her ladyship's more generous ideas, shall we say?" asked the Earl, becoming somewhat exasperated and not quite understanding his disappointment at the turn of the conversation.

"Well yes, perhaps, my lord, and—er—there is one more thing."

"Go on, Jeffries."

"His lordship was, I think, concerned for her ladyship. That is, he feared—I mean to say, my lord—" Jeffries's face had taken on a very pink hue as he attempted to phrase this latest disclosure.

"I pray you will speak plainly, Jeffries. I cannot be of help without some clue as to why I am here, now can I?"

This seemed to clear the butler's conscience enough for him to continue. "Her ladyship is—well—very beautiful, as anyone can see, and his lordship feared that she might fall prey to—to young men— unscrupulous fortune hunters."

"And he wanted me to protect her in some way?" the Earl asked incredulously, barely suppressing the laughter that had welled up inside him. Why, that was like the lamb worrying about what the lion would eat for his next dinner! It was preposterous.

Besides, protection was not at all what he had in mind for the charming Amanda Millforte. Judging by her reputation, he suspected that she was shrewd enough to see the advantage of a liaison with him and would in a short time make some overture to indicate so. It would be rather amusing to watch her maneuver, for surely she had initiated such flirtations before. But remembering that lovely face and figure, he hoped she would not tarry long. Otherwise he would have to make his own advances, a prospect he thought about with relish as he reluctantly turned his mind back to Jeffries.

"I think that may have entered his mind, my lord," the butler was saying in reply, his torso erect again.

The Earl eyed him narrowly, wondering for the first time whether any of his information was reliable. Could the imperious Jeffries have been taken in as much as his master by the beautiful lady with the fragile eyes? He had no opportunity to pursue the matter, though, for doors were heard to open at the far end of the main corridor. And so the Earl, more confused than enlightened, betook himself to the Green Salon for tea.

As Lady Millforte rose to greet him, his careful eyes swept the room. He noticed with approval that the furniture, much of it centuries old, was placed the way he remembered it. His grandmother had had a fine eye and had rearranged much of the furniture when she had come to live at Millforte. He remembered her speaking so fondly of her husband's ancestral home, and it pleased him that this woman, this opportunist, had at least seen fit not to disturb his grandmother's handiwork. If memory served him, though, the draperies and several chair coverings had been replaced. They had been, he thought, a pale green silk rather than their present rich emerald green damask.

Lady Millforte, her gaze following his, interrupted his musings by saying, "It is a lovely room, is it not? Arthur said it was his mother's favorite. I left it untouched when I went through the house, except, of course, for the draperies and those two wings chairs. They were, I'm afraid, quite shabby and sadly faded."

Lord Ainsley had to admit to himself, however grudgingly, that the new draperies made a beautiful

22

backdrop for the Oriental rug on the floor, and, he noted, for Lady Millforte—Amanda, he amended. She was now standing at the window, the draperies setting off her sea green eyes stunningly, and he was hard put to take his eyes from her.

But then his mind darted back to something she had said. "What do you mean—when you went through the house?" he asked, very much afraid of what atrocities she might have perpetrated in the ancestral home of his mother.

"Well, of course, when I came here, Arthur wanted me to feel that this was my home as well as his, and so he asked me to make whatever changes I deemed fitting."

"He did?" gulped his lordship.

"Why, yes." Amanda smiled ingenuously. "Haven't you had a walk round yet, my lord?"

"No, no—I have not really. Er—what—what did you do?" asked the Earl with ill-concealed suspicion.

Amanda spoke slowly, having decided to enjoy his lordship's discomfort for as long as possible. "Well, let me see. Of course, I did my own bedroom over. It was a pale pink, you know. Very much the first Lady Millforte's color, if her portrait is any indication, but as for me it—"

"Yes, yes, well I should expect you to do your own room. But the rest of the house. What have you done to the rest of the house?" His lordship, clearly nervous, was almost shouting.

"I must tell you, my lord, that I love this house. Arthur told me much of its history, including the terrible fire that nearly swept it away when his grandfather was a boy. So fortunate we are that that magnificent staircase remained of the original. Also the picture gallery. Do you remember it, my lord?"

His lordship, much more interested in the recent

rather than the ancient history of the house, answered abruptly. "Yes, yes, vaguely. But you have not answered my question, Cousin."

"Your question. Yes. Changes. Well, certain rooms required new draperies, as you see here. The dining room chairs required new coverings, and I did find some wonderful old tables and two chairs gathering dust in the attic. I've placed those in some of the guest bedrooms. And, of course, I had the picture gallery renovated. It would be such a shame for it to have been allowed to go to ruin. I had the leaks fixed and some of the moldings replaced—those that were damaged by the rains. It was such a dark and dingy corner of the house. I replaced those heavy, ancient draperies with light airy ones; now one can actually *see* the portraits of your ancestors," she said with a gleam in her eye. "We can take a walk there after tea if you like."

"And the rest of the house, Cousin?" asked the Earl, still dreading to hear that she had relegated some priceless Jacobean sofa table to the fireplace.

"Oh, most everything else I've kept the way I suspect it's always been. One feels an awesome sense of history here. Why should I change it?"

"Why, indeed?" echoed his lordship, his eyes widening as he stared fixedly at Amanda, and feeling for some unknown reason more annoyance than relief at this last.

Their attention was diverted as the door opened and a round-faced three-year-old bounded into the room, his nurse close at his heels. He had Amanda's black curly hair and, the Earl noticed, his father's eyes. In countenance the child bore some slight resemblance to his own mother, thought his lordship.

"Thank you, Nurse," Amanda was saying. "I will send him to you presently."

The child ran to give his mother a hug, clutching two

24

toy soldiers in his chubby hands.

"And what have we here, Victor? Soldiers? How nice!" she said, disengaging his arms from about her and taking his hand.

"And now I would like for you to meet your cousin. This is your Cousin Charles, the Earl of Ainsley. He is to be your guardian. My lord, this is Victor, the heir to Millforte."

Lord Ainsley bowed solemnly and extended his hand to the little boy. Victor eyed him suspiciously and finally thrust his hand forward.

"Make your bow, Victor," said Amanda, whereupon the heir bent very low.

Then he stared at the Earl with narrowed eyes and without turning his head asked, "What's a guarnian, Mama?"

"Well, a guardian is someone who helps take care of you, Victor," said his mother.

"Then I don't need a guarnian. I have *Mama*. She takes care of me," blurted Victor, rather upset.

"Yes, yes, of course she does," replied his lordship, somewhat discomposed by this direct attack. "And she will continue to do so. But your papa wanted me to—help her sometimes. Perhaps—perhaps I will choose a school for you," attempted the Earl.

"I don't go to school. Mama, doesn't he know that?"

"Well, his lordship—" began Amanda, but Victor, by this time glaring at the Earl, interrupted her with a new thought.

"Are you going to be my papa from now on?"

"No, Victor, he is not. Now why don't you sit down and play with your soldiers while the Earl and Mama have tea?" said Amanda very quickly as she settled him down and pulled the bell cord.

The tea tray was brought not moments later by Mrs. Havenwick, who surveyed the room with a severe

25

frown before retiring. Amanda poured the tea as she and the Earl watched Victor at his play.

"Er—why did you name him Victor, Cousin?" asked his lordship, hoping for a safe subject.

"My mother's name was Victoria. I wanted him named after her. Arthur took ill while I was carrying him, you see, and I didn't know—if—if I should ever have another," she replied, a stricken look on her face.

The Earl could not help wondering at the source of her obvious distress. "Do you not wish to marry again, Cousin?"

"No, my lord. I will not marry again," she said with a finality that made him forbear to pursue the subject.

Still trying to steer the conversation to safe waters, he asked, "Your mother—ah—when did she die? Were you very young?"

She stared at him with vacant eyes. "Yes, I was twelve."

"An accident, I believe? A fall?"

"A fall, yes, a fall," she said, as one in a daze.

"Did she look like you, Cousin?" he asked, unable to let the subject rest.

The unusual softness of his tone seemed strange to Amanda, but she replied softly, "My mother was very beautiful. She had a noble face. Magnificent eyes. She had a grace, a dignity, about her that she never lost, despite—despite everything."

He saw that her eyes filled with tears, but she seemed not to notice and continued gazing intently at her child for several moments. Her extreme distraction mystified the Earl, but before he could venture to draw her out, the somber mood was broken abruptly as Victor let out a sharp cry.

The Earl jumped out of his seat and ran to him. Amanda rose calmly and followed him. "There, there, Victor," soothed Amanda, bending close to the child.

"What's happened? You've cut your finger. Oh, dear. Here, Mama will kiss it and then Nurse will bandage it for you."

She took his hand and walked to the bell cord. Jeffries appeared a moment later. "Jeffries, please take Lord Victor to Nurse. He has cut his finger and it will need to be bandaged. Now, Victor, you go with Jeffries, and I'll come up after your bath to read to you. Would you like to hear the story about the beautiful fairy godmother?"

"Yes," he said between sobs, and allowed himself to be led away by Jeffries.

The Earl had watched this tender scene with great interest. It did not fit that such a wanton, calculating woman should be such a good mother.

"You haven't had much experience with children, have you, my lord?" she was saying.

"No, I confess I haven't," he replied, this utterance being, thought Amanda, the only humble thing she would ever hear him say. "Of course, there is my ward, but she came to us when she was ten. Catherine is my father's niece, you know. Her parents were killed in a boating accident some years ago."

"How dreadful! And what is Catherine like?"

"Kitty was a delightful child, but—but she is growing up to be a very biddable girl."

"Well," replied Amanda, bewildered at the mild disapprobation in his tone, "you must be very pleased. Isn't that what you think a female should be— biddable?"

He did not reply for a full minute, for he realized that he did not know the answer to that question. On the one hand he certainly could not abide having his will thwarted, but on the other hand, compliant females were always so insipid. And wasn't that why he had never married? All of the eligible women of his class

27

were so damned *biddable*.

But he remembered to whom he was speaking and said smoothly, "But, of course, Cousin. It is my primary requirement in a woman."

The Earl rose early, as he always did, and dressed in pleasant anticipation of a leisurely, solitary breakfast. Of course, Lady Millforte would take breakfast in bed and not alight from her room until the noon hour. Women so accustomed as she to late night trysts did not rise with the first cock crow, after all.

And so he felt a rather severe jolt when he beheld, as he entered the dining room, her ladyship comfortably seated and quite obviously halfway through her morning meal. "Good morning, my lord," she said, a glimmer of a smile on her lips.

"Yes, good morning, Cousin. Ah, do you always rise this early?"

"Oh, at least! That is, some mornings I am up rather earlier. I like to walk the hills at dawn. It's very peaceful then, and I can be—alone—with my thoughts," she said, coloring slightly and looking quickly down as if she had said too much.

His lordship shook himself. Walks at dawn? It was inconceivable. Perhaps, he thought, her state of mourning had imposed a temporary hiatus from her nocturnal activities. Yes, that would account for it. But then another thought struck him. "Surely you do not walk unaccompanied, Cousin?"

"On my own land? And at such an early hour? But of course. Else how could I be alone?"

"Oh yes, I see," said the Earl, for he suddenly did see. Clandestine meetings in the small hours of the morning might be easier to manage in the country than a midnight rendezvous. Yes, it fitted very well.

28

As his lordship strolled to the sideboard to help himself to the eggs benedict and buttered toast, Amanda abruptly changed the subject. "Higgins will be here at noon, my lord. Unless there is anything you might wish me to show you in the house, I thought perhaps you might like to have a look at the stables."

"Higgins. Hmm. I seem to remember a Staple as man-of-affairs."

"Yes, dear Mr. Staple. I'm afraid I had to pension him off and engage Mr. Higgins, oh, quite some ten months ago," said Amanda with a slight smile.

"*You* engaged Higgins?" asked his lordship, taken aback.

"Yes. For the last year of—of his life, Arthur's pain was so severe that he often could do little more than offer me advice now and then."

"And why did you dismiss Staple, may I ask?" his lordship asked with a controlled calm that was belied by the fact that he fairly stabbed his eggs with his fork.

"Coffee, my lord?" asked Amanda pleasantly, seeing that a footman had advanced into the room.

The Earl held his cup aloft but said nothing, his eyes never leaving Amanda's face.

When the footman had retired, Amanda continued sweetly. "Poor Mr. Staple was, I'm afraid, so often in his cups that his record of accounts became quite incoherent. I fear he made rather a jumble of things at the end. It took Higgins and me quite some while to set all to rights. But do not worry about Staple, the dear man. He's quite comfortable now in a cottage near the Dower House. Spends his days jaunting to and from the Boar's Head Inn, and arguing politics with anyone who will listen."

The Earl, whose concern had not precisely been the well-being of the intemperate man-of-affairs, asked roughly, his ominous brows coming together, "Cousin,

29

how long have you been managing Millforte?"

"Well, Arthur used to speak to me of business matters from the very beginning, but when he took ill, he began to instruct me in earnest. I would say near to two years, my lord," she replied with candor.

His lordship whistled through his teeth and silently cursed. This was going to be a much worse imbroglio than he had thought.

"Is something amiss, my lord? Is the toast burned, or would you like more coffee?" asked Amanda calmly.

"No, the toast is not burned and no, I would not like more coffee!" shouted the Earl, abruptly pushing his chair back and rising. "Twelve o'clock, you say? In the library, I presume? Good morning, madam!" he said as he bowed and strode from the room.

The noon hour at Millforte found Amanda, the Earl, and the pleasant-faced Mr. Higgins seated in the library. The Earl had not been pleased when Amanda had seated herself behind the great mahogany desk and motioned for the gentlemen to occupy the two chairs facing it. And he was even more rankled when Amanda began the interview.

"I don't know how familiar you are with the economics of the Millforte lands, my lord, but our eastern portion is given over largely to grazing. Mr. Higgins has been compiling the figures for the revenues from the sheep, both in wool and mutton, for the past year."

"Excuse me, Cousin," said his lordship, looking haughtily at Amanda and then turning to Higgins. "I shall require the revenues of the past *two* years, if you will, Higgins."

"Yes—er—that will be just fine, your lordship," replied Higgins, with an uncertain look at Amanda.

30

"Yes, I can tabulate those soon enough. I'm a Yorkshireman myself, you know, and in Yorkshire we always do like to look back over a period of time—kind of reflect a bit, you know—before making decisions about our sheep and suchlike."

"Fine. Now, as I was saying," continued Amanda quickly, "the pasture land is rich, and the sheep are profitable. The area around the manor and some of our northern lands are divided between apple orchards and vegetable farms. Vegetable farming is rather new to this area, as you may know, my lord. It has proved quite lucrative and, of course, is most advantageous for the tenants. You may remember that we also have quite a bit of marshland to the north. It has been my intention, and Mr. Higgins agrees with me, to drain the marshland and turn it into arable. In that way we can increase the number of vegetable farms and greatly add to the estate coffers. It will also serve to put some of our indigent tenants to work." At this juncture Amanda paused and, looking calmly at the Earl, awaited his comment.

His lordship stared at Amanda, his ominous brows knit together, for a full minute before replying. Drain the marshes? Put tenants to work? Where did she get all of these notions about pasture lands and sheep revenues and—and . . . Why, it was positively unheard of for a woman even to *know* about such things, much less discuss them. And to concern herself with financial matters, to form opinions, plans! Such unbecoming behavior was not to be tolerated!

The Earl forced himself to remain calm as he inquired of Higgins, "It is very expensive to drain marshland, is it not, Higgins?" At Higgins' rather hesitant nod he continued, "I quite agree that it is desirable to expand the vegetable farms. But it would make much more sense, would it not, Higgins, to fell some of the orchards to that purpose? That land has already proved fertile, after all, and such a course of action would be much less costly."

Before Higgins could answer, Amanda broke in, saying, "But—but, my lord, fell perfectly good orchards? Why, they are beautiful, *and* productive. We do see income from them, you know."

"Yes, Cousin, but hardly the income of the farms, you will own," answered the Earl smugly.

"My lord, the marshlands presently go to waste. The orchards do not. Certainly the more expedient course is to utilize the marshes. Why, it's being done all over the countryside. In the long run it—"

"I am not interested in the long run, Cousin," interrupted his lordship hotly. "I am interested in the next twenty years and in turning Millforte over to my uncle's heir in the most profitable state possible. Do I make myself clear?"

Seeing a dangerous glint in her ladyship's eyes, Mr. Higgins thought it wise to remind the pair of his presence. "Ahem," he cleared his throat and said, "Excuse me, but I thought your lordship would like to have a look at these figures. I've been working on them for several days now. I reckon I do enjoy discussions about sheep raising. Reminds me of Yorkshire. My home, you know. Now, these figures show the amount of wool sheared . . ."

Mr. Higgins rambled on for some fifteen minutes about sheep-related revenues, trying not to notice Amanda and the Earl glaring at each other every few minutes across the desk. The Earl asked but a few questions during this discourse, for the most part only when it was necessary to keep Mr. Higgins from some nostalgic digression about sheep shearing in Yorkshire or some such.

Finally, Amanda said, smiling, "What of the

orchards, Mr. Higgins? What income do we see from them?"

Before the man-of-affairs could answer, the door opened and the stately Jeffries walked to her ladyship and bent to whisper something. "Excuse me, gentlemen, I shall only be a minute," she said.

The Earl watched her graceful form sweep out of the room. When the door had closed Higgins said, "Now, that is one right amazing woman, if I may say so, your lordship."

"Oh?" retorted his lordship, his brows arched.

"Well, now, I don't hold with females running estates and worrying their pretty selves 'bout all these facts and figures. But truth to tell, her ladyship understands it all as well as any man. Better than most, in fact. Why, when I think of the rack and ruin I've seen estates come to at the hands of some addlepated, gaming-addicted noblemen—meaning no offense to you or your class, you understand, your lordship. But when I think— well, I'd as lief deal with Lady Millforte, that I would."

At the end of which amazing recital the lady herself reentered the room.

"Well, now, getting back to those apple orchards," began Higgins, "the fact of the matter is that the harvest has actually been increasing these past few years."

After a few minutes of listening to Higgins extolling the virtues of apple trees, the Earl finally interjected, "Have you any idea of the cost of reclaiming marshland, Higgins?"

"Why, yes, yes I do, your lordship. Now I have some figures here. 'Course these are based on a reclamation project in Yorkshire several years ago. I used to hail from Yorkshire, you know. Fine country that. Now, as I was saying . . ."

It seemed to the Earl that he'd heard about all he

could take for the present of Yorkshire and its many wonders. As if sensing his impatience, Amanda very deftly brought Mr. Higgins to a halt. "You know, Mr. Higgins, we should be quite lost without your ability to have exactly the right information at your fingertips at all times. You've given his lordship so much to think about. Do you think perhaps he needs time to digest it all? Why don't you leave the ledgers here and return, say, day after tomorrow? Would that suit you, my lord?"

"Yes, quite well," replied the Earl, grudging admiration evident in the half smile he directed to her. Once Higgins was safely dispatched, he said, a twinkle in his eye, "Well done, my dear. Is he always so—er—friendly?"

"Oh, Mr. Higgins is quite pleasant, you know. One just has to keep reminding him what question he's answering."

"I shall remember that, Cousin. We two still have something to discuss, however. Those marshlands. You have no idea what an undertaking that is. And not all marshland becomes arable, you know."

"Yes, I know all that, my lord, but—but let us discuss this as we ride out this afternoon. Perhaps the land will answer for itself. We'll ride after luncheon. Have you chosen a horse?"

"Yes, I have. You seem to have a singular knack for changing the subject, Cousin," replied his lordship, a smile curling his lips.

"Yes, well, I am pleased that you found a horse. Does it matter to you where we start? I had rather thought the eastern pasture lands would be a good place, although we will not cover all of them in one day. Then we can make our way northward."

"Yes, that will serve."

"Fine. Oh, and there is just one more thing. I want to be sure we leave time. I wish to visit the Low Cottages."

"The Low Cottages?" he repeated, mystified. Then, memory dawning, he said, his eyes narrowing, "The Low Cottages? Oh, no you don't. I know the Low Cottages and we are most definitely *not* going there."

"And, pray tell, why not?" asked Amanda, her eyes sparkling with anger.

"Because that is no place for a woman, that's why. It's filthy and stinking and disease-ridden. Besides, the whole area and its environs must be a haven for every cutthroat thieving blackguard in the county. Why in heaven's name do you want to go *there?*"

"Well, Arthur spoke of the Low Cottages, but I've never seen them, and I should, for I mean to tear them down."

"You *what?*" exploded his lordship, fairly jumping from his deep leather chair and leaning menacingly toward her.

Rising and facing him squarely, Amanda said, "I mean to tear down the Low Cottages. They are a blight on our—"

"Now, let us get something straight, Cousin. You'll do no such thing, and you'll not make any major changes without consulting me! Do I make myself clear?" shouted the Earl.

"Oh, quite, my lord. Nevertheless, I intend to visit the Low Cottages. Will you accompany me?"

"Of course not! And I repeat: You *will not* go! I forbid it!"

"*You* forbid *me,* my lord? May I remind you that you are not *my* guardian," she replied hotly, her green eyes blazing.

"But I *am* guardian of Millforte and as such I forbid you to go!" thundered his lordship, his ominous brows knit together in a very terrifying frown.

But Amanda was not terrified as she replied calmly, "Luncheon is served in one half hour. We ride immediately after that."

Chapter Three

As the wind tugged at the ringlets in her hair, Amanda, riding beside Lord Ainsley, broke her mare into a canter. The Earl kept apace, all the while watching her from the corner of his eye. She made a stunning picture, her slender figure outlined in a close-fitting black riding dress that contrasted with her stark white mare. Her lush hair streamed down her back; she had not bothered to wear a hat.

They rode westward, taking the gentle hills easily and stopping occasionally while a shepherd ushered his flock of sheep across their path. They passed some of the crofters' huts and spoke of minor repairs that were needed. At length they guided their horses in a northerly direction, and the peaceful hills began to yield to wooded enclaves and vast expanses of apple orchards. They slowed as they neared the orchards.

"You see, my lord, how rich the foliage is here. You cannot really entertain the notion of eliminating all of these trees," Amanda said lightly.

"I most certainly do, Cousin. It makes economic sense. Even you must own that it does."

"I can assure you, my lord, that your uncle's future grandchildren will not thank you for defacing the land. And all of the marshland hereabouts will *have* to be drained, if not this year, then another. Everyone in

Shropshire is talking of it."

"Are they indeed, Cousin? Well, then, we, too, have talked about it, haven't we?" he retorted, a smile curling his lips. Seeing Amanda shoot him a dark look, he quickly searched his mind for a safe subject.

"Your mare is quite a beauty. What do you call her?" he asked.

"My horse? Oh—her name is Aquitaine," she replied, somewhat miffed at the abrupt change of subject.

"Aquitaine?"

"Yes, after Eleanor. Such a marvelous lady. Don't you agree, my lord?" she replied smoothly, beginning to enjoy herself.

"Well, actually, I should have thought it rather foolish to forfeit—what was it—perhaps fifteen years —of one's life, for a mere piece of land," he said, grinning.

"Hardly a mere piece of land, my lord, you must own. The Aquitaine was *her* inheritance, and it represented a great deal of power in France. And you know perfectly well that that is *not* the point. She was a lady of great courage," retorted Amanda amiably.

"Ah, yes, for she did not allow her husband to get the better of her, now did she? Is not *that* the point, Cousin?"

"She held fast to what was rightfully hers, despite Henry's—bullying," said Amanda firmly, not willing to allow him to twist her words. But she was most displeased when he again changed the subject, so determined was he to retain the upper hand.

"Yes, well, you know, Cousin," he said in a mocking tone, "I should have imagined you'd have chosen a rather—different name for your horse."

"Oh? And what name would you have deemed fitting?"

"Ah—perhaps—Guinevere," he said silkily.

"Guinevere? Why, my lord?"

"Well, she *was* Arthur's wife, you know. And the region, of course. It is said that Arthur's legions traversed these very hills on the way from Cornwall into battle." The Earl's tone was sardonic, and he seemed determined to make some point which escaped her, but to which she knew that she must take exception. Amanda looked curiously at him as he continued.

"And then there was Lancelot. If memory serves me, legend has it that he used Lewain Castle to quarter his knights. Perhaps he and Guinevere took shelter there during their mad flight from King Arthur. Interesting times those, were they not, Cousin?"

In truth, she did not see of what particular interest the ancient adultery of Guinevere and Lancelot was to her, nor did she care at all for the Earl's insinuating tone. He was clearly baiting her, for reasons of his own, but she would not dignify his train of thought by pursuing it. He was not the only one adept at changing the topic of conversation.

"Ah, yes, Lewain. I've seen the ruins, of course. Such an imposing structure it must have been, set atop that ravine. But you must know, my lord, that 'Guinevere' would never do for my horse. Guinevere was not a heroine, you see."

"More's the pity. So, you identify with Eleanor of Aquitaine, do you? Fighting to retain her land, is that it?" asked the Earl.

"For her son, my lord? No, you are mistaken. I said that I admired her, but I, unlike Eleanor, have no intention of being punished for—disobedience," she countered, and without awaiting a reply tapped Aquitaine with her crop and set her to galloping over the lush green hills.

38

The Earl had little choice but to follow, and in a short while they came upon a small village, nestled in a wooded glade at the bottom of the sloping hills. As they slowed their horses, the Earl spied the old Norman church that had served Millforte for so many centuries.

His eyes suddenly lit up with amusement as he said, "Cousin, I should very much like to visit the vicarage. Is Mr. Trumwell still here?" It was not to be doubted that Amanda would be quite uncomfortable visiting the vicarage, and not at all well acquainted with the good Mr. Trumwell.

"Why, that's a fine idea, my lord. Do you know, the old church is by far and away one of my favorite places here. The ancient carved ceilings and the stained glass—why it's simply beautiful! And I haven't seen the Trumwells in days. Yes, do let us stop," she said with what the Earl thought was rather too much enthusiasm. Hasn't seen the Trumwells in days! Doing it a bit too brown, wasn't she? Well, he'd see how she endeavored to pull this one off. She had contrived to outmaneuver him on quite too many fronts in the course of his short visit, and though she might have bamboozled Jeffries and Higgins, surely the Vicar and his wife could not be taken in by the likes of Amanda Millforte.

Amanda and Lord Ainsley were ushered into the sunny drawing room of the vicarage by a diminutive maid, who wasted no time in bringing her mistress to them.

"Amanda, my dear, how good to see you. And you've brought the Earl. Lord Ainsley, welcome back to Millforte," gushed the very amiable Mrs. Trumwell, embracing Amanda warmly and then extending her hand to the Earl.

"Thank you, ma'am. We were riding over the estates, you see, and I espied the church, and we, well, that is,

I—" began the Earl, somehow feeling that he had to explain their unexpected presence.

"And you wanted to stop! Oh, I *am* delighted! Amanda and I certainly don't wait upon ceremony, and I should hope you won't either. I'm sure you do not like to hear this, my lord, but I do remember you from when you were in short-coats. You must come and visit at any time. Ah, and here is Vernon. Vernon, look who Amanda has brought," said Mrs. Trumwell, turning to greet the Vicar as he crossed the beamed threshold of the drawing room.

The Vicar was, as the Earl remembered, a stately though kindly gentleman, the younger son of a local baron. Tall and good-looking, his hair had turned silver-gray since the Earl had last seen him.

He strode to the Earl and shook his hand warmly. "Lord Ainsley, it is good to have you with us." He turned to Amanda and took both her hands in his. "My dear Amanda, it has been several days. I was beginning to wonder about you. Is everything quite all right?"

"Oh, quite, I assure you, Vernon. We've been very busy at the manor, what with Lord Ainsley's arrival and all. He and I have been going over the accounts, and we have been out touring the estates just now."

"My dear, you will of course stay for tea," said Mrs. Trumwell.

"Oh, Sally, are you quite sure? I fear we *are* rather imposing on you," replied Amanda.

"Amanda, what's come over you? Come now, I mean to get reacquainted with Ainsley here. You don't propose to drag him away so quickly, do you? That is, if you'd like to stay, my lord?" asked the Vicar.

In truth, the Earl was not feeling very much like company, particularly the present company. He was, in fact, most bewildered at the obvious intimacy between Amanda and the Trumwells. It was all wrong.

It was impossible! He stared blankly at Mr. Trumwell for a moment, before he recovered himself and replied, "I thank you very much. I believe our tour is almost complete in any case. Is it not, Cousin?"

"Very nearly, my lord. I had wanted to ride north a bit. But there will be time after tea."

"Wonderful. Oh, look, here comes Jimmy. Amanda, he must have seen Aquitaine. He'd not miss an opportunity to see *you,* of course," Mrs. Trumwell trilled as she glanced out the back window before turning to seat everyone.

When her maid appeared with the news of Jimmy's arrival, Mrs. Trumwell said, "Just send him in to us here, Annie. Jimmy is one of the village lads, my lord," she explained. "Lives in one of the whitewash cottages. He comes around often to do odd jobs for me, but I am persuaded it is Amanda he is hoping to catch a glimpse of. One day perhaps he'll work up the courage to ask Mrs. Havenwick if she has any chores for him. He absolutely adores the fair Lady Millforte, you see."

His lordship found his eyes widening at such disclosures by the Vicar's wife, and he began to wonder just what had happened to the Trumwells since he had last been here. He had been waiting for one of Amanda's paramours to alight, but he had hardly expected him to be a village lad, nor certainly, that the two of them would meet at the vicarage. He did not have much time to dwell on these rather sordid possibilities, however, for not a moment later a very shy little boy peeked round the door and, at Mrs. Trumwell's encouragement, entered the drawing room. He looked to be about six years old, a comely child with earnest blue eyes and straight blond hair.

The Earl listened in amazement as Mrs. Trumwell said, "Come and pay your respects to Lady Millforte, Jimmy." His lordship groaned inwardly. So Amanda's enamorato was six years old. Damn her! She'd done it again. Exactly what she had done he truly could not say, but the Earl knew only that he was becoming very irritated over this visit to the vicarage.

The little boy stammered greetings to Amanda and, when introductions were made, to his lordship. Jimmy appeared very ill at ease until Amanda took his hands and said, "How is your ankle, Jimmy? Have you taken care not to strain it?"

"Oh, yes, my lady, just as you said. Grandmama says I may not climb the trees past the lower branches," replied the little boy, pouting and casting mooncalf eyes toward Amanda.

"Well, now, Jimmy, your grandmama knows best, and you cannot hope that Lady Millforte will be there to rescue you the next time, now can you?" interjected Mrs. Trumwell, as if this same conversation had taken place before.

At this last the Earl, who had been reclining comfortably in a large wing chair by the fire, suddenly sat bolt upright.

"But, my lady," said the boy, his eyes pleading, "that was a bad tree. I been climbin' all my life and nary a mishap. If you'd care to come climbin' with me one day, well, then I could show you, an' then mayhap grandmama would let me—"

Seeing a horrified expression creep over his lordship's face, Amanda hastened to check this flow of words. "Oh, my dear Jimmy. Really I could not. You see, I don't ordinarily *climb* trees. It was just that one time, when I saw you hanging there."

"You *climbed* a tree, Cousin?" demanded the Earl, not believing his ears but no longer able to contain himself.

"Well, you see, my lord, I was out riding Aquitaine, and I heard his screams. Jimmy was caught in the highest boughs of a very large oak. He'd lost his footing, you see, and so I—well, that is, there was no one else about—" His lordship's expression at this point could best be described as thunderous, and Amanda was relieved when Sally interrupted her.

"Oh, Lord Ainsley, we were all so proud of Amanda. She saved the child's life, you know. No telling how long he could have hung on, poor dear. And he would surely have broken his neck, such a drop it was."

"I really don't know how you did it, Amanda. You know, Ainsley, she slid with the boy in her lap almost all the way down the tree, before they jumped. Jimmy sprained his ankle, and to hear his grandmother tell it, Amanda even bound it for him until the doctor could be brought. She's become a veritable heroine to the crofters, I must say," added the Vicar, not oblivious to the emotions that seemed to be boiling beneath the dark looks the Earl was casting to Amanda.

But this testimonial did not seem to appease him, the Vicar noted, and tea was at best a strained affair.

Upon taking their leave, Amanda and the Earl rode northward toward the marshlands. When he felt he had calmed down sufficiently, the Earl asked, "Cousin, am I to understand that you actually climbed a tree?"

"My lord, the child's life was in danger. Of course I climbed the tree."

"Have you no shame? A grown woman, the Lady of the Manor, climbing trees? I suppose you hiked your skirts up to do it?" he asked, calm rapidly deserting him.

"Well, of course, I hiked my skirts! You don't expect me to climb with my skirts down, do you? Why, I'd have killed myself!" she replied, her eyes flashing.

"Dammit! I don't expect you to climb at all, Cousin!" he shouted. "What in the name of Heaven is wrong with you? You could have gone for help. You—"

"Nothing is wrong with *me,* my lord. But something is very wrong with you. I could not go for help because I did not know if the child could hold on a moment longer. I did not think my consequence was as important as his life. I suppose *yours* is!" she spat back in fury.

Knowing that anything he might have said at that point would be unfit for feminine ears, the Earl swallowed the blustering retort on his tongue and glowered at Amanda for a long moment. They rode on in angry silence as the marshlands came into view.

Damn her, thought the Earl. No woman had ever pushed him to such a rage. He simply did not permit it. Why, he'd even cursed at her, of all things. What was wrong with him anyway? This would certainly never happen again, he assured himself, and schooled his features to an impassive calm.

His lordship found himself growing impatient with his grand tour, and as he was not up to a debate of marshlands versus woodlands as they applied to vegetable farming, he suggested, as politely as he could, that they head home.

"Why, of course, my lord, but there is just one more thing," she replied tranquilly.

"What? Oh, no, Cousin, don't let us start about the Low Cottages. We're going home," he said firmly, beginning to turn his horse around.

"Well, I am sorry you will not accompany me. I shall see you at dinner, my lord," she countered, and was off at a gallop.

"Damn that woman!" he cursed as he spun around to follow her. She was spurring Aquitaine to great speed, and though she was a good horsewoman, he knew that he was better. In a short while he came astride of Amanda, and as she whipped Aquitaine to move faster, he grabbed her reins and ground them both to a halt.

"Let go! You have no right to stop me!" she shouted, raising her riding crop to strike him.

He grabbed her wrist with his free hand and thundered, "Don't you dare ever raise a hand to me, Amanda Millforte!" He was squeezing her wrist very hard and in the next moment it went limp as she grimaced in pain. "Good. Now that we understand each other," he said as he dismounted, "I wish to speak with you."

"We can speak at home."

"Yes, however, the staff is a bit overly solicitous, shall we say. No, my dear," he said haughtily, reaching up for her and not letting go Aquitaine's reins, "I mean for us to take a little walk."

As he gave every indication that he would yank her down if she did not comply, Amanda allowed herself to be guided to the ground. He took her wrist roughly and led her away from the horses. She jerked her hand away and followed him to the top of the small hill overlooking what appeared to be an old abandoned crofter's hut. The day was clear and in the distance the peaks and cones of the Welsh Mountains rose beneath a blue mist.

The Earl stopped just under a gnarled elm tree and looked intently at Amanda. Her green eyes were more than usually translucent set against the perfect sky. God, but she was beautiful! He thought ruefully that there were many more pleasant things he'd rather be doing with Amanda Millforte than arguing with her. But such diversion could wait. First, he would have to curb her rather alarming breaches of conduct.

"Cousin, you simply *must* remember who you are. The Lady of the Manor does *not* go careening about the countryside, climbing trees, galloping off to the most unsavory part of the county, and I don't know what all. Why, your behavior is positively hoydenish

45

and does no credit to the name of Millforte!" he fumed.

"How dare you address me so! I'll have *you* remember who I am, my lord. You have no right to interfere with my actions, as we both are well aware. Besides which, you know very well that I do not 'climb trees,' and as for the Low Cottages, it is precisely the name of Millforte that I am concerned with. We have been making repairs on many of the estate buildings and—"

"And you put me in mind of another thing, Cousin," interrupted the Earl. "It simply is not proper for you to make decisions regarding the marshlands or production of wool, or—by God, you should hear yourself. You sound like a—like a—bluestocking!" The Earl was leaning very close to her now, one hand resting on a low branch of the tree, so that she was caught between the tree and his arm.

"Why you pompous, overbearing—" she began, her fists clenched, her cheeks suffused with color.

Suddenly the Earl did not wish to argue with her any longer. He gazed into her flashing green eyes and was conscious instead of the unmistakable desire to kiss her. Yes, he would have liked to turn the passion of her anger to something very much more pleasurable. But he had resolved to let her make the first overture, and so he merely grinned and said, "Halt, Cousin, please; *do* let us call a cease-fire." He sighed. "What can I do to make you believe that I have only your best interests in mind? And those of your son?"

But Amanda was not to be mollified. *"My* best interests? You insult me, my lord. The only interests that will ever concern the Earl of Ainsley are his own," she retorted bitterly.

His attempt at reconciliation spurned, the Earl gave full vent to his anger. "You are bent on disgracing our name, Cousin. Your mother's accident so many years ago was indeed a tragedy. All the more so because you had no mother to instruct you in the proper way to conduct yourself as befits a Viscountess!"

He could see her whole body heave with fury as she hissed through clenched teeth, "My mother did not die in an accident. And I forbid you to speak of her again!" Her eyes widened as soon as she had spoken, and her hand flew to her mouth before she turned and fled to her horse.

Jeffries heard the front door slam and turned to see Amanda, a most chagrined look on her face and tears welling up in her eyes, stumble into the house and up the stairs. From the corner of his eye Jeffries noted that Mrs. Havenwick, too, had been witness to the little scene. Not a minute later the great door opened again, this time to admit the Earl, looking ferocious as he pulled off his hat and gloves, tossed them on the trestle table, and strode up the stairs, taking them two at a time.

Jeffries looked in dismay at Mrs. Havenwick, and saw in her expression that, perhaps for the first time in their life under the same roof, they were in complete accord. There was trouble brewing at Millforte. Very big trouble. Well-intentioned though the Master might have been, Jeffries thought, he had been regrettably wrong. Her ladyship and the Earl were both too headstrong, and too proud. It was obvious that they would never agree on much of anything. And now they were all sitting atop a giant keg of powder, thought the butler, a keg of powder that would ignite without warning when the right spark touched it.

It was not until Amanda had bolted her door that she let the tears come. She threw herself on her bed and sobbed violently. She could not remember ever being so angry. Such a selfish, supercilious, domineering man! How dare he treat her that way!

Her sobs seemed to come from deep within her as she

recalled her last words to him. How had he provoked her to the point of uttering what she had never told a living soul, not even Arthur? She could have cut her own tongue out the minute the words were spoken, so horrified was she by her disclosure. Amanda's body shook, wracked with her tears for what could not be undone. And what now? Would he question her about her mother? She could not bear it if he did.

At length she felt spent, and slowly she raised herself from the bed. She walked to her dressing table and peered into the looking glass. Her hair was disheveled and her eyes red. It was several hours before dinner, and though she did not at all feel up to dining with the Earl, and would much have preferred to remain closeted in her room, she had never been one to run away and hide. Besides, she was certainly not going to allow the Earl to chase her away from her own dinner table.

Oh, but her eyes! How could she face him like this? And her head was throbbing after her rare fit of weeping. She quickly went to the washstand and dipped a clean piece of linen into the cool water. She lay on her back upon the bed, pressing the cool linen against her eyes and forehead. The sensation was soothing, and in the stillness of her room, she allowed her thoughts to wander to Arthur, as they often did when she was alone and unoccupied.

Poor Arthur. He had been such a good man. No one should have to die like that—such a painful, lingering death. Why was it that the people she loved seemed to die such painful deaths? Her thoughts flew involuntarily to her mother. Wasn't her death, in its own way, just as painful, and perhaps even slower? She felt the tears well up and forced her mind away from her mother. Not that she grieved less for Arthur, but at least she had the comfort of knowing that he had been a very happy man in the last years of his life.

She remembered when Arthur had first come to her father's house. Arthur had known her father only briefly in the cavalry many years back, but when he'd found himself passing through Lincolnshire he had visited his old acquaintance. She could still picture Arthur gazing at her so intently at the dinner table that first night. She remembered that they had played several games of chess and gone riding over the estate, rather seedy and neglected by that time. On the third day of his visit Arthur had trailed her to a secluded spot in the garden. He had gently and very simply asked her if she would marry him. She had stared at him wide-eyed, for she was but eighteen and she knew him to be about fifty. Besides, he hardly knew her!

She would never forget the next thing he said. "You must forgive my breach of conduct in not asking your father's consent to pay my addresses to you first, Miss Talbot. I do think he would welcome my suit, though. I—I—am not a poor man, and correct me if I'm wrong, but it is my impression that if he desired my suit, and you did not, that he—he would bring undue pressure on you. That, in fact, he would make things rather unpleasant for you. And I—I would not for all the world see you hurt."

Amanda felt a lump in her throat and looked up at him with moist eyes. Never before had she encountered kindness of any sort from a man, her experience limited to the men in her family. Her two older brothers were coarse and dissolute at best. Her younger brother was still a schoolboy, and her father was cruel. That this man should have understood, in so short a visit, what her life was like, and that he should have acted as he did out of concern for her, was quite overwhelming.

"Why do you want to marry me, Lord Millforte?"

"You are very beautiful, devastatingly so," he began, and seeing her look of astonishment, he went on gently. "Hasn't anyone ever told you that?" She shook her head and looked down at her hands. He raised her chin with his fingertip. "You are gracious, gentle, and—and you beat me at chess. Not many women can do that. In this short time I have come to love you very much, my dear. And though I am much older than you, yet I think I can make you happy. There is not much future for you here, is there? He has not even made an effort to present you to society, has he?" She again shook her head and he continued. "I will be blunt, Amanda. He will sell you to the highest bidder when it suits him. Do you understand that?"

"Yes, I have always known it. But I—I don't feel I know you well enough to—that is—it is not fair when I don't—I don't—"

"Amanda, I am not asking you to love me. Your company, your smile, and your wit will be enough. And I am not unhopeful that you may develop some—affection for me, as time goes on. Is the idea so unpleasant, my dear?"

She smiled up at him through her tears. He was a kind man, and that was all that really mattered. "I shall be honored to marry you, my lord."

Amanda put her hand over the compress, as if to push away the tears. It was all past, and she must dwell on the happiness, not the tragedy.

It had not been difficult to feel affection for Arthur. He was a gentle man, and he treated her with such respect and tenderness that she had often wondered, at the beginning, if she had dreamed it all. When Victor was born, her heart burst with love for both her husband and son, and she knew that despite his already evident illness, Arthur, with his wife at his side and a healthy heir in the cradle, had never been happier.

Amanda felt her body relax at these more pleasant memories, and she must have drifted off to sleep, for she was next conscious of a soft tap at the door. "My lady, 'tis time to dress for dinner."

Amanda ignored the throbbing in her head as she jumped out of bed to admit her maid. "How long have I slept, Bessie?"

"Several hours, my lady. Come, we needs must hurry if you're to be ready for dinner. That is," she said, her eyes taking in her mistress's still somewhat red-rimmed eyes and her tousled hair, "unless you'd rather I brought your dinner here, my lady. I'm sure Lord Ainsley would—"

At the sound of the Earl's name, Amanda straightened her back and brushed a few stray strands of hair from her face. "I shall of a certain dine with the Earl. The black taffeta if you would, Bessie."

"Yes, of course, my lady. Oh, and, beggin' your pardon, for it nearly slipped my mind, this message come for you just a short time ago. The footman said it weren't urgent, so I didn't wake you."

"Thank you, Bessie." Amanda read the note as Bessie began to comb out her thick black locks. It was from Lady Bosley, the Squire's wife, inviting Amanda and the Earl to dine the following evening.

Amanda frowned as she read the last part of the message: "I know you have not been out in society these many difficult months, my dear Lady Millforte, but it is past the six months now, and perhaps it will do you good to go about a bit. And we should very much enjoy seeing the Earl of Ainsley after so many years. It will be a small party with, of course, no music or dancing. You and his lordship will make ten at table, but I shall quite understand if you are not up to it."

Amanda did not doubt her feelings in this matter. She simply was not ready to go about in society. It was too soon, despite the six months. But she would have to present the invitation to the Earl, and somehow she knew that if she told him her feelings, he would insist upon going, merely to thwart her. She could not imagine that he would want to go. His behavior at the vicarage certainly did not indicate his great desire for company, and, she realized ruefully, he would undoubtedly consider the country gentry quite beneath his touch. No, it would be best to feign complete indifference, and let the Earl make the decision. Besides, somewhere in the recesses of her mind she knew that many battles loomed ahead between them. Let him have his way in the unimportant issues. She would not be fool enough to fight him on this. That could wait for things that counted, things like the marshlands and the Low Cottages.

They sat in strained silence until the covers had been removed and the footman had at last exited the dining room. Then Amanda drew Lady Bosley's message from the pocket of her gown and walked to the Earl at the far end of the table. "My lord, this was delivered to me this afternoon. It is from Lady Bosley. Do you remember Sir James and Lady Bosley, my lord?"

"Yes, somewhat. I know the Squire by reputation at all events. Live nearby, do they?" he replied, his brows coming together as he perused Lady Bosley's wide and careless scrawl.

"Yes, my lord. Sweetbriar House is but a short ride from here," she said, resuming her seat.

"Do you wish to go, Cousin?" he asked, looking intensely at her across the table.

"I will leave that entirely up to you, my lord. If you deem it fitting for me to go, then be guided simply by your own desires. You are, after all, my guest," she said demurely.

His lordship could not keep his brows from arching in astonishment at this. This was not the Amanda he had come to know in the past two days. If *he* deemed it fitting? By *his* desires? Since when did she give a tinker's damn what he thought or wanted? But then, he had not been unaware of the telltale redness in her eyes. Could his show of—well—of force this afternoon really have made a difference? His lips curled slightly at the thought, but he could not ignore a mocking voice at the back of his brain that said, "Watch out, Ainsley, or the little actress will have you beaten."

He frowned again and considered the problem. He doubted not that she itched to go. The enforced exile of the past half year or more would be torture to a woman such as she. And so his first impulse was simply to say that they would not go.

But there was another side to this. The Earl had to admit to himself that he had been most disconcerted at the Amanda he had seen thus far. Consummate actress though she might be, yet he had seen nothing of the femme fatale he knew by reputation. Would not Lady Bosley's dinner party, no matter how small, give him an opportunity to see the true nature of Amanda Millforte's character? It might be very diverting indeed to watch her single out her next lover.

He smiled at her and said, his voice all solicitude, "It is time you began to go about a bit. I think Lady Bosley is right. We are both, perhaps, in need of some diversion."

Blast him! thought Amanda. He does what *he* wants and makes it sound as if he's doing it for *me*. But she merely smiled sweetly at him, saying, "Very well, my lord, I shall send a message to Sweetbriar House at once."

Chapter Four

The Earl settled himself into a rather uncomfortable ladder-back chair in the main hall, resigned to waiting the requisite amount of time a gentleman must always wait for a woman. He considered it little short of a mental imbalance in females that they believed, universally, that the longer a man was kept waiting, the more intrigued he would be. His lordship reflected that if he ever found a woman who did not subscribe to that strange quirk of behavior, he would be intrigued indeed. He should, therefore, have been quite delighted when Amanda appeared at the head of the stairs not a moment later. But he was, in fact, anything but delighted, for this disturbed his complacent view of the universe in general and Amanda Millforte in particular. He was piqued but momentarily, however, for Amanda began to move down the stairs.

He stared at her with piercing eyes, his mouth slightly open and his breathing most irregular. Her high-waisted gown of black silk molded sensually to her form as she slowly descended the staircase. It fell below the shoulders and across the bosom under a ruffle of Belgian lace, which also served as the only sleeves. She wore long black gloves, and her only jewels were a pair of diamond drop earrings and a diamond-studded Spanish comb that adorned the soft ringlets in her hair. Her long neck was bare, its creamy whiteness broken only by a few black tendrils sweeping the nape of her neck.

He noted that her breasts were hidden and for some unknown reason this gave him a certain sense of relief. He quickly chided himself for this last, however. Why should he care a tad for the modesty of Amanda Millforte's dress? Certainly such modesty belied the true nature of her scandalous behavior, and his own momentary concern was at odds with his deliciously dishonorable intentions toward her ladyship.

Those intentions were very much on his lordship's mind as the carriage made its way toward Sweetbriar House. He glanced at Amanda through veiled eyes. It was becoming increasingly difficult to keep his distance from her. If she weren't so devastatingly beautiful, if she hadn't so much fire in her, it would have been easier. As it was, his lordship had been biding his time these three days, expecting Amanda to make the first move. Surely she must know that a certain intimacy with him could only serve to make him more amenable to whatever she wanted out of the estates. And he could not believe that her main concerns were marshlands and Low Cottages. No, such a woman does not marry a man thirty years her senior to improve the land. More than likely it was money she was after. Certainly she was sophisticated enough to know that there were ways she could curry his indulgence in whatever plans she had.

Then what was she waiting for? She had been enacting some role, the purpose of which was unknown to him. And she was a damned good actress, too. If he hadn't known her by reputation, he could easily have believed her to have been a virtuous wife turned grieving widow. Why, she had not evinced even a hint of flirtatiousness in her manner toward him. He knew himself to be not unattractive. In fact, his lordship had never lacked for willing females to delight his days and charm his nights. If he would but admit it to himself, he was more than a little rankled that the young Lady Millforte had been able to resist him for so long. Well, he had been patient long enough. It was time he took matters into his own hands.

Whatever ruminations his mind may have led him to were cut sadly short, however, as the carriage drew up at Sweetbriar House.

Amanda and the Earl were ushered into an ornate, overly furnished drawing room, and greeted effusively by the very friendly, though rather hen-witted, Lady Bosley. As she began the round of introductions, his lordship heard several gasps, and saw that all eyes were on the lovely Amanda. Only two pairs of eyes interested him. Sir James Bosley was gaping hungrily at Amanda and making no attempt to hide it. The man ought to have some manners, thought the Earl, furious. Even if his wife lived in blissful ignorance of his numerous peccadilloes, certainly everyone else did not need to read his lecherous designs on his face.

Men of Sir James's ilk commanded little respect from Lord Ainsley. His dress was overly fussy, his cravat boasting more folds than one could count, his shirt points so high that it would amaze the Earl if he could chew his food. His cuffs were ruffled and a large ring adorned each hand. He sported both quizzing glass and watch fob. His olive green brocade jacket was well cut, possibly even Weston's, for the Earl knew that Sir James considered himself something of a purveyor of London fashion here in Shropshire. But even Weston's skill could not hide the fact that he was overly plump, and that coupled with his feeble attempt to hide his balding head beneath a Brutus haircomb made him seem a foolish imitation of Prinny himself. Could

Amanda possibly see anything in all that?

But while Sir James angered him, even disgusted him, it was the other pair of eyes that worried him. The Honorable Mr. Andrew Linfield had just been introduced to them as Lady Bosley's brother, up to visit for a fortnight. "My baby brother, as you can see," she was saying. "The great disappointment of my life is that I have never been able to convince Andrew to marry. My five children all setting up their nurseries long since, and here's Andrew still a bachelor."

Had he not known her to be intellectually incapable of such machinations, the Earl would have been sure that Lady Bosley was indulging in a bit of matchmaking. But it would be just like her to chatter away, saying exactly what was on her mind, with no regard for the fact that she might be making everyone around her quite uncomfortable.

Amanda did indeed look uncomfortable, but Linfield appeared not to have heard his sister's words. He kissed Amanda's hand and seemed loath to let it go, gazing, thought his lordship, much too intently into her eyes. Linfield was about thirty, a rather handsome, well-built, sandy-haired man, and hardly the "baby" Lady Bosley spoke of. His lordship disliked him instantly.

As Lady Bosley led them to the center of the room to complete her introductions, the Earl exchanged distracted pleasantries with everyone, all the while watching Sir James and Linfield as they watched Amanda, or tried to engage her in conversation. He found himself becoming quite anxious about those two gentlemen, and he could not for the life of him understand why he cared what they did, or what she did, for that matter. Hadn't he wanted to come here to see the famed femme fatale stalk her prey? Even if she was not exactly doing the stalking, still, why wasn't he enjoying it?

His lordship was confusing himself with these rather convoluted reflections, and so he was more than a little grateful when dinner was announced. He strode quickly to Amanda, and with a proprietary clasp of her elbow made it known that he would escort her to the dining room. Linfield demured politely, but Sir James glared at him, a challenge in his eyes.

As the guests found their seats, the Earl noted that Lady Bosley did set an elegant table. The white damask cloth provided a perfect backdrop for the fine cornflower blue porcelain, and three ornate silver candelabra were spaced along the table, their dancing lights flickering over the assembled faces.

The seating arrangement did not please the Earl at all, however. Lady Bosley sat at the foot of the table, flanked by the Earl on her right and Lord Windham, whom the Earl had never met before, on her left. Lord Windham seemed a reasonable, intelligent man, a comfortably well-to-do Viscount whose passion was horsebreeding and who was devoted to his lands, just outside of Ludlow. To Windham's left sat Mrs. Trumwell, gaily holding her own with him in a spirited discussion of horseflesh. Linfield was seated next to Mrs. Trumwell, whom he all but ignored, so desirous was he of gaining Amanda's attention. For Amanda was seated, much to the Earl's dismay, between Linfield and the Squire, who occupied, of course, the head of the table.

To the Squire's left sat Lady Windham, then the Vicar, and between the Vicar and the Earl, Miss Prescott, who had also become known to the Earl for the first time tonight. She was Lady Windham's sister, a lively spinster of advanced years with a pinched nose and sharp eyes that seemed to miss nothing. She must never have been pretty, the Earl thought, but her

58

constant smile and ready sense of humor made her quite engaging.

She was at the moment conversing with Mr. Trumwell and her sister, and Lady Bosley claimed the Earl's attention as she regaled him with the latest exploits of her numerous grandchildren. Lady Bosley was a tiny, not overly plump woman who still retained some of her youthful good looks. She was totally devoted to her family and had been blessed with a mind quite incapable of comprehending her husband's notorious philandering.

But the Squire's unsavory reputation was very much on his lordship's mind as he listened halfheartedly to Lady Bosley and gazed intently across the table at Amanda. Sir James leaned toward her, almost drooling in his eagerness. To her credit, the Earl thought grudgingly, she looked uncomfortable. Or was he imagining that? His brows knit together in a deep frown as he saw Sir James put his hand over Amanda's. She quickly retrieved her hand, coloring slightly. Was she genuinely embarrassed, even distressed by his behavior, or had there been prior intimacy that she did not want revealed? He could not tell, but as he watched the Squire attempt to shovel large quantities of food into a mouth that was almost eclipsed by the ridiculously high shirt points, he could not imagine what Amanda could possibly see in such a coxcomb. Still, he thought that those two would bear close watching for the remainder of his visit.

Presently he noticed that Linfield was able to claim her attention, but the Earl was not much relieved, for the looks Linfield gave her reminded him of the mooncalf eyes that little Jimmy had cast her way. In fact, Linfield made him rather nervous, for the Earl considered him quite a threat indeed. A threat to what, he wondered? After all, Amanda had been known, or so the on dits had it, to dally with more than one man at a time. But it was not the desire for light dalliance that the Earl saw written on Linfield's face, and for some unfathomable reason, this was most perturbing of all.

Amanda, for her part, was grateful for the opportunity to turn to Mr. Linfield when the Squire's attention was diverted for a moment by Lady Windham, who asked whether he himself had shot down the delicious pheasant which had just been presented as the fourth course.

"I cannot tell you how pleased I am that you were able to come, Lady Millforte," Mr. Linfield was saying. "My sister has spoken of you often and I have very much desired to make your acquaintance. Forgive me if I presume too much, Lady Millforte, but would it be possible, that is, would you mind if I—" Linfield stammered a bit and finally blurted, "May I call upon you one morning, Lady Millforte?"

Amanda looked up at him, somewhat bewildered. What did he want with her? He was being the perfect gentleman. Was it—could it be courtship that he had in mind? Was she imagining it or did his eyes hold a certain adoration such as little Jimmy evinced? What could she say to spare his feelings but make clear how she felt? "Please understand, Mr. Linfield, that I am still in mourning. I am just not ready to—that is, it is a bit premature to—"

"But of course, Lady Millforte. I should be a loathsome creature indeed were I to pressure you at a time like this. I will return for another visit, and then we shall become better acquainted," he said, smiling warmly.

Amanda had hoped to discourage him by demurring, but that smile worried her. She tried to be more blunt. "I'm afraid I did not make myself clear, Mr. Linfield. What I mean to say is, well, to be sure, one is very much in need of friends at such a time. If you come as a friend I should be glad of some company. But—but nothing more. I shall not, even in future visits, want anything more. Do you see?" she asked softly.

"Of course, Lady Millforte," he replied, not really seeing at all but considering it a hopeful sign that he had not been barred altogether from Millforte. "Perhaps I might take you for a drive in a few days' time?"

"Yes, yes perhaps," she answered vaguely, and they lapsed into a momentary silence, for which Amanda was extremely grateful.

Lady Windham would not hold the Squire's attention for long, she knew, and she found his leering proximity quite sickening. She remembered the Earl, the day before, leaning very close to her atop that hill as he angrily and haughtily laced into her. His tone had infuriated her, but his closeness, his physical presence, had not discommoded her in the least. She peered across the table at the Earl at a moment when she felt him looking elsewhere. She knew he had been staring at her, and she found herself wishing that he could somehow wrest her from the Squire's side and take her home immediately. This was, of course, out of the question, and Amanda thought fleetingly of pleading a headache. But that was so out of character for her that she'd have everyone calling for a doctor. Besides, the Earl would never let her live it down. She would have to extricate herself from Sir James's attentions with as much dignity as she could muster.

The Earl turned his slate blue eyes upon her and she quickly looked down at the plate. Why was he always looking at her like that? She remembered his face as she had descended the stairs at home. He had been frowning at her, as usual, but even then, she had to admit, his face was handsome, his eyes, for all the seeming anger behind them, warm. Amanda had noted with some pleasure his finely tailored coat of dark gray superfine, which fitted his broad figure to perfection, and his white pantaloons, hugging his strong shapely thighs. But she had admonished herself then, as she did now. It would not do to allow herself any pleasant thoughts whatever about a man who cared not a whit for her and who held her in little but contempt.

As she schooled her thoughts away from the Earl, she became aware that the Squire had focused his attention on her once more. "My dear, I should very much like to take you riding. Perhaps tomorrow after luncheon?" he was saying.

"Oh, thank you, Sir James, but no, I'm afraid I am frightfully busy. There is much to do with the estates just now," she tried by way of refusal.

"Oh, come, come, Lady Millforte. We all have time for a little recreation, now don't we?" His grin had become openly suggestive.

Amanda took a deep breath and looked him straight in the eye. "I again thank you for the honor you do me, Sir James, but I cannot ride with you, now or at any time. I do not deem it proper, and I wish this discussion to end."

"Since when do you concern yourself with proprieties, my dear Lady Millforte?" he asked, his voice hard and his eyes narrowed. "But you may have your little game, my enchantress. We shall meet again soon."

Amanda was both indignant and bewildered by his words, but unwilling to pursue conversation with him, she turned a keen interest to her poached salmon dressed with capers.

Miss Prescott at this moment decided to engage Lord Ainsley's attention. Surely he could not be so very interested in the last lying-in of Mrs. Bosley's second

62

daughter. "How long do you plan to stay in Shropshire, my lord?" she asked.

"I do not know, Miss Prescott. We are, of course, working on the estate accounts," he said vaguely.

"Oh—is there so much to do then?"

"Well, yes, that is, no, it's all quite under control, er, that is, there are certain arrangements that have to be made," he replied uneasily.

Lavinia Prescott was wildly diverted. She had not been overly eager to attend Lady Bosley's dinner party. She found Lady Bosley a sweet bore and her husband vulgar. But indeed she had not been so entertained at a dinner party in years. The significance of the little tête-à-tête between Lady Millforte and Sir James, and the attempt of Mr. Linfield to break in, may have been lost on much of the assembled company, but she had not missed a nuance, nor, she knew, had the Earl. Even as he feebly attempted to answer her, his intense eyes kept returning to Lady Millforte. He was a very physical man, and she could almost feel the anger boil up inside him. He must be wildly jealous, she thought, and the surreptitious glances Lady Millforte cast to his lordship served only to increase her relish of the little drama.

Miss Prescott quite enjoyed her rural existence, being an avid gardener and having almost as keen an interest as her brother-in-law in horsebreeding. But she was not above collecting bits of gossip to amuse herself with, always stopping short of anything malicious. Although she was not, regrettably, attuned to all the latest London on dits, yet she knew Lord Ainsley to be one of England's most eligible bachelors. But he was also one of its most elusive, never fixing his attention long enough for a single mama to feel even a flurry of expectations for her newly launched daughter. Such marked attention as he now paid the young Lady

Millforte was indeed unusual, and she found herself wondering just what had been going on at Millforte for the past few days.

She tried another tack in her attempt to converse with the Earl. "Is it true, as I've heard, that you served in the Peninsula, my lord?" she asked.

"Yes, as a matter of fact, I did," he replied.

"Ah—special diplomatic missions, was it?"

He finally turned to her and said with an amused grin, "Let us say that I served my country in whatever ways I was able. You will forgive me, Miss Prescott, but it is not the stuff of dinner table conversation."

Any further attempt to pursue that subject was forestalled by Sally Trumwell, who was addressing Lord Ainsley across the table. "My lord, have you and Amanda spoken about the marshlands yet?"

"Yes, the subject has come up, Mrs. Trumwell," he answered a bit cautiously, thought Miss Prescott.

"Lord Windham was just telling me that he has been considering reclaiming his marshlands, and I was saying that Amanda has been speaking of the very same thing for months now," Mrs. Trumwell went on.

"Reclaiming the marshlands?" asked the Earl, turning to Lord Windham in surprise.

"Yes, I'd never thought it economically feasible, but I am beginning to consider it very seriously. It has been done with much success in some areas near Ludlow. Have you and Lady Millforte discussed it, Ainsley?" replied Lord Windham.

"Lady Millforte has—er—broached the subject, but we have not had time to discuss the ramifications," the Earl said stiffly, somehow bringing the subject to a close.

Like hell you haven't had time to discuss it, thought Miss Prescott. She would guess that the discussion could have been heard quite far and wide over the

Millforte lands. She resolved to pay the lovely young Lady Millforte a visit in the very near future, for she would want a ringside seat in the next few weeks' lively proceedings.

The Earl could not remember when he had ever been so happy to see a dinner come to an end. Miss Prescott was an intelligent enough dinner partner, and she had been shrewd enough to rescue him from Lady Bosley's ceaseless prattle, but the sight of Amanda between puppy dog eyes on one side and lascivious ones on the other was more than any man should have to bear.

Coffee was served as soon as the men had returned from their brandy and rejoined the ladies in the drawing room. The Earl saw Sir James attempt to guide Amanda to a settee in an isolated corner of the room. She was beginning to look acutely distressed, and deeming it polite at this juncture to leave, he strode toward Amanda, thanking his host perfunctorily, and took her by the arm to lead her away. The Squire glowered at him, and in fact seemed nearly apoplectic when they bade their goodnights and it was borne home to him that the Earl and not he, after all, would accompany Amanda home. The smoldering look he cast to the Earl as his lordship helped Amanda with her cloak was, for his lordship, the highlight of the evening.

"Did you enjoy yourself, Cousin?" he asked impassively as soon as the door had closed behind them.

"I found the rooms—a bit close, my lord," she replied demurely.

"Yes, a bit close," he echoed, somehow more mystified than ever about what kind of game the second Lady Millforte was playing.

The Earl could not sleep. He lay wide awake well into the night, a circumstance which he could not ever remember experiencing previously. Blast that woman, he thought. He certainly could not let Linfield or Sir James fix her attention first! It was time to seduce her and have done with it. The key was to decide when and where. She had gone through a great deal of trouble to keep distance between them. He must breach the barriers of her formality in just the right way.

His mind was not overly taxed on that head, however, for Chance was to be his accomplice that very evening.

When he could no longer abide the ceaseless tossing and turning, he rose from the bed, drew on his dressing gown, and made his way to the library. Perhaps a book would soothe his overly active mind, and make him forget the even more overly active fires within him.

As he approached the library he saw a flicker of candlelight coming from within. He was momentarily startled when a female voice called, "Who is there?" Amanda's voice.

"It is I, Charles," he replied as he entered the room. She turned to face him and he caught his breath as he beheld her. It was the first time he had seen her in a color other than black, for she was wearing a soft, flowing dressing gown that looked, in the candlelight, to be of a pale ivory to match her skin. While it was not sheer, still he thought he could discern her lovely form beneath it, and it clung to her body the way none of her gowns ever did. Her rich black hair cascaded down her back in luxurious waves that tantalized him, and he felt his blood surge within him. Had he thought himself bound by the code of a gentleman to keep his distance, he would at that moment have found it impossible to do so. As it was, he had no such scruples and did not even try.

He strode toward her. "What are you doing here, Cousin Amanda?" he demanded, his voice strong.

"I went down for some hot milk and thought I'd take something to read," she answered meekly, somewhat to her own surprise. But she rallied and asked imperiously, "And you, my lord?"

"I, too, found myself in need of some reading material." His eyes went to a little table near her, on which sat the milk and a book. He picked up the book. "Ah, *Le Morte D'Arthur*. Brushing up, are you?" he asked mockingly. "Tell me, Cousin, can you not sleep?"

Something in his tone made her answer defensively. "Why, of course I can sleep. I—I am just a bit restless, that is all."

"Ah, but of course. Well, *I* cannot sleep, Amanda, and I think it is high time we reached an understanding." He advanced a step closer. She did not move, and her eyes never left his face.

"Here we are, both of us, restless, sleep evading us, and the answer staring us in the face. I can help you sleep, Amanda," he said silkily, very close to her now. "I can make your nights most pleasurable, you know." He softly traced the line of her jaw with his fingers. "We are alone in this big house. What is to stop us?" His voice was low and husky, and as he reached for her hand, she gasped and took a step backward.

"My lord, I—" she began in a shaking voice.

"No, Amanda, no running away. No more pretense," he commanded, grasping her by the shoulders and drawing her to him. He did not give her time to reply, for in the next moment he grabbed the long black locks behind her neck and pulled her face to his. It was a bruising kiss, fierce and demanding. She pummeled his chest to repell him, but he crushed her body to him, encircling her waist with his free hand. He had *expected* her to resist; every woman did, at the beginning. Then he felt her rigid body relax, felt it begin to tremble beneath the soft dressing gown, felt her submitting to his power. She began to return his kiss, slowly at first, and then with fire. Her body was warm and compliant and he knew he had chosen his moment well. But suddenly she thrust her head aside and shoved him away from her.

She backed away, moving toward the door, with a look in her eyes that stunned him. He had been prepared for anger, for indignation. Those he could easily handle and might even enjoy. But it was not anger he read in those translucent sea green eyes. It was fear, deep, deep fear, even terror.

"No! No!" she whispered, horrified, as she turned and fled.

For several moments the Earl remained fixed where he was, unable to move. What had gone wrong? He knew the kind of woman she was, and had, given her reaction to his kiss, not misjudged her passionate nature. Was she angered that he had rewritten part of her playscript, and had she decided to feign being coy? But no, the look of terror in those haunted eyes was real enough. His lordship at once felt a great uneasiness. Of what was she afraid? Of him? Of herself? But why? A woman of her experience with men would know how to lightly spurn unwanted advances. She would not retreat in horror like some chit just out the schoolroom. There was something very wrong about all this, and he could not understand what it was.

It was with a very perturbed mind that the Earl trudged off to bed, resolving to observe Amanda very closely in the next few days and, perhaps, to have some discreet inquiries made in London.

Chapter Five

The Earl slept fitfully for the remainder of the night. At last when the sunlight began to peek through the curtains, he rose, thinking that perhaps an early walk would refresh his body and help clear the confusion in his mind. It fleetingly occurred to him that he might encounter Amanda, since such walks were her custom, but he dismissed this idea, for after last night he was sure she would remain closeted in her room till luncheon at least.

He could see why Amanda might choose dawn as a time for solitary walks, if indeed walk was what she did. The air was crisp, fresh, the dew-covered hillsides never lovelier. Silence pervaded the land, broken only by the occasional bleating of sheep or the call of a shepherd. At length he found himself atop a small hill, heather and mulberry bushes at his feet. He could see the beginning of early morning activity near some distant crofter's cottage. He thought he could discern a woman carrying water, and someone milking a cow.

He loved his own lands—Ainsley Court in Somerset, and the estates in Surrey and in the Scottish Lowlands —but he thought he had never seen a region more peaceful than these sleepy hills and valleys of Shropshire. He turned to survey the land from all sides. He frowned slightly as he perceived two figures standing in an open meadow some hundred yards from him. Even at that distance he could see that one was a man and the other a woman.

He walked forward at least fifty yards, enough to confirm his suspicion that the woman was indeed Amanda. With a sinking feeling he silently moved much closer, stopping behind a cluster of trees. And then he cursed inwardly, for he could not mistake the flaccid form and the Brutus hair comb of Sir James. They were standing about three feet from each other, talking. Amanda and Sir James! How *could* she, he thought, a feeling of revulsion sweeping through him. He turned to go, but something stopped him. He realized that an open meadow, even at this hour, was certainly not an ideal place for a clandestine meeting. The Squire might be vulgar and brash, but Amanda had too much dignity for such a rendezvous. Perhaps this was a chance meeting, then?

Although he could not hear them, his eyes were good and he could see their gestures and even perceive something of the expressions on their faces. The Squire moved toward Amanda, and she retreated several steps. The Earl frowned. Was she playing coy with him, too? But then he saw that the Squire's face did not indicate playfulness of any sort. He was clearly angry, and he advanced toward Amanda and took her by the shoulders in a rough, very unloverlike movement. Amanda tried unsuccessfully to wriggle free. Even at this distance the Earl could see her eyes. They were wide open as she looked at Sir James, and they held—oh, God, he thought—was it that same expression? Fear! She was not playing with a present lover. She was not even angry at a former lover, he thought. She was afraid!

In the next moment Sir James caught her in a crushing embrace, pressing his face to hers. He saw Amanda struggle, pound at him, even kick him, but she did not relax. She did not submit. The Earl could not

70

help a slight smile as he recalled the few moments when she had returned his kiss. Good Lord! he thought. What's wrong with me? I'm no better than he is! The Earl was angry with himself for the night before, and he was shaking with fury at Sir James.

He wanted to rush to her, to wrest her from him. And he thought at that moment that he could kill the Squire with his bare hands.

But what if he was wrong? What if he really was witnessing a lover's tiff? What a fool he would be! But he could not just stand there and watch that man use her so brutally. He would have turned his head, but that the Squire's next action brought him to his senses. Amanda kicked him and he let her go for a moment. The Earl could see Sir James's face contort itself, and then he grabbed her again and quite violently and unceremoniously threw her to the ground.

Sir James's body covered hers in a moment, and Lord Ainsley, cursing his damned pride for making him hesitate at all, bounded from his hidden vantage point and ran toward them. My God, he'll rape her if I don't get there in time, he thought. As he drew closer, he could hear her screams, and he felt a murderous rage well up inside him.

"That's enough, Sir James!" he bellowed when he was but a few feet away.

Sir James ignored him until the Earl's shadow fell upon the ground next to them. "This has nothing to do with you, Ainsley," he growled, still not moving, pinning Amanda down by her shoulders. "Get out of here!"

"Leave her alone, Bosley," the Earl said with icy calm as he yanked the Squire by his collar and heaved him to the ground away from Amanda. He quickly reached for her hand and pulled her up before the Squire had time to turn back to her.

The Squire rose, his face livid. "I'll kill you for this, Ainsley," he said, advancing toward him with clenched fists. "You are not her guardian. You have no right to interfere."

The Earl did not hesitate as he turned and landed a fierce blow to the right side of the Squire's face that sent him reeling to the ground. The Squire gasped for breath and lay stunned for several moments, not quite able to bring his plump body to an upright position.

"I have every right, Bosley. You are trespassing on Millforte lands, of which I *am* guardian. And to so violently abuse a lady! I can ruin you for this. Do you understand?"

"She's no lady, Ainsley, and you know it."

"I should call you out for this, Bosley, but that I don't think you're worth my having to flee the country for. But I warn you, I'll kill you if you ever venture onto Millforte land, or come anywhere near Lady Millforte! Do I make myself clear?"

The Squire did not answer, but struggled to his feet, smoothed his coat, and glowered at the Earl, his face beet red. He began to stagger away from them, but he turned and called over his shoulder, "You're wasting your time on a whore, Ainsley." Then straightening up, he stormed away over the meadow.

The Earl saw Amanda turn away from him, her whole body shaking, her mouth biting on her fist, as if fighting to quell her tears.

He picked up a large rock at his feet. "Damn him!" he exploded, as he dashed it to the ground.

"Amanda, I—I am sorry—that you had to be—subjected to this," he said in a low, husky voice as he strode to her. She stood with her back to him, and he gently grasped her shoulders. "I can never forgive myself. I—I should have been here—sooner."

Her head fell into her hands and her slender shoulders shook as she finally gave way to her tears. He turned her to him and she buried her head in the folds of his coat. He held her tightly and stroked the top of her head as she sobbed into his chest. After a few moments she held her head up and inhaled deeply as she tried to brush the tears from her eyes. He handed her his handkerchief. He looked at her beautiful ravaged face, at the disheveled hair covered with leaves, at the crumpled gray walking dress which fitted her lovely body to perfection. He remembered the feel of that body the night before, and he seethed when he thought of what might have happened here had he not intervened.

He was loath to release her, but he held her a few inches from him as he asked, with an edge to his voice, "Did he hurt you?" She shook her head, the handkerchief still held to her eyes. "Look at me, Amanda. I saw him throw you. Are you quite sure you are right?"

She straightened her shoulders. "I am right. I just—I just don't understand," she said tremulously. "I have known him for years. Why should he suddenly—"

"Surely you noticed that his manner last night was especially—familiar."

"Yes, and I made it quite clear to him that I would not—that I did not welcome—his attentions."

The Earl could not suppress a bitter laugh. "And you thought *that* would deter him? Come now, you cannot be that naive."

"And just what are you implying by that, my lord? I am sorry that I am not as experienced in the ways of men as you would have me," she said, her voice strong and her back stiffening beneath his touch.

"I am implying nothing. I am merely saying that you had ought not to walk abroad unaccompanied. I tried to tell you that before."

She moved out of the range of his arms and looked him in the eye as she said, "I have always traversed these lands alone. This is my home. I am not a child, you know."

"No, you are not, Amanda. Were you a child I should have a good deal less to worry about." He saw

73

her start at his use of her Christian name, as if noticing it for the first time, but he had no patience for silly formalities at a time like this. "Now I want your word that if you *must* take these walks you will have your maid accompany you." The Earl spoke too sharply, he knew. He had not wanted to scold, but somehow she infuriated him.

"I am sorry, my lord, but I cannot give my word. I have no intention of changing my accustomed habits because of one unfortunate incident. I have no idea why Sir James—approached me in such fashion, but I do not think it will happen again," she said resolutely, her sea green eyes never leaving his face.

Damn her! he thought, his ominous brows coming together. She would deliberately place herself in danger just to defy him. He clasped her by the shoulders and shook her, as he shouted, "Do I have to give you a detailed description of what almost happened here for you to understand the danger you are in? I absolutely forbid you to walk about unaccompanied. Do I make myself clear?"

"Does that include my own library, my lord?" she hissed through clenched teeth.

He released her immediately, a stricken look crossing his eyes. She regretted her words instantly. That was not fair and she knew it. Lord Ainsley's intentions had been no more honorable than the Squire's, it was true, but somehow she knew the Earl would never force himself upon her. She would not think about her own response last night, for that was most disturbing of all. She looked at the slate blue eyes gazing so intently at her. Why was it that he had the ability to bring out the worst in her, to make her say things she would never, in more rational moments, dream of uttering?

The Earl sighed but did not deign to answer her question. Perhaps he'd deserved that, he thought, upbraiding her in such a manner after the humiliation she had endured. "He obviously knows your habits and he will try again. Make no mistake about that. And if not he, then someone else. You are a very beautiful woman, Amanda. You simply cannot walk about unaccompanied." His voice had become gentler, and he began to brush the leaves and grass from the back of her dress.

His touch was soft and she felt her back tingle beneath the sarcenet of her walking dress. She tried not to think of that as she said quietly, "I do not understand. I have been a guest in his house. I have known him for years. He has never before made any attempt to—to—"

"You were married before, and then you were in mourning. You no longer have the protection of a husband. Don't you understand how that changes things?" He gazed at her in concern.

"You mean that now men feel they can take liberties with me?" she asked sharply, challenge in her eyes.

He colored slightly at that, but he refused to be baited. He would not allow his behavior to be equated with that of Sir James. Surely she must see the difference. He would never use her in such a manner. He had tried to persuade her, it was true, but that was another matter entirely. Besides, he remembered those few delicious moments when she had let down her guard and warmed to him. She had certainly not responded to the Squire in any such way. The Squire was brutal, callous, had no feeling for her, whereas *he* had—*he* had—what? he asked himself. He wanted her, but was there something more? No, he was just naturally protective of a female in distress. But when had he ever felt protective of a woman before?

He forced his meandering mind back to the ensuing conversation. "I am afraid that perhaps that is so," he said softly. He could not look her in the eye, and instead concentrated on the prickly bits of underbrush still adhering to her dress. He searched for a way to change the subject, which had become decidedly uncomfortable. "Shake out your skirts," he said, smiling slightly. "Mrs. Havenwick will likely bar me from the house if I bring you back like this."

She could not keep her lips from curling to a smile, he saw with relief, and as he gingerly pulled bits of grass and leaf from her hair, he had to fight with all his power the overwhelming desire to kiss the proud and defiant face of the woman who stood before him.

"Come, let us go home," he said as soon as she had pinned her curls back into some semblance of order.

"I will follow shortly, my lord. I—I—need to be alone for a few moments, please."

"I'm sorry, Cousin. You know I will not leave you here. You can be alone in the gardens if you must." He grasped her hand and pulled her after him. She stumbled slightly, and he realized, after several paces, that she was limping. "What is wrong with your foot, Cousin?"

"Why, nothing, my lord. Am I not walking fast enough for you?"

"Don't gammon me, Cousin. Come here." He pulled her to a nearby rock. "Sit down."

"This is foolish. I assure you I am perfectly fine."

"I had not previously noticed that you had such a decided limp to your walk," he said sarcastically. "Now sit down!" he shouted, pushing her onto the rock.

"This foot?" he asked, softly probing her right ankle. She grimaced at his touch. "When he pushed you?" She nodded and he saw her blink away the moisture in her eyes. He continued to touch the ankle and gently twist it. She gasped when he pushed the foot up from the sole of her tiny boot.

"Dammit, Amanda, did you really think you could hide this from me? And what did you hope to accomplish?" he asked in a tone he knew to be much too condescending.

"I can take care of myself, my lord. Will you please leave me alone?" she said between clenched teeth.

Like hell you can, he thought, but he merely said, "I cannot carry you all the way home, nor can I leave you here to fetch a horse. I want you to lean on me and put as little pressure as possible on that foot. Now come." He gently brought her to her feet, but she refused to come near him.

"Amanda," he said, quite exasperated, "I am well aware that you want nothing to do with me. But I am taking you home, even if I must throw you over my shoulder to do it."

She knew she had no choice, and in truth the pain was growing worse, so she allowed him to slip his arm around her and they began to walk home. She held her head high, but inside her emotions were in turmoil. She did not want his aid, yet she could not help but feel comfortable against him. She glanced surreptitiously at the handsome face, etched now in a frown as he looked down at her foot. How could he have so much disdain for her and yet evince such concern? How was it that the same man who had coldly tried to seduce her the night before could now defend her honor and vow to kill for it if necessary? He is merely acting the gentleman, she admonished herself. He would do the same for any woman. She looked away from him. It would not do to reflect too much upon that handsome face.

The Earl saw her face twist with pain as she stumbled on a clump of twigs in the underbrush. The manor had come into view. "That's as far as you go. If you press further on that ankle you will not be able to walk for a week. Up with you, now," he said as he hoisted her into his arms.

"No! Put me down! I can walk. Truly I can." She squirmed and he nearly dropped her.

"Stop it, Amanda. If it's broken you may permanently damage it. I am going to carry you and you might just as well stop fidgeting!" he commanded.

She stopped moving but she held her body rigid, as if to guard against his touch. It amused him but it made her light form more difficult to carry. As they had rather a distance to go, he said gently, "Cousin Amanda, if you will relax your body I should find it much easier to continue."

He kept his face impassive as she complied, but he could not help feeling pleasure as her warm body curled against him. She was really quite light, and there were few hills remaining until they would reach the house. After a short while she stole a glance at him, and he smiled warmly at her. She blushed furiously, and he thought she was trying very hard, though rather unsuccessfully, not to enjoy the sensation of being in his arms.

And so it was a rather congenial pair who ascended the steps to the Manor sometime later, their heads close together and their arms intertwined.

To their mutual chagrin, the entire household seemed to be awake. Jeffries's mouth fell open and his eyes rounded in complete shock as he opened the door to behold Lady Millforte in the arms of the Earl of Ainsley. The Earl simply said, "Good morning, Jeffries," and proceeded up the stairs.

Halfway up he could hear Mrs. Havenwick bellow from the main hall, "What on earth! My lady, whatever—Mr. Jeffries, what is the meaning of this?"

"Well I—I don't know, madam, but I am certain the Earl—knows—what he is doing," said Jeffries uncertainly, but with what the Earl detected as a hint of amusement.

His lordship grinned and would have been very happy to let them all think what they damned well pleased, but one look at Amanda's face quelled that idea.

"Send up her maid with fresh linen and a hot brick, if you please, Mrs. Havenwick. Her ladyship's injured herself," he called down. Whereupon a great deal of bustle seemed to ensue on the ground floor of the house, so that by the time the Earl had gently deposited her ladyship upon her bed, having shut the door behind him, not only Mrs. Havenwick, but Jeffries, a footman, and half the domestic staff had gathered outside her door to await word of her ladyship's condition.

The Earl was attempting to ease Amanda's foot from the tiny gray half-boot when her maid entered. Amanda caught her breath as he finally yanked the boot off in one quick movement. "I'm sorry. It was the only way," he said.

She nodded and her maid rushed to her side. "Oh, my poor lady. How did you come to hurt yourself?" she asked breathlessly.

"'Tis nothing, Bessie. I—I've twisted my ankle."

"You've brought the linen. Good," said the Earl, motioning for her to deposit the white cloth on the bed next to him. "And the brick?"

"I—I shall fetch it from the kitchen presently, your lordship," she said timidly, curtsying and turning to go.

"Yes, do that. But first I want you to remove her ladyship's stockings."

Bessie's eyes widened and Amanda colored and looked down quickly at the hand resting in her lap.

"I cannot very well bind an ankle that I am unable to see, and I cannot see through black stockings," the Earl sighed, mildly exasperated, as he looked at them both. "The ankle may possibly be broken, and you are wasting precious time, Bessie," he added in a somewhat admonishing tone, although he was fairly certain Amanda had suffered only a bad sprain. He strode to the window and turned his back, clearly expecting his will to be complied with.

"My lord," said Amanda, "would you please step

outside?"

"And spend half an hour extricating myself from that mob gathered out there? I think not, Cousin," he said, grinning, his face to the window.

After several moments in which he heard nothing but the rustling of bedclothes, Amanda said, "Thank you, Bessie."

"Is her ladyship ready, Bessie?" he asked.

"Yes, your lordship."

He strode to the stately four-poster bed and sat down, taking Amanda's foot in his lap. He looked up to see Bessie standing over him, expectantly. He frowned for a moment and then said, "You may fetch the brick now, and some towels. And perhaps you would inform the staff that her ladyship will be fine and they need no longer maintain their rather noisy vigil outside the door."

Bessie immediately turned to Amanda, clearly uneasy about leaving her and awaiting her ladyship's sanction before doing so. Amanda nodded, and as the maid reluctantly departed, the Earl grinned and said, "Why is it that she reminds me of Mrs. Havenwick, Cousin?"

"Why, I cannot think what you mean, my lord," she demurred, a trifle too ingenuously, he thought.

"Perhaps it is that they are both so—devoted to you," he said, looking down at the ankle. "Have they been with you long?" He began to probe the area gently.

"Bessie came to me when I was married. Mrs. Havenwick has been with me since I was a—a young girl," she replied, her body tensing as he touched a particularly sore spot.

"The ankle has swelled considerably and you can see how discolored it has become. Inasmuch as I have been able to move it somewhat, I do not think it broken. I shall bandage it and then enfold it in the towels with the hot brick. You must keep your foot very still today and

80

undoubtedly you will have to remain off it for several days."

He began very skillfully to wrap the foot in the linen. He worked swiftly but she grimaced every time he lifted her foot slightly. He stopped and began to massage the top of the foot gently. He could not help noticing the pale soft skin of the tiny foot and the small area of exposed limb.

"Try to relax," he said soothingly, as he stroked the foot and that part of her ankle that was not discolored. He looked up to see her blushing profusely. He smiled. "It will only be a few more minutes. Once I bind it the heat will ease the pain."

He bent to his task once more, and tried to distract her with conversation. "So Mrs. Havenwick has been with you since you were a girl. She was your father's housekeeper?"

"Yes. I was about twelve when she came," said Amanda, her voice flat.

"Curious that she should have been willing to leave your father, is it not?"

"She—she was very—devoted to me," replied Amanda softly.

Something in her tone made him look up at her. She was staring at the wall beyond him, and her eyes looked dull, and so very fragile. "And your father did not object?" he asked impassively, bending to his work once again.

It was several moments before she spoke. "Arthur—Arthur—persuaded my father that it would be advisable for Mrs. Havenwick to accompany me to Millforte." Her voice was stronger and she did not give him time to reply, but said, in a marked attempt at a light tone, "You do that very well. From where do you get such expertise in bandaging damaged limbs, my lord?"

The abrupt change of subject did not please him, but he responded, "Well, I did serve in the Peninsula, you

81

know. Unfortunately that campaign afforded me plenty of experience in repairing various parts of the anatomy. And besides," he added with a smile, wanting to steer the conversation away from the war, "don't you know that part of every gentleman's education is learning how to fend for himself in any eventuality?"

But Amanda did not return his smile as she said somewhat bitterly, "How nice for you. And did you know that part of every lady's education is learning how to be helpless?"

He sighed and looked into her eyes, sparkling now with the hint of anger. "I did not make those rules, Cousin," he said quietly.

"No, but you live by them," she said curtly.

"Perhaps I have never before been confronted with any of their inequities. There are those who would count me a quite reasonable man, you know."

"Do tell! How interesting," she mocked.

Feeling that this particular topic of conversation had exhausted itself, he said, "I seem to recall hearing that you, too, are rather adept at restoring bruised ankles, Cousin. May I ask the source of *your* particular expertise?"

"One cannot grow up with three brothers without acquiring some facility in the rendering of medical assistance," she said pleasantly.

"Three brothers have you? You know, you rarely speak of your family, Cousin Amanda. Where are they now?"

A warm smile crept over her face as she said, "My younger brother attained his much-longed-for pair of stripes three years ago. He's been abroad ever since. He writes often and is quite happy. He's wanted to be a soldier since the day he could talk."

"You miss him, don't you?"

"Yes, I do, rather. He is a charming boy. Although hardly a boy anymore, I dare say. He's reached his twenty-first year already."

"And your elder brothers?"

Suddenly the smile disappeared from her face and her tone became cold as she replied, "They live with my father."

He looked up at her and saw that that dazed look had taken hold of her eyes once again. He would have questioned further, but was forestalled by the re-entrance of Bessie, cradling a hot brick amid the pile of towels in her arms.

The Earl relieved her of these and dismissed her perfunctorily. Within minutes he had tied the bandage into a final knot and enveloped the swollen ankle in the towels. Amanda seemed to sink back against the bed in relief as she felt the heat penetrate her foot, and he moved quickly to prop the pillows behind her.

"I will have your breakfast sent up presently, and I shall visit with you later in the day. After breakfast I suggest you get some sleep. It has been a very trying morning for you, and—"

"But my lord, is not Higgins engaged to come this morning?"

"Yes, yes I think he is. But do not trouble yourself. I can deal with Higgins," he said smoothly.

"Oh, I am sure you can, my lord. But, you see, I should like to be there when you do," she said sweetly.

"I am afraid that is quite impossible, Cousin. You must keep very still today. Perhaps tomorrow I can carry you down the stairs, but for today I want you to stay where you are."

"Of course, my lord. That is why I see no choice but to conduct the interview with Higgins right here."

"Here? In your bedchamber?"

"Yes, why not?"

"Why not? You know perfectly well why not. It isn't fitting to conduct interviews with gentlemen from your bed," he said sharply.

"Oh, is that all? Well then, perhaps I could prevail upon you to help me to the chaise, there, next to the window," she asked, pointing to the elegantly furnished seating alcove at the far end of the room.

"No, you could not. And I can't think how that would make very much difference. Where is your sense of propriety? It's simply not decent for a gentleman to enter your bedchamber!" he almost shouted, his brows knit together.

"But *you* are here, my lord," she said ingenuously. "And did you not say, not a moment ago, that you would visit me later?"

She had caught him off-guard, and he spluttered, "Yes, well—that is another matter entirely. I am—family—after all."

"Oh, yes. How foolish of me not to note the difference. Nevertheless, this is *my* house and Higgins is *my* man-of-affairs. You will kindly conduct him here the moment he arrives," she said coolly.

Knowing full well that she was only too capable of killing herself while hobbling down the stairs if he refused, the Earl merely sighed and said, "Very well, Cousin. Now, is there anything else you require, or can you manage to stay abed until I return?"

"Why, I would not think of leaving my bed, now that you've made me so comfortable. And yes, actually, there is something I would like. Would you have the ledgers from the last quarter sent up? I should like to peruse them before Higgins arrives."

"But *I* was hoping to—" his lordship began, but then checked himself. "Oh, never mind. Fine. The ledgers it shall be," said a somewhat exasperated Earl as he bowed and took his leave.

Chapter Six

The Earl sat down to his first solitary meal since his arrival at Millforte. He found the silence in the stately dining room oppressive, and he admitted ruefully to himself that he missed the constant banter with Amanda, high-spirited though it might be.

As he helped himself to his third piece of toast with Cook's own blackberry jam, he occupied his mind with considerations upon the subject of his letter to Ridgeway. Simon Gilbrait, very recently the new Marquis of Ridgeway, had been his friend since they were boys at Eton. They had early fallen into the habit of helping each other out of awkward scrapes. Where once those had involved contriving ways of evading the wrath of the headmaster, in recent years they had rather involved extricating one another from some rather inconvenient romantic entanglements. The Earl remembered that unsavory opera dancer from whose clutches he had wrested a very hapless Simon in their first year on the Town. And just a short while ago, he thought with a sigh, there had been Camille, his own delightful, delectable Camille. So eager to please, she had purred like a kitten whenever he came near. How was he to know she'd turn into a vicious tiger when he made it known that he'd tired of her? It was so like Ridgeway to offer to accompany him on his final visit, when he bestowed a handsome new barouche upon her as a token farewell gift. Ridgeway's presence had certainly subdued her; she threw her gilt-edged looking glass at him, narrowly missing his right eye, but otherwise he escaped bodily harm.

And now there was Amanda. A mission infinitely more delicate and complex, made all the more so because he himself did not understand it. He sipped his black coffee slowly as he pondered the question of Amanda.

The ever-present talk about her in London was of a wanton woman who acquired and discarded lovers like last season's dresses, but the Amanda he knew had deported herself with the utmost propriety and dignity. The on dits he had heard over the last several years during his sporadic visits to London had all contained veiled inuendoes and been accompanied by knowing smirks, but somehow he could not recall the name of any particular man with whom she had been linked. There was always speculation at White's as to which Yorkshire baron or London nonpareil had been her latest paramour, but he could not remember the gentleman of the hour actually being identified or, for that matter, identifying himself.

He could not say why, but somehow he had to know who some of these men had been, and when she'd met them, and where. Ridgeway would be very discreet, to be sure, and if there was anything to ferret out, he would do it. *If*—he thought. And if not? Was it possible that it was all—but no, the stories were true enough. She had merely been enacting a brilliant scenario to deceive him for some spurious ends of her own. It was all part of a very carefully laid plan—except—except for last night, in the library, and this morning. None of that had been according to plan. Of that he was certain. And until he heard from Ridgeway he could not know what his next move would be with regard to his elusive hostess.

The letter to Ridgeway was no sooner dispatched than Jeffries ushered Higgins into the library.

The interview did not go well. The Earl led a blushing, flustered Higgins up the great staircase to Amanda's bedchamber, and that hapless retainer immediately plunged into a recital of projected figures for a major drainage project. The Earl was not in the best of humor, the subject of his letter to Ridgeway and the sight of Amanda wincing in pain as a result of the dastardly morning's encounter combining to make him quite irritable indeed. Amanda seemed pleased with Higgins's report, and not at all put out by the sums mentioned, but his lordship found that the projected costs made further consideration of the matter quite out of the question. When Amanda had the audacity to suggest that the Low Cottages were probably located right in the middle of stagnant swampland, and could easily be made part of the overall reclamation of the marshes, the Earl's thunderous reply reverberated through the house, and a much chagrined Higgins beat a hasty retreat from the premises.

The Earl stormed down the stairs soon after, resolving to take luncheon by himself and later to have dinner with Amanda. For he *had* promised to visit her, after all, and perhaps he would have calmed down by then. For now, he would settle down to work.

The day was not destined to be one of his most tranquil, however. As he seated himself comfortably in the library, intending to peruse the ledgers that Amanda had finally relinquished, Jeffries announced the arrival of the Honorable Mr. Linfield. The Earl received him in the morning room.

"Is Lady Millforte all right? I came as soon as I heard," Mr. Linfield was saying.

"Heard?" asked the Earl.

"Yes, about her accident. Is it broken? Her foot, I mean."

"No, no, it's not broken. And it is not her foot. It is her ankle. She's sprained it. How—ah—how did you hear about it so—so soon?" asked the Earl, eyeing the bouquet of flowers in Linfield's hand with annoyance.

"Oh, well, Lady Millforte's cook is the cousin of the upstairs maid at Sweetbriar House, don't you know? Her ankle, you say. Did you have the doctor?"

"No, no, I bound it myself."

"Do you not think it would be wise to have Dr. Pringle see it?"

"No, I do not. Nor does Lady Millforte. She is resting comfortably now and I do not wish her disturbed by *anyone,*" he said rather too loudly, a picture of the rather doddering Dr. Pringle coming to mind.

"Of course, if she is *truly* comfortable . . . How did it happen? She was out walking, I believe? Very early, wasn't it?" questioned Linfield.

"Yes, just after dawn," answered the Earl flatly.

"Did you just happen upon her, or—or—were you out walking—together, Lord Ainsley?" Linfield pressed, his eyes narrowed and his body only half seated on the cushion of the plush velvet sofa.

"No. That is—yes. We—we were looking at some of the cottages that need to be repaired."

"At dawn, Lord Ainsley?" Linfield said sharply.

The Earl did not like his suspicious tone at all, and he answered with thinly veiled hostility. "Yes, at dawn. Lady Millforte enjoys walking at that hour."

"I see. Do you?"

"Do I what?"

"Enjoy walking at sunrise."

"Er, yes, very much as a matter of fact," snapped the

Earl, and then, having had quite enough, he dispatched Linfield with all due speed, accepting his nosegay of tiny violets with well-concealed disdain. It would be orchids for Amanda Millforte, he thought. Orchids or nothing at all.

His peace was cut up once more, not five minutes later, when the Vicar and Mrs. Trumwell arrived, all concern over Amanda's injury. He blinked in amazement. How the devil did everyone already—

"Oh, our Annie is Mrs. Havenwick's niece. Did you not know?" Sally Trumwell was saying. "But then, news travels so fast in these country villages. Have you forgotten, my lord?" the Vicar's wife gushed, not awaiting a reply. "And to think you carried her all that way . . ." she prattled on, at which point the Vicar prudently suggested that she go above stairs to visit with Amanda.

Ainsley was greatly relieved, but frowned when the Vicar handed her a book for Amanda, saying, as his wife departed, "Sophocles, you know. Amanda's making her way through my classical library, rather rapidly I should say."

The Earl led the Vicar into the library and poured each a glass of brandy. "Is Sophocles really the thing for Lady Millforte to be reading?" he asked, sitting in a deep leather chair across from Trumwell.

"I cannot see why not. It is a part of our literary heritage, and Amanda is a grown woman, after all."

"Yes, yes, I suppose," asserted his lordship, for how did one argue with the Vicar about the propriety of reading material from his own library?

The Vicar proceeded to question him about Amanda's ankle, and though he was friendly enough, the Earl was uncomfortable. He did not care for the half-truths he felt compelled to utter about his "need to discuss estate matters with Amanda in the quiet hours of dawn." The Vicar smiled a bit too knowingly at this last and Ainsley drained his brandy a bit too rapidly. "Ah, tell me, Trumwell, these early morning walks of hers, are they—common knowledge hereabouts?"

"Oh, I shouldn't think so. *We* know, of course, but we were always very close to Arthur and Amanda. She doesn't gossip, you know. I would say she would not tell very many people what she did, nor when. Why do you ask?"

"Oh, 'tis of no import. Just curious."

The older man said nothing, but the sudden look of concern in his eyes told the Earl that he was a man to be relied upon, if need be.

"Do you play?" asked the Vicar, tactfully changing the subject and pointing to the carved wooden chess set in the corner of the room.

The Earl did, and invited the Vicar to a game. They played in amiable silence, broken only when the Vicar mentioned that Amanda was an excellent player. The Earl expressed surprise. "Oh, yes," Trumwell replied. "I've played with her a good deal, but not of late. She and Arthur used to play all the time; it was one of his favorite pastimes. I think she finds it difficult— painful—now that he's gone." The Vicar paused before adding, "It is time she stopped dwelling on the past, I think."

After which statement the Earl found it difficult to concentrate on the game, his mind whirling with thoughts of Amanda and Arthur. His thick brows knit together as he resolved to have the chessboard conveyed above stairs when he took dinner with Amanda that evening.

It was during luncheon that his mother's letter arrived from London. Oh, blast! he thought. He'd only

90

been absent from Town for six days! She could not *already* be entreating him to return home to escort Kitty and herself to their deadly round of routs and balls. He knew he'd have to return for Kitty's come-out ball, but that was next month.

Against his better judgment he broke the seal before finishing his plate of cold mutton. He was in no way prepared for what he found written in his mother's angular hand:

Dearest Charles:

I trust that you are well, and that you are not finding the very disagreeable task which you have undertaken to be too terribly trying.

I write to inform you of a development which has caused me great distress. I do not think we need be alarmed as yet, for it is my fervent hope that Kitty will come to her senses soon enough, but I felt it my duty to impart the situation to you, especially in the sad event that you may be called upon to take definitive action.

Allow me to elaborate by saying that Kitty has been seen several times in the past few days in the company of a young man whom I do not know. She met him for what I think was the first time at Lady Enderly's ball, just after you left. It was a shocking squeeze, and I confess I found it difficult to keep my eye on Kitty every moment. They seem to have been introduced by another young man of Kitty's acquaintance, whom I have seen at Almack's, and so presume to have *some* connections. At all events Kitty danced with this unknown young man twice that evening, and when I asked her about him later on, she could only remember his Christian name, Richard. She seems to know nothing of his family or background, and either does not know or will not reveal his name. He is an officer in the Cavalry and so must have some access to funds, but I cannot like the entire business. I've no doubt he is a younger son, and I fear he may be an unscrupulous fortune hunter, although Kitty's inheritance, while handsome, is most certainly not what one would call a fortune. It is mystifying in the extreme, Charles, and he is so very young. I do not think he is even of age. Why does he not present himself? He has not come once to call, and has made no move to make himself known to me at any of the gatherings we have both attended this week.

Kitty has not been quite right since Lady Enderly's ball. She walks around with her eyes clouded and answers one in a most distracted manner. Lady Gresham saw them together at a card party, which Kitty attended in the company of Lady Gresham and her daughter Eloise. According to Lady Gresham they spoke together for several minutes and then this Richard departed. Kitty claims that he is nothing to her and that she has not seen him outside of those two times, but to be blunt, my dear Charles, I do not believe her. She went out with her maid yesterday, ostensibly to the lending library, but Agnes returned shortly thereafter, saying Miss Kitty had forgotten her shawl and requested Agnes to fetch it. Now, Charles, when have we ever known Kitty to care a fig whether it was cold or warm, raining or not? I am persuaded that it was that soldier she met, and I have reason to believe that he may have met her in the garden here whilst I was out.

Please do not post home as soon as you read this, dear Charles, for I am not unhopeful of fixing her attention elsewhere. We have numerous engagements this week and I shall be introducing her to many eligible young men. However, you will appreciate that I did want to forewarn you, should the need for your presence here in London become urgent.

At this juncture his lordship, who had no intention whatever of making haste to London, gave way to an exasperated sigh, and pushed his plate of half-eaten mutton farther away from him as he continued reading:

By the by, my dear, Lady Gresham was here to tea yesterday and bid me convey to you her personal invitation to her daughter's come-out ball in just over a fortnight. I know how you abhor these affairs, but perhaps, if you mean to attend a select few, as you often do, you might make this one of those. I believe you have met Eloise, for she is often in Kitty's company. She is not an unpleasant girl, you know. She is actually rather pretty, I think. Nothing like her elder sister, who you may remember having met some years back. Priscilla has rather a crooked nose and wears those dreadful spectacles, and I fear is already accounted a spinster, but Eloise has lovely blond hair and a well-placed nose. I am aware that you do not altogether care for Lady Gresham, but I do think, in considering her invitation, that you might remember her very formidable position. Her friendship cannot help but improve your consequence and advance any suit you might wish to press when you decide to contract the very "eligible alliance" you spoke of. I mention this only because one must always look to the future, and lay one's path in the present, of course.

The Earl shook his head as he read this last paragraph. Why in the world he should need to cultivate Lady Gresham, the dreaded patronness of Almack's, he could not think. And he'd have his dear mother know that he remembered Eloise quite well. He'd wager she would rival her mother for her dragon tongue one day soon, given the protection of a rich, weak husband. He had never liked the friendship between Kitty and Eloise, and could not see what good would come of it.

The letter went on:

Lady Gresham mentioned one other thing to me at tea yesterday. Much as it pains me to impart such news to you, yet I should be remiss in my duty did I not. I do not know what you have observed of Lady Millforte's behavior thus far, but Lady Gresham informs me that she is currently—oh dear, how shall I say this—engaged in a romantic—liaison—with a nobleman highly placed in Shropshire. She does not know his name, but she has her information from her cook, whose husband's family comes from just outside of Ludlow. You know how reliable the servants' grapevine is, my dear Charles, and so I fear there can be no doubt as to the veracity of this story. Perhaps—I don't presume to know how one goes about this sort of thing, but perhaps you could in some way dissuade her from this disgraceful and dishonorable course, at least for the sake of her child, if not for our family name.

The Earl flung back his chair in disgust and began

pacing the floor, a deep scowl on his face. Would these stories never cease? How was it that a woman, who had not set foot inside the metropolis in nearly four years, still held the attention of the beau monde? And was he never to hear anything but vague references concerning Amanda's activities?

"Damn! damn! damn!" he exploded as he crumpled the overly long letter and threw it into the fire. He stared into the flames, his right hand resting on the black marble mantel. His face was troubled, his mouth set in a grim line, as he brooded about the enigma of Amanda.

It was thus that Jeffries found him sometime later with the unwelcome news that Miss Lavinia Prescott had come calling.

"Miss Prescott! What? Has the news reached even Ludlow?" exclaimed his lordship, and sighed. "Oh, I suppose I shall have to receive her. Show her to the Green Salon, if you would."

"Of course, my lord." Jeffries bowed and made his exit.

Ludlow! he thought suddenly. A high placed nobleman. It could be any one of a dozen such in Shropshire, but Lady Gresham's information originated from Ludlow. Surely it could not be Lord Windham. He had seemed so solid, not at all the sort. And he and Amanda had hardly spoken at all at Lady Bosley's dinner party. It seemed as if they were naught but casual acquaintances. Of course, that would be necessary cover for them, but he had not seen even a look pass between them, and he had hardly taken his eyes off Amanda all evening. He recalled that Lord Windham had shown no sign of prior knowledge of Amanda's interest in the marshlands, and surely they must have discussed that had they been intimate. No, it did not seem likely. And yet Windham hadn't seemed surprised at her involvement in such things either. Perhaps he'd do well to cultivate Lord Windham. Miss Prescott would be a good starting point, and might prove, if artfully handled, a treasure trove of information herself.

"Good afternoon, Miss Prescott," he said, closing the door to the Green Salon behind him. "Thank you for coming."

"Not at all. I do not want to disturb Lady Millforte, but I could not rest easy until I had inquired myself as to the extent of her injury."

"You—you heard about it in Ludlow?" he was unable to resist asking.

"But of course. You see—"

"Don't tell me, Miss Prescott. Lady Windham's maid has got a cousin whose niece is a kitchenmaid here at Millforte."

"Oh, no, I'm afraid you very much mistake the matter. It is the stableboy here at Millforte, William I believe his name is, whose uncle is—"

"Please, Miss Prescott. Spare me the very trying details," begged the Earl.

Miss Prescott allowed a twinkle to come into her eye. "Very well, my lord, but you must tell me everything that happened."

"There is not very much to tell. We were out walking and she twisted her foot in the underbrush."

"Out walking at dawn, my lord? Somehow you don't seem the type," she said, a smile playing at her lips and her eyes gazing unwaveringly at him.

"Yes, well, the country air—does things to one," he said vaguely, somehow very uncomfortable under her scrutiny.

"Does it, indeed?" she mused.

"Ah, yes, as I was saying—er—Miss Prescott, would you care for refreshment. Some ratafia perhaps?" He felt the need to distract her.

"Yes, I would like some refreshment. But not ratafia, heaven's sake. You don't mean to tell me *you* drink that stuff?"

"Well, no, actually, but I—"

"No, I should think not. No, I'll have brandy, if it's all the same to you."

"Brandy?" he echoed, somewhat taken aback, for it was certainly *not* all the same to him.

"Do you not stock any then?" she asked quizzingly.

"Yes, of course I stock it. That is, Lady Millforte does. Er, that is, it is stocked here at Millforte, for—for guests. I shall have some brought presently," he said curtly. As he pulled the bell cord he wondered in annoyance if Amanda would be drinking brandy in twenty years' time. Somehow he knew ratafia would not be her drink either.

"The injury was rather severe, I gather?" asked Miss Prescott, after Jeffries, eyebrows arched in very proper disapproval, had served the brandy and departed.

"No, not really. What makes you say that?"

"I can only assume so, my lord, since you found it necessary to carry her ladyship all that way," she said pointedly.

The Earl groaned inwardly. Was there nothing these confounded servants did not notice? To his chagrin he felt that he colored slightly as he replied, "I—I had reason to think it broken, Miss Prescott. I did not wish her to damage it permanently."

"Ah, I see. But it is not broken?"

"No, merely a bad sprain. She must remain abed today and perhaps tomorrow, but it will heal rapidly enough."

"Your solicitude is commendable, my lord," she said with, he noted uncomfortably, her eyes crinkling in amusement.

His lordship found the need to change the subject. "Tell me, Miss Prescott, do Lord and Lady Windham spend much of the year here?"

"At Windham House? I should say so. Not but what they don't go into London for a few weeks each year, just to see old friends. But Edmund is quite content with his horses and the business of the estate, and my sister is devoted to the tenants, you know. She is a true lady bountiful, I should say."

"She seemed a delightful woman. Tell me, ah, does she share his interest in horses, and the estate?" he pressed.

"She is not a fanatic on the subject of horsebreeding, if that is what you mean. But she is an accomplished horsewoman and certainly knows good horseflesh when she sees it. Why do you ask?"

Damn, thought the Earl, she was too sharp by far. What could he possibly reply to that? I am trying to determine if *your* Lord Windham is having a clandestine affair with *my* Lady Millforte? He caught himself up short. *His* Lady Millforte? What was he thinking?

He recovered himself momentarily, and said, his impeccable upbringing coming to his aid, "I am merely curious about my neighbors, now that I am to take an interest in Millforte affairs. Forgive me if I have been inquisitive. It was not my intention, I assure you. One feels at a loss, you know, not really having an overall concept of the region. Tell me, are there several peers in your vicinity?"

Miss Prescott, who did not for one minute believe that he was ever at a loss over anything, eyed him curiously but answered amiably enough. "Edmund is a Viscount, you must know, though the Windham lands are much smaller than Millforte. The area has one or two minor barons, and the usual squires, but that is all.

Does that help give you an overall concept of the region, my lord?"

His lordship flushed. "Well, I, that is—"

"Pray, do not apologize for curiosity, my lord. I, too, like to ask questions," she said smoothly as she rose and drew on her gloves. "Will you extend my greetings to Lady Millforte, and tell her that I shall call in a few days' time, when she is receiving visitors?"

"Yes, of course, Miss Prescott. Pray feel welcome at any time."

"I should like that. And you must visit Windham. I am sure Edmund would very much like your company. You can discuss the problem of the marshlands, for it is very much on his mind of late. Or is that Lady Millforte's province?"

"Yes, well, I should very much like to visit at Windham. Do convey my regards to Lord and Lady Windham. Good day, Miss Prescott," he said briskly, smiling as he ushered her out the door.

Blast! he thought when she had gone. He was more confused than ever. It did not seem, from all she had said, that Lord Windham would be involved with Amanda. And yet, Lady Gresham's cook's cousin or whatever he was came from Ludlow. Who else could it be? Or could it be—no—he sighed, it was not possible that it was no one at all. He had ample evidence of the uncanny ability of servants to know exactly what was going on everywhere. But how he wished—what? What did he wish? He did not know, but he found himself very suddenly in need of some fresh air.

"Jeffries," he said curtly, entering the main hall, "if any more concerned neighbors call, I am *not* at home and Lady Millforte is resting and *not* receiving visitors!" And without awaiting a reply, he strode toward the rear gardens.

Chapter Seven

As a child the Earl had been fascinated by the rear gardens at Millforte. The winding, narrow walkways lined with tall hedges gave one the feeling of walking through a maze. The pathways all led to a large open courtyard, replete with intricately carved fountains and clusters of flowers, and presided over by an ancient oak tree that local legend insisted had been planted in the time of King Arthur. The gardens had delighted his childhood imagination, but now it was their promise of solitude that drew him.

He made his way to a bench in the center of the courtyard. The late afternoon sunlight filtered through the branches of the old oak to illuminate the gardens at set intervals. He closed his eyes, the scent of jasmine assailing his nostrils and the only sound the delicate splashing of sparrows, bathing in one of the ornate fountains, as oblivious to him as to the light April chill. He opened his eyes and stared at the sparrows. He could not do what they did—pursue what he needed or wanted, oblivious to the outside world. He had always prided himself on doing just that, on not caring a damn what anyone thought. But that was before Amanda. Could he take her for what she was and not care what she had been and the world be damned? He thought not. Even *he* could not do that. And what *was* she, dammit? He had no evidence of anything. Nothing that was real. All that was real were those translucent sea green eyes and that luscious tumble of black hair.

His head jerked sharply in response to a sound coming from the far end of the courtyard. He could not place it at first, and then realized that it was a voice.

"Whoa! Steady you go. Nice horses," it said. A child's voice. Victor.

He got up and walked toward the northwest corner of the garden from where the sound seemed to come. Behind a cluster of blackberry bushes stood a white wall that stretched partially around the courtyard. There, atop the wall, sat Victor.

"Victor, what are you doing here?"

"Better get out of the way, Cousin. You'll get runned over," Victor shouted, his little hands extended in front of him, moving up and down rather rapidly.

"Run over? What on earth do you mean?" asked a truly puzzled Earl.

"I'm riding in my carriage, and my horses are very wild. But I can handle 'em," said the child proudly, his little bottom bouncing up and down upon the wall.

In spite of himself the Earl smiled. "I should say you can. I've no doubt you'll be acclaimed a nonesuch in no time at all. But—ah—perhaps you could rein them in and we could talk a bit," said the Earl, looking around and satisfying himself that there was no one else about.

Victor beamed and brought his horses to a halt. "Do you want to climb into my carriage, Cousin? I'll give you a ride."

"No, er, thank you, Victor. Ah, are you here all by yourself, Victor?"

"Yes. 'Cept for my horses."

"Well, yes, but what I mean is, where is Nurse?"

"Oh, she has the vapors again on account of poor Afena getting into the house and jumping on my bed."

"Afena? Who is Afena?"

"Afena. You know, my dog. I call her Afena because she's so smart. She understands everyfing I tell her," answered the little boy.

Enlightenment dawned and the Earl smiled. "Do you, perchance, mean Athena, Victor?"

"Yes, that's just what I said. Didn't you hear me, Cousin? Afena is my dog, only Nurse cannot abide dogs in the house, and when Afena gets into the nursery she has the vapors. That's why she's lying down."

"Wait, wait, Victor. You're going a bit too fast for me. Where—where did you get the name *Athena* from?"

"Oh, that's easy. Mama says that in the olden days, in a faraway place, there were mighty gods—girl gods and boy gods. Afena was a girl god and she knew *everyfing*. Didn't *you* know that?" he said, beginning to sound impatient.

"Well yes, actually, I did. Now as you were saying, Nurse has the vapors, and so you were sent out here on your own?"

"Oh, no. Nurse sent me to Mrs. Havenwick. But she's busy in the linen room. There's nofing to do there."

"Oh, I see. And *then* what did you do?"

"Well, Mrs. Havenwick said I should go to Cook, but Cook is busy making blackberry pie. She says she has to make a special dinner for my lord and lady tonight, but I don't understand why. Mama can't even get out of bed."

The Earl's eyes widened somewhat at this bit of intelligence, and he wondered where Cook got her ideas from. "Then why did you not stay with Cook, Victor?" he asked.

"'Cause I don't like blackberries. Pooh! So I just came out here to ride in my carriage."

"But you should not be here alone. Won't you be missed?"

"Oh, no, they never miss me in the afternoon. Cook will think I went back to Mrs. Havenwick, and Mrs. Havenwick will think Nurse got over the vapors, and Nurse will think—"

"Yes, yes, I see, Victor. But you know, you could get hurt and no one would know."

"But I'm very, very careful. And anyway, now *you're* here. Will you play with me?"

The Earl sighed, realizing finally that it was useless to talk logic to a three-year-old. "But I'm afraid I don't know any games, Victor."

"Not know any games? You must know *some* games," Victor said, incredulous. When the Earl shook his head, the little boy added, "Well, if you don't know about the boy gods and the girl gods, and you don't know any games, what *do* you know?"

"Well, I, that—" The Earl found himself at a rare loss for words.

"I know," said Victor, deftly sliding down the wall and taking the Earl's hand, "I can *teach* you games. Let's play hide and seek. You close your eyes and I hide. Then you find me."

The Earl, who remembered full well how to play hide and seek, could think of nothing he would rather have done less. But Victor was his ward, after all, and recalling the initial hostility with which the child had greeted him several days ago, he decided that it would be prudent to acquiesce.

Victor's hiding places were rather obvious and the game progressed rapidly. The Earl's hiding places were even more obvious and Victor was delighted. When it was Victor's turn to hide again, the Earl swiftly glanced around the courtyard, expecting to catch a glimpse of Victor so that he could avoid finding him for a little while. But he did not see the child right away, as he had before, and so he began casually to peek behind bushes and under the benches. When after several minutes he had not found Victor, he began to search in earnest. Five minutes later the Earl was frantic.

"Come on out, Victor. I can't find you. You've won the game," he called, rapidly circling the courtyard. Still no Victor.

"Victor, you come here this instant. The game is over!" he shouted, his apprehension making him quite angry by now.

At length he heard a giggle. He was startled because it came from above him. He looked up and beheld Victor, sitting astride a low horizontal branch of the ancient oak tree.

"You couldn't find me. I won! I won!" exclaimed Victor.

"Yes, you did. Now come down from that tree, Victor," said his lordship sharply.

"No," retorted Victor. "I'm riding Zeus."

"You're doing what?"

"I'm riding my horse. His name is Zeus. Isn't he beautiful?"

The Earl chose to ignore the fact that that particular branch of the mighty oak did bear some resemblance to a horse, and said, "Did your Mama tell you about Zeus, Victor?"

"Oh, yes. Mama said Zeus was a boy god. He was the king of all the gods and he was in charge of the thunder and lightning."

The Earl frowned. What could Amanda have been thinking, filling his mind with such things? "Victor," he asked, "does your mama know you climb trees? Or Nurse, or anyone?"

"Maybe. They never said. Do you want to climb up here with me?"

"No, Victor. I don't climb trees. But I want you to come down. You'll have to find another horse. This one is too dangerous. I don't want you climbing trees. Do you understand?"

Victor eyed him narrowly but did not move.

"Victor!" shouted the Earl angrily, and the boy complied, somehow slithering down to the ground.

"You're not my papa. You can't tell me not to ride Zeus," said Victor, his lips set in a decided pout.

"No, I am not your papa. But I *am* your guardian, and I am afraid you'll have to mind what I say. Now come along," replied the Earl firmly, taking the little boy's hand in his own and pulling him toward the house.

As the Earl led Victor up the stairs, he noticed with some degree of amazement that the boy did not quite know whether to cry or to smile.

They found Mrs. Havenwick on the top landing. "Mrs. Havenwick," said the Earl brusquely, "you will please see that Victor is properly supervised for the remainder of the afternoon. I found him quite unattended in the gardens just now, and I trust that such laxity of duty on the part of the staff will not be repeated."

Mrs. Havenwick's eyes widened in astonished fury at such words. She reached out to Victor and pulled him to her enormous bosom in one sharp motion, almost as if she were wresting him from the mouth of an evil giant. She glowered at the Earl, her gaze meeting his, as she said pointedly, "Come, Victor. 'Tis time to visit your mama."

Victor looked up at the Earl with a sheepish half-smile. "Good afternoon, Victor. You go along to your mama now. Perhaps I will see you tomorrow," said his lordship softly, adding a clipped "Good day, ma'am" to Mrs. Havenwick before he turned and marched back down the stairs.

His lordship paced the library, the morning room, and finally the gardens again in an attempt to soothe his slowly burning temper. He was deeply distressed over the events of the day. The assault upon Amanda and her consequent injury, Linfield and his nosegay, his mother's letter—why, it was the outside of enough! He was a reasonable, even-tempered, fair-minded man, but how much could even such a man as he be made to bear? And now this—this irrefutable evidence of the utter mismanagement of Victor's care! At least *that* situation was easily rectified. He would set Amanda straight on that head at dinner tonight.

It was this latter resolve which occupied his mind as he took his tea, and so it was a very self-possessed, if highly charged, Earl who knocked at Amanda's door just before dinner.

Upon entering, his eyes flew to the empty bed and in the next moment fell upon Amanda, standing at the window farthest from the bed. "Cousin Amanda, what in the name of Heaven do you think you're doing?" he said harshly, trying to ignore how beautiful she looked in the lavender silk dress that set off her porcelain-like skin and her black hair.

"Why I'm watching the sparrows in that tree," she said, smiling and pointing out the window.

"Don't trifle with me. What are you doing out of bed?" he demanded.

"Oh, well, I truly was in need of a bit of exercise, you know. The pain is very much lessened and one certainly cannot remain abed all day when one is perfectly healthy, now can one?" she replied lightly.

"One certainly *can* and *will!* I shall assist you back to bed immediately," he said firmly, advancing toward her.

"That is very kind of you, I'm sure, but I am not quite

106

ready to retire. I should like to walk around a bit first. I shall be terribly sore if I go back to bed so soon." She moved slowly away from the window, limping only slightly.

"I have a good mind to make you terribly sore if you don't! You have no idea what damage you can do to that ankle if you press on it too soon. You must remain abed tonight and tomorrow. Now, let me help you," he said in a loud voice as he put his arm around her back and under one arm.

"Don't you dare ever threaten me! And take your hands off me! I shall do perfectly well on my own. Perhaps you'd better come back when your temper is mended." She tried to wriggle free of him, but he bent down and in one swift motion lifted her unceremoniously over his left shoulder and carried her to bed.

"Damn you, Ainsley, put me down!" she shouted, her fists pounding his back.

He gently lowered her to the bed. "Watch your language, my little firebrand. It doesn't become you," he said, grinning mockingly at her.

Her face was flushed and her eyes blazed as she arranged her skirts about her, but he was saved her angry retort by a knock at the door. Bessie entered followed by a footman, both carrying trays laden with what looked like a five-course dinner. He watched Amanda seethe in silence as the servants set a tray for her and a bedside table for him.

As soon as the door had closed behind them, she fumed, her teeth clenched, "You are arrogant and overbearing and you have no right whatsoever—"

"Aren't you going to eat your turtle soup, Cousin?" he interrupted nonchalantly.

"No, I do not want any soup!" she replied sharply.

"But you *must* eat. Else you'll have no strength in you to fight me at every turn."

"I fight *you*? Are you not quite forgetting that it is *you* who—"

"Alas, I am forgetting nothing. Now, eat your dinner and let us table this rather edifying discussion for the moment. Cook seems to have taken special care with the glazed duckling and we would not want to appear ungrateful, now would we?" This time his smile was warm and his tone almost soft, and she could not help but evince a glimmer of a smile in return.

"Well, I confess I am rather hungry. Tell me how you spent your day, my lord. I trust it was more interesting than mine was?" she asked.

Thus they ate their dinner engaged in surprisingly amiable conversation, and it was not until coffee had been served that his lordship broached the topic uppermost in his mind. "I must bring to your attention a matter which greatly distresses me, Cousin. I encountered Victor this afternoon in the rear gardens. He was sitting astride the surrounding wall and was quite alone."

"Ah, yes, I had meant to take this very matter up with you earlier, but that you distracted me with your rather puerile display of superior physical strength," she replied. His eyes narrowed at this and she went on, "I will thank you not to disrupt the routine of this household and to remember that it is not your place to reprimand my servants."

"Your servants are negligent in attending to Victor, and it is definitely my place to put a stop to it. Are you not concerned that Victor was unattended?"

"I hardly think that a few minutes by himself will do him great harm."

"A few minutes? You cannot know but that it was several hours. Nurse had the vapors, so he said, something about his dog, and he went from Mrs. Havenwick to Cook, and finding both occupied, made his way to the gardens. He even intimated that this was a rather common occurrence. What kind of household are you running here?"

"A rather efficient one up until this week, it would seem. Victor cannot come to any harm there, and he would never leave the gardens. Really, you refine too much upon it.

"I suppose he cannot hurt himself scaling walls? And would it interest you to know that I found him in one of the branches of the huge oak tree during our game of hide and seek?"

"You played hide and seek with Victor?" she asked, her eyes widened, a smile playing at her lips.

"Well, yes, actually—he—he wanted to play a game, and it seemed as good as any," he said uncomfortably.

"Indeed," she said smoothly.

"That is neither here nor there. The point is that he climbed that tree and seated himself astride one of the lower horizontal branches. And he's done it before, I can assure you. He claims the branch is his 'horse.' Why, he even has a name for it!"

"Does he indeed?" she asked, raising her coffee cup to her lips.

"And that puts me in mind of another thing, Cousin. Are you aware that he calls his dog 'Athena'?"

"Oh, yes. She's a darling little Irish Setter pup. I shudder to think what Nurse will have to say when she reaches her full size, though."

"I don't care what the dog looks like, Cousin. It's the name. What did you tell him about Athena?" he asked, pushing his cup away from him and rising from his chair.

"Why, that she was very wise—the goddess of wisdom in fact," she answered, her eyes narrowed in curiosity.

"And Zeus? You told him about Zeus, as well, did

you not? His 'horse' is named Zeus. Did you know that?" he said angrily.

"In truth I have not had the pleasure of meeting Zeus. How very clever of him! He's always been a precocious child!" she said sweetly.

"Clever! Cousin, have you no concept of what you are doing? Filling his head with all manner of indecent stories of the Greek gods. Have you no sense of propriety at all?" he shouted, by this time pacing the floor in front of her.

"Well, of course, I don't tell him the *indecent* ones, my lord." She grinned. "You truly must not refine so much upon it. He was frightened during a thunderstorm one night. I told him about Zeus and his thunderbolt and that Zeus was probably angry at one of the other gods and that it had nothing to do with us."

"That's all very well, but the fact remains that you blithely fill his head with things not fit for drawing room conversation! Next, I suppose you'll be reading him *Oedipus Rex* for a bedtime story!" ranted the Earl, his brows coming together ominously.

"Fustian! You know very well I would do no such thing!"

"Ha! But you admit to having read it yourself!" he snapped, leaning rather closely to her, his smoldering face towering over hers.

"Well, of course I've read it. Haven't you?" she replied strongly.

"That is another matter entirely," he said flatly, straightening up and schooling his face to some semblance of calm.

"Ah, yes, I might have known. Well, then I suppose you'd not have me read the Bible either. Have you lately taken a close look at what is contained in *that* book, my lord?"

The Earl felt his color rise and walked to the window

nearest the bed. "It becomes clear to me that there is only one feasible course of action. It is time Victor had a governess."

"A governess? Why, he's only three years old!" she exclaimed.

"A governess, yes. The very thing, I am persuaded. She will provide moral guidance, proper supervision, and a firm hand," he replied, deciding he quite approved of his own idea.

"His mother can provide all the 'moral guidance' he needs at this 'turning point' in his life, I assure you," she said mockingly. "And a firm hand? A schoolboy needs a firm hand, my lord, not a child just out of swaddling clothes. As to supervision, do you actually mean to add a fourth person to my household whom Victor can evade? Surely you jest. The whole notion is preposterous." Amanda's eyes blazed and her body tensed upon the bed.

"Rest assured that I am quite in earnest, Cousin. As to your ability to guide the child in what is decent and proper—well, we need not even discuss that! And it is never too early to accustom a child to the proper discipline. Your tendency to coddle him is rather alarming."

"Coddle him? You've just accused me of not hovering over him enough. Pray decide in which direction I err before flying into such a passion, my lord!"

"I shall advertise in the *Gazette* for a governess without delay," he said firmly, his back to the window.

"You will do no such thing! This is my house and I'll not have you interfering!" she erupted, sitting bolt upright and attempting to swing her legs over the side of the bed.

"Stay where you are!" he shouted, striding to the bed. "*I* am Victor's guardian, and *I* shall make the

111

decisions regarding his upbringing!"

"No, my lord, you are mistaken. We are *both* Victor's guardians. Now, of course, the time will come when he shall be in need of male guidance, and I will most assuredly call upon you. For now I think it best you leave his care to me. He is *my* son, after all," she said quietly, falling back against the pillows.

Damn! he thought. Would they never agree on anything? And where was that footman? This discussion was not improving his humor in the slightest. He stalked to the bell cord and pulled fiercely on it. The footman appeared almost momentarily, bearing the rather massive library chess set in his arms.

Amanda turned questioning eyes toward the Earl. "A welcome diversion, do you not agree, Cousin?" he said with a slight smile, peering at the slender form that was quite dwarfed in the rather huge bed and thinking that diversion was indeed what he needed.

"Yes, I suppose, my lord, but I really would prefer not to—that is—I have not played in quite a long while," she said softly, her eyes downcast.

"So the Vicar tells me. Are you perhaps afraid your acumen has suffered irrevocably in the months since you've played? Do you not accept my challenge for a game then, Cousin?" he asked smoothly, looking intently at her.

She raised her eyes to his. "But, of course, I accept your challenge, my lord."

"Excellent," the Earl said smugly, drawing his chair very close to the bed, for the servant had placed the chessboard on Amanda's bedtray.

The Earl's nerves were taut. He was incensed with Amanda, for she seemed to delight in thwarting his every wish. And yet he could hardly tear his eyes away from her as she rested against the pillows and the down bedcover, her soft lavender dress caressing her figure and barely exposing the whiteness of her throat.

The opening moves of the game were routine. Amanda seemed to play competently but without much ingenuity. The Earl found himself watching Amanda more than the board. He strove for concentration.

"I do not know many women who play chess. Most of the ladies of my acquaintance prefer a sociable game of whist," he said, advancing his bishop.

"Really? I'm afraid I do not care for games of chance," replied Amanda lightly.

"Do you never take chances, Cousin?"

"Not very often, my lord. One must always consider the consequences," she said softly. He gazed intently at her for a long moment, until she said, "Your move."

The Earl advanced his rook onto the board. "I find the game most interesting. One can draw many parallels to life as it truly is."

"Do you mean that the king is the most important figure, the one everyone makes a great fuss over, while the queen is in reality infinitely more powerful?" she asked with a smile, her pawn moving to block his lordship's bishop from attacking her queen.

"No, I was rather thinking of the knight. One must always be wary, for the knight is treacherous. He can infiltrate the King's fortress without warning," he said as he moved his black knight within attack range of Amanda's queen. As she contemplated the board, he added, "For instance, if you are not careful, the black knight will steal away your queen. And then where should the king be?" His tone was insistent, as if emphasizing some hidden meaning, but Amanda's face was impassive.

"Then I suppose my queen will have to exert her power and take your bishop," she said with a smug look.

"What the—" he blurted. "Very nice, Cousin. It seems the queen has a few tricks of her own." Damn, he thought. He could not let her beat him. It was unfair competition. How could he keep his mind on the game when they were alone in her bedchamber and those green eyes peered out at him across the bed? This game had been a fool idea to be sure. He concentrated on the board.

"But now you see she is endangered," he said as he moved his rook.

"And so the white knight rescues the queen," countered Amanda, blocking the black rook with her knight.

"But then he should carry her off, at least according to the fairy tales, should he not? Like Guinevere and Sir Lancelot?"

"No, my lord, that would not do, for, of course, her allegiance is to the king."

"Always, Cousin Amanda? Is the queen always so loyal?"

"Always, my lord," she said quietly, and then, "Check, my lord."

His lordship blanched. How had that happened? He had not anticipated this when he'd suggested the game. He moved his knight in defense of the king, but to no avail. He opted for a dignified exit. "My compliments, Cousin. You play well. Perhaps tomorrow you will grant me the opportunity to redeem myself," he said, a smile playing at his lips.

"There is always the opportunity to redeem yourself, my lord," she said smoothly and then added, "And now if you'll forgive me, it has been a difficult day, and I should like to get some sleep."

And I'd like to help you do it, he thought regretfully, as he bade her good night and departed.

Chapter Eight

Amanda was perched on the second landing of the great staircase, both hands on the wooden banister, when the Earl alighted from the dining room just after breakfast.

"Cousin! What on earth—" shouted the Earl as he looked up. He did not stay to finish his sentence but bounded up the stairs two at a time until he reached her. He immediately slipped his arm around her shoulder, holding her firmly in place. "Now just wait a minute. Where do you think you are going, dressed like that?"

"You do not approve of my walking dress, my lord? I know it is not in the first cut of fashion, but still I think it serves," she said amiably, holding the flounced black skirt a bit away from her and inspecting it.

"Don't gammon me. You know perfectly well what I mean. Why are you wearing a walking dress, when you are most definitely *not* going walking? I shall assist you down the stairs, if you insist on going, and install you upon the chaise in the morning room. You may receive visitors, or write letters, but you *may not get up* until I come for you! I thought all that was made very clear yesterday."

"Clear to you, perhaps, but not at all clear to me. I am very much in need of fresh air, and so, if you would excuse me, my lord, I shall be on my way." She wriggled free of his arm and took a careful step down.

"Incorrigible termagant! Here, you must not do that alone. Stairs of all things!" he said, exasperated, moving toward her and attempting to scoop her into his arms.

"My lord, please," she said, her voice lowered and quite urgent. "If you insist on carrying me down the stairs, we shall have the entire staff and half the village atwitter with the news in half an hour. Really, I cannot bear another day of Bessie's strange looks and Mrs. Havenwick's 'harrumphs,' not to mention Sally Trumwell, and Miss Prescott and—"

"All right. All right! Your point is well taken, Cousin," he agreed, grinning. "Just lean on me, then, and put as little pressure as possible on that foot."

When they reached the bottom, his lordship tried to steer her toward the morning room, but she stood firm. "I have some brief business in the library, before I go out to the gardens, my lord," she said pointedly.

"Very well. As a matter of fact, I have some business in the library myself," he retorted, unwilling to relinquish his hold upon her.

The Earl seated Amanda in one of the deep leather chairs in front of the desk and walked behind it. She was quite obviously miffed by this, but he forestalled any objection by picking up the piece of paper on the desk and beginning rapidly, "I wish to read this to you before I send it off to the *Gazette*." Whereupon he read aloud his very carefully worded advertisement for a governess for the three-year-old Viscount.

"Very prettily worded, my lord. Quite futile, however," she said, rising and advancing to the desk, "because as I said before, there shall be no governess for Victor at this time. I thought that was made perfectly clear yesterday," she continued in a cool tone.

"Clear to you perhaps, but not at all clear to me," he said smugly.

Her eyes flashed. "There will be no governess here until Victor is ready for lessons!"

"Well, then, did you not say Victor is precocious? If you insist on lessons, then lessons he shall have. Immediately!"

"You are not putting that child into a schoolroom! Why, it is too preposterous to discuss!"

"Then let us not discuss it! Any child capable of naming his dog 'Athena' and his imaginary horse 'Zeus' is ready for lessons. And any mother who teaches him the things you do has no right to object!" he shouted, his brows thunderous.

"This is *my* house, and *I* shall hire the staff *when* I deem it proper! You are overstepping your bounds, my lord," she retorted, leaning forward and snatching the paper from his hands.

"Give me that, this minute!" he shouted.

"I think not, my lord. I shall put it where it belongs." She turned her back on him and walked, unevenly, but as quickly as possible, to the fireplace.

He was at her back in a moment. "Oh, no you don't. This has gone far enough." He tried to wrest the paper from her hand, reaching from behind her, but she shielded it with her body until she had crumpled it. She moved to toss it into the fire, but he pinned her arms to her body.

"Give me that, you little termagant!" he growled, pressing her arms with increasing force and so pulling her closer to him.

"Let me go! Or do you suppose it will improve your consequence to best a woman, an invalid one at that, in a wrestling match, my lord?" she said, trying in vain to twist out of his grasp.

"Ah, so you admit you are an invalid. We've made

117

progress!" His lips touched her hair as he spoke. "As to a wrestling match, I should like that very much. But I don't think you would lose, you know," he said huskily, and in the next moment he spun her around, keeping one arm still tightly around her, and brought his mouth down on hers with an angry force.

She jerked her body and tried to turn her head away, but he held her fast. His lips engulfed hers demandingly, but she kept herself rigid. He knew that if he held her long enough she would submit, for she was not, he was certain, indifferent to him.

Amanda's arms were pinioned between her body and his, and she could not pull free. She was no match for him physically, she knew, but she would not allow a repeat of that night in the library. Submission to him now would put her in his power. She kept her body stiff, and her teeth clenched. She felt a tingling in her legs and her back and realized that she longed to succumb to it. But the voices in the back of her head kept saying, "No, no, you cannot give in."

He tried to force her mouth open with his tongue. Her lips parted slightly, but she hastily clamped her mouth shut. He seemed taken aback by her steadfast refusal to relax her guard, and he slackened his grip momentarily, whereupon she jabbed at his stomach with her elbow.

He released her angrily and she spun away from him, the notepaper still crushed in her hand. She threw it into the fire and said, her voice barely above a whisper, her breathing irregular, "You have once again indulged in a puerile display of superior physical strength. I am duly impressed. It does not change the fact that there will be no governess at Millforte until *I* hire one, and I will thank you not to forget that!"

"No, my dear firebrand, I shan't forget anything about this morning. But I am not at all pleased at having to rewrite that advertisement. It would seem that *you* are the one indulging in a puerile display of the sulks," he countered, grinning rakishly. "And now if you will excuse me, I have work to do."

Amanda's fists clenched at her sides. How dare he dismiss her from her own library! How dare he treat her so! But short of throwing something deadly at him, she could not think how to dislodge him, and she did not care to amuse him by trying. And so with her head erect, she turned and slowly exited the room.

So angry was she that she hardly noticed the pain in her ankle as she marched purposefully toward the rear gardens. Only when she had reached the courtyard, well out of earshot of anyone and everyone, did she allow her injured foot to stamp and a "Damn you, Ainsley! Damn! Damn!" to escape her lips.

She began to pace the courtyard restlessly, but realizing that the strength in her ankle should be husbanded, she sat down on one of the stone benches, only to rise again a minute later to resume her agitated pacing. Thus, alternately pacing and forcing herself to be seated, did she continue for some time, contemplating the fact that the Earl's visit was proving more difficult than she'd ever imagined, in more ways than one.

The grin had vanished from the Earl's countenance as soon as Amanda had left the room. In an erratic hand he scribbled a second advertisement to the *Gazette*, this one rather less painstakingly worded than the first. He threw the quill down and rose abruptly as soon as it was complete.

"Damn that woman!" he exploded, beginning to pace the room, his hands digging savagely into the pockets of his finely tailored coat. She *would* confound his every effort to make changes or decisions of any kind, despite the fact that it was obvious that *he* could view the managing of Millforte much more objectively than *she*. Of course, he did have to admit that things were not nearly so bad as he'd expected them to be, but still there were some very distressing goings-on that he would have to make an end of presently. Yes, he would win in the end; he had to, of course. But still, he had not been prepared for such vehement opposition, nor had he ever encountered its like before.

He paused abruptly in front of the fireplace, and watched the last bit of the writing paper collapse and burn. He stood there for a moment, his eyes blurred and his temper somewhat quelled by the steady shooting of the flames. He shook his head and sighed inwardly, for he could not hide from himself the fact that the source of his extreme agitation was not the clash of ideas between Amanda and himself.

Dammit! he thought. He had not meant to press himself on her again in such a manner. But they were standing so close, and even in her anger she was so alluring, so—so—exciting. He was only human, after all. But if he was angry at himself, he was even more piqued at Amanda. Why did she resist his advances so? She was not indifferent to him—he was certain of that. He had known it that night in the library, and even now, for just a brief moment, he had felt it. She had repelled him out of fear the first time, but this time, when she had not allowed herself to succumb, there had been no fear, only anger.

Did she perhaps fear her own desires? But why? Certainly she was no stranger to passion. Or was she? That made no sense, and yet in another way, it was the only thing that *did* make sense. Of course, there had been Arthur, but remembering his gentle character and their tremendous age difference, he doubted whether

the word *passionate* would have described their
relationship. There had been Arthur, *but had there
been others?* Common sense told him that, of course,
there had. But a deeper instinct stirred inside him,
making him doubt. He simply *had* to know! There
must be some way to find out, he thought, resuming his
pacing.

Windham! He would start with Windham. He was a
likely candidate, after all—a "nobleman highly placed
in Shropshire," his mother had said, and the information had come from Ludlow. He must make his closer
acquaintance; he must see just how devoted he was to
that wife of his, and just how satisfied he was with his
horses and his land. Yes, he would go straight away. He
was already dressed in breeches, and a morning visit
such as this would be unremarkable in the country. In
his eagerness he did not remember to seal the newly
written advertisement for mailing, which document
remained askew upon the desk where he had left it.

At length Amanda tired of her pacing, and the
silence in the courtyard began to seem oppressive. She
was still greatly distressed and felt the need of exercise,
but her ankle could not tolerate much more walking,
she feared.

I shall ride, she thought. The company of Aquitaine
and the sensation of the wind in her hair and her body
fairly leaping across the fields had never before failed
to calm her temper or raise her spirits. She could not
change to her riding habit, of course, for the staff
would raise a terrific fuss should they see her, and
Ainsley—ugh! She could not bear to think what he
would do. She might have been pleased at his seeming
concern for her welfare, and indeed almost was after
yesterday morning. But by the evening she'd realized

that it was not consideration for her, but merely his need to control everything and everyone around him, that motivated his vigilance.

Well, she was certain that she would have no difficulty riding, and so vexed was she with his lordship that she would ride even so. She kept her gait cautiously slow as she made her way to the stables.

"But, beggin' your pardon, my lady, you havin' injured yourself and all, I'm thinkin' that maybe you oughtn't—that is—" the gentle Williams stammered when she appeared at the stables requesting Aquitaine.

"I appreciate your concern, Williams, but I do assure you that I am quite all right. I'm just going for a short ride. Now if you please, my horse," she said firmly.

The groom's weather-beaten old face looked doubtful. "Won't your ladyship reconsider?" he said almost mournfully. "His lordship was here just a bit ago, and in a rare takin' he was, and well, I do think he'll be mighty distressed when he finds out—that is—he bein' the one as seen to your injury and all."

"His lordship has been most kind, I'm sure, but he is not your master, now is he?" Williams shook his head. "But I am your mistress, and I wish to ride. You would not ask me to collect my own horse, now would you?"

"Oh, no, of course not," he said hastily and disappeared into the stables.

He brought Aquitaine around and helped her to mount. "Beggin' your ladyship's pardon, I didn't mean—it was only—"

"I know. His lordship does fly into quite a rage. But you needn't worry about that—I shall take care of the Earl's temper. And there's no need to mention my ride to him at all, is there?"

"No, my lady," he said uncomfortably, as she smoothed Aquitaine's mane affectionately.

"By the by, Williams, did his lordship say where he

was going?"

"He asked me how long it would take to ride to Ludlow, my lady."

"Hmm. Ludlow. I wonder—well, in any case, that's east, so I shall go west," she said, more to herself than to him, before she took her horse off at a canter.

Amanda spurred Aquitaine to a gallop as soon as they reached the first of the open meadows. Aquitaine took the gentle hills easily and seemed as glad of the exercise as she. Her body felt exhilarated as the wind whirled around her, and her head began to clear. Above all she must remain cool-headed and calm, she told herself, for it seemed that every display of temper only served to amuse the Earl and make him feel more superior. And, heaven knew, he didn't need any help in that quarter.

But still, she must take *some* definitive action to make it clear that she would brook no nonsense where the welfare of her child and his inheritance were concerned. If she did not beat him to the draw, she would probably find even the local workmen hesitant to do her bidding. Williams was just a beginning, she feared.

The marshlands—she somehow had to formulate an expedient plan for that particular project. And the Low Cottages—those did not need a plan, merely a word from her, and if she acted quickly, perhaps it could be done without his knowledge. However, she must first see them—but, of course! How foolish not to have thought of it! She was already riding westward. She was sure she would find the Low Cottages if she followed her instinct. Besides, everyone always said that as soon as you came close, the stench would lead you straight to them. That prospect did not please her, but then, she did not expect to be pleased by the Low Cottages. That was why she meant to tear them down, and then, of course, when the area had been drained, the soil properly prepared, to build whitewash cottages, each with its own little farm.

She smiled to herself as she turned Aquitaine in a more northerly direction. Yes, she would best him yet. There would be little the Earl could do once she had seen to it that the Low Cottages had been razed, and of course, he'd have to agree to their rebuilding. Even *he* could not condone leaving her tenants homeless, worthless and beneath his notice though he might think them.

The lush green hills gave way to wooded enclaves, and as she slowed Aquitaine, the mare skillfully wended her way over the brambles in the underbrush and between the trees. At length the foliage became sparse and the ground less firm.

"Now, take it slowly, Aquitaine. Don't let us get mired in a bog."

They rode for some way on ground that was damp but did not give way under them. Amanda guided Aquitaine over a series of hills, rather stark but firm, and surveyed the surrounding terrain. She could see stagnant pools of water ahead of them, and as they drew closer she could smell them as well. How this must flood in the rains, she thought, and instinctively looked up to see a noncommittal late April sky. It was not actually blue, the sun barely shone, but the clouds were not especially threatening either.

Amanda guided Aquitaine downhill, and that discerning mare found herself a firm path on which to tread as they continued farther into the marshes. In the distance Amanda could perceive several huts in what seemed a small valley, and she prayed that the ground would hold them. She could not know if those huts were a part of the community of Low Cottages but trusted that her sense of smell would guide her.

In this she was correct, for as they pressed on, more huts came into view in the valley just below them, and a dank and putrid odor began to waft toward them. Even Aquitaine reared her pristine white head and seemed to object rather strenuously to the proposed course. "Come now, old friend. We cannot turn back now. I shall enjoy it less, I assure you," she said, stroking the mare's fine coat and urging her toward a gentle incline that would lead them into the valley.

They first came upon a cluster of decrepit huts—to call them cottages was to award them a status they could not merit. They were of a muddy brown earthen material, their thatched roofs pitifully sparse. She knew they must have no flooring, probably not even rushes to give them a semblance of cleanliness. Smoke rose out of several holes in the roofing, and she pictured a crude firepit in the center of a primitive room.

There were no people about and somehow she hoped none would appear. But she felt compelled to travel the length of the valley, and she veered Aquitaine so that they could follow its contour. The dirt roadway seemed to turn a corner and then another group of hovels came into view. These were more numerous and set closer together along an unpaved street, and it was obvious that this was the main part of the "village."

A ditch ran the length of the roadway, some yards from the cottages. The water was filthy, and a foul, fetid odor rose from it. She gulped and inhaled the scent of what might have been a mixture of human waste, dead animals, and she could not think what else. She thought she would be sick, but a moment later a door opened and she knew she had not seen the worst.

An old woman emerged from a hut just across the roadway. She stooped almost to a hunchback, and her hair lay like matted straw upon her head. A small child followed her out. He wore a tattered, ill-fitting gown of some sort, possibly the vestiges of swaddling clothes he had long since outgrown. He looked to be about two or three. Oh, God, Victor's age. She turned her head away but forced herself to look again. The child looked very thin and his feet were bare. The clouds had begun to cover the sky, hiding the sun and bringing a chill down on the land, and she found herself wishing she had a blanket in which to wrap him. He was tugging at the old woman's skirt and pointing to Amanda. The old woman finally looked up and gazed blankly at Amanda on her white mare. Amanda smiled but the woman returned only a glassy stare, her partially open mouth revealing several brown teeth and no others. Amanda tore her eyes away and moved on.

She passed several more cottages and farther on saw figures moving. A pair of mangy dogs sniffed about, searching the ground in vain for edible scraps. A woman was washing clothes in a large basin. Amanda wondered with a sickening feeling where the water had come from. Two children were running about barefoot, their hair unkempt and clothes threadbare. A little girl was chasing a boy, and she squealed in delight when she caught him. Children are children, Amanda thought, and wondered in despair what these two had eaten for breakfast. Beyond them the road turned and Amanda espied a cluster of trees which almost hid a thatched roof structure, larger but no less dilapidated than the cottages. An old gig and ancient nag stood in front. Was this a shop or tavern or— Presently from inside came the rise of drunken male laughter, and Amanda thought it prudent to retreat.

She turned Aquitaine round and retraced their path. A second woman now bent over the wash basin; the children still ran about. But then, suddenly, the little girl looked up and Amanda saw several ugly red sores on her face. Amanda clutched at her stomach to stanch a wave of nausea. I've seen enough, she thought. Enough to know my instincts were right.

"Come Aquitaine, take us home," she whispered to the mare, tapping her gently with her crop.

Aquitaine pressed forward, searching for an exit from the valley. They came upon a narrow path which seemed to wind its way up the hill, albeit among some rather tangled underbrush. Aquitaine carefully began the climb, but when they reached the top, the earth seemed more boggy than the area where they had first descended. The mare gingerly took a few steps and, sensing success, several more. She jumped a shallow gully that crossed their path, but the earth gave way beneath her and she could not lift her front legs from the thick mire.

"Come now, you can do it, Aquitaine. Just several quick steps. The ground just beyond is firm." She stroked the horse's mane to reassure her, but she was not much alarmed. None of the marshes in this part of the land was particularly dangerous. Farther north, she knew, the bogs became treacherous, but here they were more an inconvenience to the traveler, and of course, impossible for the farmer.

Several minutes later the mare was able to raise her legs, and cautiously made her way to more solid ground. Amanda kept her at a moderate trot, in case they should encounter murky ground again.

It was not long before she heard the sound of horses approaching. She wondered fleetingly whether a shepherd might have to chase stray sheep up here. She rather doubted it. Who, then?

She was to know soon enough. Two rather scrawny gray horses drew up alongside Aquitaine. If Aquitaine was not pleased with such close proximity to such inferior specimens, Amanda was even less comfortable with their riders. Both had an unshaven, unclean look, and they leered at Amanda. One had a flushed face and a rather enlarged nose; the other had a long gash over his right eye.

"And what have we here, eh, Amos, in the middle of nowhere? A lady, I do declare," the one with the long gash said mockingly as they drew up to Amanda.

The narrow path had brought them very close, and Amanda surreptitiously tapped Aquitaine to make her go faster.

"Not so fast," said the man called Amos, the one with the red face, catching Aquitaine's reins and bringing her to a halt. "We just might fancy some company, ain't that right, Gus?"

"Well, I'm afraid I must be going. Now let go the reins and let me pass, if you please," she said firmly, with more confidence than she felt.

"I don't think you heard my friend right, little lady. We be in the way of wantin' some company," said Gus, his voice hardening as he dismounted from his horse. "Now come on down here, little lady," he added, his arms outstretched, his grin revealing uneven brown and yellow teeth and his breath rancid.

Amanda, duly frightened by this time, knew she must stay on the horse at all costs. She sat erect in the saddle.

"Stubborn little filly, ain't you?" said Gus when she had not moved. "Hey, Amos, what you suppose a fine lady like her'd be carryin' in her purse?"

Amanda found herself sorry she did not have a reticule with her, much as it would horrify her to give it to them. "Do you gentlemen know who I am? This is Millforte land, and I am Lady Millforte. Now I suggest you let me pass or the consequences for you will be dire indeed."

"Well, now, see," said Amos, leaning close to her, his

whiskey breath assailing her nostrils, "we don't hail from these parts, and that name don't mean much of anythin' to us, 'cept maybe that you carryin' plenty of blunt, you bein' such a fine lady and all."

"But I don't *have* a purse, I can assure you. I just went out for a little ride," she said, hiding her fright behind an exasperated sigh.

"For a little ride, up here in the bogs! Hah! Mayhap it be that you ain't such a lady after all, even with them fancy clothes and that horse. No lady'd come up here, not by herself, no how. Come on down, and hand over the blunt," said Gus, reaching for her hand. She jerked it away, holding firmly to the reins.

"I have no money. Now let me pass!" she said angrily, kicking her heels into the mare. But the man called Amos tightened his grip on the reins, dismounting clumsily, and Gus grabbed her right arm and began to pull her down.

"Take your hands off me!" she shouted, hitting Gus with her riding crop and holding herself firmly in the saddle with her free hand.

"Damn bitch," muttered Gus furiously, as he reached for the crop.

Amos meanwhile began pulling at her from the other side. He was none too steady on his feet, but she found herself fighting both of them, her legs and arms flailing at them. She heard her dress tear from the back, and then Gus, who had managed to wrest the crop from her iron grip, yanked her off the horse. A pain shot from her injured ankle up to her hip.

"Now," he said, his voice hard, "maybe you'll behave yourself, little lady. Where you be keepin' that purse?"

"But I told you, I haven't one," she protested.

"Hey, Gus, how 'bout them earrin's? Rocks like that'll fetch a bundle. Give us the earrin's, your la'yship," said Amos, staggering a bit toward her.

"I will not! This is an outrage!" she said, turning as if to mount her horse, but the man called Gus grabbed her arm and Amos pulled at one of her diamond earrings.

"Ouch! Take your hands off me!" she shouted, her free arm jabbing at the drunken Amos. She felt alarmingly helpless. Her ankle pained her greatly by this time and she doubted whether she could mount without assistance. Nor could she run, and in truth, the muddy ground would make it very difficult to cover any distance in a short time. Besides, the one called Gus, stone cold sober, could without a doubt outrun her.

Amos kept tearing at her earring, and Gus began to pull at one of her hands. She was afraid to move her head lest she tear her earlobe. "What are you doing?" she cried, the pain in her ear increasing.

"You may not have a purse, lady, but you got a ring, ain't ya?" asked Gus angrily.

The ring and the earrings—gifts from Arthur. The family jewels. How could she let them have them? She had other earrings, at least. But the ring—the ring had been given to Millforte brides for generations.

"Here, wait," she said, grimacing from the pain in her ear, and from the arm twisted in Gus's hold. "I—I'll give you the earrings—if you—if you'll let me go after that."

"Well, now, that be better," said Amos, letting go the fingers that were wrapped around the diamond drop earring.

"Not so fast, Amos. We'll get the earrings, all right, but I ain't about to let this little ladybird fly away so fast. We ain't had a woman in weeks. You so drunk you forget that, Amos? Well, *I* ain't drunk. Come 'ere, little lady. You comin' with me," he said, pulling her after him away from the horses.

130

"No, you let me go," she cried desperately, punching him with her free hand and trying to kick him.

"Oh, no you don't. Ain't no woman never got away from Gus, when he'd set a mind to her," he shouted menacingly, and grabbing her free arm at the elbow, he yanked her toward him and pitched her into the gully. She was so light that she spun back with great force. She felt her weak ankle buckle under her, and her body fell to the ground. She felt her head come down on something hard, and she found that she could barely lift her eyelids. She heard the drunk speak.

"Now see what you done, Gus! She may be dead. There's blood a' spoutin' behind her head. You go in and get them earrings."

"Never mind the earrings. Let's get out of here," said Gus hastily.

"How 'bout the horse? That'd fetch up a bundle."

"You crazy, you drunken fool? If she's who she said she was, everyone in the county'll know that horse. Let's get the hell out o' here."

She thought she heard the sound of hoofs retreating, but in the next moment all light and all sound disappeared, and she was plunged into darkness.

Chapter Nine

As the Earl handed his reins over to Williams in front of the stables, he felt relieved to be home. The sky was getting darker every minute and the clouds were ominous. Williams looked at him rather strangely, he thought, as if quite disconcerted to see him. "Is everything all right, Williams?" he asked.

"Yes, well, of course, your lordship. Just, er, just that dark sky has me a bit worried, you know," said the groom uncertainly.

His lordship remained unconvinced, but let it pass, for he was in rather a hurry to see Amanda. He had been gone for several hours, and his visit to Windham House had greatly improved his humor. He had found Lord Windham and his Lady just emerging from the stables, having witnessed the birth of a most promising foal. They had been walking arm in arm, and as they recounted to him the story of the unique parentage of this particular foal, they had seemed so in harmony with each other that he found his suspicions vanishing into thin air.

Later over brandy, he and Windham had amiably discussed horses, then politics, and finally, the economy of large country estates. He had found that his first impression of the Viscount, at Lady Bosley's party, had been correct. Windham was a levelheaded man, well informed in the most up-to-date farming techniques, and they discussed some of the virtues and problems of Shropshire soil.

Eventually the conversation turned to the marsh-lands. It annoyed the Earl that Windham's opinions were so much in accord with Amanda's, and he felt his suspicions begin to rise again, until Windham said, "I understood the other night that Lady Millforte had some interest in reclaiming her marshlands. If that is the case, I should be happy to discuss my findings in the matter with both of you. . . ."

No, Windham did not sound as though he knew Amanda well at all. And he was plainly more interested in his lands than in Lady Millforte. The Earl remained noncommittal on the rather delicate subject of the Millforte marshlands, but when they parted he had the distinct feeling that here was a man he could respect, and whom he would see again.

Against his will his lordship found himself reviewing Windham's statements about the marshlands as he rode home. Ridiculous, he told himself. Obviously the economic balance of the Windham estates differed from that of Millforte. Windham might need his marshlands to survive. Millforte, much larger and seemingly much more productive, did not. He would explain all of that clearly to Amanda, and certainly she could be made to see reason.

He did not wish to argue with her, and he most certainly hoped that she had not walked about too much during his absence. A poorly healed ankle, even after a mere sprain, could plague one for years, he knew. And so, as he left the stables, he hurried to the house and immediately inquired of Jeffries as to her ladyship's whereabouts.

The good butler had not seen her all morning and presumed her to have been resting in her room. The Earl knew better and, after ascertaining that she was neither in the library nor the morning room, walked to the rear gardens. Still not finding her, he went in search of Mrs. Havenwick.

He found her in a tête-à-tête with Amanda's maid in the hallway outside her ladyship's bedchamber. The maid curtsied and fled as he approached. "Mrs. Havenwick, have you seen Lady Millforte?"

"Er—why—yes, your lordship. Her ladyship is—er—resting, she is. Plumb fagged out after yesterday's mishap is what," said that stout lady, her eyes wary and her arms folded as she moved to stand in front of Amanda's door.

"Well, I must say I am relieved to hear that she is resting. Now if you will excuse me, Mrs. Havenwick, I should like to see her," he said firmly.

"Er—well—wouldn't your lordship be wanting to change his clothes? You've just come from riding, have you not?" she said, and he might have agreed, as he looked down and realized that his boots and the bottoms of his breeches were indeed caked in mud. But somehow her tone bothered him; it was too—ingratiating. He was sure she was hiding something.

"Stand aside, if you please. I shall see her now," he commanded, peering menacingly down at her.

"B—but, your lordship, she isn't decent!" said the housekeeper, almost pleadingly, but reluctantly stepping aside.

"Then she can put on a dressing gown!" he said, annoyed, as he knocked on the door. There was no answer. He shot a dark look at Mrs. Havenwick and entered the room. It was empty.

"Where is she?" he demanded, turning to the housekeeper again.

"Oh, she—she merely needed some fresh air. You probably missed her in the gardens," she stammered most uncharacteristically.

The Earl looked intently at her. "Are you telling me the truth?" he asked in a tightly controlled voice.

134

Seeing her pained look, he added, "Good God, woman, don't you understand I mean her no harm? Now where on earth is she? She can't have gone far with that ankle. Has something happened to her? How can I help her if you conceal her whereabouts from me?" He grabbed her shoulders as he shouted this last.

She put a hand to her mouth and her eyes filled with tears. "I beg your pardon, my lord. I—I just don't know where she is. Bessie helped her dress after breakfast, and then, and then—no one saw her after that, 'cept Williams, and he—he—" She began to sob and pulled a handkerchief from the pocket of her dress.

The Earl dropped his arms. "Williams? What's he got to do with this?"

"She—she—went riding, my lord. She's been gone several hours and—" The Earl didn't wait to hear the rest, but bolted out to the stables, grabbing his cape on the way.

All that Williams could tell him was that Amanda had left after breakfast and that she'd said something about heading west. "Why didn't you tell me when I arrived, Williams?" he demanded.

"I beg pardon, my lord. I should have done, I know, but I kept hoping that she'd come back and you'd not—not—"

"That I'd not find out she'd been out? Dammit, Williams, why did you let her go?" he asked angrily.

"I tried to stop her, truly I did, but she—read me a lecture about my duty, and—"

"Never mind. I can well imagine. Saddle my horse, quickly!"

Two minutes later the Earl was galloping off, cursing himself for his abominable temper. The servants were terrified of him, and Amanda— Oh, God, what had he driven her to?

He rode westward for some time, glancing every so often at the ever-darkening sky, and trying to consider

135

where she might have gone to be out these several hours. Suddenly he felt the wind rise, and the raindrops began to fall in a slow but steady stream in the next minute.

Damn! It was going to pour, and he had no idea where to look for her. She had been very angry with him, perhaps justifiably so, he thought ruefully. If he knew Amanda at all, he had to guess that she would attempt to do something that would infuriate him. A short ride with that ankle would have been enough, but she obviously hadn't been satisfied with that. The rain by this time had begun to fall in sheets, and he could only hope that she hadn't been fool enough to ride through any marshlands on such a cloudy day. She might have, though, she with her plans and projects. Her projects! No, even she wouldn't do that. Or would she? If she was angry enough—what better assurance of incurring his wrath than venturing to where he had expressly forbid her to go? The Low Cottages! Of course, that is just where she would go!

He veered his horse northward and pulled his cape more tightly around him against the driving rain. He prayed that the horse knew the terrain well enough not to fall into a quagmire. He thought he remembered the approximate location of the Low Cottages, though, and guided the horse accordingly.

Only once did the gray falter. The Earl had been unsure of the way and had slowed to a walk. The horse stepped off the narrow roadway and sank several inches into the mire. It took some minutes of coaxing until the horse pulled his way back to the road. They rode more slowly than he would have liked, so strong was the wind and so heavy the rain, but at length, the Earl spotted several huts in what looked like a narrow valley, and he rode toward them. He kept to the high ground, but followed the row of miserable cottages. He could not have been sure that these were indeed the

Low Cottages but that the stench, even in the rain, was unmistakable. His sharp eyes searched the valley below and the murky terrain ahead and to the side. There was not a human being in sight. All sensible persons have taken shelter, he thought, no matter how miserable a shelter it be.

He felt a sinking feeling in his stomach, for he could see no sign of Amanda or Aquitaine. Presently he heard a whining sound, from somewhere behind him. A horse. Despite the pounding rain he was sure of it. Might it be—with no further thought he steered the gray toward the sound, somehow avoiding the ever-threatening mud. Again the whine, and then suddenly the stark white head of a horse rose from a gully some yards ahead. Aquitaine!

He spurred his horse and galloped forward. Aquitaine lifted her head and gave a shrill cry. The Earl stopped the gray short and jumped off. Aquitaine was standing in the gully, and there next to her lay Amanda, curled on her side, her arms covering her face as if to shield herself from the storm.

"My God!" he blurted as he leaped into the ditch. He bent to her. Her eyes were closed, her face partially hidden. "Amanda," he said gently, "can you hear me?" He saw the blood at the back of her head, and for a moment was afraid to touch her, so still was she.

But her eyelids flickered slightly and she tried to turn her head toward him. "My head—dizzy," she mumbled haltingly.

"'Tis all right. I'm here now," he said as he gingerly picked her up and carried her out of the gully. She lay limp in his arms, but her eyes opened slowly. He stared down at her beautiful, pained face, for a moment oblivious of the rain. He felt an unaccustomed surge of fierce protectiveness. "My God, what happened?" he rasped, and then cursed his impatient tongue. This was hardly the time. "Never mind," he amended, striding

137

toward his horse, but she clutched weakly at his sleeve.

"Two—two men," she whispered brokenly, and his arms tightened about her as a sick feeling of dread overcame him.

"Did they—hurt you?" he could not help asking in a tortured voice.

"No—only my head—ran away," she stammered, and then her eyes closed.

The Earl cursed fluently, but he wasted no more time. He must get her home. He saw that Aquitaine had climbed out of the gully. Knowing he had no choice, he set Amanda carefully down on her feet, turning her to him and propping her against his body. Quickly he reached for Aquitaine's reins and secured her to his own horse. He lifted Amanda once again and somehow managed to mount his horse, Amanda in his arms. He pulled her close to him in the saddle and drew his cape around her.

Her body sagged against him, and he kept one hand about her waist lest she slip away. He turned the horse around and brought him to a mild canter, Aquitaine in tow. He had always deplored the dictates of fashion by which his tailor had talked him into the overabundant capes now favored by gentlemen, but for once he appreciated the several layers and numerous folds of the cloak, for the rain had not abated and the cape was ample enough for both of them.

"Only my head," she had said, and with that the Earl had to quell his tumultuous feelings. And that gash on her head was bad enough. That and this rain—he had no idea how long she'd lain in that gully. Long enough to contract a terrible chill. He rode on with grim determination, telling himself that she would be right and taking comfort in the feel of her steady breathing against him.

He had covered her head as best he could, but at length he felt her stir, and her head came up just above the cape. She turned slightly to look at him and he felt her body tense as she tried to edge a bit away from him. He smiled ruefully to himself. He did not quite know whether to be flattered or dismayed that Amanda, just barely conscious, was so aware of him as to feel the need to avoid him. But at least he felt himself calming down.

He pulled her closer. "You aren't very strong yet. I do not want to lose you. Relax, Cousin Amanda," he said gently.

She allowed herself to fall back against him, her head nestled into his chest. Despite the driving rain and the dire circumstance, he found the sensation quite pleasant.

But the rain, rather than slackening as he'd hoped, became even heavier, and fell with such force that it was difficult for the horses to keep their footing. He moved to draw the cape tighter around them, concern for Amanda mounting. Her dress was soaked through, and it would not be long before she began to shiver violently. Presently, his horse began to weave erratically, undoubtedly unable to see through the downpour. And the Earl feared that the animals would very soon become hopelessly mired in a bog.

"All right, old chap," he murmured to the gray. "I see there's no help for it but to seek shelter. Though Heaven knows the land here is barren enough. Not even a crofter's hut—"

The head of wet, wavy black hair chose that moment to peek through the cloak. Amanda seemed more awake now, her eyes wide open. He was much relieved, but still wanted her head down. "My dear, you must—"

"There *is* a hut. Not far. The horses . . ." she interrupted, her voice weak but clear enough.

So, she'd heard him, he thought. Well, at the least she'd not object to the hut. But where— And then he recalled the abandoned hovel they'd seen the other day. They were standing atop a hill, engaged in a rather fiery conversation. No, he could not forget that, and he thought the hut must be just southwest of where they now were.

Amanda resisted all his attempts to cover her head, her eyes sweeping the sodden fields. The Earl rode on, trying to keep the horses on solid ground and fearing with each passing minute that he had miscalculated the direction. For the terrain, slightly hilly, yielded little more than a deal of mud and an occasional tree.

"Cousin, look," the soft voice called to him, "over there, to the left." He turned his head and had to strain his eyes to see, partially hidden in a low valley, a thatched roof and the barest hint of a small, dilapidated hut. "Is that not the one we saw that day on—"

"Yes, it is. Thank you, Cousin," he said a bit too curtly. How had *she* found it so easily? He unceremoniously shoved her head down under the cloak and turned his horse westward, blinking back the rain all the while.

The Earl assisted Amanda to dismount and caught her as she stumbled against him. But then she righted herself and refused to be carried into the hut. None too pleased, he whisked his cape off and onto her shoulders and grasped her firmly by the elbow to lead her inside.

The hut was bare, the floor earthen. But though it was damp, at least no rain leaked through. He eyed the floor uncertainly. She seemed steady enough, but surely she ought to sit down.

"I am right, Cousin. The horses . . ." she began, and he smiled in amazement.

He brushed a wet curl from her cheek. "I'll only be a moment," he whispered, and went outside.

He was back quickly, leading the horses inside. He did not relish sharing a room with the cattle, but they needed to be sheltered from the rain, and two more bodies would, after all, help to warm the hut. For there was no kindling for a fire. He looked at Amanda and frowned. By now she was shivering. He swept his cape off her and shook it. Her black kerseymere dress was sodden, and he knew what must be done. But he feared her reaction when he broached it.

Bracing himself, he looked down at her and said quietly, "Amanda, you are soaked through. You will catch your death in that dress. You really needs must remove it, my dear. I shall turn around, and you can cover yourself with my cape."

"No, I—"

"Amanda, please. You can become very ill. At the least let me wring the dress out, and then you can put it right back on if you wish."

She shook her head, her sea green eyes wide with distress. "No, Cousin. I thank you for your concern, but that will not be necessary," she said with quiet dignity.

Damn! He gritted his teeth, somehow knowing he could not move her. There was no Bessie here, no servants gathered outside the door. She lowered her eyes and he scrutinized her, a jumble of emotions warring within him. He felt rage at her attackers, anger at her reckless behavior earlier and her foolish adherence to proprieties now, and fear for her health. Sighing, he drew the cape around her shoulders once more.

He needed to warm her but did not imagine that she would allow him to pull her closer. Instead he stepped round to examine the wound at the back of her head. It was no longer bleeding and did not look as terrible as he'd feared. "Does it pain you much?" he asked, coming back to face her.

"It is s-sore, that is all. And I am not nearly so dizzy as before," she replied, trying to keep her teeth from chattering. She still had not looked up.

141

He nodded gravely and brushed some of the hair from her face, attempting to ring out the wet locks. It was then that he noticed the blood on her left earlobe. That had not come from the fall and he felt that mounting dread again. He *had* to ask, and perhaps, after all, the question would distract her from the cold. He put his hands lightly on her shoulders. "Cousin Amanda, can you tell me what happened? Please look at me." He spoke soothingly and she raised wary eyes to him. "I must know the extent of your—injuries. And the men must be apprehended."

He felt her tense at that, and she looked down again. "Men, my lord?" she asked shakily. "Surely you are mistaken. I was thrown. Some noise—an animal perhaps—frightened Aquitaine and she bolted."

His brows knit together in a frown. Had she actually forgotten what she—but no, she knew very well. He lifted her chin with his forefinger. "My dear, you do malign a most surefooted animal with that particular clanker. Now let us try again. There were two men. You may go on from there."

"I am perfectly fine, my lord, but for this gash on my head, and I cannot think—"

"Amanda! If you force me to I shall examine you more closely. We can start with that dress—"

"That—that will not be necessary, Cousin," she said with an attempt at dignity. She stepped out of his grasp and over to one of two small shuttered windows recessed in the earthen walls. The shutter dangled open on a broken hinge. She closed it and leaned her head against it as she hesitatingly recounted what actually happened. His body went rigid with fury as he listened. And when she spoke of those vile cutthroats yanking her from her horse, he had to steel himself not to gather her into his arms. He stayed close behind her, and when she'd finished he turned her slowly around. He did not know whether to believe that they had not raped her.

142

He knew she would be mortified to tell him that.

He did not touch her, but his eyes bore into hers. "Amanda, these kind of men—they stop at nothing. I must know the truth. If they hurt you—"

"Please, Cousin. I understand what you are asking. But I have told you all. Truly." She placed a delicate hand on his forearm and spoke urgently. "You needn't pursue them. They—they've gone away."

For one wild moment he wondered if she was afraid that he would endanger himself pursuing these villains, then chided himself. She does not care for you, Ainsley. You are just another male to be evaluated according to his usefulness. But that thought fled from his head as rapidly as it had come. It just did not fit. The callous, designing woman and the charming, dignified lady were not one, and the reality was here with him. And somehow he thought that she did care, much as she endeavored to hide it.

"Amanda—"

"Cousin, I am right," she repeated calmly, gazing steadily at him out of innocent, fragile sea green eyes.

Finally, he breathed a sigh of relief. He covered her hand with his. It was ice cold. "You are freezing. Come away from the window."

He led her to the center of the room and pulled the cloak more tightly around her. It fleetingly occurred to him that he ought to take her to task for the hoydenish behavior that had led them to this pass at first stop. But the notion dissolved as he beheld that white face, still streaked with wild strands of black hair, the eyes regarding him now with a curious mixture of fear and trust. He felt her body shiver, and this time drew her closer. His hand involuntarily came up to stroke her cheek. "Amanda," he said hoarsely.

"I—I was so frightened," she whispered, but now she did not seem frightened, did not back away from him.

He did not mean what happened next to have

occurred, but his face was so close to hers, and it seemed the most natural thing in the world. He brought his lips to hers very gently, tentatively, as if awaiting her reaction, and she clung to him, so that he began to kiss her in earnest, feeling a fire within him that, despite the wetness of their clothes, he would not have thought possible. He moved his hand under the cape to her back, and began to caress her, to move his hands up and down until he thought the heat of his hands would sear right through her.

Every rational part of her being told Amanda to back away, not to let him touch her. She meant nothing to him. He was amusing himself at her expense. But somehow the gentleness of his tone, of his touch, and finally of his kiss belied that. She could not have kept her distance had she wanted to. For when his strong arms caught her in his embrace, when his insistent lips crushed hers, she wanted only this, to be here, with him. The persistent voices at the back of her head kept saying no, he has only contempt for you, but her back tingled as he ran his hand up and down her spine, and when he whispered her name into her hair, over and over, she shooed the voices away and gave him her lips again, her hand stealing to the back of his neck. Her whole body seemed to quiver uncontrollably as he touched her, and she felt a wave of fire go through her such as she had never known before.

Her response further inflamed the Earl, and every part of his being ached for her in a way that he had not felt for any other woman. He thought he could take her now, that she wanted him as much as he wanted her, but he knew she would regret it later. In a flash he realized that he would, too, and still holding her, he pushed her gently from him and looked intently at her flushed face. She looked suddenly hurt—hurt that he had begun or hurt that he had stopped? He couldn't tell.

"Forgive me, Amanda, I—I meant no—disrespect," he said huskily.

She merely looked at him, a bewildered look in her eyes. How could she believe that, or understand it, he thought, when even he did not understand it? He wanted to explain that this was different from that night in the library, or even this morning, but how could he, when he didn't know why? He still did not know what she was, or had been. Could she have changed so much? Or could all the purveyors of gossip have been so mistaken? He hoped Ridgeway would be quick about a response, for he would surely go mad if some explanation were not forthcoming.

Of one thing and one thing only he was certain. He was no babe in the woods where women were concerned, and he knew that, the heir notwithstanding, no man had ever kissed her like that before. He did not know why that was so important to him, but somehow it was, and it was undoubtedly that knowledge which had given him the fortitude to push her from him. He knew he had to lighten the mood now, somehow, or he would never be able to keep away from her.

"Are you never to address me in any other way, Amanda? I have a Christian name, you know," he said with a smile.

"Very well, Cousin Charles," she said demurely.

"Vixen," he said, smiling and stroking her pale cheek with his fingers.

He moved to scan the hut then, and found some straw mats piled in a corner. After ascertaining that they were not crawling with anything unsavory, he spread several on the floor near the wall. He motioned for Amanda to sit.

"The rain may not let up for several hours. We cannot very well stand the whole time." He noted that she had stopped shaking but it was still very cold and damp in the hut and he was afraid that she would catch a terrible chill. But she didn't move; she merely looked at him wide-eyed. He could not blame her for doubting his sincerity. He had given her ample reason to distrust him, he thought with chagrin.

He finally sat down first, and then he extended his hand to her. "Come, Amanda," he said very gently. "You will need your strength to fight a fever that will most surely beset you. You must try to rest. And your ankle—I'd almost forgotten. The pain must be terrible."

She smiled weakly and reluctantly sat down, several feet away from him. He sighed. He had obviously broken the mood only too well. "Amanda, you are drenched to the skin. You can become very ill. I have not a blanket nor a fire in here with which to warm you. Come here." He took her hand and she slowly slid near him. He put his arm around her, under the cape, and drew her close. He gently pushed her head down onto his shoulder, and with his free hand he began to caress her cheek, her hair, and to trace his fingers around the curve of her ear.

Despite herself Amanda snuggled closer to him, and felt her body relax under the soft stroking of his fingers over her face. It was cold and wet outside, even inside this spartan hut, but she could not remember ever feeling quite so warm and comfortable. It made no sense, she knew, and a part of her was still wary. It must all be part of a calculated plan to seduce her, to use her for his own callous pleasure. But why had he said what he had just now? A man bent on seduction would not, she thought, apologize for a kiss. Still, she knew she ought to get up and put several safe feet between them, but somehow, her legs wouldn't move, and her eyes began to close.

He pulled her closer when he knew she was asleep, and he listened to the steady drone of the rain. He hoped it would abate soon. He had seen men die from a chill that began with an innocent rainstorm, and he shuddered at that. His hand moved across her shoulder and he became aware that he was touching her bare flesh. He felt for the fabric of the dress and realized it was torn. A worried frown crossed his face as he wondered again whether she had told him the truth when she said those men hadn't hurt her.

Fool woman, he thought. Going to such lengths just to thwart me. She undoubtedly would never have ventured there alone—would have taken a groom at the very least—had I not made such a fuss about it. I should have just accompanied her there and been done with it. He felt he would never forgive himself if she came to harm because of his bullying. Bullying! That was probably just what she thought. She was Eleanor of Aquitaine, fighting for her land, and he was Henry II, bullying her, trying to imprison her for disobedience.

He looked down at the beautiful, innocent face at his shoulder. He must remember in the future that such bullying was not the way. In the future! What was he thinking? He was due back in London in a week at the latest. There was no future for them, not for the Earl of Ainsley and a woman of Amanda Millforte's reputation.

As he had done numerous times this past week, he thought about that reputation, about all that he had heard of her over the years. He had only been in London intermittently during the past four years, leaving every time he was needed for some delicate mission on the Continent. He could still not recall anything specific, just those veiled innuendoes about Amanda being linked with half the House of Lords, and about her escapades in the Shropshire countryside. He had certainly seen no evidence of any such behavior in Shropshire, and it struck him as curious that, having spent only one season in London some four years ago, her name was still bandied about with a twitter and a smirk in the clubs and at the most proper ladies' teas. Yes, it was curious indeed.

If Ridgeway failed him, he would have to make inquiries himself, and in any case, he knew that he would have to return to London soon. It somehow startled him to realize that he did not at all want to leave, and that with all the glitter and amusement that London had to offer, he had never been half so amused, nor found life nearly so interesting, as he did in this sleepy corner of the Shropshire hills.

At length the loud thumping of the rain on the thatched roof gave way to a light pitter-patter. After a few minutes he shook Amanda. "Come, let us go. The rain has abated, at least for now."

As she opened her eyes, they widened, and he saw her cheeks color as she realized where she was. He stood and held his hand out to her. She rose and when he opened the door he saw that, indeed, all that was left of the storm was a misty drizzle. He led the horses outside and secured Aquitaine's reins to the gray's. Then he went back inside for Amanda.

The cape had slid from her shoulders and he bent to retrieve it. As he moved to sweep it round her once more, his eyes fell upon the tear at the back of her dress, just below the shoulder. He had not seen it earlier; perhaps the torn flap had clung to her when she was dripping from the rain. Now it fell away from her body, revealing the whiteness of her skin, across which was an ugly scar, several inches in length. His hand instinctively touched it, an act he instantly regretted, for she stiffened and when he looked into her eyes he read deep mortification there. He stared at her, eyes questioning, for several moments, until she must have felt obliged to reply.

"A carriage accident. Several years ago. It—it never healed. I was struck—by a splint of wood which tore

148

my skin," she said falteringly.

He looked steadily into her eyes and thought, You are a poor liar, my lovely one. But such distress and almost pleading did he read in her eyes that he did not press her for the truth.

As he tenderly placed the cape about her shoulders, he felt the overwhelming desire to kiss her again. With much effort he restrained himself, for he very much wanted her to trust him, and he could not jeopardize what little trust she might now have.

Amanda, humiliated at what her torn dress had revealed, and rather afraid that her response to his embrace might very well lower her esteem in his lordship's eyes, fought herself not to dissolve into quite unaccustomed tears. She was saved from these only by the knowledge that his eyes held solicitude and warmth and not a particle of their usual mockery and arrogance.

Yet, as he ushered her out of the hut and lifted her onto his horse, she found herself wishing that he would not smile at her quite so engagingly. She had been foolish to let her emotions override her rational sensible self, and as the Earl mounted behind her she tensed and quickly inched away from him.

"None of that, Amanda. We must guard against the cold," he whispered into her ear, and pulled her back against him. His breath on her ear and neck sent a delicious warm flush throughout her body, and she did not try to push away again. Rather she allowed herself to relax, and a little sigh of pleasure unwittingly escaped her as her head came to rest against his lordship's chest.

He smiled and permitted himself to stroke the top of her head just once, before he turned his attention to the horses and the trip home.

Chapter Ten

For the second time in as many days, the Earl of Ainsley appeared on the Millforte doorstep with Amanda in his arms. Her body had gone limp as soon as they alighted from the horse, as if her last reserve of strength had finally deserted her. The Earl had caught her up into his arms, and this time Jeffries's face showed only relief that her ladyship had been found, relief and then anxiety when he saw that she did not look at all well. His impeccable training was such that he did not say a word, however, as he swung the door open to reveal the main hall, instantly buzzing with servants all clucking concernedly and craning for a glance at their ladyship.

"Some brandy, Jeffries," whispered his lordship as the butler relieved him of his soaking cape. "And you'd better send for the doctor," he added, though he did not really see that the rather ancient Dr. Pringle, who had been at Millforte since before he was born, would be much help. He himself had had enough experience treating exposure during his years on the Continent, he thought, but there was, after all, the head injury. Better have the doctor look at that, he supposed. At the very least he would provide some laudanum.

Jeffries nodded and the Earl proceeded up the great staircase, ignoring the "Oh, my's" and "My poor ladyship's" floating up behind him.

At the top landing he was met by a very agitated Mrs. Havenwick, her fat hands cupping her cheeks as she spoke. "What's happened, my lord? Is she hurt? Where did you find her? Oh, my poor lamb! Do set her down and I shall attend her at once," she cried, the rising hysteria of her voice becoming a near bellow at the final command.

The Earl was not at all pleased at being thus accosted, much less commanded, by a woman who had proven herself totally inept at handling Amanda or her son. He did not wish to waste a moment's time, for Amanda had begun to shiver anew, despite the warmth of the house. But as the housekeeper's rather wide girth fairly prevented him from passing, he said brusquely, "Send me her maid, Mrs. Havenwick, with several hot bricks and extra blankets." He then moved to wriggle past her, but she suddenly looked hurt, and he added impatiently, "I shall send for you as soon as I need you, Mrs. Havenwick." To this the housekeeper took definite umbrage, for she lifted her nose and her chins into the air, and her mighty bosom heaved, but she did finally step aside for his lordship, Amanda aloft, to pass.

The Earl thrust aside the coverlet and the down comforter and gently placed Amanda on her bed. She was shaking violently by now and he quickly threw the comforter back over her. He started to unbutton her dress at the neck, and despite her physical distress her hand immediately flew up from beneath the comforter to grab his.

"No—n—no!" she said in a shaky voice, twisting and trying to turn her back to him.

He was pleased to see some fight in her—anything less would have been alarming—but he wished all the same that her maid would make haste. Amanda pushed at him with her hands, but she was weak, and as he paid not the slightest heed, her efforts soon became halfhearted. When he had succeeded in disengaging countless buttons and hooks and had still only made his way to the top of her bosom, he opened the dress just that much.

"Leave m-me alone!" she managed to shout, her eyes flashing, color rising in her cheeks. Her right hand swung up as if to slap him, but he caught it midair.

"Don't be a fool, Amanda," he said urgently. "You are very ill."

He pressed the comforter against her chest and then started working on the multitude of buttons on the left sleeve. These buttons were very much smaller, and stood side by side in a neat little line from the wrist to the elbow. His large hands had great difficulty manipulating the tiny buttons, and his mind unwittingly drifted to the observation that medieval chastity belts could not have been as effective as the latest designs in fashionable dress.

Finally, Bessie came scurrying into the room, several woolen blankets in hand. "O—ooh—my lady! What can have happened to my ladyship *this* time, my lord? Oh, 'tis ill, she is! I can tell," she babbled, her voice near to breaking.

"Come here, Bessie," the Earl said without preamble. "I want you to take off all her clothes—underclothes as well—but keep her covered all the while. These woolen blankets will be best. Do you understand? Take off everything. She is soaked through and will catch her death in these wet things. Put her into a warm nightgown, but a loose one. And be quick about it. I shall wait right outside the door." Bessie had turned pink and then scarlet at his words, and Amanda glared at him, but he did not waste time appeasing either of their sensibilities.

Jeffries met him in the corridor outside her door, having just brought the brandy himself. The Earl was touched by his concern, for surely such was footmen's work. He smiled his acknowledgment and Jeffries said, "I have sent word round to Dr. Pringle. I would expect him within the hour, my lord, if there is no undue delay. Is there anything else you require, my lord?"

"No, and thank you, Jeffries," said his lordship, and as he regarded the butler's erect frame, his face a mask of silent concern, he marveled at the discipline that kept him from asking the obvious questions. At length he said, "Jeffries, we will undoubtedly be besieged by well-meaning neighbors who will have heard every manner of incorrect tale regarding her ladyship's misadventure. You will kindly inform them all that her ladyship was waylaid by two highwaymen, on our own land, somewhere to the south of the marshlands. She fought them off, and they neither hurt her nor succeeded in robbing her of anything, but she fell into a gully and gashed her head, and then was drenched by the rains. I carried her from the gully. That, by the by, is the truth, Jeffries, and you may tell the servants as well. They will be agog with curiosity and I had rather they be told the correct story than keep embellishing one of their own invention. For your information alone, Jeffries, your mistress is a very brave woman, for it was not merely her jewelry that they wanted. They would have attacked her person had she not fought so fiercely. You understand, of course, why I'll not have that to be got about. In any case, neither her ladyship nor I will be receiving today, and possibly not tomorrow either. I only hope she does not develop a dangerously high fever. Oh, and I had almost forgot. I will want to speak with the magistrate. Amand—er—her ladyship gave me a fairly detailed description of her attackers and I should like them to be pursued as soon as possible. I cannot say when I shall be free to see him, but have him await me in the library."

At that moment Bessie opened the door, her face very white as she said, "She is bad, your lordship. All those blankets piled high and still she shakes and shakes."

His lordship nodded gravely. "Bring up the hot bricks, please, Bessie, and some luncheon for us both. Hot soup and some cold meats will be fine." She curtsied and flitted away, and he turned to the butler as he took the tray of brandy from him. "Send the doctor up as soon as he arrives, of course," he said. Then after a pause, "Please see to the household, Jeffries, and—and—thank you." Jeffries favored him with a warm smile and bowed slightly as the Earl turned to enter the room.

Amanda's body was wracked with shudders, her movements visible even beneath the layers of blankets. He set the brandy down on the bedside table and quickly poured a glass. He noted appreciatively that Jeffries had provided a second glass, knowing, no doubt, that the Earl would need it almost as much.

He sat down upon the bed and as he lifted Amanda from behind the shoulders, he said softly, "Drink this, Amanda. It will warm you up." She leaned forward but so violently was she shaking that it was difficult to steady the glass. When the brandy finally went down she choked and tried to push his hand away.

"No, you must," he said, pulling her up a bit higher and holding her closer to him. She took a second gulp without choking, and then a third. He put the glass down and she grasped his arms.

"So c-c-cold," she whispered.

"I know, but you are safe and warm now. The shaking will stop soon. Lie back and I will cover you," he said, but her small hand clung to his arm as he

154

settled her in. He realized that his own coat was rather wet. He wriggled out of it and took her hand in his.

After a short while he felt the shaking subside just a little, and he did not move when Bessie knocked and entered with two hot bricks wrapped in linen. He merely instructed her in placing them between the bedclothes and ignored her somewhat astonished gulp as she spied my lord and lady holding hands. She retreated in silence, as did the upstairs maid, who almost dropped the lunch tray when she entered the bedroom at his lordship's beckoning.

The Earl propped Amanda up upon several pillows, and midway through the piping hot barley soup, the terrible shivering seemed to stop, and Amanda took the spoon from the Earl. "I can manage now, I think," she said a bit unsteadily, with as much dignity as she could muster.

She refused most of her food, however, despite the Earl's entreaties. "Some—some of the bread, perhaps. And some wine. My throat feels dry. But I simply cannot abide the meat just now." She grimaced and looked rather sick.

He remembered her head. "Are you still dizzy, Amanda? Does your head still pain you?"

"Yes, I suppose I am a bit dizzy." Her head moved from side to side. "It has become so hot in here." She looked down at the bed. "Why must I have all these blankets? Can you not take them away, my lord?"

The Earl was alarmed and put the back of his hand up to her cheek. It was already warm. "Very well, but you must eat a bit more." He removed the extra blankets, leaving only the down comforter. He searched his mind momentarily for a way to distract her from her discomfort. His eyes fell upon her bedjacket, a pale mauve confection of silk and lace that was visible above the comforter. "Shall I help you out

155

of your bedjacket, Amanda?" he asked, a hint of mockery in his voice.

"Certainly not. I am quite comfortable, thank you," she managed to retort, her voice weak but her flashing eyes giving him some degree of optimism regarding her health.

"Good. Then if you are quite comfortable, I'm persuaded you will want to eat some more of your lunch, my dear," he said, grinning.

Amanda gave him a rather disdainful look and turned to her food. She merely nibbled at it, though, and drank a bit of wine. At length he helped her to lie back against the pillows. She tossed about and complained of the heat. His chair was placed right next to the bed, and he leaned over her. "Shall I remove the comforter, then, Amanda?" he asked in jest, a smile playing at his lips, for he knew that only a sheet lay between the cover and the lady.

"No, you shall not. I am quite fine, I do assure you," she snapped.

"I am much relieved. Now perhaps you will settle down and allow yourself to sleep. That is the best cure, you know, my dear." He said this last rather gently, and she seemed mollified, for he could sense her body becoming less tense, but still she did not close her eyes.

"You may go, now, my lord," she said quietly, but no less commandingly.

He was quite taken aback by her tone, and rather annoyed, but then he remembered that such augured well for her recovery. "I shall go when you are asleep, Amanda, and I must remind you that you were not to call me 'my lord.' I believe we discussed that in the—er—earlier?" he said smoothly.

"Ah, yes, *Cousin,*" said a sleepy voice, whose owner finally closed her eyes and fell asleep.

*   *   *

The Earl poured himself a brandy and had just taken a long sip when Jeffries knocked and announced the arrival of the doctor.

Dr. Pringle looked even older than the Earl had imagined. His wrinkled face was quite pink and atop his head stood a shock of white hair that seemed to stand on end. His body was rather bent, but he was not precisely stooped. Rather, his body seemed to slant downward as he walked, so that it looked as if he were about to fall flat on his face. He never did, however; he merely advanced several paces in a straight line, falling farther and farther forward as he did so, and when he seemed to be tilting too low, he would stop, preferably with the aid of some obstruction such as a chair, straighten up just a bit, and begin again. This he did several times as he made his way across the large bedchamber to the stately four-poster bed.

It was not, to say the least, a posture that inspired confidence, and the Earl rather reluctantly rose to greet him.

The doctor bowed so low in acknowledgment that his lordship momentarily thought to help him rise. But Dr. Pringle managed to accomplish this himself, and said, in a voice more raspy than the Earl remembered, "Had a run-in with the highwaymen, did she? Dastardly doings, that's what I say. What kind o' country is this when a lady isn't safe to go about her own land? And such a one as she—right nasty coves, no doubt 'bout that. Hit her head, butler said. Caught in the rain, too, is that so? Ah—well, there she is. What seems to be the trouble?"

The Earl merely gaped open-mouthed at him, but before he could collect himself enough to reply, the doctor bent to Amanda, touching her brow with the palm of his hand. "She's sleeping," said the good doctor.

"Yes, I know," said the Earl with controlled calm,

"but she's feverish."

"'Course she is. Exposure to the elements, you know. Worst kind of fever and chill. How long was she exposed, m'lord?"

The Earl was relieved to hear that the doctor was capable of uttering at least one complete sentence, and this unaccountably gave him just the bare minimum of faith in Dr. Pringle's medical abilities. He answered the question and then volunteered a very cursory and abridged account of Amanda's injuries and what he himself had done thus far. He omitted the ankle altogether.

"Well, you did right to keep her warm, m'lord. Ah—brandy—good idea. So she stopped shaking, did she? And now the fever's bound to build. Not much can we do about it, I'm afraid. Bathe her in lukewarm water if the fever gets bad, 'specially her legs. Someone ought to stay with her overnight, seems to me."

The Earl waited for him to say more, and when he did not, finally asked, "And what of the head injury, Dr. Pringle? Does that need to be watched?"

"May have dizzy spells. May hurt some. Head's mighty strong, though. It'll heal. Needs plenty of rest. Give you some laudanum to ease the pain. Help her sleep, too." The doctor unbent from the bed, and turned as if to leave.

"B-but, doctor," spluttered the Earl, quite beside himself, "are you not going to examine her ladyship?"

"Well, don't know but what I can see well and good enough what it is ails her. But p'rhaps I had ought to listen to her chest and such." He looked with squinting eyes at the Earl as if trying to recall something about him. "You're Ainsley, isn't that right? Old Millforte's nephew, they say. You're not her husband then, are you?" The Earl shook his head and the good doctor nodded. "Ah, her intended, then. Well, you *had* ought to leave us now, while I examine the little lady."

"Er, yes, well, I am not her intended either, you understand. I am guardian of the heir and the estates. I—er—came from London to—er—help Lady Millforte."

"Seems you came just in time then, to help, I mean," the doctor replied, chuckling at his own attempted jest.

The Earl was not happy to leave Amanda to the mercy of a doctor who might have difficulty remembering why he had been summoned at all, but feeling he had no choice, he said, rather crisply, "I shall send her maid in presently. I trust this will not take long."

It did not, indeed, take very long. Bessie was not in the room much above four minutes before the door opened and Dr. Pringle catapulted out of the room, the top portion of his body preceding the lower by a full half minute at least.

"Chest clear. Throat not inflamed. 'Course it may be early days yet. Always danger of the pleurisy developing. Main thing to watch is the fever. Rising steadily, I should think. Left the laudanum on the bedstand. Come by tomorrow, I will. Afternoon, m'lord," said the aged medical man as he executed a stiff half-bow, straightened his body, and made a tilting exit down the corridor.

The Earl found Bessie wringing her hands inside Amanda's bedchamber. "She's bad, your lordship, I just know it. What are we to do? Oh, what are we to do?" she wailed.

He strode to the side of the bed. He put his hand to Amanda's cheek and frowned. The fever was rising; unfortunately the ancient doctor had been right in that. She was still asleep and he wondered whether the doctor had looked into her throat at all. She was not dangerously hot, and he thought it most prudent to let her sleep. He turned to the maid.

"At the moment we will allow her to sleep, Bessie. You will sit here and watch her, and send for me immediately if she either wakes or shows any signs of acute distress," he said brusquely.

The maid, wide-eyed with fear, nodded dumbly, whereupon the Earl, after cautioning her against any sighs or moans or sobs which might disturb her ladyship, gathered up his coat and made his way down the great stair to see whether the magistrate had yet arrived.

It was not until he neared the library that the Earl realized that he had actually put his still damp, hopelessly wrinkled coat back onto his frame. He would *never* have done such a thing in London, he thought, and imagined that his valet would be profoundly shocked. The magistrate could wait, he decided, and strode back toward the stairs.

Darby was indeed shocked when he beheld his master, Hessians muddy beyond recognition, coat crumpled beyond redemption. The Earl allowed himself to be divested of these as well as his shirt and breeches, enduring in patient silence Darby's mutterings about the ignominy of finding oneself still dressed in morning clothes, and filthy ones at that, in the late afternoon. He submitted to the valet's ministrations as the latter arrayed him in a charcoal gray coat and white pantaloons, but his lordship balked at the overly precise cravat Darby began to arrange. Taking matters into his own hands, he flipped the cravat over quickly several times, creating a simple, if asymmetrical knot. He hastily buttoned his own waistcoat and briskly existed the room, leaving his gray-haired manservant to gape in astonishment after him.

The Earl found the local magistrate awaiting him in the library. That short, stocky man, heretofore unknown to the Earl, was quite beside himself with awe at being in the presence of one so exalted. He assured the Earl that the chief county magistrate, Lord Coninghill, would of a certain have come himself were he not detained in London on business. The Earl started at this; he had not seen Coninghill in many years and had quite forgotten that his seat was in Shropshire. They had been old school friends, a fact which he forsook to relate, for the magistrate seemed acutely embarrassed, even mortified, that such a dreadful crime had taken place within his territory. When he said he would do all in his power to apprehend the villains, his lordship believed him.

When the magistrate had gone, the Earl sat for several minutes behind the desk, his fingers massaging his weary brow. He was concerned for Amanda's health, to be sure, but he feared even more for her safety once she was well. Even if he could contrive to keep watch of her while he stayed at Millforte, he would have to leave at some time. She was much too headstrong to heed any of his advice and none of the staff seemed in the least bit capable of keeping track of her.

"Good God, Ainsley, you look awful!" exclaimed the Vicar as he advanced into the room without ceremony. He watched the Earl's head jerk up in response.

"Oh, Trumwell, I—"

"I know. You are not receiving. I'm afraid I rather bullied poor proper Jeffries. I shall go if you want me to, but I—well—I thought maybe I could help," the Vicar said. He watched his lordship crane his neck a bit, as if looking beyond him, and he grinned and added, "I am quite alone, as you see." The Earl colored but smiled weakly. The Vicar thought fleetingly that his dear Sally, who brought sunshine wherever she

161

went, would do wonders for Amanda in a day or two. She would be a disaster in the library just now, though, and he had not mentioned to her his destination.

"It's good of you to come, Trumwell," said the Earl, beginning to rise. The Vicar motioned for him to sit, and his lordship, indicating that the Vicar might do likewise, continued, "She's asleep now. The fever is rising and we shall have to guard her closely. But truly, there is not—"

"Ainsley, I'll be blunt," interrupted the Vicar. "I naturally want to know how Amanda is, and if you should need me, I am at your service. But that is not why I've come. I assumed you'd have the sick room under control. Forgive the presumption, Ainsley, but are you not troubled by more than her health?" Actually, the Vicar did not think it presumption at all. Why, even if he hadn't surmised as much from the untoward events of the last two days, one look at Ainsley's face would have told him there was more to all this than there seemed at the outset. He watched Ainsley's eyes narrow as the latter regarded him intently.

"If I'm out of line, Ainsley, I would that you will say so, but I cannot stand on ceremony where Amanda's well-being is concerned. Ainsley," he said, leaning forward and speaking urgently, "is there any connection between this heinous attack today and yesterday's mishap?"

Ainsley sighed and looked quite exasperated. "Only in the sense that Amanda does exactly the opposite of what she knows to be my wishes. She knew that I did not approve of her solitary walks at dawn, and I had expressly forbid her to go to the Low Cottages."

The Vicar struggled to keep a grin from his face. He could not imagine anyone forbidding Amanda to do anything. Whatever can have possessed a man as intelligent as Ainsley to commit such folly? Ainsley obviously was not in the mood for seeing the humor in anything, though, and so the Vicar schooled his mind to the very serious subject at hand. "The Low Cottages—is that where she was? By herself?" he asked.

"Yes—I—that is—we had a bit of a row and she was very angry—and—well, you understand I will not have this to be got about—but you know she's been speaking of tearing them down. I won't hear of it, of course. In any case, she was on her way back when two men—when it happened."

"What exactly did happen? A robbery attempt?"

"Yes. Quite unsuccessful. She—she fights like a tiger," said his lordship.

"Does she indeed?" asked the Vicar, a smile creeping into his eyes. Actually, were it not for the very real danger which had threatened Amanda, this entire conversation was rather amusing. The good Vicar could not help wondering what else Ainsley had said he "wouldn't hear of," and exactly when the Earl had seen her "fight like a tiger." Amanda was a bit headstrong, to be sure, but surely not a tiger? He continued in a serious tone, however. "Was she hurt? How did she hit her head?"

"Yes, she fell into a gully when they—er—in the struggle. Her head hit a rock and she was knocked senseless, and then the blackguards fled. Then, of course, the rain started."

The Vicar gazed piercingly at the Earl for several minutes. "There is more, is there not, Ainsley? Does it have to do with yesterday?" he pressed.

Ainsley looked at him searchingly, almost as if sizing him up for the first time, but at length he replied. "It—I—Trumwell, no woman should be made to face in a lifetime what Amanda has been through these two days. The incidents are not related, I do assure you, but, well, the cutthroats she encountered today wanted more than to rob her. She fought them, but I think it was only her fall against the rock that saved her from—from . . ." He was obviously loath to go on, and here the Vicar, who felt almost sick, interjected.

"I was much afraid of that," he said quietly. "It is vital that these rogues be apprehended. And what about yesterday, Ainsley? How did she hurt her ankle?"

The Vicar was gratified that his friend did not hesitate this time. "She was walking alone. I happened to have arisen unaccustomedly early. I have not—er—slept well of late," he said. The Vicar's lips twitched as he restrained a smile. He thought he understood something of why Ainsley could not sleep. Ainsley went on, "I, too, went out to the meadows. I espied her in the distance, standing next to Sir James. He seemed—angry—and he—well—to make short work of it, Trumwell, he pushed her to the ground and flung himself—that is—" the Earl's face was livid as he recalled the scene.

"Pray, do not force yourself to—to continue, Ainsley. I take it you—arrived on time?" the Vicar asked, quite shaken. When Ainsley nodded, he continued, "I had always thought him a bad lot, but to stoop to such disgusting conduct! It quite sickens one. And Amanda. What she must have felt. Have you thought to press charges?"

"Heaven knows I should like to see that swine put away. But I cannot—Amanda would be humiliated beyond reason. She would have to leave the county. She can hardly bear it that *I* know—that I was there. You realize, of course, that you must never let on that—"

"You need not even say it, my friend. Do you think any threat lingers from that quarter?"

"I have made it clear that he will have to deal with

164

me, and so I think not, but I may have to return to London in the near future. Perhaps you will be able to convince Amanda to remain at the manor, or at the least not venture forth unaccompanied. I—she—does not give the slightest credence to what I say," said his lordship with a sigh.

The Vicar merely smiled enigmatically and nodded his head slowly, but to himself he thought, You have a good deal to learn about women, worldly though you be, my friend. As a reply was clearly expected, he said soberly, "You may rest easy, Ainsley. I will do my utmost, should the need arise."

"I'm sure you will, sir, but you cannot guard her constantly. How has she managed to keep out of scrapes before?"

The Vicar repressed a smile. "In truth, Ainsley, I cannot say that—well—what I mean to say is— Amanda led a rather—shall we say—uneventful life before—before—" The Vicar felt himself color and the Earl interrupted.

"Before *I* came here?"

"Well, yes, actually, now you mention it," replied Trumwell a bit sheepishly, for he did not see a way out.

The Earl sighed and shook his head. "It would seem that she and I bring out the worst in each other."

"Oh, I would not say that, Ainsley," said the Vicar amiably, and rising from his seat, he added, "and by the way, what exactly *is* the worst in you?"

"Never mind, Trumwell. I don't doubt that Amanda will give you quite an earful the moment my back is turned," said the Earl with a grin.

And with that, a much heartened Vicar took his leave.

Chapter Eleven

"Never you mind about calling his lordship, Bessie," Mrs. Havenwick was saying as Amanda sensed herself drifting back to wakefulness. She felt a dream slip away, a dream of Spain, the Spain her mother had spoken of, warm and golden in the summer sun.

"Imagine him coming here and giving orders like he was Lord of the Manor. Well, he ain't, not of this one, and I'm the one as ought to be taking care of her ladyship, like I've always done," Mrs. Havenwick continued.

Spain was gone, but Amanda's eyes remained closed. Her eyelids burned, as if she'd been in the sun too long.

"But he'll be frightful angry, Mrs.," ventured Bessie in a tiny voice.

"Imagine him thinking as I'm not able to nurse my lady. The nerve! Now, don't just stand around like a ninnynammer, Bessie. Put the kettle near the fire. I don't want the water to be cold, and I'll be wanting to refill the basin, I'm sure. She's fearful hot, she is."

Amanda was, indeed, feeling very hot. It had not been the Mediterranean sun, after all, that made her face and arms burn. She opened her eyes. Despite the voices, she half expected to see the Earl standing over her. Instead she saw Bessie at the side of the bed, wringing her hands and gazing anxiously at Amanda. She turned her head slightly and saw Mrs. Havenwick leaning over the washstand, dipping strips of linen into the water basin.

Mrs. Havenwick sat down on the bed. "You're awake, are you? You've had a good sleep, my lady. 'Twill help you win your strength back." She touched her rough, fat fingers to Amanda's brow. "It's very hot you are, my lady. The water will cool you off." As she said this she began to bathe Amanda's face and neck with the wet cloth. The warm water created a cool, delicious sensation on her skin, but somehow she found the sight of Mrs. Havenwick, her puffy face encased in wrinkles, her enormous bosom hovering above her as she lay in the bed, rather disappointing. A handsome face, framed with dark wavy hair, Amanda thought unwittingly, would have been much more to her liking.

Suddenly a flood of memories came rushing toward her. The gully, the rain, the crofter's hut. She remembered the Earl covering her with his cape, pulling her to him, engulfing her in his arms. She felt herself blush, and knew that she must push that face with its slate blue eyes out of her mind. It would not do at all. She had yielded to her emotions this morning, but it had been a mistake that must not be repeated.

Further images flashed through her mind. The Earl carrying her to bed, feeding her the soup, the awful shivering. She blinked away the images; she could not bear for him to have seen her so helpless.

Mrs. Havenwick was unbuttoning her nightgown. Amanda felt the warm water caress her chest, her belly. Suddenly she remembered the Earl unbuttoning her dress, pressing the comforter against her. She squirmed inwardly at the thought of the liberties he had taken. She must ensure that such a thing never happened again. She did not know how Mrs. Havenwick had contrived to supplant his lordship at her bedside, but she knew the housekeeper would be more than happy to keep it that way.

"I do not wish him to come here again, Mrs. Havenwick," she whispered.

"Who, my lady?"

"The Earl, of course," replied Amanda, her voice stronger.

"Now, don't you trouble yourself, my lady. I intend to care for you, just as I've always done," said Mrs. Havenwick. Amanda smiled but Mrs. Havenwick's attention was caught by a knock at the door.

Bessie opened the door just a bit and said, "'Tis his lordship."

"One minute, Bessie," Mrs. Havenwick said. She arranged Amanda's nightgown and the covers above her and glanced nervously at the door. "Now, my lady, he only means the best for you. Truly, he does. Why, did he not go out after you, with the storm clouds already a-gathering?" Amanda colored and Mrs. Havenwick went on. "Ain't nobody can counter him anyway, excepting you, my lady, and you not in any condition to go hollering at him now. He'll behave the gentleman, I know that at least."

"Mrs. Havenwick, how can you possibly—" Amanda was saying, her eyes wide with indignation, as his lordship entered the room. She clamped her mouth shut when she saw him, and cast sullen eyes at both the housekeeper and the Earl.

"Well, my dear, you are looking a bit stronger," he said amiably, walking to the bedside and trying to ignore the tension in the room. He placed a book on the bedside table. "It would seem your little nap was highly beneficial." He eyed the water basin and the wet linen. "How long have you been here, Mrs. Havenwick? Has

168

her fever risen? Why was I not informed?" As he said this he glanced meaningfully to Bessie, who had retreated to a far corner of the room at his entrance.

The look was not lost on Mrs. Havenwick. She glanced anxiously from Amanda to his lordship, and, folding her arms and heaving her bosom, she turned to the Earl. "I came to look in on her ladyship, my lord, and finding her color high and her body indeed warm, I sent Bessie for a kettle of water. There was no need to alarm you, my lord. I have been nursing her ladyship since she was a girl, after all. It ain't proper for a gentleman to attend her in such a manner. Cook is fixing you a nice dinner, my lord. You go on and have your dinner and I shall attend my lady."

The Earl waited patiently for Mrs. Havenwick to finish her little speech. He had sensed Amanda's feeling of relief as the housekeeper spoke; it was clear that Amanda had put her up to it. In spite of himself he had to admire the housekeeper's utter nerve in so confronting him. He would not waste his ire on the servant, however.

He spoke calmly to Mrs. Havenwick, but gazed pointedly at Amanda all the while. "I thank you for bespeaking my dinner, Mrs. Havenwick. You will kindly have it sent up here. I shall dine with Lady Millforte. And you needn't concern yourself about her care. I am not a stranger to nursing, as she knows. I shall, of course, call for her maid should I need her," he said smoothly, and bent to feel Amanda's cheek. "I see you've brought the fever down for now, Mrs. Havenwick. Excellent. Lady Millforte and I are most grateful, I am sure. Good afternoon, Mrs. Havenwick."

Amanda smoldered as the Earl straightened up and waited for Mrs. Havenwick, whose mouth had quite fallen open, to leave. The housekeeper looked from lord to lady, mumbled her customary "harrumph," and patted Amanda's hand before she marched herself out of the room.

The Earl turned to Bessie, who was looking down at her nervously twisting hands. "We'll have an early dinner, Bessie. You may go now," he said, but the maid was at the door before he'd finished.

He pulled the velvet chair up to the bed. Amanda turned her head away from him. He was not quite sure to which of his many sins she was reacting at this point.

"Mind your manners, Amanda. You have company. Now, how do you feel? Are you very uncomfortable? Does your head still hurt?"

She turned back to him and said, "I am feeling fine, my lord, and I do assure you that I am not in need of any company. I do not consider it appropriate for you to be here."

"Ah, but then perhaps you will consider that it is *I* who am in need of *your* company," he said silkily, but finished more forcefully, "and you need looking after in your present state, whether you care to admit it or no."

"Then if you must visit, pray be seated on the chaise in the seating alcove. You, who have so oft spoken to me of the proprieties, seem to regard none." She spoke coolly, but unaccountably, she began to blush, and he thought he knew what was troubling her.

"Ah, then it is my proximity that worries you," he said, grinning. "But I do protest that I have always, at least while—*here*—with you, acted the perfect gentleman. Surely you cannot argue with that."

"I most assuredly can, but I do not—do not wish to discuss it," she snapped.

"And if I have not always behaved as a gentleman in other—er—circumstances, I do apologize, although I cannot say that I regret it, Amanda," he said, his voice suddenly very soft.

170

Amanda swallowed and her blush deepened. "You should not be here, my lord," was all she could say.

"Charles, or Cousin Charles, if you must," he corrected. "You do wrong me, Amanda. I have only your best interests at heart."

"You said that once before."

"And so I meant it, both times. Come now, if I were going to seduce you it would hardly be in your sickroom with all the servants hovering about, now would it? Besides, you have forgotten that a basic element in seduction is the ultimate willingness of the capitulating party," he said in a very husky voice.

To his immense delight, Amanda blushed a deep shade of crimson.

There was nothing that Amanda could say. She turned away, acutely uncomfortable. She wanted to shout at him and order him from the room, but when he spoke so softly, so intensely to her, she felt terribly weak, and much to her dismay, a very pleasurable warm ripple glided over her body. She was supremely grateful when Bessie and a footman entered with their dinner.

Amanda ate very little of her dinner. Conversation was desultory; the Earl regretted that there seemed to be no topic that they could discuss amicably. At length his lordship said, "You are not very talkative, my dear. Are you feeling poorly again?"

"I am quite well, as I said before. You have had your dinner. Perhaps now you will leave me to my rest."

"I'm afraid I cannot, as you well know, my dear. Dr. Pringle was quite specific on that head."

"I was not aware that you had such confidence in Dr. Pringle, Cousin Charles," she said smoothly.

He ignored her comment. "We have a long evening ahead of us, my dear. I thought perhaps I should read to you," he said rather gently, his eyes warm.

She did not want him here. She should order him out of her room without delay. All the voices at the back of her head told her so. But when he looked at her in just that way, she somehow could not.

Her eyes searched his face as she said a bit weakly, "I—I should like that very much, my lord—er—Cousin. Do read from *Electra*. I am just now in the middle of it."

His lordship did not want to argue further with her, but lust and murder in ancient Greece? Really, she ought not to be reading such things! "Sophocles is hardly what I had in mind, Amanda," said the Earl sternly. "I am reading Shakespeare. Shall I read from this then?" He picked up the book he had placed on the table.

"Well, I do rather enjoy my Shakespeare, I must admit. What play are you reading?"

"*The Taming of the Shrew*," he said complacently.

"*The Taming of*—oh, no, Cousin," she objected rather strongly. "I am afraid that particular play is not very much to my liking." The Earl frowned and she added disdainfully, "I might have known that is the sort of thing you'd read."

"And just what is—"

"I suppose I shall simply have to go down to the library to choose another," she interrupted with a sigh.

"You'll stay where you are, madam!" he fairly shouted, jumping up from his seat at bedside. "Oh, very well," he said in exasperation, "*Electra* it shall be."

And so the Earl settled himself down to read *Electra*, thinking that Petruchio would never have approved. But then, Petruchio had never met Amanda.

The Earl was awakened twice in the middle of the night as he lay crumpled and curled in the velvet chair near Amanda's bed, his long legs inadequately supported by a damask ottoman with tasseled fringes.

Amanda had fallen asleep somewhere in the middle of *Electra*, and as she seemed reasonably comfortable, the Earl had set himself up with the chair and ottoman, and allowed himself to drift into a light sleep. His years of service on the Continent had taught him to sleep lightly if he needed to, wary of every sound. A fever always worsened at night, and he could trust no one else in the household to attend Amanda.

He woke the first time when she stirred restlessly in her bed. She was very hot and complained of a headache. He woke Bessie and bade her bathe her mistress until she cooled down. When the maid beckoned him back into the room, he gave Amanda several drops of the laudanum and brushed the wet strands of hair from her face as she drifted back to sleep.

The second time he was jarred from sleep by a scream.

"No! No!" Amanda was shrieking as she frantically clutched at her face with her hands and tossed from side to side, the bedclothes a jumble under her. "No, Father, no! It isn't true!" she cried.

The Earl sat down on the edge of the bed and grabbed her hands. "Amanda, wake up! It's all right! You are dreaming. Amanda, look at me!" He shook her gently, but when her eyes opened they held a faraway look. He was sure she did not know who he was. Just as well, he thought, considering that it was probably three o'clock in the morning or some such, and she would take great exception to his presence.

"Dreaming. I have been dreaming," she said slowly, as if to convince herself. Then her eyes widened with a look of anguish. She tried to lift her head from the pillows. "Victor!" she said. "Don't let him find Victor!"

173

"No, Amanda, he shan't. I promise. Now go to sleep. You are safe. Victor is safe. Go to sleep," he said softly, thinking that laudanum did strange things to one.

She smiled a fuzzy smile and relaxed against the pillows. Her eyes closed and she seemed to fall into a peaceful sleep.

Which was more than his lordship was able to do, for he found that, weary though his body was, his mind was racing. What kind of family had Amanda come from? She seemed terrified of her father, and she could not mention her mother without evincing a great deal of distress. He wondered if it all in some way explained her marriage to his uncle. She had given no indication that her marriage had been unhappy, yet it did not seem the sort of union a young girl would willingly enter into. But she had not, at least according to what he remembered his distraught mother writing him at the time, been forced in any way. Had she indeed been coerced, there could have been none of the snide references to her as a calculating opportunist.

None of it made sense, as indeed, nothing about Amanda had since he'd arrived, and his tired mind finally gave up and he began to feel sleepy. He would doze for the next couple of hours, he thought, and rouse himself in the early dawn. He had not deemed it politic to tell Amanda that he would stay the night, and he knew there would be hell to pay should she wake and find him there. Unfortunately for his lordship, his body was more tired than he knew, and it managed to adjust itself to the ridiculous position he'd placed it in all too well, for the Earl slept very soundly indeed.

So soundly, in fact, that the next sound he heard was Amanda's agitated, "Cousin Charles! Wake up!" He opened his eyes and slowly lowered his feet, sitting up as he did so.

"Amanda—oh—I—uh—good morning," he mumbled.

"Good morning, indeed, Cousin!" said Amanda sharply. She was sitting bolt upright in bed, holding the comforter nearly up to her shoulders. "Perhaps you would be good enough to explain what in the world you are doing here at this hour of the morning!"

He was not quite awake enough to think of any coherent reply, and so he simply said, "I suppose I've been sleeping."

"So it would seem. I was under the impression that you had been given quite adequate accommodation here. If that is not the case, indeed, if something is amiss, you need only say so, and adjustment can be made. There is no need, I assure you, to—"

"Amanda," he interrupted, quite awake by now, "you know very well there is nothing wrong with my accommodation. You have been very ill—although heaven knows you don't sound very ill right now. But you have been running a very high fever and you simply had to be—watched—through the night."

"Ah, I see. And, of course, in a house full of servants, there was no one so qualified as you," she said sarcastically.

"Something like that," he said, coloring slightly.

"I would not have thought it of you. To take advantage in such a manner."

"Oh, come now," he said, incensed as he felt a crick in his neck and an ache in his back, "you cannot for one minute believe that I would—why, if I were bent on such a course, it seems to me that yesterday morning would have been a much more opportune time. Do you not think so, Amanda?" he asked silkily, standing up and looking down at her. Her eyes flashed and he added, "Although, if memory serves me, that could hardly have been construed as my taking advantage of you, now could it?"

Her eyes widened as if in disbelief and she turned a deep crimson. He could have bitten his tongue out.

"Amanda, I—I did not mean it. Forgive me," he said gently.

"You will kindly remove yourself from my room. You have quite overstayed your welcome, Cousin," she said icily.

He looked down at her with warm eyes, searching her face for some sign of forgiveness, but her chin jutted firmly out, and her eyes were cold. Damn! he thought. No woman had ever exasperated him the way she did. He had never even had to *try* to win a woman over, and now here was this woman, with whom he could not even carry on a polite conversation. Why, it was uncanny the way she managed to provoke him to act like a cad, and worse yet, to feel ashamed of it later.

He took a deep breath and sighed wearily. "I shall send your maid to you, Amanda. Please remember that you are in desperate need of rest. I shall visit with you after breakfast," he said quietly, and betook his aching body out of the room.

"Damn you, Ainsley, or Cousin Charles, or whoever you are!" she shouted, throwing a pillow toward the closed door when he'd left the room. She yanked the covers off her and swung her legs over the side of the bed. As she did so she sat up abruptly and a wave of dizziness hit her. Her head began to ache violently, and she slowly lowered herself back down into the pillows. She would await Bessie's assistance, after all.

Her head might ache, but she did not feel feverish and though she might not be completely well, still she did not feel nearly as weak as she had yesterday. It was imperative that she dress and leave her room immediately after breakfast. The Earl must not find her here. At all costs she must keep her distance from him. She must place their dealings back on the businesslike plane on which they had begun, and that was best accomplished, she knew, in the library.

She thought of the warm eyes he had fixed upon her a few moments ago. It had taken all of her willpower not to succumb to their entreaty. It was becoming increasingly difficult to resist the slate blue eyes, that very engaging smile of his, and the gentle, husky voice. But she must; she could not trust him. She had believed in him for those few moments in the hut; it was impossible to doubt him when he looked at one in just that way. But now good sense prevailed, and she knew that that interlude had meant nothing to Ainsley. If anything, she had been right in presuming, when he'd pushed her away from him yesterday morning, that she had somehow displeased him, confirmed his disdain for her. Certainly his ungentlemanly comment today was proof of his contempt.

Yes, she had simply got to keep him at a distance, and she must not evince any dependence at all. It only served to make the Earl more domineering.

And she would certainly not be dictated to in matters of the estate. She remembered suddenly the Earl's advertisement for a governess. Well, she would find a way to forestall the arrival of any such person, and meanwhile, she would finish what she'd set out to do yesterday. She would send for Higgins and set her project under way immediately. It would feel very good to best the Earl in this matter of the Low Cottages, and she thought his lordship's character would certainly benefit from the realization that he was not, after all, omnipotent.

Chapter Twelve

The Earl had gratefully allowed himself to be put to bed by Darby when he had staggered into his room in the early morning, a rather twisted relic of the man he usually was. He had given orders to be awakened for an early breakfast, and having partaken of this excellent repast, his lordship felt somewhat refreshed. He made his way down the stairs to the library, thinking that a few moments' quiet reflection on the problem of Amanda would do him good.

The problem of Amanda was staring him right in the face, however, as he entered the library, for there sat the lady herself behind the great mahogany desk.

"What the—Amanda! What are you doing out of bed?" As he said this he realized that he'd said it too many times in the last two days, and he could not help thinking, quite ruefully, that though he'd wanted to take her to bed ever since he'd first met her, a sickbed had been quite far from his mind.

"I am working, Cousin," she said calmly. Indeed, she had several ledgers open before her, and was engaged in tallying lists of figures. "Higgins left these figures for me. There are several minor decisions that must be made with regard to production of wool and mutton in the northeast section. Perhaps you would care to be informed as to the details, Cousin?" she asked in a very businesslike tone.

Indeed, he did *not* wish to be informed of the details, but she did not await his reply. Rather, she launched immediately into a detailed discussion of the economy of the northeast section. So involved did she become in what was an obvious attempt to distract the Earl from other topics, and so nervous lest her attempt fail, that she rose from her chair and began to pace the dark oak floor. Her discussion of the minutiae of the sheep industry at Millforte actually became quite animated, but the Earl recognized it as a desperate ploy to keep the discourse between them anything but personal. She waved him to one of the soft leather chairs, and he settled back to enjoy her performance. It was made all the more amusing by the fact that she had, no doubt unwittingly, chosen to wear a deep mauve dress of crimped crepe that became her exquisitely.

He knew he ought to order her straight up to bed, for though she seemed strong now, she would undoubtedly suffer a relapse. But he also knew that she would pay him not the slightest heed. And so he sat, his mind only partially attending the content of her speech, but his eyes following closely as the slender figure, so gracefully set off in that dress, moved about the room, and his ears remarking the intelligence and determination in that voice.

He made what he thought were suitable replies at suitable times, but the vicissitudes of wool and mutton production were much effaced in his mind by the vicissitudes of his relationship to Amanda.

He had hoped yesterday, in the crofter's hut, that there had been some subtle—alteration—in their relationship, and that perhaps she would come to trust him. But now she seemed more guarded than ever. With chagrin he admitted to himself that his ill-advised, quite unforgivable parting comment, coupled with his presence in her bedchamber at six o'clock in the morning, had gone a long way toward producing this morning's obvious attempt to act as though yesterday had never existed.

"Cousin, are you attending?" she asked, standing once more behind the desk and evincing mild impatience as she ran her fingers down a column of figures. He had the uncomfortable feeling that he had been asked a question about those figures, and indulged in a moment of rather unaccustomed stammering before the door of the library burst open and their attention was claimed by a most remarkable spectacle.

Into the room catapulted a noisy entourage the like of which his lordship had never before encountered, led by a rather muddy, yelping, bouncing Irish setter puppy. Close on the heels of the dog was Victor, his clothes muddy beyond recognition, his dirt-caked hands held close to his face as he sobbed and quite incoherently tried to address his mother. He was followed by a frail-looking woman gasping and sobbing and talking all at once, looking as though she was about to faint, and whom the Earl surmised could be none other than Nurse, no doubt having the vapors. Williams, cap in hand and a most abject expression on his face, timidly brought up the rear.

The Earl had risen as soon as the door burst open, and now from the corner of his eye he saw Amanda calmly walk around the front of the desk toward Victor. He thought he detected a smile touching the corners of her mouth. She bent slightly to Victor, but straightened up almost instantaneously, for a new disturbance called her attention.

Into the library stormed the formidable Mrs. Havenwick, her face quite puckered with anger as she carried on a heated exchange with a fat woman in a white cap and a once white apron covered with what might have been blackberry juice. The wearer of the apron his lordship took to be Cook, and Cook, looking quite as formidable as Mrs. Havenwick herself, was leading a sobbing, terrified scullery maid by the ear.

The cacophony of noises and the rag-tag look of the motley assemblage were indeed far beyond anything his lordship had heretofore experienced. Had such a thing occurred in his own home, he thought complacently, he would have cowed them all with one fierce stare and sent them scurrying back where they belonged. Had his mother been confronted with such a sight, he had no doubt that she would have swooned and fainted on the spot, thereby terminating the discord as the entire staff united in their efforts to revive her. In fact, he thought, any well-bred lady ought to faint, or cry out, or have the vapors, at the very least.

But Amanda did none of these. The hint of a smile had not left her lips, nor did her serene face show even a crease of anxiety. She took Victor's hand, and standing in front of the assembly, she raised a clarion voice. "Ladies, and good sir," she began, and gave all a stern look merely by widening her eyes. A hush immediately fell upon the room and she continued quietly. "That you have all come to me with very pressing concerns I have no doubt, but I can hear no one when you all speak at once. Now, I shall begin with Victor." She bent to the still sobbing child and said, "What is the trouble, Victor? Why are you crying?"

Victor rather brokenly began to tell his story, with Amanda frequently interrupting to question him or repeat back what he'd said in order to verify it with Nurse. The gist of the contretemps was that Athena, the yelping oversized puppy, had not been content to roll about in the mud with Victor outside, but had led Victor, Nurse, and Williams a merry chase up to the nursery, which was now decorated with paw prints and footprints of muddy brown. Nurse was demanding the expulsion from the manor of the dog and the head groom, who had introduced the dog in the first place, or she would pack her bags this very day, as being nursemaid to a dog, not to mention the dirtiest little boy she had ever seen, had not been part of the prescribed position, after all. Victor was pleading for Athena, and Williams, after apologizing profusely for so disturbing her ladyship, asked if she was feeling quite well after yesterday's mishap, and didn't she know that boys will be boys, and every boy needs a dog, leastways every English boy, didn't her ladyship agree?

Her ladyship whispered something to Victor which quieted him, and then she stood erect and faced the others. The Earl saw that she swayed slightly, as if overcome by dizziness, and he moved forward surreptitiously. But Amanda took a deep breath, steadied herself, and lifted her head to speak. Satisfied that she would not collapse under the strain of her illness and this unprecedented onslaught, the Earl sauntered to the fireplace. He reclined against the chimneypiece, a bemused expression on his face as he prepared to watch Amanda unravel the chaos before them.

"Williams, you will please see to it that the dog remains outdoors. When she is much older and calmer, she may be permitted inside. If Victor must run amuck with her, you will keep watch over him; see that he enters the house through the kitchens, where he can be washed down. Nurse, I believe that Victor understands that he will be permitted to keep his dog only if he is careful to keep her out of doors. Victor does not want to lose his beloved Nurse, you know, and as the dog seems devoted to him, I think Victor and Williams together can prevent further mishap. You will try to remember, however, Nurse, that neat and clean is *not* the normal state for little boys. You must learn to tolerate a bit of dirt; it all comes off with soap and water, after all."

Williams smiled gratefully at this little speech, and Nurse sniffed, a bit put out still. But Victor, obviously having inherited his mother's propensity for shrewd diplomacy, went to Nurse and clamped his little arms around her skirts. This was all that was needed to melt the last of Nurse's anger, for she put her arms around the boy and led the little group away, all, including Athena, quite mollified.

The next group was not dispatched so easily, each party seemingly possessed of a different set of facts concerning the same incident. What the Earl gathered, while the scullery maid whispered, Cook threatened to turn her off without a character, and Amanda tried to talk with Mrs. Havenwick, was that it all had to do with the butcher.

"Where is Mr. Grimsby now, Cook?" asked Amanda.

"He's below stairs, your ladyship. Says he won't leave till he gets what's owed him. Accuses me of stealing his money. But I swear I paid him every penny Mrs. Havenwick give me, I did."

The Earl wondered momentarily why this butcher scrupled to show himself upstairs. No one else apparently did. Why, it was just the sort of ramshackle household arrangement he had expected would be de rigeur here at Millforte. He checked his irrational mind at this last, however. There was nothing ramshackle about the way Amanda addressed her servants, and he knew it. And besides, it was obvious that they held her in the highest respect.

"Now, Sarah, Cook gave you the money for the butcher each time, is that not correct?" asked Amanda quietly.

"Yes, your ladyship," the scullery maid said timidly, effecting a slight curtsy.

"Well, then, did you give the money directly to the butcher, Sarah?" Sarah's eyes were down and she nodded. "Sarah, look up at me," said Amanda somewhat forcefully. "Answer me again." The scullery maid started to whimper again, and then sob, and

Cook snatched her ear again, and called her various unsavory names, more, thought the Earl, to prove to all and sundry how superior she herself was than to castigate the maid. Mrs. Havenwick begged leave to dismiss them both, and find a new butcher, but at length Amanda succeeded in extracting the story.

It seemed that Sarah was keeping company with a smooth-talking young man, who came around much too frequently to please Cook, and who had been such a gentleman, according to Sarah, as to suggest that he himself should deliver the payments to the butcher, and so to save his dear Sarah the arduous trip. The villain in the story finally uncovered, the Earl had no doubt that Amanda would dispatch each of the grieving parties with impunity. Her next statement surprised him, however.

"Cook, take Sarah belowstairs to await our decision in this matter. You will kindly offer Mr. Grimsby a cup of tea and tell him his payment will be forthcoming." Amanda spoke with a grace that would have done justice to the highest seat of royalty in the realm.

"Well, Mrs. Havenwick, what do you say to all of this?" asked Amanda when the two had gone.

"My lady, the maid is a silly girl. I thought she'd be trouble from the beginning, but I thought it'd be trouble of a different sort, if you take my meaning," Mrs. Havenwick replied in a remarkably soft voice.

"Yes, I do. Let us see if we cannot save her from trouble of any kind in the future. She is guilty of nothing more than foolishness, is that not correct?"

"Yes, I suppose, but—"

"Mrs. Havenwick, she must be taught the evils of keeping company with slippery-tongued young men. Put the fear of God into her, as well as fear of being turned off without a character if she ever becomes embroiled in any other such coil." Amanda saw that the housekeeper still looked doubtful and she went on,

"Come now, we must give the girl a chance. There have not been any complaints about her up until now, have there?" Mrs. Havenwick shook her head. "Then that is settled. Now, do pay Mr. Grimsby whatever he claims is due him, and see that he goes away placated. It will not do to have him bearing tales about Millforte all over the county."

"Very well," consented Mrs. Havenwick, and ventured, "And the rascal what done all the mischief? Peter his name is. Will you be wanting to call in the authorities?"

"I do not want him to make trouble for Sarah. Is he in service hereabouts?"

"No, my lady. Never did an honest day's labor, that's my guess."

"Well, then send him straight to me when next he shows himself. I shall see him safely dispatched well outside the county. That is all, I think. Oh, but there *is* just one more thing, Mrs. Havenwick. I know it has not always been easy for you, with Cook and all. But this is all the home she's ever known. And she does make a surpassingly fine blackberry pie. Please contrive to rub along peacefully with her, for my sake, Mrs. Havenwick?" said Amanda amiably.

Mrs. Havenwick actually smiled. "I'll do my best, my lady, that I'll promise. Er—if you will excuse me, my lady, hadn't you ought to be resting in bed? I can bring your ledgers to you there if you like."

The Earl had been all but forgotten during this exchange, so quiet had he been and so far effaced from the center of the room, but Mrs. Havenwick turned and gave him an almost conspiratorial wink as she said this last. He was indeed shocked to be thus recognized by the housekeeper, but Amanda's reply was most predictable.

"Now don't *you* start, Mrs. Havenwick. I'm fine and I've work to do. So do you, do you not?" she said good-naturedly, and the housekeeper exited on cue, shaking her head as she did so.

The minute the door had closed, the Earl began to applaud. "My compliments, madam. Your highly developed sense of diplomacy is second to none," he said with a smile, thinking that he could have used her with him during the War. Why, she had averted disaster on every front. Not a single retainer was leaving, even that confounded dog was staying, and she'd managed to preserve the housekeeper's authority and just about everyone's dignity. He wondered unwittingly whether he would have been so successful.

Amanda smiled and bowed her head slightly in response to his accolade. But in the next moment she moved quickly to the nearest chair and grasped its back. She bent forward slightly and he saw that her face was flushed. The Earl rushed to her side and put his arm around her to help her sit down. She moved out of his grasp.

"'Tis nothing, truly. I am fine, Cousin. Just a delayed reaction to—to all this," she said, her arm sweeping the room.

He had seen enough to know that she did not indulge in physical reactions in response to a bit of riotous commotion. She looked quite faint, however, and he was alarmed. "It is nothing of the kind, Amanda, and well you know it." He put his hand to her cheek. She tried to turn her head away. "You are ill, my dear. Come, you belong upstairs," he said gently.

"Indeed I feel very strong, Cousin, and as I told Mrs. Havenwick, I have work to do. I am expecting Mr. Higgins this morning," she said, a bit tremulously, he thought.

"Are you now?" he asked, wondering what she could be up to. She started to walk toward the desk, but he grasped her by the shoulders. "How dare you jeopardize your health in such a manner, when you have

186

many responsibilities, not the least of which is your son!"

"Fustian! You know perfectly well I am not endangering my health. I have business with Higgins which—"

"Which can wait, Amanda," he said sternly, gazing intently into the sea green eyes which flashed anger.

"Kindly remove your hands!" she demanded, squirming under his grasp.

"No, Amanda. Not until I have seen you safely upstairs."

She glared at him, but her breathing had become heavy, and she finally allowed him to lead her toward the door. She labored up the stairs, taking rather deep breaths, he thought. Once inside her bedchamber she spurned the bed and insisted on being seated on the chaise in the seating alcove.

"You will please see that Higgins is sent to me as soon as he arrives," she said, a bit breathlessly.

"No, Amanda. The only visitor you shall have today will be Dr. Pringle."

She swung her legs off the chaise and made as if to rise. "Cousin, you have absolutely no authority over me. I say Higgins shall—"

"Amanda!" he said earnestly, sitting down on the chaise and taking both her hands in his. "Stop going on as if nothing happened yesterday. You were injured. You caught a chill. You have been seriously ill; you are still not out of danger. Surely your good sense should tell you that." She gave him a wary look but allowed herself to recline once more upon the chaise.

He still had not let go her hands, but she felt his grasp become gentle and his voice caressing, as he added, "And stop pretending that nothing happened between us, Amanda. It just won't wash, you know." He smiled that devastating smile and his warm eyes almost burned into her. She felt a flush overtake her, and it had nothing to do with her health. Oh, God, she thought, it would be so wonderful to be able to trust him.

The Earl was well aware of that flush, and knew he had got to find some distraction for them both. Else how was he ever to keep her *in* her bedchamber and himself *out* of her bed?

As such he went in search of Jeffries to bespeak a chessboard for now and luncheon for later. He encountered the butler in the morning room and was given a report of the latest Millforte visitors. "Mrs. Trumwell and Miss Prescott came to inquire after her ladyship just before tea yesterday, my lord. Lady Bosley came early this morning. And you've just missed—er—Mr. Linfield, my lord," said Jeffries, his eyes falling upon a nondescript vase which held a cluster of violets.

The Earl followed Jeffries's glance and he frowned. "I—I thought the flowers would look better here than—than anywhere else, my lord," said the butler.

"I quite agree, Jeffries." The Earl smiled, thinking that Jeffries, who had picked the one room in which Amanda seemed to spend very little time, was a rare butler indeed.

Jeffries had the chessboard sent up, and the Earl and Amanda spent several agreeable hours absorbed in the game. The Earl won both games, which Amanda took in surprisingly good measure. The companiable mood continued throughout luncheon, much to the Earl's delight. The cold pheasant was excellent, the claret more than passable, and Amanda, sick or not, a lovely sight as she reclined upon the chaise in her mauve dress, her luncheon perched on a bed tray. The Earl had drawn a comfortable high-backed chair up to the chaise, and wishing to stay clear of controversial subjects, which any topic concerning Millforte seemed to be, he did not object when Amanda began to question him about the War.

"Not enjoyable, no. I would not expect that you would consider war to be that. But I seem to remember Arthur mentioning that you had played a role in some rather delicate—shall we say—diplomatic negotiations. Surely you would have found that stimulating?" she asked.

"Arthur spoke of me to you? He knew what I was doing?" he asked, a bit too abruptly.

"He mentioned you on occasion," she said, seemingly bewildered.

He digested this bit of information but did not think it wise to pursue the subject. Instead he answered her question. "It *was* stimulating much of the time, that is true. But there are other things that one sees. There is great ugliness—I do not just mean the death and destruction of war. But in my capacity I saw an underside to human nature that I wish I hadn't. Men who would sell their souls, and their country, to the enemy for money, money that they would throw away in the most exclusive gaming hells and brothels of Europe."

"Englishmen did that?" she asked very quietly.

"Yes, some of them ruffians, down and outers. Others—I am afraid there were a few who were quite well connected to the ton. It is amazing to what depths of shame greed can drive one," he replied, his voice trailing off. He searched for a way to change the subject, but there was no need. Amanda understood and did it for him.

"And since you've come back, have you been in London or have your estates claimed most of your time?" she asked in an attempt at a light tone, her eyes never leaving his.

"The estates do require much looking after, as you can well understand. But I cannot say that I mind. It is rewarding work. I make periodic appearances in

London when there is someone I particularly wish to see, and I do attend an occasional party. But the social whirl can be quite tedious, I do assure you," he said with a smile, shaking off the rather somber mood of a moment ago.

"Oh, but I cannot believe that London is all *that* dull. Why, the beau monde flock there in droves every Season, do they not?" asked Amanda, amused.

"The beau monde flock to London, I am persuaded, to gossip about one another, and to outdo one another in the outrageousness of dress or the extravagance of balls and routs and whatever else they can conjure up. Everyone comes because no one wants to be discussed in his own absence. The on dits can be rather cutting, you know." He said this last rather earnestly, but it did not seem significant in any way to Amanda. He sipped his claret, suddenly pensive.

"I have only been there once, and that visit a very short one, but still it seemed that there was much in the way of amusement. The country is much more to my liking, of course, but others quite seem to thrive on town life. Are you saying that you do not?" she inquired, smiling.

He looked away for a moment. Somehow her question jarred him. He knew that London bored him; he could not abide the pettiness of society, and although he enjoyed the company of a few good friends, there were few others whom he really cared to see with any regularity. Certainly there were no women who could hold his interest for very long. Even his mistresses, who might satiate him physically, did not interest him. But London and the beau monde were the center of existence for men of his rank and fortune. Why did he not thrive on it, as Amanda said? And what else *was* there? He was devoted enough to his estates, he loved the land, and he savored quiet evenings with a book in hand. But even these evenings never gave him a complete feeling of satisfaction. In truth, Amanda's seemingly innocent question quite unsettled him because he had suddenly come face to face with the fact that there had been tremendous emptiness in his life until—until what?

He could not bring himself to finish his thought, but he felt a faint though unmistakable stirring in his stomach as he looked back at Amanda, her sea green eyes holding a look of concern as he hesitated in his answer. He was too uncomfortable with his thoughts to do anything but endeavor to change the subject.

"Perhaps I am jaded," he replied. "London can be quite gay, and one can always find entertaining companions. And then there is always the Marriage Mart for high diversion." He grinned.

"The Marriage Mart?" She pushed her tray away and he removed it to the floor.

"Yes, Almack's. Have you never been there?"

"Yes, Arthur did take me, but I have never heard the Assemblies referred to quite that way."

"I'm afraid my mother would be much chagrined to hear me speak so irreverently about that sacrosanct institution. But Marriage Mart it is, if one would but observe the quaking debutantes, the obsequious, social-climbing mamas, the down-and-out gamesters hanging out for heiresses—why, it is wildly diverting, I do assure you," he said quite dramatically.

"Such a bleak picture you paint, Cousin. Do go on," urged Amanda, her eyes sparkling with amusement.

"Actually it is not as bleak as all that. If one maintains a sense of humor, one can even enjoy oneself. But—oh—heaven help the gentleman, and even more so, the young lady who breaks one of the venerable rules." He put his lunch table away from him.

"Such as?"

"Ah—well, one must never, never dance with the

same twittering damsel more than twice in one night, lest the hapless gentleman find himself quite irrevocably betrothed by morning," he said in a near whisper, pulling his chair as close to the chaise as it would go.

"Oh, no!" She laughed.

"Oh, yes! And every young lady must secure permission from one of the dragon ladies before allowing herself to be engaged for the waltz."

"Oh, you *are* irreverent, sir! And who, may I ask, are the dragon ladies?"

"Why, the Patronesses, of course. Actually, only one is a dragon lady, but the name is somehow fitting. Did you not meet them? Let me see, there is Lady Jersey, and the Countess Lieven, and Emily Cowper, and the true Dragon Lady, Augusta Gresham. They say she breathes fire." He leaned forward and whispered this last conspiratorially.

Amanda could not contain her laughter. "Oh, no, you can't mean it. I do recall them as perhaps a bit— overwhelming, but—but— And why must a lady obtain permission to dance the waltz?"

"Have you never danced the waltz, my lady?" asked the Earl in mock horror.

"No, I haven't, I'm afraid."

"Well, then, you must allow me to teach you. We can walk through the steps, until you are well enough for the more strenuous movement of the dance." His tone was light but he looked steadily into her eyes and Amanda blushed and looked down.

It was not his logical self but something deep inside him which caused him to say softly, "It is another rule of the polite world that a lady never refuses a gentleman a dance without a very good reason, and preferably compensates by sitting out with him over a cup of lemonade. Now which shall it be, the waltz or the lemonade?"

She had recovered herself and lifted her eyes to meet his, a tentative smile on her face. "You must know that I cannot abide lemonade. The waltz it shall be, sir."

He helped her to rise and watched the dress of crimped drepe fall softly about her body as she did so. He took her hand and led her to the center of the room.

They stood facing each other. His voice was very low as he said slowly, "Now, let us see. The gentleman places his arm about the lady's waist, just so. And the lady's arm rests on the gentleman's shoulder, yes, just so. And then, he takes her hand in this manner. Do you see?" He peered down into her eyes and she slowly nodded, her body trembling slightly as they assumed the correct position.

"The movement is not difficult, really. A simple one-two-three step, like this," he said, his voice grown husky as he began to lead her slowly through the dance. They walked through the steps several times and gradually began to accelerate their pace until they were gracefully executing the waltz about the room. Neither seemed to miss the music.

The Earl drew her closer and felt the warmth of her body as she periodically brushed against him in the course of the dance. For a few minutes he was totally unaware of his surroundings, and then suddenly his eyes widened as he looked down at the head of lustrous black hair that hovered near his chest.

This is madness, he thought. She is ill. She must not exert herself. And she will never learn to trust me if I do not contrive to keep my distance from her. But he did not move to stop the dance. She fitted too comfortably in his arms, and her body moved too much in harmony with his. He was only human after all.

Amanda, too, became totally unaware of her surroundings. She closed her eyes and felt herself floating about the soft carpet as he held her in his arms. And once again, as in the crofter's hut, the only reality was those arms around her.

This is madness, she thought. I ought to banish him from my room permanently. It is not proper—not safe—for him to be here. But even as she thought this, she knew that she would not be the one to stop the dance. She opened her eyes and found him gazing intently at her.

Their eyes locked for a long moment and somehow they were dancing more slowly, their bodies closer together. The Earl thought he saw a flicker of anxiety cross the translucent eyes as they stared out at him. He did not want her to pull away from him and thought that conversation might help. "May I ask, Amanda, what your impression of London was, during your visit?" he said lightly, accelerating their pace once again.

"Well, it was some time ago, as you know. I remember being quite overwhelmed by the throngs of people and by the fact that one was always so busy. It was very gay, of course, and the brightly lit ballrooms and resplendent attire of the haut ton were a sight I could not soon have forgotten." Suddenly she seemed far away, her eyes glazed as she appeared lost in memories. "But I have also," she said, her voice lowered and her eyes focused on him once again, "retained the impression that London can be a very cruel place if—if—one is not—well received."

He looked at her intently for a moment. "And were you not well received, Amanda?" he asked softly.

"Oh, Arthur's friends were most kind. We had many invitations, to be sure," she answered, trying a little too hard to be gay, he thought.

"But?" he asked, and when she did not answer, he said, "But you were not well received by some? My mother, for instance?"

"I—I am sorry, Cousin. I should not have said anything at all." She lowered her eyes and her body

194

became tense.

"Nonsense. Do not apologize. My mother can be a very charming woman when she wants to be, but I fear she suffers from an exaggerated sense of her own consequence. And you may not believe this, but she is convinced that I do not have sufficient sense of mine."

Suddenly she laughed and turned her face up to his. "You are quite right, Cousin. I do not believe you."

"'Tis true, nonetheless," he said, delighted that he'd made her laugh. She did not do it often enough, he thought. "Why in her most recent letter, which I received only two days ago, she advised me that I should contrive to improve my consequence, and that ingratiating myself with the Dragon Lady herself was the most efficient means of doing so."

"No, oh no! You are quizzing me!" she exclaimed, nearly choking with laughter, and relaxing once again in his arms.

He felt as if he never wanted to stop the dance, but his conscience finally got the better of him, and he said, "I fear I quite tire you out, Amanda. I'm afraid it is most irresponsible of me to do so."

"Oh no," she said spontaneously, "I am not the least bit tired." The moment the words were out, she blushed a deep shade of pink and looked down.

The Earl gradually slowed their pace. At length they were standing still, but their arms had not moved. She had not looked up and he slowly disengaged the hand that held hers. He placed his forefinger under her chin and gently lifted her face to him. "Promise me the next waltz as soon as you are well," he said very softly.

"Yes," she whispered, and he fought himself not to bend his head to hers so that their lips would meet.

He was saved that exercise in willpower, which no man can truly be expected to win, by a knock at the door, which caused them both to jump rather abruptly apart.

Chapter Thirteen

The upstairs maid, that very same who had nearly dropped the lunch tray the day before, entered with a letter on a silver salver. "Begging your pardon, your lordship, your ladyship," she said, curtsying but unable to keep her eyes from widening in wonder as she beheld my lord and lady standing rather close together, facing each other in the middle of the room. "A footman bid me bring this to you, my lord. 'Tis a letter just arrived by special messenger."

The Earl took the letter and the maid collected the lunch things before exiting the room. He silently led Amanda back to the chaise and sat down in the high-backed chair before breaking the seal. A frown creased his face the moment he began reading. He knew his mother would not write again so soon if the news were good.

"Damn!" he muttered under his breath as he neared the end of the letter. He recalled himself immediately and his head jerked up. "Excuse me, Amanda, it's just—"

"Bad news, Cousin?" she asked quietly.

"Rather, I'm afraid," he said, his brows coming together. "How dare the chit—oh, I'm sorry, Amanda. You cannot possibly know what I am talking about, can you?" he asked with a slight smile. Amanda shook her head and he went on, "Well, perhaps I really had ought to explain what has transpired, since it will necessitate a change in my plans."

Amanda nodded, and he said, "Two days ago I received a letter from my mother, as I mentioned before. The admonishment about my social obligations was merely an afterthought, the real purpose of the missive being to inform me of a rather alarming development concerning my ward, Kitty. Kitty, as I may have told you, is just turned eighteen and is making her come-out this Season. It has quite put my mother in a pucker, what with all the new clothes, and taking stock of all the eligible men about Town, and accepting more invitations than anyone can reasonably be expected to honor. My mother is enjoying it all immensely, or was until this—this situation came about.

"It seems that just after I left, Kitty met a rather spurious young man, a soldier whose name and background she either did not know or would not reveal. The young man refused to present himself to my mother, but she had reason to believe that he and Kitty met secretly several times. So said the first letter."

"Oh, Cousin, I am so sorry. And you have not said a word. How worried you must have been these two days," she said softly, her voice all concern, her eyes looking into his. She moved to sit straight up upon the chaise, a very attentive look on her face.

"In truth, I—I have not refined too much upon the problem. I have had—other things—on my mind," he said slowly, unable to take his eyes from her face, which was now very close to his. "And I had thought, as did my mother, that Kitty would come to her senses." He looked down at the letter. "She hasn't," he said, his voice growing stronger and his right hand tapping the letter as he held it in his left.

"What has happened?" asked Amanda.

"At a ball several nights ago Kitty very recklessly danced three dances with this—this—soldier of fortune." He looked up to see Amanda's brow arched and smiled at her. "I was not jesting when I said that such was a solecism most judiciously to be avoided. A young girl can quite ruin her reputation by doing that. And if that were not bad enough, she was later seen emerging from a darkened terrace with the very same young man. This unfortunate set of circumstances was reported to my mother by none other than the Dragon Lady, you must know," he said rather dramatically, a look of mock horror on his face. "And naturally, my dear mother swooned immediately, and—well—I shall read this," he said, looking down at the letter.

"Those dreadful palpitations began again in my heart, and my dear son, I must tell you that I truly did think I was about to draw my last breath."

He looked up again, grinning, and saw that Amanda was attempting to suppress a smile of her own. "In any case, her sudden ill health made it impossible for this young man to evade her further." He looked down and began to read.

"And, oh, my dear Charles, he introduced himself as a Captain Smythe, but I must tell you that he did not look anything like a Smythe at all. That he is a man with something to hide I cannot doubt. He was most evasive about his people, and only kept insisting that his intentions are honorable. Which I can well imagine that they are, unabashed fortune hunter that he is. I have forbid Kitty to see him, naturally, but I have little hope that she will obey. I am afraid, Charles, that you really must come home, before she does something utterly scandalous."

He omitted the very last paragraph, some drivel about the thought that perhaps he would welcome the excuse to extricate himself from the unsavory company of the second Lady Millforte. He folded the letter and gazed earnestly at that very same second Lady Millforte, whose lovely face was lined ever so slightly with concern.

"I am afraid I have no choice," he said at length, rising from his seat and beginning to pace. "This idiotic little ward of mine will ruin herself inside of a week if I do not do something. I shall start by wringing her damn little neck!" he declared angrily, his brows coming together and his voice rising.

"Oh, Cousin, you really must not—"

"I beg your pardon, Amanda. I must learn not to use such language—"

"No, no, Cousin. I was not commenting on your—er—expressiveness. Simply on the fact that you intend to go there and wring her neck."

The Earl went to the bell cord and pulled it. "That is only a beginning, ma'am. After that I shall—I shall lock her up until she learns what behavior is befitting a young lady of her rank and station!"

A maid entered and the Earl requested his valet be sent to him. He moved to stand beside his chair and placed his hands on the seat back. He looked at the hint of a smirk on Amanda's face. "And I suppose you have a better suggestion, my dear?"

"Oh, I would not presume to advise you, dear sir. But—well—this is, I am persuaded, a matter of great import, and so I would feel rather remiss if I did not express to you my—er—opinion in the matter," she said hesitantly.

"Indeed?" He arched his brows. "Did anyone ever tell you, my dear, that you are a very managing female? But do go on, let us hear what *you* would do in my place," he said good-naturedly as he sat himself down in the chair once more, a rather smug smile on his face.

Before she could begin, however, they were interrupted by the Earl's valet. Amanda waited as his lordship walked to the door and spoke in low tones to the servant before resuming his seat and his very smug look.

"I believe, Cousin, that the first thing I would do would be to recollect what sort of girl she is. Did you not tell me that Kitty is rather a biddable girl?" Amanda began.

"And so she was, until my back was turned," he said, his mouth turning down in annoyance.

"Yes, perhaps it *is* your absence which has caused this departure from obedient behavior, or—or perhaps it is simply the fact that she never before had reason to do aught but what she was told. You do remember your Shakespeare, do you not, Cousin? Juliet was the most obedient of daughters until she met Romeo. I fear Kitty must, at the moment, feel her affections most strongly engaged."

The Earl's frown deepened.

"Tell me about her, Cousin," continued Amanda.

"She is the usual sort of girl just out of the schoolroom, I suppose. Thinks of little else but her new dresses and bonnets, and which ball she will next attend."

There was a note of disparagement in his voice and Amanda wondered just what he thought young ladies *should* concern themselves with. Certainly not the difficulties of tenant farmers nor the repairs of the estate cottages.

"She is a bit frivolous, then, shall we say? And is

Kitty possessed of a romantic nature, Cousin?" Amanda asked.

"What exactly do you mean, Amanda?"

"Is she given to daydreaming? Does she read silly romantic novels?"

"In truth, Amanda, I must say that I have no idea *what* she reads."

"No? I must say I find it curious indeed that you would not take more of an interest in Kitty's reading habits. You seem inordinately concerned with *mine,*" she said with a hint of sarcasm.

He colored slightly. "That is another matter entirely. She—she has my mother to guide her, after all."

"Ah, yes, of course. I, on the other hand, have no one but you. But let us get back to Kitty. Has she never spoken of the kind of man she wants to marry? Has she been much enthralled with the splendor of London society?" Amanda went on good-naturedly.

"She seems happy enough, I suppose. She has spouted, now you mention it, some nonsense about love, about not caring for title nor fortune, but this will pass, to be sure."

Amanda cocked her head and looked searchingly at his face. "And do you not credit love, Cousin Charles? Is every woman interested only in rank and fortune then?"

"If the chit herself is not, then rest assured that her mother is," he said, rather too harshly. "Love within marriage is a luxury few can afford," he added before he realized that this might be a rather unfortunate remark, given Amanda's own marriage. He deliberately lightened his tone. "And you, Amanda, what is *your* opinion of love and marriage?"

Amanda kept her face impassive as she replied coolly, "As you say, Cousin, love is a luxury few can afford."

He looked steadily at the composed face before him. He was somehow disappointed by her answer. "Yes," he said flatly. Yes, it is a luxury few can afford, he thought, and those who can afford it . . . Those who can, Charles, he admonished himself, know better than to mix the two. Love was something physical that happened between a man and his mistress. It had nothing to do with marriage.

"But let us get back to Kitty," he continued. "Perhaps she *is* of a romantic nature, as you suggest. It does not change anything. I must, in any case, put an end to this foolish affair."

Amanda smiled in a way that reminded the Earl of a parent's indulgent smile to a child. "Can you not see that for a girl of a romantic bent, a good part of the young man's appeal is the very mystery surrounding him? And if he has revealed himself to her but sworn her to secrecy, so much the better. It is then a great adventure. Furthermore, should the match be frowned upon, should she indeed be forbidden to see him, the sense of adventure is heightened, and might even precipitate quite dire consequences."

"Perhaps, Amanda, perhaps," he sighed. "Now pray tell, how do you propose I deter Kitty from either bringing utter ruin upon herself or becoming embroiled in a disastrous marriage?"

"Oh, Cousin, I am sure I could not presume to advise you—" she began, her eyes wide with innocence.

"Oh, of course not, Amanda. But do overcome your scruples and tell me anyway," he urged, his eyes twinkling.

"Well, first of all, I would not let her know the reason for your sudden return to London. You can invent something else, I am sure." He blanched at this assumption that such prevarication was quite natural to him. Amanda ignored him, however, and went on.

"And I would most assuredly not forbid her to see him, Cousin. On the contrary, you must invite him to call."

"I will do no such thing. Really, Amanda, I had thought you—"

"Cousin," she said calmly, "Kitty will contrive to see him no matter what you do. You have so much as told me so. Surely good sense will tell you that it is infinitely preferable that they meet under your watchful eye rather than privately in a dark corner of the lending library or some such. I am persuaded that between you and your mother it can be managed that they never have a moment alone together. It would seem to me that discourse between lovers would be decidedly— unexceptionable—with a third person always in attendance. Do you not agree, Cousin?"

The Earl stared at her for a moment, his eyes wide as he considered what she said. He rose from his chair and strolled to the window. "There is merit in what you say, Amanda; I can see that. But what will be the end of such an affair?"

"You must make the acquaintance of the young man, of course. By the by, Cousin, he is you say, a fortune hunter. Is Kitty, then, an heiress?"

"She will come into a comfortable income at the age of three and twenty, or upon her marriage, but it is not what one would call a fortune."

"Then, naturally, you will take pains to make that quite plain to him. Also you might simply tell him that her inheritance will not be released until she reaches the age of three and twenty. To a young man, five years will seem a very long time."

The Earl could not help wondering if such prevarications as she now suggested did indeed come naturally to *her*. His mind jumped unwittingly to the doubts about her that had always plagued him. But no, he had been all through that. He would not give credence to all those unfounded rumors. At least—well—he would see Ridgeway in London. The one advantage of this whole distasteful situation was the prospect of clearing his mind with regard to Amanda.

"Go on, Amanda," he said after a moment.

"All the while, Cousin," she continued, "you and the Countess must endeavor to keep Kitty very much occupied with all manner of parties and routs, and you, sir, must introduce her to every eligible Corinthian you know."

Managing female, he thought. I ask for a bit of advice and she has my every waking moment organized for the next fortnight at least.

"Oh, now be fair, Amanda, such a round of parties will be sheer torture for me, and well you know it." He smiled, leaning his right elbow on the windowsill. "Now tell me, you who are full of such sage advice, from where does your experience in these matters arise? Certainly not from growing up in a house full of brothers."

"No, not at all. Actually, Cousin, I do not know, except to say that I read a great many silly romantic novels in my girlhood." She smiled.

He walked over to the chaise. "I do not believe you. You were never that frivolous. I would guess that you were a very serious young girl. Tell me, Amanda, were you never given to simple foolishness and laughter?"

She rose and walked ahead of him toward the window. "There was little place for—laughter—in my father's house," she said quietly, and then turned to face him. "But you, Cousin, we are forgetting your rather pressing problem."

"Yes—I—I suppose I had ought to make haste to leave." He ought, in fact, to be very happy for the excuse to leave Millforte. Hadn't he come here with the intention of making this visit as short as possible? Why then did the prospect seem so unappealing? And why did those fragile sea green eyes gaze up at him in just that way? He cleared his throat, and his eyes searched her face. "But I fear that the timing is—inauspicious. You are not well, and there is much that is as yet unfinished—with regard to the estates."

She did not know what to make of those slate blue eyes, boring into her as if trying to read her innermost thoughts. She looked quickly down at her hands. She meant to keep her tone light, but somehow she did not succeed. "Cousin, I—I am truly not that ill, and you know very well that I shall be cosseted and ministered to by the staff until I am ready to scream, or run away—"

"Yes, that is exactly what concerns me. Who will go after you—that is, you—you must have a care, Amanda. Do not go about unaccompanied. If you must go out, take your maid, or a groom, or someone. Promise me you will not do anything foolish," he said. His voice had grown louder, but it held none of its usual harshness, and as she looked up into his eyes she saw that they were warm. Somehow she found herself wishing he would simply shout at her with his accustomed arrogance. She would be furious to be sure, but at least then she would not be plagued by the turmoil of emotions that now engulfed her. Now she felt—she did not know what she felt, only that there was danger for her in the intensity of those warm eyes. That she keep the conversation light was imperative.

"But, Cousin, you know I am incapable of foolishness. You've said so yourself," she countered, a glint in her eye.

"Amanda!" he said menacingly.

"Very well, Cousin. I have no wish to be cudgeled again, nor—nor anything else. I shall be careful, I promise."

"Good. I should not be long gone."

"Then—then you do mean to return, Cousin?" Now, why had she asked that? she wondered. She ought to be very happy indeed that he was leaving. She had not wanted him here in the first place. Why, then, did the prospect of his departure seem so unappealing?

"Of course, Amanda. Did I not say I had—unfinished business here?"

"Ah, yes, the estates."

"Yes, the estates," he echoed, his voice soft. "There is much that I have yet to learn, to understand—about the business of the estates." He took a step closer to her and his eyes locked hers. She wished that he would not stand so close, but she could not seem to move herself away.

"I should dispatch this rather unpleasant affair as soon as possible. I would I may return in not much above a se'nnight. You will remember to rest, Amanda?" he asked quietly.

Oh God, she thought, he must not look at her that way. But she could not take her eyes from his face as she answered, "Yes, Cousin, I shall."

"And you will not forget that you have promised me that next waltz, Amanda?" he pressed, his voice low and husky.

She could almost hear his heart beat, so close was he. Somehow she must lighten the mood, or she would be lost. "I shan't forget," she said, and then added, a twinkle creeping into her eyes, "Perhaps I should practice while you are gone, Cousin, in order to perfect my step."

The Earl's face became thunderous. "You will do no such thing!" he said forcefully, grabbing her hands and pulling her even closer. "You do it well enough as it is. Do I make myself clear, Amanda?" he added commandingly.

"Oh, yes, Cousin, quite clear," she said as demurely as she could, her eyes wide with innocence.

"Good," he said, his brow still furrowed. Then suddenly he released his hold on her, retaining only her right hand, and took a step backward.

He raised her hand to his lips, holding it there a moment longer than necessary, his eyes burning with intensity as they searched her face. "Good day, ma'am," he said abruptly without smiling, his eyes never wavering.

"Good day, Cousin," she echoed calmly, and suddenly, he turned and was gone.

When all was in readiness for his departure, the Earl spent a few moments in conversation with Jeffries. "Keep watch over her, Jeffries," he was saying, "inasmuch as you are able. I would very much prefer that she remain within the gardens, but if she must venture out, see that she has someone accompany her. Send someone after her if necessary."

"Of course, my lord, I shall do just as you say," said the butler, his face impassive and his head erect. "Is there anything more?"

"Yes, there is. Sir James Bosley, Jeffries, is under no condition to set foot on Millforte land. He must not be permitted anywhere near the manor nor in the vicinity of Lady Millforte. I cannot emphasize enough the grave circumstance which necessitates such a stricture. Do you understand, Jeffries? He is a danger to Lady Millforte," he said, his voice low but strong, his face etched in a frown.

Jeffries's brows had arched upon hearing the Earl's words, but he recovered himself almost immediately. "It shall be as you say, my lord. I shall not relax my vigil."

"I appreciate that, Jeffries, and oh, there is one thing more," the Earl said, his face relaxing.

"Yes, my lord?"

"Violets, Jeffries. They are rather—out of place here, do you not agree?" A glimmer of a smile touched his lordship's lips.

Jeffries permitted himself a smile as well. "I *quite* agree, my lord. I shall contrive to keep the violets—er—as little in evidence as possible. Have no fear on that head."

"Excellent, Jeffries," he said smugly, and shortly thereafter took his leave, confident that Jeffries, a rare man indeed, would most conscientiously carry out his orders.

Amanda remained motionless at the window, staring out at the lush side gardens, for quite some time after the Earl left. She ought to feel immense relief at his sudden departure, she thought. It was sooner than she'd dared hope it would be.

Presently she began to pace the room. Somehow she did not feel relieved at all. In fact, she found that she was rather restless, a sensation to which she was quite unaccustomed. She ought to rest and thought perhaps a book would soothe her nerves.

Amanda walked to the bedside table, upon which several books were neatly stacked. She carried them to the chaise and sat down, swinging her feet up as she did so. *Electra* was on top of the pile of books. She opened the book to where she'd left off, but as she began to read, it was the voice of the Earl that jumped out at her from the page. She remembered his resonant voice intoning the haunting words of Sophocles, and suddenly she thrust the book aside. There was a strange feeling in the pit of her stomach, and she found that she did not at all care to read Sophocles.

The next book was *The Taming of the Shrew.* Cousin Charles's book. Well, she certainly had no desire to read that. "Taming" indeed!

Amanda took the third book into her hands. *Le Morte d'Arthur.* She turned it over and over but did not open it. She remembered the Earl's comments to her that day when they had first ridden out over the estates. He had likened her to Guinevere. Why? He had taunted her with it, at that time and during their first chess game. What relation had she to Guinevere? And did he see himself as Lancelot? Lancelot, the shining knight brought to Camelot by Arthur to help protect the realm? Arthur had trusted Lancelot, as he had loved his wife. But they had not been able to help themselves. They had fallen in love and they had betrayed the king.

Suddenly Amanda felt dizzy. The words she had been thinking whirled about her head. Arthur had trusted him, had loved his wife. Arthur brought him in to protect the realm, to oversee the estates. But they had not been able to help themselves. They—no! no! No, she thought, it was nothing like that. She had no feeling at all for the haughty Earl, and he only contempt for her.

She rose from the chaise and found that she was shaking. She certainly was not in love with Charles. It would be foolhardy to allow herself to be so taken in, for surely he would do nothing but trifle with her. Yet she could not forget the intensity of his words yesterday in the hut, nor the gentleness that he sometimes evinced. Nor could she deny to herself for very long the strange sensations he invoked in her every time he came near. Such did not constitute love, that much was certain, but still, she chastized herself, she had no right to have any such feelings for a man, what with poor Arthur gone not much above six months. She remembered the times the Earl had kissed her, and how hard it had been to resist him, how she had not really wanted to. What was wrong with her? She must quell such feelings once and for all. She would not betray Arthur's trust, nor his love. And she would not succumb to the rakish charms of the Earl of Ainsley. Besides, she would never marry again. One kind and caring man was more than any woman had a right to expect in a lifetime, and she had already been so blessed. She would never entrust her life to another. She had seen too much cruelty to take such a risk.

Amanda paced from the window and back again to the chaise. She could not erase the image of his face from her mind. She had to admit that she would miss that face, as well as their repartee, which, no matter how vociferous, was almost always amusing.

She sighed. Certainly life would be somewhat prosaic without him here. But this was pure fustian! She was not a silly romantic chit mooning over an impossible swain. She was a grown woman who knew where her duty lay. And there was work to be done. Yes, she would throw herself into her work. That would serve to quell those disturbing stirrings at the bottom of her stomach.

Thus resolved, and abandoning the idea of rest for the remainder of the afternoon, Amanda made her way to the library. She had not really done any work in several days, and she found quite a proliferation of papers on her desk. They were arranged in neat little clusters, for the servants, who had strict instructions not to discard any papers on the desk, could not seem to resist stacking them in perfect little piles, according to size and shape rather than any concept of subject matter. Thus, any sense of order was completely lost, and Amanda sat down and began to sort through them. There were several messages from the bailiff regarding minor cottage repairs, and Higgins had sent some papers to sign. She smiled at a letter from an old friend, but was disturbed not to find one from her brother. He had not written in a while. She supposed he was still in France, but she always felt better when he confirmed his whereabouts and his continued good health.

Her eyes next fell upon a letter in a handwriting she did not for a moment recognize. It was unsealed, addressed to the *Gazette* in London. Ah, of course, it was the advertisement for a governess. So he *had* written it. She might have known. But why had he not sent it? Had he simply forgotten or had he never intended to send it? Had he merely been trying to frighten her, subdue her with his superior show of power, or did he really believe that Victor needed a governess? She read the advertisement. She noted that it was not as well composed as the first, justifiably consigned to the fire, had been, and that it was written in a jerky hand. He had been very angry, she recalled. So had she, for that matter. She could not remember ever being spurred to such anger by anyone, and her mind immediately jumped to her rather spontaneous flight to the Low Cottages.

The Low Cottages! She had almost forgotten her plans for them. She must send for Higgins today. It would be best to put her plan into action at once. There would be nothing the Earl could do when he returned to find that the Low Cottages no longer existed. She found a clean sheet of writing paper and dipped her quill in the inkwell. She hesitated. She had warned him of her intention, yet for some reason she felt that she was being underhanded. Her eyes unwittingly returned to the unsealed letter to the *Gazette*. Had he meant to send it or not? If he had not, he would be even more furious if she actually had the Low Cottages razed in his absence, furious and perhaps, she thought, perhaps hurt as well. She chided herself immediately for that thought. He is impervious to hurt, she told herself. He considers himself too far above everyone to be so touched by such an action. She would send for Higgins immediately, she resolved, but somehow, she could not manage to compose a message to the man-of-affairs.

At length she pushed the writing paper away. She needed some fresh air, she thought. She must take herself to some place devoid of association with the Earl of Ainsley, for he was disturbing her peace of mind, even now in his absence, and this she simply would not allow. To that end she rose abruptly and betook herself to the rear gardens to calm a restless disposition that had no right to be restless at all.

Upon leaving the manor, his lordship made one rather brief stop at the vicarage, entrusting the good Vicar to do all that was in his power to see that Amanda remained safe and in good health.

And so it was not much above an hour after he had received his mother's letter that he found himself seated in his carriage, rumbling eastward toward London. As the Earl watched the lush green hills of Shropshire disappear outside his window, he became increasingly depressed. He recalled his trip from London to Millforte. He had rather enjoyed it, for he had been looking forward to some amount of amusement once he arrived. Well, he *had* been amused, but not in the way he had anticipated.

He was not at all sure what had happened there. He only knew that there was that strange stirring in the pit of his stomach, and that he very much wished he were going in the opposite direction. He had been very sure of everything a few short days ago. Now he was certain of only one thing—he had not wanted to leave Millforte. If he were to be thoroughly honest with himself, he had not wanted to leave Amanda. But that was absurd! She was just another woman, after all. And a damned troublesome one at that! A man with his experience did not allow a pair of fragile green eyes and a tumble of black hair to so disturb his serenity. And with this particular woman, he chided himself, whether her reputation had any basis in fact or no, he was playing with fire, in more ways than one.

He felt fire every time he went near her, yet he would not seduce her—he had discovered that yesterday. And the other alternative was simply impossible. Even if the on dits had all been false, he had no intention of— So what in hell, he asked himself, was he doing? He was playing with a fire that could never be quenched.

No, he told himself, he had best set his mind on the task ahead. That would certainly help him forget a lady who by all rights ought to be more easily forgotten.

So successfully did the Earl distract himself with thoughts of the task that awaited him, in fact, that as he approached London, two days later, he had quite worked himself into a fury regarding his wayward ward. He would wring her damn little neck, and that was only the beginning!

Chapter Fourteen

Kitty Berenson jumped out of the carriage and ran up the stairs of the neatly landscaped townhouse. She was simply dying to see Anne, her oldest and dearest friend. And though the Warings had only just arrived this morning, Anne's mother had insisted that Kitty might visit. Breathless, she glanced back at the carriage, imagining the housekeeper's frown at her lack of decorum. But Kitty felt only relief at being freed of those sharp eyes for a time. The stern-faced woman had been dogging her every step ever since Aunt Ainsley had decided that neither Kitty nor her maid could be trusted. But such could not be helped, Kitty knew.

And then Anne's petite form appeared in the doorway, and Kitty squealed in delight. They embraced right there on the steps, the housekeeper and a startled footman notwithstanding. Anne led Kitty inside to a sitting room where Mrs. Waring was supervising the removal of holland covers. She encouraged them to escape the boxes and the dust and retreat to Anne's room for a nice long cose. Kitty thought wistfully that Anne was the most fortunate of girls, for her mother was utterly kind and understanding. Aunt Ainsley had always been kind in her way, but she had such strict notions of propriety, especially now that they'd come to Town.

She could not help saying as much to Anne when

they reached her bedroom and sat together on the canopied bed. "And so you see, one must always trouble to be very pretty behaved indeed. London is so different from the country."

"Poor Kitty. I thought you would be totally enchanted with London society. Why, a Season is all you've talked about for years. I was the one who looked upon it with trepidation. Has it truly been trying for you?"

"Oh, no, no. It's simply wonderful, Anne. One must, I suppose, accustom oneself to the watchful eyes of all the dowagers. And you will think me dreadful for saying this, after all the Ainsleys have done for me, but this past week has been much, much better, because Cousin Charles has been out of town." At Anne's questioning glance she went on. "Since we've come to London, he and Aunt seem to discuss nothing else but my future. Why, I think she's actually made *lists* of men! Before he left I thought I should go mad if I heard the words 'eligible' and 'suitable' one more time!" Kitty exclaimed.

"But my dear Kitty," replied Anne, stifling a giggle, "you can hardly marry someone who is neither eligible nor suitable."

"Yes, I know. But if you saw what passes for suitable—why, any man with some degree of fortune and any piddling title, no matter how old or deformed he be, is considered suitable!"

"Oh, Kitty," said Anne, her eyes swiftly taking in her friend's delicately chiseled face, her golden hair, and the two dimples that framed her mouth, "you must have a house full of beaus already, with the Season barely under way. I cannot believe that anyone will force you to marry a deformed old man. Truly you exaggerate."

"Yes, but only a bit," replied Kitty, her blue eyes twinkling. "You see, young men are considered, by Aunt and Ainsley, to be too wild and unsettled. I tell you, most of the 'suitables' are old. Why, Cousin Charles is said to be one of the most eligible men on the

Marriage Mart, and look how old *he* is!" squealed Kitty, wide-eyed.

"Why, he can't be much above thirty-four or thirty-five, from what Mummy has told me."

Kitty nodded. "He's thirty-five."

"Well, that is hardly old, dear Kitty. I think it gives a man a chance to acquire some polish, after all," replied Anne.

Kitty shuddered. "Polish indeed! Eloise says he's had a string of French mistresses."

Anne's eyes widened, but they were interrupted by a maid bearing a tray of refreshments. "Who is Eloise?" she asked when they were alone again.

"Oh, Eloise Claredon. She is the daughter of Lady Gresham—the Marchioness of Gresham, I should say. Lady Gresham is one of the Patronesses of Almack's, and according to Aunt, worth 'cultivating.' Aunt considers her a friend, but I think she is secretly terrified of her, so afraid to offend is she. I've even heard Lady Gresham called the Dragon Lady." Kitty whispered this last, and then continued. "Well, in any case, Eloise is just our age—her ball is in a few weeks. Aunt thinks *I* ought to cultivate *her.*" Kitty reached for a glass of lemonade and began munching a biscuit.

"Do you like her?" asked Anne.

"Eloise may be pleasant enough when she wants to be, but she is a terrible gossip—I shudder to think what she must say about me when I'm not with her."

"Oh, Kitty. Who could possibly have an ill word to say about you? You are the most guileless creature imaginable, and so beautiful—surely everyone must adore you."

"In London girls do not adore other girls who are beautiful. But in truth I do not hold court like the great beauties, though I do not lack for dancing partners." Anne's brows went up in surprise but Kitty continued. "I am persuaded that girls like Eloise do not make

216

friends exactly. Not real friends, such as we are. Her only interest is in capturing the attention of the right male. You simply must watch her flirt and push herself forward at Almack's."

"London sounds dreadful. Oh, Kitty, I am sure I should never have come. Large parties frighten me, and I have not the wit nor the desire to flirt and scheme to catch a man. And I shall never, never go to Almack's, even though I think Thomas was able to secure vouchers."

"Of course you'll go to Almack's. My dear, dear Anne, you are gentle and very, very pretty to look at, although you will not credit it. You are not fair, but your brown hair frames your face perfectly. And you have beautiful deep brown eyes. You will take very well, I am sure."

Anne shook her head. "Almack's is way above my touch. I do not want a duke nor an earl, nor even a viscount. Mummy has never concerned herself with rank and position before, but every so often now she reminds me that our lineage is old and respected and I must aim as high as I can. But truly, Kitty, I want only a simple country life, with a man who loves me and loves the land. I do not want to live in a mansion with hundreds of servants, nor be hostess for hundreds at dinner."

"I should not mind it, I don't think. But I do not think that shall be my lot either." Kitty's eyes became dreamy.

Anne looked at her with narrowed eyes. "You little minx. You've been keeping something from me. You've not said a word about your beaus. I'd expected you to be chattering ceaselessly about at least ten. Kitty, you have not—there is not one special one already, is there?"

Kitty blushed and took her friend's hand. "You must not tell anyone, Anne. And in truth, I have your

217

brother to thank for it."

"Thomas? What has he to do with it?" asked Anne, her eyes wide with curiosity.

"Oh, where shall I begin? It is as if the world has turned inside out for me. It was just above a se'nnight ago, Anne, at Lady Enderly's ball. I was talking with Thomas and Lydia. She is charming, Anne. You will indeed be fortunate to have her for your sister."

"She *is* wonderful, and Thomas dotes on her. But pray do not digress. What happened next?"

"Well, suddenly a young man strolled over to us. A captain in the Cavalry, just returned from abroad. Thomas introduced him as his friend, and then—and then Richard asked me to dance." Kitty's blue eyes sparkled and she was smiling a soft smile, lost in her own thoughts.

"And then what? Oh, Kitty! Do attend! You have not told me anything about him!"

"Haven't I? Let me see. He is very, very tall and very lean, and he has wavy brown hair and lovely hazel eyes. I remember that I did not want that first dance to end, for I could not bear to go back to Aunt and be forced to dance with another stodgy 'eligible'—and so we sat out the next dance over lemonade. He told me then, and later when we met in the next few days, about his life with the Regiment, and about some of his dreams. He has had his colors for three years now."

"Kitty—you are not contemplating a life following the drum?"

"If I had to, I would, to be with Richard. But—oh—it is truly fortuitous! You see, he has come back to England with the intention of selling out. He said he had been rather tiring of the life. It was beginning to lose its glamour for him, but he could not think what else to do—"

"He is a younger son?"

"Yes, and so, of course, soldiering had once seemed

218

so logical, but he does not have the wanderlust that so many of them have. And then, you see, Providence smiled down at him and he only just recently received word of an inheritance from a maternal relation. It is a large family—he does not know why the legacy went to him, but so it did. It is not a fortune, but a quite comfortable income, including an estate in Essex, and an excellent stable of horses. Richard has a passion for horses and dreams of breeding racehorses. Oh, Anne, forgive me. How I do go on! You cannot possibly be so interested—"

"Oh, fustian! Of course, I'm interested, and I own I cannot wait to meet him!"

"You shall. Tonight perhaps. You will be at the Cheswick's ball, will you not?"

"I think so. Mummy spoke of so many invitations," Anne said nervously.

"Oh, but of course you will. And you will be quite a success, lovely Anne. I shall introduce you to everyone I know. And I do so want you and Richard to meet. His manner is mild and his voice gentle and he—he is good and—and he loves me, Anne," she said softly, color rising in her cheeks.

"Dear Kitty. I am so happy for you. And he must indeed be special, for I do recall your requirements on that head," said Anne, a mischievous grin on her face.

"Whatever do you mean?"

"Do you remember those endless summer days at Four Oaks, when we plotted passionate courtships and enchanting weddings? You were always the romantic one. No simple soldier for you, nor even a straight-forward earl or duke. Oh, no. Rather an impoverished earl reduced to smuggling in order to retain his ancestral lands. Or a duke whose title and fortune had been wrested from him by a nefarious cousin who was trying to kill him. Have you forgotten?" asked Anne.

"Oh, but Anne, indeed I am being unfair, for I have

not told you all. You see, he is not a simple soldier. That is, there are—complications," Kitty said, a bit warily, Anne thought.

"What sort of complications?"

"He—well—he has certain family problems which he must resolve before he makes himself known in the proper way to Aunt Ainsley," replied Kitty hesitantly.

"You mean he has not presented himself to her?" asked Anne.

"No—he *did* do so—several days ago—but he cannot at this time reveal his true identity. There has been no crime committed, or anything in that way, but his family has been very wronged and he must uncover the villain and set all to rights. It is such a coil, for he must go about in society in order to do so, yet remain as much in the background as possible."

"Kitty," said Anne, her voice becoming a trifle harsh with anxiety, her eyes narrowed, "has he told *you* his real name, or this wrong he must undo?"

"No," said Kitty slowly, "but that is merely because he does not wish to put me in the position of having to lie to Aunt Ainsley. Oh, Anne, he really is the most considerate of men. He simply does not want me embroiled in any way."

Anne looked doubtful. She was beginning to fear that her friend would be deeply hurt. "But Kitty, how can Lady Ainsley countenance his addresses?"

"Well, she does not—exactly—countenance them," said Kitty uncomfortably.

"What do you mean, 'not exactly'?"

"You see, Richard was reluctant to present himself at all—circumstances being what they are—and when he finally did—well—Aunt was not best pleased. I do not know that she can possibly have found out that I met him in the lending library but I think she did. And then at the Fenicott ball—oh, Anne, I have been such a fool. We—we got carried away, Richard and I, and we danced together too many times—I am still not accustomed to the arbitrary rules of society. And we were only out on the terrace a moment, but Aunt swooned when she found out, so of course Richard had to present himself, and—oh—it was too terrible, Anne! She has forbid me to see him!" Anne was alarmed by her friend's despairing tone and even more so by the anxiety she saw in Kitty's eyes. Kitty was the eternal optimist, never perturbed for long by anything.

"But surely there must be a way to bring her round, Kitty."

Kitty shook her head, and Anne realized that she was right. Perhaps if the Dowager Countess knew Thomas, he might vouch for Richard, but as it was that would not answer. Above all, Kitty said she feared that her Aunt would send for the Earl.

"Oh," said Anne flatly. "I hadn't thought of that. And is he so terrible, then?"

"Cousin Charles is terribly proper and—and—stuffy, and he has the most frightful temper. Why, even Aunt is afraid of him! One does not cross the Earl of Ainsley, Anne. I learned that early on. But now my loyalty, indeed my whole future, belongs to someone else. And I fear that if Cousin Charles is apprised of this, he will find some way of separating us permanently." Kitty spoke very quietly, almost in a whisper, and there was fear in her eyes. Had she wailed hysterically, Anne would have been less alarmed, would have been confident that Kitty was merely bringing one of her romantic fantasies to life. But this was a calmer, more mature Kitty than the girl who had visited Anne at Four Oaks last year, and Anne felt her anguish.

"But then, Kitty, surely you must not seek him out tonight. You must not arouse Lady Ainsley's suspicions in any way."

"I know that, but the Duchess of Cheswick's routs are said to be such sad crushes. Why, one can quite lose one's party and never find them again. Besides, Richard will look for me, and I shall not be able to turn away. I just couldn't, Anne. If only I could help him clear his name, but I know that is something he alone must do."

Anne nodded, but when Kitty left sometime later, she was filled with a sense of foreboding. It quite overshadowed her own fears about attending her first ball, for she was certain that something unfortunate would happen tonight.

The Earl strode up the steps of his mother's London house just before teatime. He told the butler to announce him and began to pace the floor in the front hall, a fierce look on his face. His right hand slapped his gloves into his left, and he quite scared away several hapless servants who needed to cross the front hall. Happily for the domestic staff, it was not long before the Earl was instructed to ascend to his mother's sitting room.

He kissed the rouged and wrinkled cheek and sat down in a plush tufted chair opposite the chaise upon which his mother reclined. "Dear Charles," she said dramatically, her hand going immediately to her breast, "thank God you have come."

"As you see, Mother," he said dryly. "I am pleased to see you looking so well, despite recent events."

"Always a kind word for your mother," sighed the Dowager. "Thank you, my dear, and I must say that you look none the worse for the ordeal *you* have been made to suffer. At least I have been able to rescue you from the clutches of that woman. That is some consolation, at any rate."

"Yes, well, Mother," he said, schooling his face to an impassive mask, "you must know that I intend to return to Millforte as soon as this unfortunate affair with Kitty is over."

"Why, Charles, you cannot be serious! Surely there cannot be so much to do there? Why, I do not ever remember you giving so much time to your *own* estates."

The Earl hesitated only a moment before saying, "Yes, I know, Mother, but then the affairs of my estates have never been quite so—er—confusing. But let us speak no more of it. Tell me about Kitty."

Whereupon the Dowager launched into a dramatic recital of the events of the past week, ending with the ill-fated occasion upon which the young man finally presented himself. The Earl found himself thinking that either Kitty had been particularly ingenious in devising ways of seeing this young man, or his mother had been particularly careless in her chaperonage. Knowing how his mother got rather involved in gossip sessions with her friends, and even in a card game or two, he suspected it was a little bit of both. But it would not do to argue the point now. The damage was done.

"I do not know whatever could have possessed her to behave so scandalously," said the Dowager.

"Come now, Mother. Dancing in full view of hundreds of people can hardly be called scandalous, even if she did do it three times," said the Earl, repressing a smile.

"Why, Charles," said his mother, quite taken aback. "I do believe you make light of this whole rather dreadful situation."

"On the contrary, Mother. I may think society's rules absurd, but I do not for one moment discount the irreparable damage a young girl like Kitty can do to herself by flaunting them. Now, is there anything else you can tell me about this soldier, this Captain Smythe, as he calls himself?"

"In truth, he is a rather nice-looking young man, and would be quite unexceptionable were it not for his specious behavior, and that name he has given himself.

And, of course, the fact that he is a younger son can hardly recommend him for our Kitty. But I take heart now that you are here, Charles, for I am persuaded that you will make her see reason. Her affections simply cannot be so totally engaged in so short a space of time. It has only been a week, after all. Surely she is imagining an affection that cannot be there, for how much can happen in a week?"

The Earl looked at her sharply, and then turned quickly away. "As you say, Mother," he said impassively, but her words echoed in his mind: How much can happen in a week? He wondered that himself, but it was not of Kitty that he found himself thinking.

"Charles," his mother was saying, and he shook himself out of his reverie, turning back to her. "We have not much time," she continued. "I am expecting Lady Gresham to tea, actually within a very few minutes. I am afraid you may be obliged to stay."

"Very well," he said with an exasperated sigh, "and to what ghastly rout am I expected to escort you and Kitty tonight, may I ask?"

"The Duchess of Cheswick's." The Earl frowned ominously and his mother hurriedly added, "Yes, dear, I know it will be a shocking squeeze, but you really *must* begin introducing Kitty around. You know so many more eligible young men than I, to be sure."

The Earl grimaced. "Very well. I shall endure it for Kitty's sake. But I do warn you—not many more. Now tell me, does Kitty know you have sent for me?"

"Why, no. I thought it best to say nothing until your arrival."

"You have done wisely, Mother. I shall see her at tea, I presume?" The Dowager nodded. "Good. Let us say nothing of the reason for my return to London. In fact, I shall not indicate that I am in any way aware of what has transpired. Will this soldier of hers be at the Cheswick's, do you suppose?"

"I can only assume so, for Kitty has gone about in a quite heightened state all day, very unlike the fit of dismals of the two days past."

"Fine. You must point him out to me at the earliest opportunity. I should like to observe him from a distance, and undoubtedly, the Duchess's crushes being what they are, Kitty will contrive to meet him, despite your vigilant chaperonage."

"I assure you, Charles, I shall be most diligent—"

"On the contrary, Mother, after I arrive you must relax your guard, for I would very much like to see them together, unbeknownst to them of course. It should not be too difficult to be unobtrusive in such a crowded ballroom."

"Why, Charles, I do believe you *were* engaged in espionage activities during the War, despite your protestations to the contrary."

"Now, Mother, I did no such thing. And that is neither here nor there. I simply would like to observe firsthand just how far this little affair has got to, in order to know best how to deal with it. I trust we are in agreement, Mother?"

"Of course, Charles, whatever you say. And now, perhaps we should go down to tea."

The Earl had not seen the Marchioness of Gresham since last Season, but he could see that his memory was in no way faulty. She was the Dragon Lady, indeed, and in fact, looked more the part every year, as her girth increased and the wrinkles in her face formed a more indelible scowl. The image was further enhanced by the hideous olive green turban sitting atop her head, a large ruby set among its many folds. But she was all smiles as she paraded into the drawing room, extending her hand to him. "But what a charming surprise, to be sure, Lord Ainsley. And how very cagey your dear mother is—not a word to us."

"The pleasure is all mine, dear Lady Gresham," he

said, rising and taking the proffered hand with a stiff formal bow.

The next moment the wide form of the Marchioness moved aside, revealing two young women, who, though actually quite tall, were dwarfed by the formidable Marchioness. "And may I present my daughters, my lord, Lady Priscilla and Lady Eloise Claredon."

The Earl executed two more rather formal bows, and cast an accusing glance toward his mother, who had not mentioned the Gresham daughters, but that lady seemed quite unaware as she bustled about seating everyone. He would very much have liked to stand against the mantel, from which vantage point he could remain detached from the proceedings, but his mother would have none of it. Despite his fiercest stare, he ended up in a wing chair, the Dragon Lady on one side of him and her younger daughter on the other.

He gave each of the sisters a cursory glance as he mechanically held up his end of the inane conversation. Priscilla, whom he had not seen in a while, was, as his mother had indicated, not blessed with the most beautiful of faces. The spectacles and matronly lace cap did not help, he thought. Eloise did have a rather pretty face to recommend her, but twice he caught her batting her eyelashes at him in the most obvious ploy known to man, and it made him want to roar with laughter. Eloise's tone with him was deliberately sweet, and she appeared quite demur, but when she thought he was looking elsewhere, he caught her face in an unguarded moment. She seemed to have a natural grimace and he had no doubt at all that she was her mother's **daughter** in more ways than one.

Lady Gresham was addressing him, he realized, and with difficulty he gave his attention to the formidable woman in the oversized olive green turban. "I do hope Lady Ainsley relayed my invitation to Eloise's come-out ball. We shall be most honored to have you there,

226

my lord. Eloise and Kitty have become the dearest of friends, you must know," she said ingratiatingly, but he was spared further discourse as a maid entered with the tea things.

The Earl took advantage of the diversion to rise from his seat and saunter over to the fireplace. Not a moment too soon, he thought, for Lady Gresham began hinting broadly about the extraordinary musical and artistic talents of her younger daughter. He managed, just barely, to keep his face composed; had he been in close proximity of Lady Gresham and the extraordinary Eloise, he doubted whether he could have maintained the proper decorum.

And so it was that Kitty did not at first notice him when she entered the drawing room several moments later. She immediately went to his mother and kissed her on the cheek. The Earl thought he had never seen her look better; her eyes sparkled and there was a healthy glow to her skin. She had grown into a lovely young woman, and he decided that the sooner they found her a suitable husband, the better they would all sleep.

He watched her turn to greet her guests, and it was not until she straightened up, after rather stiffly embracing Eloise Claredon, that her eyes fell upon his lordship. For a moment she was rooted to her place, and he watched the color drain from her face. She tried to speak but her lips were trembling, and her face was completely white.

He moved forward in the next moment, actually fearing that she might collapse in a faint at the feet of the Dragon Lady. But she recovered herself almost immediately and advanced toward him. He took her hand and kissed it. "My dear Kitty. Such a pleasure to see you. London truly does agree with you. You have never looked lovelier," he said softly.

"Thank you, Cousin Charles. I—that is—it is a very

227

pleasant surprise to see you. We—we were not expecting you so—so—soon," she said haltingly, a brave smile planted on her face.

The Earl could see out of the corner of his eye that conversation had continued quite normally as his mother poured the tea. He was relieved that Kitty's lapse had gone unnoticed by everyone but him. As he led Kitty to a place on the sofa next to Eloise, he reflected that he needed no further proof than the look on her face to know she was up to something she ought not to be. And it also struck him that she knew perfectly well why he had suddenly come to London. She might be silly and romantic, but he suddenly realized that his ward was not at all a fool. He would do well to heed Amanda's advice and tread very warily in his dealings with her.

After he had seated Kitty, he resumed his comfortable pose at the fireplace, and listened with half an ear to the feminine chatter. Really, it was unfair of his mother to subject him to this. Was not this evening to be torture enough?

Lady Gresham was telling his mother, in all confidence of course, that she had it on very good authority that old Lord Griswold had quite been in his cups the other night at White's and had gambled away the last vestiges of the Griswold fortune. "They say he hasn't a feather to fly with, poor man, but of course, one never knows for sure, does one?" she was saying, a malicious curl to her lips.

The Earl involuntarily grimaced and turned his eyes toward the younger women. He found the conversation not much more tasteful. Eloise seemed to be filling Kitty's ears with tales of which debutante had been cut by which socially essential matron, and did Kitty know that Agatha Gelfrey really *was* going to accept the Marquis of Dellworth, although how she could pos-

228

sibly, when he reeked of brandy and suffered from the gout, Eloise simply did not know.

Suddenly the Earl heard his name, and realized that Lady Gresham was addressing him. "But, dear Lord Ainsley, we are being rude, are we not, my lord, boring you with all our woman's talk?" she said, her voice dripping charm and sweetness. He thought the talk more appropriate to vipers than women, but said nothing. "Tell me, Lord Ainsley, was your trip to Millforte satisfactory?" she asked, and encountering a warning glance and a sideward jerk of the head from his mother, he dutifully resumed his seat to the right of Lady Gresham.

"My work there is coming along quite satisfactorily, yes," he replied impassively, and with some degree of finality to his tone, but the lady was not to be deterred.

"Oh, I *am* glad. I was saying to Lady Ainsley just the other day that it was most unfortunate that so fine and upstanding a peer as yourself had to involve himself with such—well—you know—in such a situation. One hears so many things. Of course, they may not all be true, but even if a mere half of the stories are, well, I say, it does quite offend one's sense of decency, does it not? But the subject must be painful for you, my lord. And tell me . . ."

The Earl felt himself stiffen with fury and was grateful that she herself changed the subject, for in the next moment he would have, and none too politely at that.

As conversation shifted to this evening's revels, he groaned inwardly. He looked from the Dragon Lady to her daughters to Kitty, but a tumble of black hair and fragile sea green eyes would not leave his mind's eye, and he thought that there was only one woman with whom he cared to dance.

Chapter Fifteen

Amanda had found herself quite unaccustomedly restless following the Earl's departure, unable to concentrate long on anything. For two days she had not been home to any callers except Sally and Vernon Trumwell, and though they were dear friends, Vernon's very piercing looks and Sally's ceaseless, cheerful chatter were a bit much for her.

But today she determined to take hold of herself. She could no longer tell herself that she was ill, or suffering the aftereffects of a dreadful experience. She had to admit that what was distracting her was a very disconcerting image of slate blue eyes and wavy brown hair that would not go away. Fool, she told herself. How could she let a man like that get to her? A man who spent all his time screaming at her and pointing out her faults. Well, not quite *all* of his time—there were those other moments, after all. But she must not think of that. She must think of the mockery in his tone, not the warmth in his eyes.

Amanda decided that it was time she receive visitors, and told Jeffries so as she made her way to the library after breakfast to settle down to work. She still did not feel up to deciphering Higgins's notations and figures, but she could at least catch up on personal correspondence.

There was still no letter from her brother. It had been several months, and though that was not entirely unusual, yet she was concerned about him. She would write to him, although she was not sure whether he would get the letter, and if so, when. But it always made her feel better to know she had tried to communicate with him. He was all the family she had—he and Victor. The agony of growing up in their father's household had brought them very close together, and she missed him terribly. She did not consider her father and two older brothers family. She had not seen them for four years and most fervently hoped she never would again.

But the truth was that she was very frightened that she *would* see them again, or at least her father, very soon. He had not dared to come near Millforte while Arthur was alive, but news of Arthur's death must have reached him by now. She tried not to think of it, but lately the nightmares had begun recurring, the ones that had plagued her in the first year of her marriage. They were terrible nightmares, in which her father came back and it started all over again. She always tried to tell herself, once daylight came, that it was *her* house and she could bar him from it, but she knew that if he was determined, which he would be, especially if he needed money, he would get to her somehow.

Once in a weak moment during the last year of Arthur's life, she had told him of this fear. He had answered quite cryptically that he would try to make some provision in his will that would preclude her father coming near her. She had not understood then what he meant and now, six months after Arthur's death, she still did not comprehend it.

A chill went through her as she thought of her father. Arthur had understood her feeling of dread, and he had protected her. But Arthur had not known the worst of it. She had never been able to utter the words. Even Mrs. Havenwick, who had stood by her all these years, did not know, for she had come afterwards . . .

Amanda shook herself out of her reverie and began writing a cheerful missive to her younger brother. She was thus engaged when Jeffries interrupted her a short while later to say that Mr. Linfield had come to call and was now in the morning room.

"I did tell you, did I not, my lady, that Mr. Linfield has—er—come to call every day since you've been ill? He has left a nosegay of—er—violets each time," Jeffries said, emphasizing "violets" with such distaste that Amanda wondered what could have given him such a dislike of them.

"No, you had not told me, Jeffries. But it doesn't signify," she said amiably, curious as to what could have come over the normally punctilious butler. And she wondered why he had put Mr. Linfield in the morning room. It was her least favorite room and she almost never received there.

As she entered the morning room, Mr. Linfield rose and handed her a nosegay of violets. Out of the corner of her eye she could see a spray of the flowers in a vase on a side table. They must be yesterday's bouquet, she thought, and as she looked down at the delicate nosegay in her hand, it occurred to her that they were not, after all, the most interesting of flowers. But she extended her hand and smiled as she said, "Mr. Linfield, how kind of you to come."

Mr. Linfield gazed back at her warmly. Too warmly, she thought. "Lady Millforte, you cannot know how much pleasure it gives me to see you up and about. I have been quite worried about you," he said.

Amanda walked to the bell cord and pulled it. Jeffries appeared immediately. "Please see that these are placed in water, Jeffries," she said, handing him the flowers, "and some refreshment for Mr. Linfield, if you would."

When Jeffries had bowed himself out, Amanda sat down on a pale pink settee and motioned her guest to a chair opposite her. "Thank you for the flowers, Mr. Linfield. They are very—delicate," she said, for want of a better word.

"It is my pleasure, Lady Millforte. They are indeed delicately beautiful, as you are," he said earnestly.

Amanda thought that though she might be many things, *delicate* was not a word she would have chosen to describe herself. But she merely changed the subject by saying, "Jeffries tells me you have called every day. That was very good of you, but hardly necessary, you know."

"My dear Lady Millforte, it was the least I could do, after all you have been through. I do hope you are feeling well today. You look just perfect, but I would not want to detain you if you are in need of rest. Your butler said you were in the library when I came in. I pray you have not been driving yourself to work overmuch."

She could not say why, but Amanda began to feel Mr. Linfield's solicitousness rather cloying. She surprised even herself when she next said, "I think I am able to gauge myself quite well, Mr. Linfield. I do know, after all, when I needs must rest."

"Oh, of course you do, Lady Millforte," he countered rapidly. "I would be the last person to think you had anything less than supreme good sense."

Amanda found herself not in the least bit mollified by this last statement. If anything, it made her quite ashamed that she had spoken in such a manner to a man who meant her no harm. He was not the Earl, after all. She was therefore very much relieved when Jeffries entered bearing a tray of sherry and biscuits. He set it down on the table in front of Amanda and left.

"Sherry, Mr. Linfield?" she asked.

"If you will have, Lady Millforte, I should indeed enjoy a glass."

Amanda was not accustomed to drinking much of anything before luncheon, but somehow she felt in need of the sherry. Besides, she was sure Mr. Linfield would not drink if she did not. There was an uncomfortable silence for a few moments, filled only by the sound of the sherry as Amanda poured two glasses.

As she held her glass to her lips, she asked amiably, "And are you enjoying your stay here in Shropshire, Mr. Linfield?"

"Yes, yes, I must say I am. The countryside is very beautiful," he replied, and they lapsed again into silence as both sipped their drinks.

"I am hoping, Lady Millforte," ventured Mr. Linfield finally, "that you will one day soon feel well enough to accompany me for a drive through the countryside. I know that you may not be feeling quite the thing just yet, but perhaps in the next week you would so honor me."

For some reason she could not fathom, Amanda felt as if she was ready to scream. She knew she spoke with undue harshness as she said, "Mr. Linfield, you are in error in assuming that I am not feeling quite the thing. In truth I feel rather strong and I am sure the fresh air would do me no harm." Now, why in the world had she said that? She had no wish to drive with Mr. Linfield. Quite the opposite, she knew that she must discourage his attentions. The mooncalf eyes she remembered from Lady Bosley's dinner party had not been her imagination, after all. They were gazing at her right now.

"Please forgive me, Lady Millforte. It was presumptuous of me to speak so. You, of course, would know better than anyone whether you are inclined to take the air just yet. And I should be most delighted to take you out tomorrow, or right now, if you would like. I have my curricle here."

Amanda merely stared at him for a moment. Would he never stop apologizing and agreeing with her? It was maddening. And whatever had possessed her to speak in such a way to him? Feeling that she must have offended him, she felt she had to make amends in some way. "Thank you, Mr. Linfield. I—I do feel the fresh air would be beneficial, but perhaps—perhaps not a drive in the curricle just yet. But—but would you care to see the rear gardens, Mr. Linfield? They are actually quite interesting."

It was obvious from the bedazzled expression on his face that her guest was anything but offended. He followed her out to the rear gardens like a grateful puppy dog, and she thought with dismay that her suggestion had been a mistake. She kept up a running monologue on the history and structure of the rear gardens, so to keep the conversation impersonal. When he once more began to steer the talk to Amanda, she countered by asking him about his own estate.

Linfield spoke rather animatedly about his estate in Warwickshire, which included some farm land. Linfield, it seemed, was an avid farmer. As he spoke of his work and his hopes for the future, Amanda interrupted with occasional gestures, enough to seem politely interested but not enough, she fervently hoped, to give him the impression that his plans for the future were any particular concern of hers.

Amanda thought he would never leave, and was extremely grateful to Jeffries when he came to tell her that Miss Lavinia Prescott had come to call. Mr. Linfield, thankfully, took his leave straightaway, expressing the hope that she would yet honor him with a drive in his curricle.

Jeffries had ensconced Miss Prescott in the Green Salon, and Amanda retired there as soon as she had dispatched Mr. Linfield. Miss Prescott was standing at the large picture window to the right of the fireplace.

"Miss Prescott, how nice to see you," said Amanda, advancing into the room.

"Lady Millforte. It is good to see you looking so well. I do hope you are on your way to recovery," said Miss Prescott, turning from the window.

"Yes, I am, thank you, and I must also thank you for coming to call, as I know you did several times."

"'Twas nothing, my dear. Everyone has been concerned for you."

"Do sit down, Miss Prescott," said Amanda, taking a seat herself.

"Ah, tell me, Lady Millforte, that was Mr. Linfield who just left, was it not?" asked Miss Prescott as she sat next to Amanda on the sofa.

Amanda realized with chagrin that the picture window afforded a lovely view of the circular drive in front of the manor, and of course Miss Prescott would have seen him depart.

Involuntarily Amanda sighed. "Yes, Miss Prescott, it was. And do call me Amanda, please."

"Very well, my dear, but then you must call me Lavinia. Now tell me, Amanda—this is not the first time I have seen Mr. Linfield here. Please forgive me if I am being presumptuous, but you are not encouraging him in any way, are you?"

"Good heavens, no." Amanda sighed again. Somehow she was not at all offended by her visitor's curiosity. But she did feel very, very tired and more than a little concerned about Mr. Linfield's attentions. "Quite the contrary, Lavinia. I have been trying to find a way to discourage him. But he—he does not discourage easily."

"No, I do not imagine he would. He is quite smitten, you know, Amanda," said Miss Prescott, a benevolent smile on her face.

"Oh, dear. I feared as much."

"Yes, but, my dear, taking him to the rear gardens hardly sounds like discouragement, you know."

"I know, Lavinia. I know. I realized my mistake as soon as I'd made the suggestion."

"I take it Mr. Linfield is not exactly—your sort of man, shall we say?" asked Miss Prescott, her head cocked and her eyes alert with unabashed curiosity.

"No, he is not. In truth, Lavinia—well—it is most unkind of me to say so, I am sure, but I was never more grateful than when Jeffries came to inform me you had called. Why, I thought I should go mad. He—he agrees with everything I say. He refuses to find any fault with me at all!"

"Oh, I see," said Lavinia, her eyes crinkling with amusement. "You would rather like a man who would disagree with you, and perhaps, find a fault or two?" Lavinia thought with relish that Amanda and Ainsley were even better suited than she'd ever imagined.

"Well, yes, I suppose I do enjoy a good argument now and again. That is—no, Lavinia, I—I do not want *any* man. I—I am in mourning," stammered Amanda, blushing and looking down quickly at her hands.

Lavinia smiled a knowing smile. "Of course you are, my dear. But—"

"Oh, Lavinia," said Amanda quite suddenly, "please do forgive me, for I have been quite remiss in my duties as hostess. Would you care for some refreshment? Lemonade, or sherry, perhaps?"

"Sherry would be lovely, thank you, Amanda," replied Lavinia, bemused, though in truth she would much have preferred to pursue the topic at hand. But it was obvious that Amanda was uncomfortable and she did not wish to distress her.

Amanda pulled the bell cord, and in a moment the butler appeared with a tray bearing sherry and biscuits and some lemonade as well. "I did not know Miss Prescott's preference," he said as he set the tray down and departed.

Amanda poured the sherry and handed Lavinia a glass. She declined to take any for herself.

"Tell me, my dear," said Lavinia as she sipped her sherry, "what will you do the next time Mr. Linfield comes to call?"

"In truth I do not know. How does one discourage such a man?" asked Amanda anxiously.

"One does not, I think, discourage him. Rather, I think the best course would be to provide him with a new object for his affections," said Lavinia, her tongue tracing her lips with relish at the thought.

"Lavinia!" exclaimed Amanda, wide-eyed with amazement. "I do believe you mean to engage in a bit of matchmaking."

"Well, my dear, 'tis a little hobby of mine, but mind, I don't indulge myself very often these days. Only for a special friend every now and then," confided Lavinia, her eyes alight.

"Do you have anyone in mind?"

"No, child. But I shall uncover someone. Have no fear of that. You leave Linfield to me. And now, my dear Amanda, I am persuaded you must be all puckered out and much in need of rest. I shall leave you now." Lavinia downed her sherry and rose.

"I have much enjoyed your visit. Please feel free to call again," said Amanda, rising and walking with Lavinia toward the door.

"Thank you, Amanda, I shall. And please remember

that in me you have a friend, should you ever have need of me."

"You are very kind, Lavinia. I shall remember," replied Amanda, taking Lavinia's hands for a moment.

"Oh, and Amanda. One thing more. The Earl is due to return in the near future, is he not?"

"Yes, I believe so," said Amanda, her eyes suddenly narrowing.

"Do be careful my dear. He will not take kindly to Mr. Linfield's visits."

Amanda looked suddenly pale as she said quietly, "I am afraid you much mistake the matter, Lavinia." And then she seemed to rally, for she added, rather more brightly, "The Earl's interests here are the business of the estates and Victor. My activities are no concern of his, after all."

Like hell they aren't, thought Lavinia, but she merely said impassively, "As you say, my dear." She followed Amanda out to the main hall, thinking all the while that Amanda was very much in love with the Earl of Ainsley, and very much unaware of that fact. It was all coming along quite as she'd thought it would, and she looked forward with amusement to the Earl's return. In the meantime she must turn her fertile mind to the problem of the infatuated Mr. Linfield.

After the ordeal of tea in his mother's drawing room, the Earl was more than a little grateful to Ridgeway for his dinner invitation. It gave him an excuse to escape his mother's house and to arrive late to the Cheswick ball.

"Charles, good to see you," said the brown-haired, blue-eyed Marquis of Ridgeway as he rose to greet his friend in the study of his London house.

"And you, my friend," said the Earl, taking the

239

comfortable chair by the fire which Simon had indicated.

"Back a bit earlier than expected, are you not, Charles?" asked Simon as he walked to a side table on which sat a decanter and glasses.

"Yes, I am. My ward, Kitty, has got herself mixed up with some fortune-hunting soldier."

"Well, you will deal with it with the utmost expediency, I am sure. I met Miss Berenson the other night, by the by. A fetching little thing. I imagine, Charles, that this will not be the last little affair you'll have to break up before she's safely settled. I don't envy you, but then, if memory serves me, you have dealt with women a good deal more difficult than your innocent young ward, and you seem to have come through quite unscathed, haven't you? Brandy?"

"Yes, please," Charles said, permitting himself a smile. "I shall need to fortify myself for this evening." Simon handed him a glass of brandy and took the seat opposite his.

"Now, let me guess," Simon began. "To what abominable entertainment has the dear Dowager committed you tonight? The Beckenhurst musical soiree? No, I think not. I know of three card parties, but no, to launch a young lady such as Miss Berenson, there can be only one place—and you have my most sincere sympathy, old man. You didn't come to ask me to accompany you, did you?" said Simon, his brows suddenly arching in mock horror.

"No, Simon, that is, not exactly. Nor did I come to discuss that troublesome chit under my care. You received my letter, I presume?" said the Earl, leaning forward as he took a sip of the brandy.

"Yes, I did, Charles, and I cannot say that I thank you for it. I have been to no fewer than three balls, two card parties, and one afternoon garden party in pursuit

240

of the requested information."

"Not to mention spending a great deal of time at White's and perhaps at Mrs. Townsend's as well, my friend?" queried the Earl, a gleam in his eye.

"Yes, well, all in the line of duty, as they say," replied Simon, downing some of his brandy.

"Just so," said the Earl, "but now tell me, what were you able to ferret out?"

"Charles, it's the damndest thing. I keep hearing the same things you've heard. I've asked many subtle and some not so subtle questions, and I've done a good bit of eavesdropping. The on dits are quite consistent. She began amusing herself, shall we say, with any number of men, all respected peers, soon after her marriage to old Millforte." Simon noticed the muscles in the Earl's face tighten, but as he said nothing, the Marquis went on. "The Beau Ton seems to think he took her away from London when he got wind of her activities, and he never brought her back after that. But that seems not to have deterred her. I can only conclude that she made such an impact when she was here that her various paramours followed her out to the country. Though how she accomplished that under her husband's nose I cannot conceive, for they seemed to have lived rather quietly out there in Shropshire. No wild house parties—the kind where that sort of thing goes on all the time, if you know what I mean."

The Earl nodded, his brows knit together, his elbows resting on the arms of his chair, as he tapped the fingers of one hand together with those of the other. He said nothing, and Ridgeway continued. "Tell me, Charles, is she *that* beautiful—is she so compelling that—that men would follow her anywhere?"

The Earl's frown deepened, and he stared at Simon without speaking for a full minute. "Names, Simon. Are there any names? Surely in that time there must be one man who has boasted of the liaison."

"Charles, that is what is so strange about the whole thing. There is nothing tangible, just as you said in the letter. No names, no dates, no places. Just talk. It makes no sense. Ah, there is something else. Something that I have realized, rather than uncovered, though I cannot conceive that it will be of any help to you."

"What is that, Simon?"

"Well, I have spent a good deal more time than you in London these past few years. I must have arrived from abroad several months after your uncle's marriage, for I do not believe he and Lady Millforte were still in London. At any rate I do not recall ever meeting Lady Millforte. I do remember that the on dits were full of her name at the time, and the stories quite outrageously scandalous. But gradually the talk ebbed, as talk will, you know."

"Yes, but even on my infrequent visits to town I can recollect hearing her name bandied about," interrupted the Earl, somewhat irritably, thought Simon.

"To be sure, the scandalous Lady Millforte was never far from the tongue of any truly devoted gossip monger. But do you know, Charles, the very curious thing is that the on dits have arisen again with renewed vigor in the past few months. I cannot think why—she has been in mourning, has she not?"

The Earl nodded and Simon continued. "It makes no sense at all, Charles. Why should the Beau Monde care so much to discuss a woman it has not seen in nearly four years? Oh, and do you know that the latest on dit is of a liaison with Lord somebody or other in or about Ludlow? That's near Millforte, is it not?"

"Yes," replied the Earl, setting down his glass of brandy. "Does anyone know his name?"

"I've drawn a blank, once again. I tell you, it's uncanny, Charles. One would think the stories

242

amounted to nothing at all, but her name would hardly stay on the tip of every gossip's tongue, and for so long at that, were there not enough veracity to support them."

The Earl sat very still, staring at the fire. He did not speak for several moments, and finally Simon broke the silence. "Charles, are you feeling quite the thing?" he said, somewhat perturbed.

Suddenly the Earl stood up and walked to the fireplace. He turned to face his friend, a smile on his face. "Yes, I am feeling fine, Simon. Truly fine indeed. You have answered all of my questions; you have told me everything I needed to know."

"But Charles, I have told you nothing. Hardly more than you already knew. The stories are—"

"Are just that, Simon, stories. I think I knew it all along, but somehow, I had to be sure. Why Simon, one hour in her company would serve to assure you that she could not possibly conduct herself in such a reprehensible manner. I only hope she never finds out about these tales—she would never forgive me if she thought I had—had doubted her for a moment." He said this last more to himself than to Simon, his voice remarkably soft, and his friend rose from his chair, staring openmouthed at the Earl.

"Why, Charles Ainsley, I do believe you have f—"

"Have been appalled that a woman could be so abused by a callous society? You are quite right, Simon," interrupted the Earl briskly, after which Simon closed his mouth, sat back down, and decided to hold his peace.

"And I must now do all in my power to clear her name, Simon," continued the Earl earnestly. Simon shot him a questioning look and the Earl answered, somewhat apologetically. "She is my kinswoman after all, and it is my mother's family name that has been besmirched. Naturally, I must do what I can to repair the damage that has been done."

"Naturally," echoed Simon, a smile playing at his lips as he looked into the face of his friend. He found a new expression there, a softening of the hard masculine features, a warmth in the eyes, that had never been there before. Charles might not want to admit it, to his friend or to himself, but Simon had no doubt at all whatever as to the effect the lady in question had had on the Earl of Ainsley.

"And now, Simon, we have a difficult task before us, if I may be so presumptuous as to call upon you a second time."

"At your service, Charles," said Simon, by this time rather amused by the whole thing.

"They say that where there is smoke, there is fire. But when it becomes obvious that there has been no fire, well, then someone has created the smoke. Would you not agree?" asked the Earl with a self-satisfied smile.

"I suppose so," said Simon doubtfully.

"Well, then, we must endeavor to ascertain who has created the smoke. Four years' worth of unfounded rumors that have quite set the Ton on its ears. Why would anyone bother?"

"If I am following you, Charles, you are surmising that someone has engineered this. It seems fantastic—but it would be quite a malicious piece of work were that the case."

"Yes, and malice has only one or two purposes—to hurt one party, to benefit another, or both. We must first decide who has been most hurt by this."

"Keep going, Charles, I follow," said Simon, his interest quite piqued as he reclined in his fireside chair and watched his friend leaning against the chimney-piece.

"My mother takes great pride in her family name, so

244

naturally it has been distressing to her," said the Earl.

"But it has in no way altered her life. She is still looked upon with the greatest respect by everyone in the Ton," Simon added.

"Very true, Simon. Then there is the late Lord Millforte. Presumably *he* had heard the disreputable stories, and that is why he took his wife back to the country. I do not know that he was so enamored of London society, but still, his life certainly was affected in some way."

"Yes, Charles, but he is dead now—what—half a year or more? The on dits are as—er—infamous as ever, shall we say," said Simon, choosing his words very carefully now.

"Which leaves, as the intended victim—" began the Earl.

"The second Lady Millforte," finished Simon.

"Just so. The second Lady Millforte. But for the life of me, Simon, I cannot conceive of who would bear her malice," said the Earl, his eyes narrowed.

"She has no enemies that you know of? Beautiful women often do, you know," Simon said quietly.

"She does not make enemies, Simon. Why, you should see the way she—" The Earl stopped short when he caught Simon looking up at him, a grin on his face. "Well, never mind. In any case, Amanda is simply not the sort who makes enemies, not knowingly at least," he added, taking his seat once more.

"Following your own line of thought then, Charles, it may be someone who bears her a grudge of which she is unaware—"

"Or someone who had and still has something to gain by making sure she rusticates up in Shropshire for years. Not that she has in any way minded—or even been aware—but has not the effect of all this been to close the doors of polite society to her?" Charles asked, an edge to his voice.

"I would say so, yes."

"Well, then, I must discover who it is who would go to so much trouble to see those doors closed, mustn't I? And if I may prevail upon you once more, old friend, to help me—I shall only be in London a short time. It is very important that I arrive at some satisfactory conclusions before—before returning to Millforte. If you would not mind, do attend a few more balls for an old school friend. Ask questions. Find out in any way you can who might bear her a grudge, who might have wanted her buried out in Shropshire. I can do my share of eavesdropping, but I certainly cannot come right out and discuss the matter. I am family, after all, and I do not doubt that half the Ton must be well aware that I have just spent the last week at Millforte. Well, what say you, Simon? Shall it be the Duchess of Cheswick's or Mrs. Townsend's tonight?"

"Oh, I suppose Mrs. Townsend's girls will keep until another night," sighed the Marquis, and then he added, a glint in his eye, "It is most heartwarming, I must say, to see to what lengths a man will go for the sake of his mother and her family name." But the Earl cast him a dark look and he said no more about it then, or during the excellent dinner that followed.

Chapter Sixteen

Kitty was definitely enchanted as she stepped into the enormous ballroom of Cheswick House. Eloise had said it was to be one of *the* events of the Season, and Kitty did not doubt it. She had never seen a ballroom more magnificent. Hundreds of lights flickered from brass sconces, and exquisite chandeliers hung throughout the room, their myriad crystal pieces scattering the light of the flames.

One entire wall of the ballroom consisted of French doors, which she could see led to a series of graded terraces and out to the formal gardens below. Flowers were arranged in huge bunches everywhere, including the balcony on which the orchestra sat perched. But most splendid of all, thought Kitty, were the guests, arrayed in their astoundingly elegant silks, brocades, and jewels.

She was very grateful that Aunt had insisted that she have a gown made especially for this occasion. The dress was cut in the high-waisted style, with a slip of pale pink satin partially covered by a robe of white lace. She wore a single strand of pearls that had belonged to her mother, and Aunt's dresser had caught her hair up in soft curls. She did not need anyone to tell her that she was looking her best, but there was only one person's opinion that really mattered anyway.

She looked in vain for Richard as she followed the

Dowager across the ballroom to where the chaperones were seated. At length she espied Anne and her mother and beckoned them over. The Dowager and Anne's mother renewed their acquaintanceship, and Anne and Kitty moved off to the side to join a gathering of young people. Anne looked lovely, her brown hair and eyes set off beautifully in a gown of ivory crepe. It was not long before she and Anne found their hands claimed for the quadrille just forming, and their dance cards began to fill rapidly.

Richard had accompanied Thomas and Lydia into the ballroom. In a way he had felt that he should not come to the Cheswick ball at all. He could do Kitty more harm than good by meeting her, and yet he could not bear the thought of his beautiful Kitty craning for a glimpse of him in the crowd all evening, and then returning home despondent, wondering why he had not come to her. And if he was completely honest with himself, he desperately wanted to see her. It had been nearly three days, during which time they had had no communication of any sort. He missed her terribly, but even so, he must be firm tonight in pointing out to her the course of action they must now follow. They must forbear seeing each other until he had uncovered the villainy which had been perpetrated against his family. They would have a private understanding, of course, but they would have to be patient before declaring themselves to the world, or even to Kitty's family. He loved her too much to use her ill in any way, and it grieved him that he might be the cause of her estrangement from her aunt and her guardian. To Kitty it had all been part of a great adventure, but he could not help thinking that his courtship had been terribly shabby indeed. She deserved much better than that.

He had not meant it to be this way. In fact, such a coil

had been the farthest thing from his mind a mere two weeks ago. He had come to London with the intention of completing the legal work necessary to claim his inheritance and to see about selling out of his Regiment. He had been shocked when Thomas, whom he trusted implicitly after their years on the Continent, had informed him of the unfortunate situation in which his family had become embroiled.

And then there had been Kitty. Catherine Berenson. The timing had been all wrong—in fact it could not have been worse. But even after that first dance, he could not have turned away had he wanted to. There was something about her delicate face, her golden hair, the way her blue eyes looked up at him when he spoke, something about her that he could not resist.

Even as his mind conjured her picture, he caught a glimpse of her executing a graceful dance with a rather tall, good-looking man dressed in the height of fashion. He felt a stab of jealousy, but forced himself to melt back into the crowd. He did not want Kitty to see him; it would not do for her to seek him out. Thomas would arrange a rendezvous later in the evening, and he had to be content with that.

In the meantime, he had work to do. In truth, he had not been very successful these two weeks. He felt no closer than he had at the beginning to uncovering the villain he sought, but still, a crowded ballroom was a fertile field of inquiry. A snippet of conversation here, a delicately placed question there, were his only hope of picking up clues.

On one side of the ballroom, near tables of refreshments, were ornate, partially curtained archways. As he stepped behind a curtain he came face to face with a rather guilty-looking couple engaged in a tête-à-tête. He quickly moved away and strained his ears to catch fragments of dialogue emanating from the ballroom.

"Oh, but Mother, he is quite unexceptionable, I do

assure you," said a very anxious youthful voice.

"I am sorry, my dear. He will not do for you. You have already given him one dance and that is enough. Do I make myself clear?" said an authoritative voice.

Richard moved on, still behind the archways.

"Really, old chap. Chits just out of the schoolroom are simply not in my line. Shall we adjourn to the Card Room?"

Richard continued on to where a group of chaperones were seated. He could see only a few of them—those seated far to his left. He was unable to see more than the feet of those whose conversation he could hear.

"Well, my dear Priscilla, I have done a good night's work. I'll not allow history to repeat itself. Pity I could not have been so—shall we say—imaginative when it was your turn."

"Mother, let us not go all through that again. Truly I am quite content."

"I must say, my dear, that the human animal shall never cease to amaze me. Everyone seems to take such relish in it—why, a clever person can quite set the world by its ears. Remember that for the future, my dear."

For some reason a shiver went through Richard. There was something very cold and calculating about that speech. It did not at all sound like the average hopeful mother of a young girl. And so it went. One conversation more inane than another. More social-climbing mothers instructing more hapless daughters, more cynical Corinthians rating this season's crop of debutantes, some even taking wagers on who would catch whom in the marriage sweepstakes.

Richard was exasperated. He would get nowhere like this. Perhaps Thomas would have better success—at least *he* could engage in polite conversation in an attempt to garner information, while Richard was for the moment forced to stay very much in the background. As such he moved out into the crowd to seek Thomas out again, anxious also to know when his meeting with Kitty would take place.

Despite the late hour, the Earl and Ridgeway found to their mutual disgust that there was still quite a lineup of carriages waiting to arrive at the doorstep of Cheswick House.

"There's no waiting at Mrs. Townsend's, you know, Charles," said Simon with a grin, as they sat in the stationary carriage. "Sure you would not care to turn the carriage around?"

"No, afraid not. As you said, all in the line of duty, old boy," replied the Earl.

"Hmph. That is all very well for you. But what do *I* do tonight besides eavesdrop?" asked Simon amiably.

"Ah, my good man. While I am engaged in pursuing my wayward ward, you will have the opportunity to mingle with the Pink of the Ton. You might wander into the Card Room and question a few gentlemen who've downed a bit too much of the spirits. You might flatter a few choice dowagers—they are always eager to impart gossip, you know. And do not neglect the fair young ladies—they are like sponges, absorbing every *on dit* so they can repeat it and imagine themselves sophisticated," said the Earl in his mocking tone.

"Now, Charles, you can ask many things of me, but the new crop of debutantes is definitely not in my line, as you well know."

"I do know that, Simon. And I certainly don't blame you. I have avoided them judiciously these many years. Which reminds me, I must stay clear of the Dragon Lady. Did you know she's launching another daughter this year?"

"Yes, so I've heard. Don't tell me old Lady Gresham has her eye on the bachelor Earl!" exclaimed Simon.

"Is not your reputation enough to disqualify you?"

"It would seem not. I have already been subjected to one recital of the girl's accomplishments and fear that she'll have the chit in my lap if I so much as close my eyes. But you know, Simon, it occurs to me that perhaps you ought to make the acquaintance of the fair Eloise." The Earl saw his friend's brows shoot up and he quickly added, "One dance would be sufficient, I do assure you. Eloise is a veritable treasure trove of nasty gossip, I am persuaded. And she is perhaps still guileless enough to reveal her sources."

"You would make me do all this just for your mother, Charles?" asked Simon out of the corner of his mouth.

"Why, of course," answered the Earl, smiling. "I would, after all, do likewise for you—and your mother."

It was a full half hour before they were able to disembark in front of the stately pillars that marked the entrance to the mansion. Simon promptly began to fulfill his assigned duties, and the Earl, assuring himself that Lady Gresham was nowhere near his mother, went to greet his fond parent.

The Dowager Countess was enjoying an animated conversation with an old flame, and she turned somewhat reluctantly to speak to her son.

"Where is she, Mother?" he asked perfunctorily.

"Why, she is on the dance floor, dear. Her hand has been claimed for nearly every dance. And no wonder—she looks truly beautiful tonight, Charles. I am sure even your critical eye will approve the lovely gown and—"

"Mother, please, I am not at all interested in Kitty's attire, merely in her whereabouts. Do you see her dancing at this very moment?" he asked, helping his mother rise from her chair.

"Well, no, actually, I do not. But the room is so very crowded. I am persuaded that you will find her presently. Or she may have gone in to supper. The

Marquis of Fritchley was to escort her, you know."

"No, I did not know. Well, thank you, Mother. I shall commence looking for her," he said, mildly annoyed, and turned toward the center of the ballroom.

He negotiated his way around the periphery two times before satisfying himself that his ward was indeed not on the dance floor. A glance into the banquet hall revealed that she was not partaking of supper either, and the Earl began an agitated search of the various public rooms of the house.

Kitty prayed that her exit through the French doors had gone unnoticed. She tiptoed down several graduated terraces, and found herself on a stone pathway lined with hedges. She advanced uncertainly for several yards until she heard her name whispered in the night air. She followed the sound, turning as the path did. "Richard!" she exclaimed in the loudest whisper she dared.

"Sssh!" he said, putting his finger to his lips and taking her hand. He led her along the path, which twisted and turned among the hedges. They passed several open areas with benches and flower beds, but Richard kept walking until he found an arbor, almost completely enclosed by hedges and trees.

"Oh, Richard," said Kitty, "I have missed you so."

"And I, too. I saw you dancing earlier. I had all I could do to refrain from approaching you. You look more beautiful tonight than I have ever seen you," he murmured, pulling her close.

She felt a shiver go through her body. "Richard, I do not know how I shall endure this. And you must know, something dreadful has happened. Cousin Charles has returned to London," she whispered.

"The Earl?" he asked.

Kitty nodded. "I saw him at tea. He has not said

253

anything to me as of yet, but I do not doubt of his reason for being here."

"Have you seen him here tonight?"

"Not yet. But he will come sooner or later, and I am frightened of what he might do."

"Very well, Kitty," he said, holding her away from him and leading her to a bench set beneath the overhanging leaves. "What I had originally meant to say to you is even more important now. We cannot continue this way. It can only lead to undesirable consequences. It will be very difficult, I know, but I fear we must not see each other again until—until I have avenged my family name. At that time I will ask permission of your guardian to pay my addresses to you." Richard saw Kitty's eyes fill with tears as she shook her head disbelievingly.

"And you know," he said very softly, taking her hands in his, "I have never asked you in so many words, but tell me, my beloved Kitty, will you consent to be my wife?"

Kitty struggled to stem the tears and nodded her head, a faint smile on her lips. "You know I will, Richard. And I would go anywhere with you, endure any hardship—"

"I know that, Kitty, but when we wed it shall be with full blessing of Church and family, and we shall make our home together in Essex. Now, Kitty, attend; you must not try to see me. If you must get a message to me, do it through Thomas, and I will do the same."

"All right, Richard, but please, may I know your direction in case—in case I should need to contact you in a hurry?"

"Kitty, I do not want you to contact me," he started to say, but seeing the desolate look on her face, he consented. "Very well, but you must send a servant with any message, and only under dire circumstances. Do you understand?"

"Yes, of course, Richard."

"And Kitty, you must never, under any circumstances, come there yourself. Kitty, promise me—it would be disastrous for you to appear there. It is a street where only gentlemen have rooms and no lady would venture there alone. Is that clear?" he said rather sternly.

"Yes, Richard. I fully understand."

"All right, my love," he sighed, and gave her his direction. Then he rose and took her hand. "And now, we must go back before your absence from the ballroom is remarked," he said gently.

"Richard," said Kitty in the softest of voices, "this is the last time we shall see each other, and I cannot bear the thought of dancing with all those other men."

"Don't you think it was torture for me to watch you on the dance floor, knowing that of all men, I could not claim even one dance? But it shan't be for long. I shall work diligently to set this matter to rights," he said, looking down at her delicate face, framed with silken hair that was faintly illuminated by the moonlight. "Kitty, we must go back," he said hoarsely, taking a step closer to her.

"Yes, Richard," she breathed, moving closer to him, her face turned up to his.

The Earl was becoming increasingly piqued as he searched unsuccessfully for his ward and, he feared, that unscrupulous young man. He had made the rounds of the house and ended up back in the stifling, overcrowded ballroom. He accepted a glass of brandy from a passing footman and let his eyes scan the dance floor once more.

Oh, blast it all! Whatever was he *doing* in this place? He had much rather be in the country, in one particular part of the country. He'd already seen two different heads of lustrous black curls glide by. Each time he'd felt his heart beat erratically, until the head turned and he beheld a face that had neither sea green eyes, nor that chiseled nose, nor ... He chided himself for behaving like a schoolboy. He had a job to do, and unpleasant though it might be, he must put personal concerns aside for now. All of which made him even more furious at his troublesome ward! Where the devil was she?

Unable to bear the closeness of the ballroom, he slapped his drink down on a table and strode out to the formal gardens. Here he continued his search, but the task was disagreeable to say the least. Twice he stuck himself on the thorns of the rosebushes, and once nearly pounced on an embracing couple, before discovering that it was the wrong couple!

He resolved to proceed with caution from then on. The path along the hedges seemed to delight in twisting and turning into various enclaves, almost as if it were made for clandestine lovemaking. At length he heard voices behind a curved hedge.

"Stop looking at me like that. It is for your own good. We must—" a man was saying.

"Of course we must, but I cannot bear to leave you now. It may be weeks, months even," whispered a feminine voice.

"It's not fair, Kitty; I am only human, after all," said the man huskily, after which the only sound was a faint feminine moan and the rustle of clothes.

The Earl felt his blood boil and for a moment was riveted to his spot. Then he sprang into action, rounding the hedge in seconds. He saw the couple, locked in a most shocking embrace, and advancing forward, shouted, "That's quite enough, Captain Smythe!"

Kitty and the young man instantly jumped several feet apart. "Cousin Charles!" whispered Kitty, her hand flying to her mouth, her eyes wide with horror.

"How dare you!" the Earl growled between clenched teeth. "How dare you behave in such a disgraceful manner, Catherine! And as for you, sir—any man who would so abuse a young girl—"

"Please, Lord Ainsley, I meant no disrespect, I do assure you. It is not at all what you think—" said the young man in some earnest.

"It matters not what I *think,* Captain, but what I *saw* and *heard.* And I tell you this—if you come anywhere near my ward again I shall call you out!" seethed the Earl, taking care to keep his voice down so as not to attract attention.

"But, my lord, you have not—"

"There is nothing to discuss, Captain. You are forbid access to Miss Berenson from this time forth. And you, miss, come here!" he said menacingly, his temples vibrating with fury.

Kitty meekly moved toward the Earl. "You will plant a weak smile on your face. You may touch your hand to your brow once or twice as we stroll calmly into the ballroom. When we reach my mother, I will explain that you are not feeling at all the thing, and we shall take our leave. Is that clear?" When Kitty nodded, he added, "And you, Captain, are to remain here for some time before entering the ballroom, and for God's sake find another entrance!"

He took Kitty by the hand and pulled her after him. He sensed her turn for a moment back to the Captain but he jerked her forward.

The only sound in the carriage on the way home was the muffled sound of Kitty sobbing into a handkerchief. The Earl had no intention of discussing the matter as the carriage rumbled its way over the cobblestone streets, and the Dowager, who had exited the ballroom on cue, did not dare ask questions.

Once inside his mother's drawing room, the Earl helped his mother to a chair and ordered Kitty to be seated. His brows were knit together in an ominous line and his voice was harsh as he spoke. He kept his eyes on Kitty but addressed the Dowager.

"Her behavior tonight was completely shameless. I regret that the only course open to us is to betake her to the country. As far as Kitty is concerned, the Season is over!" Kitty gasped but he continued. "Perhaps next year we may try again to introduce the ungrateful wretch to polite society, but for now, she will clearly benefit from a year in the country, during which time she may ruminate upon the proper behavior befitting a young woman of quality!" His voice had risen to a loud and angry pitch, and Kitty cowed beneath his rage.

"Very well, Charles," the Dowager said quietly. "When shall we leave?"

"You will rouse the servants early tomorrow to prepare the luggage. I want you gone by noon. I shall make it known that Kitty is not well and is in need of country air. As she took her leave early tonight for reasons of health, I daresay it will not arouse comment. Now get you off to bed, Catherine. I have no wish to see you again," he said in disgust.

When she had gone, the Dowager asked, "Charles, what exactly did happen?"

The Earl tried to curb the harshness in his voice as he briefly recounted the scene upon which he had stumbled.

"Oh dear, it was as I had feared," she sighed, reaching for her vinaigrette.

"Yes," he said, his face still dark with fury. "I am sorry, Mother, that you must bury yourself at Ainsley. I know how you do enjoy the Season. But I see no other way."

"Of course, Charles, you are right," she said calmly, wishing that he, too, would calm down. "I suppose we must be grateful that she has not already ruined herself. And let us hope she will quickly forget that unscrupulous young man."

"I have no doubt she will, Mother. What can Kitty know of love, after all?" he said in a strange tone that the Dowager could never remember hearing from her son before. She shot him a questioning look, but his only reply was a curt "Goodnight," as he kissed her cheek and left the room.

Kitty dismissed her maid as soon as Agnes came in to help her undress. A plan was only vaguely forming in her mind, but Kitty knew that she would not sleep tonight. She sat down in a chair by the fire, silently letting tears roll down her cheeks. She had been frightened of Cousin Charles tonight, very frightened indeed. But she would not let him ruin her life.

Kitty waited until she heard no more movement about the house. Then she stepped out of her ball gown and quickly donned a traveling dress. Hurriedly, she packed a single bandbox, which she could hide under her pelisse, and then rapidly drew on her bonnet, boots, and gloves. Into her reticule she stuffed her few jewels and her pin money. She had little, but it might pay for one night's lodging if need be. She prayed that such would not be necessary, and took one last look around her room. Suddenly an idea came to her. She pulled up the bed covers and rumpled the sheets, and then took a nightgown from a drawer and threw it on the bed. Let them be confused as to when she had left, she thought. And then pulling her fur-lined pelisse around her shoulders and closing it in front to hide the bandbox, she stealthily made her way down the stairs and let herself out the back door.

Kitty walked several blocks before she dared hail a hackney, for there were a few stray people still about and she did not want to attract attention anywhere near her aunt's house, as a girl alone climbing into a hackney

259

certainly might.

She was thankful that she had been able to prevail upon Richard to reveal his direction. She felt a pang of conscience that she was about to break her promise, but a few hours old, not to go to his rooms under any circumstances. But these were not just *any* circumstances. This was a dire emergency and she would somehow convince him that, truly, this was the last promise she would ever break.

The hackney driver tried unsuccessfully to dissuade her from her course, as did the sleepy manservant who opened Richard's door. "You should not be here, miss. If you would tell me your name, I am certain the Captain will call upon you in—"

"I shall not leave here until I have seen your master," she said defiantly, after which the servant shook his head and motioned for her to enter.

He led Kitty into the sitting room, cold now as the fire glowed with its last remaining embers, and went to rouse his master.

In less than ten minutes Richard dashed into the room, still buttoning a shirt that he had just thrown on. "Kitty, whatever can have possessed you?" he gasped, not sure whether to be angry at Kitty or frightened at the sight of her forlorn figure shivering in the cold sitting room.

"Oh, Richard," she cried, coming toward him, "the most dreadful thing has happened. Cousin Charles has ordered me back to Ainsley, to stay at least until next year. Aunt is to take me there in the morning. Don't you see, Richard? They will never let you near me, and I shall never see you again!" Her voice rose, tears beginning to roll down her cheeks.

Richard was beside himself. It was the middle of the night, Kitty had come alone to his lodgings, and he was in his stockinged feet. Why, he had barely got his britches on! The entire situation was a potential disaster. Somehow he had got to convince her to return home before her absence became known. But she turned from him with moist eyes and he found himself moving toward her.

"Kitty," he said gently, taking her hands in his. "Kitty, look up at me. Listen carefully. It is very dangerous for you to be here, my love. You must return before your absence is noted. It will not be for long that we are separated. As soon as I have resolved my problems, I shall explain all to Ainsley and ask his permission to pay my addresses to you. When he sees that we have both behaved with propriety, and that your feelings have remained the same, well then, he will relent. Rest assured, my love, that it is only a matter of time."

Kitty shook her head and stared at him wide-eyed. She sniffed as if to check her tears and said, her hands clutched tightly to his, "You do not understand, Richard. It will be a matter of pride, *his* pride. He will never, never give in. And then he and Aunt will contrive to marry me off to some antiquated peer and—"

"Kitty, don't you realize that they cannot force you to marry anyone you do not wish to?"

"You don't know the Earl, Richard."

"Kitty, my beloved. We must be strong and do the right thing."

"I *am* being strong, Richard. That is why I came here tonight. I know that there is only one course of action open to us now," she stated calmly, looking him full in the eye.

He dropped her hands. "And what is that?" he asked, quite afraid of the answer.

"We must elope. We—"

"Kitty!"

"Please, Richard, hear me out. It makes a great deal of sense. We shall no longer have to worry about my guardian, and I can help you in whatever you must do as regards your family. Your problems are my problems, after all, Richard."

"Kitty!" he exclaimed, grabbing her shoulders. "Did it never occur to you that you are under age, and that the course you suggest is highly dishonorable? In addition to which, I will never involve you in my rather ugly family problems!"

"But there is a way to get married if one is underage, is there not? There is a place—I do not know the name, but it is just across the border in Scotland, I believe—"

"Yes, Kitty, yes I *know* about Gretna Green. But I refuse to take you there."

"You don't—you don't want to marry me, Richard? Is that it?" she asked softly, her eyes downcast.

Good God, this just wasn't fair. How was a man to maintain any code of honor at a time like this? "Oh, Kitty," he said in a very low voice, pulling her to his chest and putting his arms around her. "Such a foolish question. You know very well that I want to wed you. But not in such an ignoble way." He began to stroke the fine blond hair and he felt her arms steal up around his back. "And you are aware, my foolish girl, that Gretna Green is approximately four days from here? How do you propose we travel together all that way without your reputation being torn to shreds?"

"We can travel as brother and sister, can we not? And from all that I have heard about such things, I own society will forget very quickly as long as I return a married woman," she murmured, her head comfortably pressed against his chest.

"I would that society's memory were indeed that short, my love," he said, and thought grimly of his own family. "But it is not just that. We shall wed in a church, Kitty, with our families in attendance," he added with what he hoped was appropriate firmness.

"Richard," she said, picking her head up and looking him in the eye. "I shall not return to Aunt's house. If

262

you will not take me to Scotland, where we may be wed, I shall go elsewhere by myself."

"Kitty, my sweet child, you can't mean that. Where on earth would you go?" he asked gently, still holding her.

"I am not a child, Richard, and I mean what I say," she said quietly.

There was something about the resolute set of her chin and the tranquility of her tone that made him drop his arms and stare at her. What was he to do? He could not very well allow her to wander about the countryside by herself. Somehow he believed her when she said she would never go home. He shuddered when he thought of what would happen to an innocent young girl traveling by herself. He certainly could not let her stay the night in his lodgings, and in any case, what would they do in the morning?

He sighed. "Very well, my love. It shall be as you wish," he agreed, and cupping her delicate face in his hands, he kissed her very gently on the lips. He was rewarded with a shy smile, and then he said, "I must finish dressing and assemble my things. I shall have tea brought for you and the fire lit."

He called to his manservant to see to the lady's comfort and to pay the hackney driver and dismiss him, for he felt it safest to hail a new one when they were ready. He slowly climbed the stairs to his room, his mind racing furiously as he tried to devise a plan by which he might take Kitty to wife honorably. As he entered his room the idea came to him. They *would* travel as brother and sister, as Kitty had suggested, and with any luck they would get away with it, but their destination would not be Gretna Green. No, he had a much better idea.

Chapter Seventeen

"No! No!" Amanda screamed as she ran through the field of grass. But her father followed relentlessly, his heavy stride steady despite his bloodshot eyes and his slurred speech as he growled her name. "Not again!" she cried over and over, pushing herself ever faster.

And then suddenly, blocking her way, was the steep rise of a mountain. She could hear her father just behind her and cried out in despair, until she espied a rope hanging from the top of the mountain. But how could she climb all that way? She could not possibly—

"Yes you can, Amanda," came a voice, a man's voice, from above. She looked up but could see only a tree with deep green leaves. "You can do it, Amanda," came the voice again. "Just hike your skirts and climb." Charles. It was Charles's voice.

"But Victor. I must—" she began frantically.

"Victor is here, Amanda. He climbs very well. Now come quickly!"

Oh, God, could she do it? It was so steep, and she was so frightened. But her father was closing in on her, his reeking breath on her neck. Terrified, she hitched her skirts and began to climb. "Whore!" her father roared after her, and she climbed faster.

"Charles!" she screamed. "Charles!" She thrashed about, her whole body perspiring, her voice becoming raspy. She gasped for breath and then, suddenly, opened her eyes. She was in bed, her bed. She sat up, shaking. The bedclothes were rumpled. She took several deep breaths and brushed the damp hair from her eyes. Oh, God, she'd been dreaming. Another dream of her father. But this one was different. What was Charles doing in her dream?

And then, for the first time, she remembered the last nightmare, that night she was ill and Charles had given her laudanum. She realized now that he'd been here when she awoke, screaming in fear. He had held her, comforted her, and put her back to sleep. Why, he must have been here all night! She looked about the moonlit room wistfully. He was not here now to reassure her, to— She swung her feet over the side of the bed. Of course, he was not here now! Nor should he be! He did not belong in her life, nor at Millforte, and certainly not in her bedchamber in the middle of the night!

She felt chilled and slipped on her silk wrapper, then began to pace the carpeted floor. This dream was most disturbing, and not just because of her father. He terrorized her nights, but such was not new. What *was* new was Charles—the Earl, she amended—calling out to her. And she had gone to him, or at least tried to. Why, she'd even called him "Charles"!

She wondered what she had revealed to him about her father in her delirium the night of her illness. She was persuaded it could not have been much, for he had said nothing. Of a certain he must never know how frightened she was, nor what her father had done. And she must not come to depend on him—neither awake nor asleep! She must stand on her own, protecting her son and herself. It was the only safe way. Yet in the dream, the Earl had meant safety.

No! She could never fully trust him, nor any man. She lit a taper and sank down onto the velvet chaise in the sitting alcove. She would not attempt to sleep again this night. Idly she picked up the first of the several books on the table next to her. *Le Morte d'Arthur*. No. She had no wish to read of Lancelot and Guinevere. The next book was *Electra*. She could still hear Charles's—that is, the Earl's—voice, reading to her. Sighing, she set it aside. Oh, Lord, why did she miss him so much? She meant nothing to him. All her better sense told her that, and yet she could not keep his face from her mind's eye, nor his intense, slate blue eyes, nor his arms, gently encircling her as his lips—

"No!" she actually shouted aloud and then finally settled back with the last book, *The Taming of the Shrew*. Silly of her not to wish Charles to read it to her, she mused. It had naught to do with them, after all. She was certainly not a shrew, and he was most definitely *not* her lord! Resolutely, she opened Shakespeare's play and began to read.

When the first rays of sunlight stroked her eyelids at dawn, she lay reclined on the chaise, the book still in her lap. She looked down at the leather volume and frowned. *The Taming of Shrew*? Whatever could have possessed her?

Darby knocked gingerly on his master's door. Never before had he awakened the master at the ungodly hour of eight o'clock of the morning, unless specifically requested to do so, which was rare enough indeed.

"Go away. I said not before noon. It can't possibly be noon," growled the Earl from inside the room.

Darby opened the door and walked silently toward the bedside. He reached for the dressing gown that was draped on a nearby chair and stood next to the semiwakeful form of the Earl. He held the dressing gown poised in the air so that his lordship might slip into it.

He kept his head erect and his face impassive as he said, "Forgive me, my lord, but there is a messenger here from Lady Ainsley. It is very urgent."

"Oh, blast it all! What can she possibly want now? I just left her a few hours ago," the Earl muttered as he slowly lifted himself from the bed. Darby helped him into his dressing gown, and the Earl tied the sash and distractedly smoothed his rumpled hair. "Well, bring him up here. I certainly don't intend to appear downstairs like this," his lordship said.

"Yes, my lord," said Darby, and flitted away.

The footman who entered the Earl's room within a few minutes was clearly very nervous. He stood twisting his cap unmercifully with his hands as he said, "Beggin' your lordship's pardon for intrudin' at such an hour. I know that—"

"Yes, yes, well, go on, man. What does my mother want?"

"Her ladyship fell into quite a swoon, my lord, and is beside herself, I should say, on account of Agnes—" he began.

"Agnes? Who is the world is Agnes?" demanded the Earl impatiently.

"Agnes is the girl what is Miss Kitty's maid, my lord. Well, Agnes ran straight away to her ladyship's room with the news."

"News? What news?"

"Miss Kitty's bolted, my lord. Gone with but a single bandbox, she is," replied the footman uncomfortably.

"What do you mean 'gone'? She has left the house? Just like that? When?" asked the Earl, bearing down furiously on the footman.

"Can't anyone say, my lord. Agnes went to wake her early, and—and—she just weren't there."

"Goddamn!" exploded the Earl, his fists clenched. "And I suppose the entire household knows about this?"

"Well, my lord, beggin' your pardon again, but it would be hard for anyone not to know—what with all the shoutin' and wailin' that's been goin' on. But—but, if I may say so, my lord, there isn't a one among us who doesn't love Miss Kitty. We ain't about to bear tales about town."

The Earl eyed him narrowly, wishing he could believe him. But he wasted no more time, and within three quarters of an hour found himself in his mother's sitting room.

"She left no note, and no one heard her leave?" he asked after listening to his mother's rather emotional recital of the morning's events.

The Dowager rested upon her chaise, vinaigrette in one hand and a handkerchief in the other. Her hair was disheveled, and there was a blanket across her knees. Her maid stood about attentively. "No, Charles, on both counts. And the servants are up very early, you know."

"Of course. We must assume that she left in the middle of the night. In fact, I doubt that she slept at all, regardless of the disarrayed bedcovers."

"Oh, Charles, it is too dreadful. And we have not a clue as to where that soldier resides," said the Dowager, putting the vinaigrette up to her nose and clutching at her breast with her free hand. Her maid mopped her brow with a wet cloth.

"I hardly think it would matter at this point," said the Earl grimly, his hands rigid at his sides. He was furious at Kitty and he thought he could kill that soldier, but he tried to curb his anger so as not to distress his mother further.

"Whatever do you mean?" she asked.

"They would hardly have stayed at his lodgings, Mother. That would get them nowhere. No, if I am not mistaken, they will have left quite some hours ago, and are well on their way to Gretna Green right now." He laughed bitterly to himself, thinking that he had done exactly what Amanda had warned him against, and the lovers had done exactly what she had predicted they would.

The Dowager moaned and lay her head back on the chaise. "Oh, dear. I have tried so hard to bring Kitty up properly, and it has all come to naught. I have failed miserably, Charles."

"Now, Mother, all may not be lost. I shall pursue them without delay, and with any luck, I may overtake them. My valet is at this very moment packing my things, and I gave orders for my fastest coach to be readied."

"At least I did *something* right, my dear son," she said, smiling weakly and patting his arm. "I knew you would take the matter in hand. But I fear Kitty's reputation will be damaged beyond repair."

"Not necessarily, Mother. Last night she left the ball early on pretense of being ill. Keep that pretense alive. Circulate it about that she is ill with fever and must keep to her bed for several days. And see that the servants do the same. Your footman informs me that they are quite loyal to Miss Kitty. Since it is obvious that the truth cannot be hidden from them, we shall give them the opportunity to prove their loyalty."

"Very well, Charles. But please be careful. Do not drive within an inch of your life." The Earl hid a grin as he reassured her and made a rapid exit.

Once home, he dashed off a brief message to Ridgeway, informing him that family business must take him out of town for a few days and that his friend should carry on. And then, his orders having been carried out most efficiently, he set off in his traveling coach. He had taken but a small amount of luggage, and only a groom accompanied him. Darby had not been best pleased to be left behind, but the Earl needed to travel as simply as possible. He himself was driving, and once out in the country, he took what he thought the likeliest road north, and spurred his horses to great speed.

Thomas Waring was worried about his friend. Richard had been quite shaken by his encounter with the Earl of Ainsley, and Thomas was sure that, if he had slept at all, which was unlikely, he would welcome company for breakfast. Thomas knocked at the front door and was quite overset when Richard's manservant informed him that the Captain had left precipitously in the middle of the night with a very young lady who did not look at all the type to come to a gentleman's lodgings in the middle of the night.

Thomas's first thought was that perhaps Anne would know something, since she was in Kitty's confidence. As he entered his mother's rented town house, he felt very grateful that Anne was an early riser. He would not like to alarm the household by demanding that she be awakened. He found his sister alone in the dining room, eating her breakfast. But as it was, she was duly alarmed, and completely surprised, when Thomas related all that transpired.

"Oh, my God, Thomas? What can we do?" she asked in a whisper.

"Well, if I could figure out where they'd have gone, I'd go after them. If Ainsley gets to them first, I've no doubt he'll call Richard out."

He saw Anne shudder. "There can be little doubt as to where they've gone, I think. They've gone off to elope."

"You mean to Gretna Green? No, Anne. That is not like Richard at all," said Thomas, reaching for the cup of coffee that Anne poured him.

"But it is very much like Kitty. Believe me, I know her well. She is of a very romantic nature. I don't doubt that it was her idea. Besides, tell me honestly, Thomas, if that were the only way you could wed Lydia, would you not do it?"

Thomas grinned. "All right. You've convinced me. I shall set out after them straightaway."

Anne insisted he eat something first, and then suggested that she had ought to go with him. To his vociferous protest she calmly replied, "You are afraid the Earl will call Richard out. And so he probably will, for Richard will have compromised Kitty's reputation beyond repair. You wish to find them before Ainsley does, but pray tell, what good will it do Kitty's reputation to be seen jaunting about the country with two men instead of one? You are neither one related to her, you know. At least if there is a female present, we may salvage something of the situation, and I've no doubt it would placate that dreadful Ainsley."

Thomas could not doubt her logic, nor could their mother. And as his estimable sister needed no more time than he to pack and ready herself, they shortly set off together for the north road to Scotland.

The Earl spent the first two hours of his journey alternately berating himself and his blasted temper, and cursing the foolhardy runaway couple.

He would not enjoy the drive. He had not been in London even twenty-four hours and here he was back on the road again, this time well aware that every minute counted. He was so furious at Kitty that at times he felt he ought to leave her to her fate. But he knew he could not do that. She was so very young—he could not let her ruin her life. But truth to tell, he did not know what he would accomplish by overtaking the couple, unless he found them before nightfall. Even then, it would be difficult to keep the whole affair hushed up enough for Kitty's reputation to remain intact. Once night fell, however, it would be too late. He could not know whether Captain Smythe would attempt to take advantage of Kitty before the wedding ceremony, though he did not actually think Kitty would be fool enough to succumb. But, of course, as far as society was concerned, it made no difference. The truth was that, when all was said and done, Kitty might have no choice but to marry this spurious Captain Smythe.

But that was only part of the reason that his heart was not fully committed to this pursuit. He resented careening about the countryside after this silly child. He would much have preferred to have remained at Millforte. He missed Amanda, and found that he very much wanted to see her again. Ridgeway's findings, or lack of findings, had not in any way shocked him. In fact, he would have been surprised had Ridgeway indeed come up with any evidence to support the rumors about Amanda.

He had not had much time to think about what he and Ridgeway had discussed, so caught up in Kitty's nefarious adventures had he of necessity been. But as he held the reins over the long monotonous road north, he felt an unmistakable sensation of relief creep through him. He had known all along—well—almost all along; his instincts had been right. He could not wait to see Amanda again. They had been playing games long enough, doing an elaborate dance to sidestep each other. It was time they had a very long talk.

As such he became increasingly frustrated at the prospect of continuing north for several more days, when in fact every part of his being ached to go west.

Several hours outside of London the Earl espied a posting inn, and as he had eaten no breakfast, he decided to take an early luncheon. Besides, it was just possible that the errant couple had stopped here, perhaps at dawn, for fresh horses and something to eat. It would be wise to ensure that his conjecture as to their destination was correct. He could not imagine that he could be wrong, but better to find out now than in two days' time.

And so began a pattern that would repeat itself over and over. He questioned the innkeeper and his wife, who revealed that travelers of quality had indeed come round earlier. "A Mr. Brown and his lovely sister off to visit their mother what is sick, poor dear. Such a beautiful girl, with golden hair, and the prettiest bonnet . . ." the innkeeper's wife went on.

So he had been right. But "Mr. Brown?" Why, that was almost as bad as "Smythe"! At least they had the sense to travel as brother and sister, but then, not everyone would be as gullible as the innkeeper's wife. The innkeeper looked as though he'd believe anything for the right amount of money, and the Earl found himself hoping that Kitty's "Mr. Brown" had plenty of gold coins with him.

By nightfall a much perturbed Earl still had not overtaken them, though all evidence told him his northern route was, indeed, correct. Now it seemed that they would *have* to marry, he thought angrily. But he could not give up. The late afternoon of the second day found him at a crossroads, however. For the innkeeper at the rather rundown King's Crossing Inn insisted that it was a westerly direction they had taken from there. A housemaid and the innkeeper's daughter corroborated the story, and so, against all his instincts, for such was *not* the way to Gretna Green, the Earl proceeded west.

By midmorning the next day he was thoroughly confused, and more than a little vexed. At every stop he had confirmed that the couple were indeed heading west. But where the devil were they going? Surely this Captain Smythe-Brown could not have gone so far out of his way just to confuse his pursuers. The Earl thought grimly that perhaps he had no intention of marrying Kitty at all. But no, if it was her money he was

273

after, Gretna Green could be his only destination. So where the hell—

Presently the Earl realized that the terrain was beginning to look very familiar. It made no sense, but every testimony had led him to this very road in Shropshire, the one he'd taken to Millforte. Damn the chit! What was he to do now? There was not another posting inn for quite some way, nor any sign of the couple, nor anyone to ask. Oh, blast it all! He'd had enough of Kitty and her spurious Captain! They'd already spent two nights together at all events; the damage was done.

Besides, he guessed that he was no more than an hour from Millforte. And suddenly his need to see Amanda seemed much greater than Kitty's need of him. And he reminded himself that he had no idea where to go from here; perhaps Amanda *would* have. She seemed to possess quite a store of good sense, although he did not particularly relish telling her of the display of temper that had led to this mad flight in the first place.

And so it was that the sixth day after he had left Millforte, the Earl once more appeared on the doorstep of that stately manor. The door was opened, as always, by the upright Jeffries, but the Earl thought for one moment that he detected, rather than the surprise he would have expected on the butler's normally impassive face, a decided look of anxiety. It was so fleeting that his lordship told himself he was being fanciful.

Jeffries greeted him with his usual warmth and informed him that her ladyship was in the library. "I shall announce you without delay, my lord," said the butler.

"Never mind, Jeffries. I shall go myself," said the Earl, and strode quickly to the library, giving only a passing thought to the fact that he was bringing all of his traveling dirt with him.

He knocked softly on the closed door and entered immediately. Amanda rose from her desk as soon as he came in, a slight smile on her face. She glided toward him and extended her hand. God, he thought, but she was exquisite. He noted that she looked pale, even strained, but she said quite calmly, "What a pleasant surprise, Cousin Charles."

"The pleasure is mine, I do assure you, Amanda," he responded, raising her hand to his lips. It was almost uncanny the way she managed to appear so calm all the time. She was not in the least bit ruffled by his unexpected appearance. For a moment he found himself staring at her. She was wearing the same black muslin and lace dress she had worn on the first day he had come to Millforte. He looked at those translucent sea green eyes and that luscious hair that tormented him in his sleep. She did not say a word, but stood before him, her eyes searching his, and he finally remembered his manners.

"Amanda, do forgive me for this unexpected intrusion, but the strangest thing has happened."

"Cousin Charles, before you begin, there is something I must tell you," she interrupted.

"Yes, of course, my dear, but allow me to explain my arrival first. You see, the day I arrived in London, or rather, that night, there was a ball. I found Kitty—"

"You must listen to me, Cousin. My brother is here," said Amanda.

"Your brother? Why, how nice for you, Amanda. I know how you have missed him. But do let me finish, for I need your advice. Then you shall tell me all about your brother," the Earl went on rapidly, his voice growing louder as he continued. "You see, I found Kitty and that soldier of fortune in the garden at the Cheswick ball, in a very secluded spot in the garden, you must know. And I suppose I should have followed your advice, but that I was simply beside myself with fury and—"

"Cousin, my brother has brought a girl with him. He wants to marry her," Amanda interjected, her voice also a bit louder.

"My felicitations. I wish the couple happy. But do attend, Amanda. At this point I am sure I do not know what to do. You see, I gave them both quite a set-down, and told Kitty that it was off to the country for her the very next morning," the Earl explained, his voice by now quite loud, for he had the feeling Amanda was not listening. He began to pace the floor as he felt the frustration of the whole affair welling up inside of him. "I was awakened early the next morning by the dastardly news that the two of them had—"

"Charles!" shouted Amanda, coming toward him. "You are not attending me!" She put her hand on his arm and he stopped pacing, very aware of that hand and the fact that she had used his name without a title for the first time. He stared into her eyes.

"My brother is here," she repeated, her voice firm, "and he has brought a girl with him." Suddenly her voice became very soft, and there was a pleading look in her eyes. "He loves her very much, Charles, and he wants to do right by her."

Suddenly his eyes widened and enlightenment dawned. "Kitty," he said, almost under his breath. "Your brother is—is Kitty's soldier of fortune!" he spluttered. Amanda sighed and dropped her hand.

The Earl began to pace the room furiously, his brows knit together at their most ominous. "How dare he! How dare he treat her so! I'll murder him! Where are they, Amanda? Where are they?" he shouted menacingly.

"Calm down, Charles. I will take you to them presently," said Amanda quietly.

"Calm down? Not a chance, Amanda. And I'm going to wring her neck while I am at it. The ungrateful, disobedient chit! What kind of man is he anyway, Amanda? An elopment of all things! Why the hell did he not present himself and pay his addresses in the appropriate manner? Why this charade of Captain Smythe? Where is he? It's no use attempting to protect him, Amanda!" he raged.

"Charles, don't you know why he did it?" asked Amanda tensely.

"No, I do not, Amanda. I do not know why a young man chooses to behave so disgracefully, and to ruin a young, innocent—"

"He did it because of me," said Amanda, her voice strangely flat.

"What are you talking about?"

"He did it because of me, because of—of—all of the things—they are saying about me—in London," she said with difficulty.

The Earl stopped dead in his tracks. "How do you know about that?"

"Richard told me just now," replied Amanda quietly, looking down at her hands.

He came to stand before her. "Amanda, I—" he began softly.

She looked up at him. There was moisture in her eyes, but her voice was angry as she said, "Which was more than you ever did, Charles. Why did you not—"

"Oh, come now, Amanda. What did you expect me to say, 'My dear Lady Millforte, in London they tell the most scandalous stories of your amorous activities. Tell me, are they true?' Really, Amanda—"

"No, I suppose it was better to assume they were true and act accordingly. Oh, my dear Lord Ainsley, so much is clear to me now," she said bitterly.

"Just what do you mean by that?" he retorted.

"That night in the library. I could not comprehend why you spoke to me that way. It just did not make sense. But now, of course, 'tis perfectly clear. If the lady is so generous with her favors then why should you not have your share!" she shouted.

"Amanda! Stop talking like that!" He stepped closer and took her hands in his.

She quickly pulled away. "Well? Was it not just that way, Charles?"

He blanched at the memory of his behavior that night. "Amanda, I—I cannot deny that. But you must believe that I have regretted it ever since. From that time onward I realized—"

"You realized what, Charles? Oh, come now—you shall lead me a dance no longer. What a superb actor you have been! That day in the hut—and 'promise me the next dance, Amanda.' Oh, you have been very good. I thank God that despite the things you said, and the way you looked at me, I always knew at the back of my mind what contempt you harbored," she spat out, turning and crossing to the fireplace.

The Earl did not know when he had felt so miserable, nor out of control of his situation. He strode toward her and put his hands on her shoulders. "Amanda, you are wrong. Very wrong. Before I met you, of course I believed the on dits. You were a name without a face. I had no reason not to. But as soon as I arrived I began to doubt, and after a while I knew they could not be true."

His voice was soft and as he turned her round to face him she felt a shiver go through her. She wanted so much to melt into his arms, but she knew that she must not. Her instincts had been right and she would never trust him again. She forced herself to hold her head erect and look him coldly in the eye, and after a moment he dropped his arms from her shoulders and sighed.

"Dammit, Amanda! I have never shown so much restraint with a woman in my life. Do you think I would have done that did I not have the utmost respect for you?"

He thought he saw her eyes fill with moisture, but she quickly turned away and walked to the window to the right of the desk. "I think we have quite exhausted this subject, Charles," she said coolly. "You hold the future of two human beings, my brother and your ward, in your hands. What are you going to do about them?" she asked quietly.

The Earl thought the predicament of the runaway couple very trifling compared with the problem he was now having with Amanda, but he would have to deal with them sooner or later. Somehow he found that his anger at them had completely dissipated. He came to stand near Amanda at the window which overlooked the rear gardens.

"What kind of prospects does he have, Amanda?" he asked tiredly as the couple suddenly came into sight, strolling arm in arm in the courtyard.

She told him about Richard's inheritance and his plans for the future, what little he had been able to blurt out when the rather disheveled couple had appeared on her doorstep in the early morning. "Richard never had any intention of going to Gretna Green, you know. He considered that a highly dishonorable course."

"But he went north from London," said the Earl, perplexed.

"He did not want Kitty to know that he intended to bring her here. Do you know that she arrived at his lodgings in the middle of the night and threatened to run off by herself if he would not carry her to Gretna Green?"

"What had he intended to do once he got here?"

"All he could think of was to leave her with me until such time as he could declare himself to be Richard Talbot and hold his head up in society. He had only been in London a very short time when he met her. And, in fact, had only just found out about—about the—stories circulating. His friend Thomas Waring informed him upon his arrival in London that something untoward was afoot. Thomas, by the way, is the one who introduced Richard to Kitty."

"And how does Thomas know Kitty?"

"I believe, if I understood it correctly, for they were both talking at once for a full half hour when they arrived, that Thomas's sister, Anne, is Kitty's oldest friend," Amanda replied, turning to look at the Earl, a slight smile on her face.

"Ah, yes, I have met Anne, I believe." He stared again at the couple down below and sighed. "If they truly have formed a lasting affection, then I have no wish to interfere. I will insist that they wait until the end of the Season, however, for Kitty is very young. If at that time she is of the same mind, I will countenance the wedding."

"Thank you, Charles," said Amanda, her hand lightly touching his arm. "He will be a good husband to her."

"I wish them happy," said Charles softly, looking into her eyes. She quickly dropped her hand and looked away. "In the meantime, I must, I suppose, join forces with Richard to see if we can ferret out the source of these disgusting stories," he continued.

"No, Charles, I beg you will not—" Amanda began, but stopped when the door burst open.

"I say, Mandy—" Richard called, and then he stopped short, Kitty at his heels. "Oh!" He gulped. "Your lordship—I—I—" he spluttered, his eyes widening at the sight of his sister standing not a foot away from the Earl of Ainsley!

Chapter Eighteen

"Cousin Charles!" gasped Kitty, moving slightly out from behind Richard.

"As you see, Kitty," the Earl countered smoothly, bowing slightly.

For one moment after that there was silence, everyone seemingly frozen in place. Finally Amanda moved forward toward the couple. "Well, come in, Richard, Kitty. I think perhaps we might all sit down. There is much to talk about."

Amanda ushered the rather reluctant couple to the comfortable leather sofa, and she turned to the Earl, motioning for him to join them. He sauntered over to the fireplace, which stood just to the side of the sofa, and assumed a comfortable pose, leaning one arm on the mantel. Amanda took a chair directly across from Kitty and Richard.

"I must say you two led me a merry chase," he said sternly.

"I—I am sorry, my lord. I am afraid I had little choice," said Richard quietly.

"You could have come to me, could you not, and explained your situation? Even waking me in the middle of the night, once Kitty had come to your lodgings, would have been preferable to this mad dash across the country," the Earl admonished, looking from Richard to Kitty and back.

"Forgive me, my lord, but I had reason to believe that you would not be—amenable to talking with me. I—I did try—in the garden sir, if you remember," replied Richard.

The Earl frowned. "And if you will remember, Richard, your disgraceful behavior with my ward gave me ample cause to murder the pair of you!"

"It would seem that you missed the first part of our conversation, my lord," Richard ventured.

"What I heard could hardly be construed as conversation!" exclaimed the Earl, whereupon Kitty blushed a deep red, and Richard shifted uncomfortably in his seat.

Then the young man took Kitty's hand in his and looked directly at the Earl. "What you did not hear, my lord, was my telling Kitty that we must not see each other again, until such time as I was able to declare myself openly to your lordship and beg leave to pay my addresses in the prescribed manner."

The Earl was silent for several moments. He was painfully aware that it was his fit of temper which had precipitated this entire escapade. "You were two nights on the road. I assume, Richard, that you conducted yourself as a gentleman," he said at length.

Suddenly Kitty jumped up from the sofa. "Cousin Charles, what can you be thinking?" she exclaimed.

"Sit down, Kitty!" said the Earl rather fiercely. "For a girl who thinks nothing of arriving at a man's lodgings in the middle of the night and then jaunting about the country with him for two and one-half days, you have no right to take exception to such a question."

Kitty did as she was told.

"There has never been any question of—unbecoming conduct, my lord. And we traveled as brother and sister," said Richard.

"So I was told. Well, perhaps we may salvage

something of all this, after all. Although how we may explain Kitty's absence from London for some five days for the moment escapes me." The Earl could see that Kitty and Richard were regarding him nervously. He had kept them in suspense long enough. He sighed and then, taking several steps toward them, said, "Kitty is very young, Richard. I wish her to have a London Season. If, at the end of that time, you are both still of the same mind, I shall give you my blessing."

Kitty's hand flew to her mouth and her eyes filled with tears. "Thank you, Cousin Charles. Thank you," she mumbled.

Richard rose from his seat and walked to the Earl. He shook his hand. "You shan't regret this, my lord, I promise you. I love her very much, and I—I will take good care of her," said Richard, his voice strong for the first time.

The Earl looked from Kitty to Richard and smiled. "The pleasure is all yours, Richard. Let her lead *you* a merry chase from now on."

Richard walked over to Amanda, who was now standing up beside her chair, and they embraced. The Earl saw that she, too, had tears in her eyes. He did not want to bring up the next subject, but he knew it must be said.

"This little episode is not finished, however. You will all kindly recall that there was a reason that Richard did not—er—make himself known at the outset. Richard, I fear that you and I have quite a bit of work to do—"

"No, Charles," interrupted Amanda, but her sentence was never completed, for there was a knock on the door and Jeffries immediately entered the library.

"Pardon the intrusion, your lordship, your ladyship," said the butler, bowing his head, "but there are a young man and young woman here, wanting most urgently to speak to your ladyship. Something about your brother, my lady."

All eyes flew to the door as a commotion arose in the doorway. Jeffries stepped aside, his normally impassive face looking quite shocked at this breach of protocol, for into the room marched a small, brown-haired young lady followed by a tall, good-looking man.

"Thomas!" exclaimed Richard, jumping up. "What are you—"

"Anne!" gasped Kitty.

"Lord Ainsley!" blurted Thomas, his brows shot up in surprise.

The Earl nodded in response, and for a moment after that no one spoke. Everyone, the Earl noted, was gaping at everyone else, trying to make some sense of the scene. Finally he broke the silence.

"You, I presume, must be Mr. Thomas Waring," he said, striding toward the middle of the room.

"Yes, my lord. I—" began Thomas, much flustered.

"You are surprised to see me? Let us guess, Waring. You were perhaps hoping to reach Richard before I did and somehow help him avoid my wrath?" asked the Earl, a decided glint in his eye.

Suddenly Amanda bustled forward. "Do come in, Mr. Waring," she said amiably, and then turning to Anne, "And you must be Anne. I have only just met Kitty today and she has already spoken of you. Come and sit down, my dear."

Amanda led Anne to the sofa, and the Earl thought that her gentle tone had a calming effect on everyone. The group seemed to visibly relax, and Amanda made all the necessary introductions. The Earl ambled back to his pose at the fireplace and Amanda, once she had seated everyone else, turned to Jeffries, who had not moved from the doorway.

"Jeffries, please inform Cook that we will be six for luncheon. I should like to dine in one-half hour. I am persuaded our travelers must be very hungry indeed. Oh, and do bring some refreshment—sherry will be fine, I think."

"Amanda," said the Earl, "I should think lemonade for—"

"No, Charles. The girls have had as trying a day as the rest of us, you must own."

"Very well, my dear. As her ladyship says, Jeffries," he said, grinning, and was rewarded by an angry look in those green eyes.

"Now, where were we?" continued the Earl. "Ah, yes, Mr. Waring is surprised to see me here. I, in turn, am somewhat taken aback to see him, but upon reflection I find it most commendable that he has tried to help his friend. But Miss Waring, I do confess my inability to comprehend why *you* chose to join this mad cross-country pursuit."

His lordship was even more nonplussed by the clear, steady voice in which the diminutive girl answered. "'Tis really very simple, my lord. We were concerned, Thomas and I, about Kitty's—reputation, you see. I felt that if we did indeed overtake them, it would much improve matters if she were to be seen traveling with another female."

"Ah, finally we encounter one person who has acted with a modicum of common sense in this whole idiotic affair. I commend you, my dear," said the Earl, bowing slightly.

Thomas and his sister both looked rather uncomfortable and the Earl smiled and said more softly, "I am afraid you are too late to help your friend, Mr. Waring. You see, I have already decided not to murder him. Rather, I have told both of these errant, though very determined, young people that at the end of the Season, if they are both of them steadfast on this course, I shall countenance a wedding."

Thomas shot a surprised look at Richard and said

285

nothing, but Anne leaned over to Kitty, who sat next to her on the sofa, and took her hands. "Oh, my dear, dear Kitty. I am so, so happy for you," she said in a soft voice. "You see, everything *has* worked out."

His lordship looked over at Amanda, standing behind the sofa, and was much gratified to see her regarding him with a most indulgent smile. Perhaps he could yet make some headway with that proud and headstrong lady.

Jeffries entered at that moment and served the sherry all around. As soon as he had departed, the Earl strolled to stand next to Amanda behind the sofa.

"Now that we have perhaps cleared the air, we have, ladies and gentlemen," the Earl began, "two problems remaining to us. I believe that Mr. and Miss Waring have provided the solution to the first by their rather unexpected arrival." Several bewildered faces turned to him and he continued. "Yes, I think this solution will do nicely. There is the problem, you all must know, of how to explain Kitty's absence from London for some five days without setting all the nasty tongues wagging. Thus, we shall all arrive back in London together and shall give out the story that it was recommended that Kitty take several days of country air in order to cure the indisposition that she has suffered since the night of the Cheswick ball. We have all, therefore, been on an outing, a visit to an elderly aunt of mine in, say, Warwickshire. That should satisfy the worst of the gossip mongers, that is, if Mr. and Miss Waring have no objection to complicity in such a havey-cavey affair," said the Earl, grinning as he said this last.

"Not at all, my lord," said Thomas. "We came here to be of help. When do you suggest that we leave?"

"I suppose we had ought to leave as soon as possible," he replied, rather reluctantly, turning to Amanda, who stood not three feet away from him.

"But not before luncheon," said Amanda.

"But not before luncheon, Waring, as the lady says," echoed the Earl.

"My lord," said Richard, standing up. "You mentioned two problems. The second, I assume, is that of—"

"Precisely, Richard. You and I must work together now to uncover—"

"Ahem," Jeffries interrupted from the doorway. He looked most distressed, which was so unlike him that the Earl became alarmed. He started forward but Amanda put her arm out to stop him. He looked up at her as he felt her hand on his sleeve, but she turned to the butler.

"What is it, Jeffries?"

"Ah—excuse me, your ladyship, my lord," he said, bowing, "I'm sure I do not know what can be done, but—but—Miss Lavinia Prescott and Mr.—er— Andrew Linfield have come to call," Jeffries said reluctantly, his shoulders just a trifle hunched over.

"Oh, dear, this *is* a busy day," Amanda remarked.

"Linfield! What is *he* doing here, Amanda?" demanded the Earl a bit too harshly, he realized.

Amanda's fingers tightened on his arm. He looked down at the delicate white hand that was partially hidden with black lace and felt even angrier at Linfield.

"He is a guest in my house, Charles," she whispered. Then she said calmly to Jeffries, "I cannot very well turn them out, when it is so obvious that I have visitors. Show them in, Jeffries, and tell Cook we shall be eight for luncheon."

Lavinia Prescott was delighted. She had seen several hats and pairs of gloves, including a woman's, on the trestle table in the hall. And Jeffries had appeared decidedly uncomfortable when she and Linfield had, purely by accident, appeared at the front door together. Amanda must have some very interesting visitors indeed.

Lavinia was not disappointed. The first thing she saw upon entering the library was Amanda quickly removing her hand from the coat sleeve of the Earl of Ainsley, from whom she stood not a foot away.

Amanda moved toward the doorway and ushered Lavinia and Mr. Linfield in. She performed all the proper introductions, but as she gave no reason for the sudden appearance of all these people at Millforte, Lavinia began to speculate wildly. That pretty fair-haired girl was sitting very close to Captain Talbot. So close that their knees were almost touching, and no one seemed to mind in the least. Hmm, she thought. There must be something there. Strange that Amanda had never mentioned anything.

Lavinia's musings were cut regretfully short, however, by Jeffries's announcement of luncheon. As they all strolled out to the corridor, Lavinia found herself watching the petite dark-haired girl. Anne, she believed her name was. Such sensitive eyes, and such a pretty smile.

When they entered the dining room, Lavinia noticed two nosegays of violets on either end of the sideboard. Must be yesterday's and today's offerings, she thought with a chuckle. The table, she noted, held a large basket of deep red roses. The ivory porcelain, trimmed with gold, looked lovely on the ecru tablecloth, and Lavinia marveled at the grace of Amanda's table, which of necessity must have been hastily arranged.

The little group seemed fairly relaxed, all except Lord Ainsley, who hadn't stopped glaring at Linfield, and Linfield, who kept glancing covertly at Amanda. Lavinia moved closer to Amanda, who was talking with Anne. "Your house is simply beautiful, Lady Millforte. The frescoes near the ceiling in this room are exquisite," said Anne, and then glancing about the room, added, "And I do so love flowers. Ah—violets! How delightful they are!"

Lavinia thought her eyes would pop out of her head. Violets! Out of the corner of her eye she noted that the Earl's face, too, held an arrested expression. The child likes violets! And such a sweet child, too. She wondered—well, it was worth a try, but she would have to work very fast. She smiled soothingly at the Earl.

Amanda had made some polite reply to Anne, and Lavinia distracted her for a moment. She whispered a hastily devised seating arrangement and a few instructions into her hostess's ear and said, "Trust me, my dear."

She was gratified that Amanda followed her suggestion, and within a few moments they were all seated. Amanda and the Earl sat across from each other, at the head and foot of the table. Anne sat between Linfield and Lavinia, and she hoped the Earl would not have the apoplexy over the fact that Linfield was next to Amanda. Amanda's brother and the golden-haired girl, Kitty, were cooing at each other across from her, and there was little doubt as to what was afoot there, although not a word was said about it.

Amanda was talking animatedly to Anne's brother, as Lavinia had instructed, so that Linfield had no choice but to turn to Anne and herself.

"It is so refreshing to find someone who appreciates flowers, Miss Waring," said Lavinia. "And do you like the country, then?"

"Oh yes, I love the country. This is my first Season in London, but I own I shall not be sorry to return home," said Anne candidly.

"Mr. Linfield, you, too, if I am not mistaken, prefer your estate to the bustle and chaos of London. Is that not so?" asked Lavinia.

"Why, yes, actually," said Linfield to both of them, smiling and, Lavinia noticed, looking at Anne for the first time now that he was forced to talk to her. "I confess I am a devoted farmer."

"Are you?" asked Anne animatedly, her eyes looking directly into Linfield's. "I think that is wonderful. 'Tis so sad when men own land and do not appreciate it. Where is your estate, may I ask, Mr. Linfield?"

The conversation from that point needed no help from Lavinia. She turned to the Earl. He had finally stopped glaring at Linfield and instead sat watching Anne and Linfield deep in discussion, a rather amused look on his face.

The potato soup had been replaced by a delicious plate of cold glazed duckling, and as Lavinia helped herself to a slice, the Earl leaned forward and whispered, "My compliments, madam. You are a shrewd judge of human nature. I could not have done better myself."

"Thank you, my lord. I thought you might approve," Lavinia replied, a gleam in her eye.

After the third cover had been removed, a most delectable trifle was served, but Lavinia felt it was time for her next move. She grimaced and shifted uncomfortably in her chair. Her hand went to her brow, and she sighed rather loudly.

"Miss Prescott," said the Earl, "are you feeling quite the thing?"

"Oh, I suppose. I confess I do feel a trifle warm."

Anne turned away from Linfield for the first time. "Miss Prescott, may I help you?" Lavinia sighed again. Anne called to Amanda, deep in conversation with Mr. Waring and Captain Talbot. "Lady Millforte, could we perhaps open one of the French doors?"

"Why, what—" began Amanda as she looked toward them. "Why Lavinia, my dear, what is it?"

"Oh, 'tis nothing. I—I do not know. Mr.—Mr. Linfield—could I—prevail upon you—to—to—drive me home? Perhaps if I could lie down for a bit—"

"Lavinia, you are more than welcome to rest here, you know," said Amanda.

"Thank you, my dear, do forgive me, but I fear I will be much better off at home. That is—if—if Mr. Linfield does not mind . . ." Her voice trailed off.

"Why, of course not, Miss Prescott," said Mr. Linfield, more than a little reluctantly, thought Lavinia, delighted.

"Do you have your—your carriage here, Mr. Linfield?" Lavinia asked, breathing unevenly.

"Why, yes, Miss Prescott. You shall be most comfortable, I do assure you."

"Thank you, Mr. Linfield. Then perhaps—perhaps you would not—mind—if—if—Miss Waring were to accompany us. She is so kind and would be—a comfort to me—I am persuaded."

Linfield needed little convincing. His eyes fairly lit up at the idea, and Anne blushed a lovely shade of pink.

"Miss Waring, would you—" Lavinia began.

"I shall be delighted, Miss Prescott," Anne said softly.

Out of the corner of her eye Lavinia saw Thomas Waring frown and open his mouth as if to say something, but Amanda forestalled him. "Perhaps, Mr. Linfield, you will allow me to offer the assistance of one of my grooms. It is a long ride—he can drive if you should tire, and he would, of course, act as chaperone for the ride back," said Amanda.

Lavinia saw Thomas Waring relax in his seat, and Linfield said, "Thank you, Lady Millforte. You are most kind. I shall, of course, accept your offer."

They were gone within minutes, and the Earl thought he saw Amanda heave a sigh of relief. He smiled, thinking that the machinations of Miss Prescott, who, he had no doubt, was as healthy as a horse, were little short of brilliant. And Amanda's notion of the groom certainly helped tremendously, for Linfield could ride home with Anne in the carriage while the groom drove. Anne seemed a pleasant enough young girl. It would be amusing to see if anything developed from the afternoon's activities. But in any case, Linfield seemed to have been weaned from Amanda, and the Earl was heartily gratified by the fact that Amanda had apparently been a most willing participant in the entire charade. He smiled at her now, but she returned him a cold stare.

"My compliments, Amanda. You and Miss Prescott have done a good day's work between you," he said smoothly.

She glared at him and said frostily, "I cannot think what you mean, Charles." Suddenly she rose from the table, excused herself, and gracefully exited the room.

The Earl stared after her, his face a mass of emotions. He stood up, barely aware that Thomas, Richard, and Kitty gazed unabashedly at him as he threw his napkin down, muttered "Damn!" under his breath, and marched out of the room.

"Now just a minute, Ainsley," called Richard, somewhat anxiously, rising from his seat. He did not at all like the menacing look on the Earl's face as he followed Mandy out of the room. But Thomas pulled him back into his seat.

"Take it easy, old boy," said Thomas.

"No, Thomas. You have no idea what a temper that man has."

"But I think your sister *does* know. Let them settle it themselves," replied Thomas.

"Why should I allow my sister to be subjected to his—his unbridled wrath?"

"He'll not harm her, Richard," said Thomas quietly. "I think he is in love with her."

"What are you talking about?" exclaimed Richard.

"If you two would stop making sheep's eyes at each other, you might see beyond the end of your fingertips. It's as plain as pikestaff to me. Although I do not know if *he* knows it yet." Thomas grinned broadly.

"But it's impossible! Not Cousin Charles, Thomas," declared Kitty, quite incredulous.

"My dear Kitty," said Thomas, much amused, "I do assure you, it is quite possible. You see, in the end, even the best of us succumb."

"Well, I'll be damned!" blurted Richard, and then, "Oh, begging your pardon, Kitty."

Thomas saw Kitty look quite adoringly at Richard, and before they became too oblivious of their surroundings, he said, "I say, Richard, what about this Linfield chap? Do you know him? I cannot like it that Anne has gone off with a man I've never met, but I did not see a way to stop her without creating a scene."

Richard turned back to Thomas. "I agree that you had little choice, Thomas. But you needn't worry. Mandy would never have allowed Anne to go off like that had he not been perfectly unexceptionable. Nice-looking fellow, too," said Richard, but then his eyes went to Kitty's, and he took her hand, and Thomas could see that they were lost to him.

He sighed and rose from the table, intending to take a walk toward the stables, thinking wryly to himself that the horses would probably provide better companionship today than anyone else.

The Earl knocked softly on Amanda's door. He was feeling very frustrated, even angry, but he could not afford a fit of temper now. "Amanda," he called gently, "we must talk."

"There is nothing to talk about. Please leave," came the answer from within.

His lordship hesitated only a moment before opening the door. Amanda was standing at the window. He shut the door behind him and walked toward her.

"Amanda," he said, coming to stand next to her, "I

293

do not want to leave this way. Surely you—"

"Charles, I have made very clear how I feel. That you see fit to burst into my room uninvited has not given me cause to change my mind."

"Amanda, I—I made a very human error. But after that, I do assure you, my motivation was quite different." His voice was soft and his eyes warm. He did not know what else to say.

But Amanda turned cold eyes on him and said, "Had you not ought to prepare for your journey, Charles?"

"Amanda!" he said fiercely, grabbing her by the elbows and pulling her close. "Can you really tell me that there has been nothing between us, nothing that is worth saving?"

"Whatever was between us was a sham, Charles, a complete sham," she replied, her voice flat and aloof.

He dropped his hands. "Very well, Amanda. It shall be as you wish," he said quietly. "But there is one thing more which we must discuss. I need your help. Richard and I must now join forces to try to uncover the source of the—the distasteful stories which have circulated about. We must put a stop to them once and for all. Your name must be cleared."

"No, Charles," she said adamantly.

"Of course it must. And now I needs must ask you please to think—I know this is painful for you, Amanda—but do think—is there anyone who for any reason may have taken you in dislike, or who may have been unwittingly hurt by you?"

"No!" Amanda protested. "I'll not have the two of you to be gadding about London like two white knights on some misguided mission to avenge my honor. There is nothing wrong with my honor and I will not have any part of this. Do you understand?"

"You are being ridiculous, Amanda. There is no question of dishonor, but still your name must be cleared. I would I could have spared you this, my dear, but in truth you could not hold your head up in society today."

"Then society be damned!" she shouted between clenched teeth. "I have no need of them. Oh, go away, Charles Ainsley, go back to your London society and leave me in peace!" She put her hands to her temples and turned away from him.

"I cannot do that, Amanda," he said softly.

"Why, Charles?" she demanded, facing him once again. "Could it be that you still doubt? You have to trace the on dits so you may have unequivocal proof? Is that it? Is she a whore or is she not? Is that what you wondered all the time you were here, Charles?" she shrieked, her face white with fury.

"Amanda, stop it this minute!" shouted the Earl, seizing her by the shoulders.

"That's what you thought all along, isn't it, Charles? That night in the library, and then in the crofter's hut. No wonder you think nothing of entering my bedchamber unbidden at all hours—"

"No, Amanda! No!" he yelled, shaking her.

"Why bother avenging my name? Let the on dits thrive! You're wasting your time on a whore—is that not what the Squire said, Charles? Only then I did not understand. He was right, Charles. Go away and leave me alone! Do you hear me, damn you? Just go!" she screamed, her eyes filled with tears. She turned her back to him, her head bent and her arms wrapped around herself, hands clutching tightly at her elbows. She was stiff and silent for several minutes. He knew she was trying to stem the tears and longed to take her in his arms. But he knew that would be a mistake and so kept his distance.

At length Amanda picked her head up, straightened her shoulders, and turned to stare out the window. "Please go now, Charles. You have had your say," she said very quietly.

"Amanda," he breathed, moving behind her and putting his hands on her shoulders. "Can—can we now begin anew?" He felt her stiffen under his touch.

"No, Charles," she said, her voice cool. "There is nothing between us. Nor has there ever been. And I ask you again to give up this—this mission. It is humiliating in the extreme."

Charles dropped his hands from her shoulders and stood to her side, turning and looking into her eyes. He sighed. "Then if it is too late for us, Amanda, at least let it not be too late for them. You don't suppose I can allow Kitty to marry Richard if it means that every door of polite society will be closed to her, do you?"

He saw Amanda's brow furrow with anxiety and he added gently, "Please think, Amanda. Is there anyone who might have imagined herself—or himself—wronged by you in any way? People do make enemies without meaning to."

Amanda's voice was flat and lifeless as she said, "In truth, Charles, I know of no one. No one at all. Unless—but that is too preposterous."

"What is it, Amanda?"

"Well, I have only just remembered something," she said, turning to face him, "but it cannot possibly have any bearing on this—this situation. But—well—I do recall that Arthur was meant to have married someone else before he met me. They were not betrothed, but it had been arranged that he would go to meet her with the purpose being to contract a marriage. I have no idea who the woman was—I did not know even then—but it was on his way to her family seat that Arthur stopped off to visit with my father. He—he proposed to me several days after he arrived."

"Thank you, Amanda. I do not know if this will be pertinent, but we must try every manner of inquiry. I—I must go now. But I shall return soon, and we shall have a very long talk, Amanda. And I shall hold you to your promise of the next waltz," he said intently. Then he brought her hand to his lips for one moment and strode from the room.

Lavinia allowed Linfield to escort her up the stairs to Windham House. Anne remained in the carriage.

"Thank you, Mr. Linfield," Lavinia said. "You have been most kind. I am sorry to have taken you away from your luncheon."

"Think not of it, Miss Prescott. Indeed, I have quite enjoyed the ride," he replied good-naturedly.

"I am glad to hear that. It does ease my conscience somewhat. You know, Mr. Linfield, if I am not being too presumptuous, I did notice that you enjoyed Miss Waring's talk of her first impressions of London. It occurs to me, if I may say so, that you yourself might very much enjoy the gaiety of London. Perhaps you might consider a visit to the metropolis."

"Curious that you should mention it, Miss Prescott, for I have—er—very recently, considered the very same thing. But I fear I am not at liberty to do so." He said this last hesitantly.

"Why not, Mr. Linfield?" asked Lavinia, trying to keep the corners of her mouth from turning up into a grin.

"Well, I have rather befriended Lady Millforte of late. She is living very quietly now, and I am afraid that perhaps she has come to look forward to my little visits and would perceive it as—as an insult were my attentions to cease," he said quite uncomfortably.

Lavinia had to muster all of her strength of character to reply in a serious tone. "Do not trouble yourself on that head, Mr. Linfield. Lady Millforte is in mourning, and very much prefers to live quietly. I know her well and I do assure you that she will not think it amiss if you go off to London. No, Mr. Linfield, you do go on your way, and leave Lady Millforte to me."

"Very well, Miss Prescott. You have set my mind at ease. Do you have a rest now. I pray that your indisposition shall be of short duration," he said, smiling, his step light as he walked back down the stairs and on toward his carriage.

The Earl's face was grim as he assisted everyone to board the two waiting carriages in the circular drive at Millforte. Kitty and Richard would ride with him, and he elected to drive rather than sit and watch the two of them stare longingly at each other for hours at a time. Anne's eyes sparkled as she allowed Thomas to assist her into his carriage. She seemed to have enjoyed the afternoon well enough, thought the Earl wryly. Thomas regarded the Earl with a rather bemused expression which his lordship found infuriating and for which he did not care to know the reason.

Amanda had embraced Richard and the two girls and shaken Thomas's hand warmly. Now she said good-bye to the Earl with the same formality with which she had greeted him that very first day in her library. And the Earl knew that the wall she had erected around herself now was ten times thicker than any that had existed then, and he did not know how he would breach it.

But breach it he would, he told himself, no matter what it took, or how long. For as he looked into her eyes as she mouthed her cold good-bye, he saw deep anguish there, and he knew that she was suffering as much as he. Well, he would be back, very soon if it could be managed, and there would be a reckoning. Pride could be carried just so far, after all.

Chapter Nineteen

It was not until he had put quite a bit of distance between himself and Millforte Manor that the Earl was able to take his mind off the mistress of the manor and concentrate on the task ahead of him.

He realized that although he had quite easily resolved the problem of what story to tell the concerned and the curious about Kitty's absence from London, he had not even considered the problem of what to tell his mother. If he told her the truth of Richard's identity, she would undoubtedly fall into a swoon from which she was not likely to recover for days. And protestations of Amanda's innocence at this point would not help at all, not without concrete proof of the falsity of the stories. The Ton would have a titillating time of it indeed, trying to uncover a link between Kitty's trip to the country and Lady Ainsley's sudden decline.

No, he thought, his mother would have to forgive a departure from the truth for the sake of ultimate family harmony.

It was obvious, then, that if he was not to take his mother into his confidence, he could certainly not allow Kitty to go on seeing Richard. And he had seen enough today to know that they could not be kept apart if both were in London. Besides, he realized,

Richard's presence in London presented a problem of another sort. He could not very well continue to call himself Captain Smythe, only to appear later as Captain Talbot, betrothed husband of Catherine Berenson. And were he to present himself now as Richard Talbot, the snubs he would receive would only be more damage needing to be undone.

There was no help for it. The Earl knew now what must be done, and so after the next stop, he had the groom drive and climbed inside the coach with Kitty and Richard. He explained the problem of his mother. "You must see, Kitty, that she would never accept Richard under present circumstances. Much as I find it distasteful to be less than forthright, I think it best that, until those circumstances change, we give the impression that this entire affair is terminated." Kitty's lower lip protruded in a decided pout, and he was prepared to quell her inevitable objections. But he was very pleased when Richard did it for him.

"Kitty, we must heed his lordship. If our future happiness can be assured through some temporary hardship, then so be it. I have told you before, I would not see you estranged from your family. The Earl is right. I am in no better position to see you openly than I was before. And now that I think on it, Ainsley, my very presence in London is particularly ticklish. I naturally want to do my part to unravel this web of deceit surrounding our family names, but I cannot very well do it as Richard Talbot. And I know," he said, smiling, "that Richard Smythe was looked upon at least by some as a rather havey-cavey fellow."

"Precisely, Richard. I have cudgeled my brain these last several hours over this very dilemma. If you will both be guided by me, I think we can manage to pull this off." Richard nodded and Kitty, after a moment's hesitation, assented as well. "Good. Now, Richard, I do think it best that you absent yourself from London altogether. Has the legal work been completed for you to take possession of your inheritance?" asked the Earl.

"No. It will not be for several weeks that—"

"All right. I thought as much. Allow me then to offer you the use of my estate in Surrey. 'Tis not far from London, and I have several fine horses stabled there. When we reach London I shall compose a letter of introduction to my estate manager. I think it best if you were to leave the very day after we arrive. The less you are seen, the simpler our task, I am persuaded."

Kitty started to protest but Richard firmly forestalled her, patting her hand as he accepted the Earl's offer.

"Now, Kitty," the Earl continued, "I intend to tell my mother that I have dispatched this matter satisfactorily and that you will be guided entirely by me, which is, in fact, the truth. You will be contrite over the trouble you have caused, which you ought in any case to be, and you will allow yourself to be squired about London in the usual fashion. A few days' mild distress will be expected, but after that you must enjoy yourself. No moping about the house, and you must not refuse to see any callers. I shall make sure my mother does not force the attentions of any one particular gentleman upon you, but I do expect you to be charming to all. Is that quite clear?"

"Yes, Cousin. Quite clear," Kitty snapped, and the Earl smiled in satisfaction.

They traveled late into the evening, finally disembarking along with Thomas and Anne at the Black Stallion Inn. Since all had stopped there at different times within a very few days, their arrival of necessity caused a deal of comment. But the crest on the Earl's traveling coach, the imperious authority of his voice, and the gold sovereigns he handed the proprietor

301

seemed to quell any overly abundant curiosity.

After a reasonably palatable dinner, the Earl composed a message to the Dowager, to be sent by mail coach the next day. He informed her that Kitty had been found, and that she should give out the story that Kitty had gone with her guardian and some friends on a visit to the country, so to recover from her indisposition. Even if the message arrived only one day before his little party did, thought the Earl, it would have been worthwhile.

Kitty enjoyed a long gossip with Anne after dinner, and that seemed to cheer his ward somewhat. That and the fact that Richard was always at her side, gentle and encouraging, whenever she seemed apt to become dejected. But the Earl noted that Richard was not moved by the fluttering of feminine eyelashes. When Kitty would have quietly led Richard off to an adjoining room where they might be private, it was Richard, not the Earl, who reminded her that this was a public inn and such behavior would not do at all. The Earl found his opinion of this young man rising steadily, and the remainder of the trip passed uneventfully.

It was in the early evening two days later that the Earl's traveling coach drew up at his mother's house. Kitty was suitably contrite, and if the Dowager thought it amazing that Kitty was not quaking before her formidable guardian, she said nothing.

"It pleases me that you have come to understand the wisdom of what we are trying to do for you, Catherine. You are indeed fortunate that the Earl has saved you from a most disastrous course, and has contrived to salvage your reputation as well. Not many girls who run off as you did are so fortunate," intoned the Dowager as she rested upon the velvet settee in the drawing room.

"Yes, Aunt," said Kitty meekly, standing before her. "I—I am truly sorry for having caused you concern."

"That's a good child. And you understand that you may not see that—that Captain Smythe again?"

Kitty shot an anxious look toward the Earl, and he quickly came to her side. "Kitty understands that she must be guided by me, Mother. There will be no Captain Smythe in Kitty's life," he interjected, quite truthfully, he told himself. He turned to Kitty. "Is that not correct, Kitty?"

"That is correct, Cousin," she said in a tiny voice, her eyes on her shoes. She seemed most grateful to be dismissed a few minutes later.

"Well, my dear Charles, you have indeed wrought miracles. She seems a good, compliant child once again. And where, may I ask, is that unscrupulous young man?" asked the Dowager.

"I have taken care of the young man, Mother. You need have no fear on that head. Now, tell me, did my letter reach you?"

"Yes, it came just this morning, and I have already told several of my friends about your little excursion to the country," replied his mother, smiling.

"Excellent. I had hoped you would. Have you an invitation for some event or other tomorrow evening? I think it important that she be seen as soon as possible," said the Earl, reclining now in a wing chair to the side of the settee, his long legs outstretched.

"There is the Wilcox soiree, and the come-out ball for the Pickwick twins."

"Take her to the ball. Half the Ton will be there, no doubt. Dreadful bores, come-out balls, but they do have their uses." The Earl's lips curled in a smirk.

"I shall certainly do that. And—ah—might I prevail upon *you* to make an appearance, Charles? It might help if it were seen that all was well between Kitty and

303

her guardian."

"Hmm. Well, perhaps I may," he said, thinking that it would be as good a place as any to pursue his task. He declined his mother's invitation to dinner and then, flicking some dust from his coat sleeve, asked in seeming nonchalance, "Er—tell me, Mother—I find myself idly curious about something. Before he wed the second Lady Millforte, Arthur was supposed to have married another. Do you recall who it was?"

His mother looked at him with narrowed eyes, but replied, "There had been no formal engagement, you understand, Charles, but yes, I do recall. Arthur had approached the Greshams with the possible intention of marrying Priscilla Claredon."

The Earl's eyes widened. The Dragon Lady's spinster daughter was to have married Arthur Millforte? That was news indeed. He recovered himself quickly and visibly relaxed in his seat, trying to appear only mildly interested.

"I would imagine, then, that the Marchioness was rather—er—disappointed when he married Amanda Talbot," he remarked casually.

"Disappointed is hardly the word, Charles. She was furious. There had been no announcement, of course, nor had he even met poor Priscilla, but still, expectations had been raised. And to pass over a marquis's daughter, and Lady Gresham's daughter at that, for the daughter of an obscure baron, one so young and so obviously unsuitable—well—you can imagine, dear Charles, that she did not take it very kindly at all. And one could not help but sympathize, for Priscilla was already two and twenty at the time, and one knew that there would be no further opportunities. A girl like that—well—she needs must be snatched up in her first Season, while she is fresh, or I fear there is little hope. It is indeed fortunate that Kitty is so pretty to look upon, and she does not lack for charm, I should say."

"To be sure, Mother. But tell me, did Lady Gresham say anything to you at the time?"

"There was very little she could say, Charles, for she would not speak ill of my brother to me. She merely said that it was indeed a shame that our two families were not, after all, to be united. It was Emily Cowper who told me how enraged she truly was. Dear Emily said that Augusta was quite beside herself, even ranting about taking revenge for the dishonor against her daughter. There was no dishonor on Arthur's part, of course. Fool he may have been, but that is all. Naturally, Augusta knew that, and her comments were made in the heat of her distress, and I am sure she was most contrite afterwards for having such evil thoughts. In fact, she became quite a bit friendlier after that, even asking occasional questions about Arthur's new wife. She knew that I, too, was displeased with the match and she was quite sympathetic about it. I know you do not care for Augusta, Charles, but she has, you know, been a comfort to me."

"How kind of her, to be sure, Mother," said his lordship dryly, and shortly thereafter took his leave.

The Earl was more than happy to turn himself over to the ministrations of his valet. Darby was delighted to see him and seemed to derive some sort of grim satisfaction from the fact that the Earl's clothes were in as disreputable a state as Darby had known they would be. As he unpacked his lordship's portmanteau, he expressed doubt that a single cravat contained therein would ever again be fit to wear. And Darby knew of a certainty that those particular black Hessians, neglected through so many days of travel, could never, ever again be worn in polite company.

His lordship most gratefully allowed a hot bath to be drawn for him, and as he submerged himself in the steaming water, he felt the fatigue of the last several days slowly begin to dissipate. He would much have preferred to stay home for the evening, but he did not want to lose any time. Besides, after what his mother had just imparted to him, he was very anxious to speak with Ridgeway. And he would speak to Richard tonight as well, for the younger man would leave London in the morning.

As the hot water began to soothe his sore and tired muscles, the Earl reflected upon what he had just learned. Lady Gresham, it seemed, perceived herself as having a grievance against Arthur. Certainly that could be extended to include Amanda, but still, it was too preposterous to consider. Indeed, he had never considered the Marchioness a kind woman, but this piece of malice would have gained her nothing. How far would even the Dragon Lady carry revenge? And why now were the on dits becoming more lively? It did not make sense, and he thought that, in any case, it would be very difficult, if not impossible, to prove the source of the rumors. Perhaps, he thought, there was more here than one could see at the outset. He would start by learning more about the Claredon family than what he knew. Ridgeway ought to be rather a help in that quarter.

Fortified by a glass of brandy, the Earl allowed himself to be arrayed in evening dress. He took a moment to compose a letter to his estate manager in Surrey, bidding him see that Richard was made comfortable, and left the house, directing the coachman to carry him to Richard's lodgings.

His lordship gave Richard the letter, declined his offer of refreshment, and took a seat opposite him in the cozy first-floor study.

"Richard," began the Earl, "I know that you spent some time in the past weeks trying to find some clues as to the source of the unfortunate rumors."

"Yes, I tried, Ainsley, but I am afraid I came up empty-handed," said Richard, waving his hand in a gesture of futility.

"I understand that, Richard, but you see, it is just possible that you heard something—a snippet of conversation, perhaps—which might have a significance you could not know of," the Earl suggested, reclining in his seat.

"Ah, yes, I see. What can I tell you? I spent a good bit of time at the clubs. There was the usual talk of politics, the latest wagers at Gentleman Jim's, and then of course, the talk of women," said Richard, sipping a glass of brandy.

"And?" pressed the Earl.

"Lady Pynchon is this Season's Incomparable, you must know. The odds are heavy as to whether she lands a duke or a marquis, or has to settle for an earl, no offense intended, of course," Richard informed him, smiling.

"All the dukes and marquises are welcome to the fair Lady Isabel. But do go on," said the Earl, grinning.

"There is always talk of certain favored members of the demimonde, of course. And, let us see, last week's news seemed to be that the enchanting Lady Claibourne was no longer under the protection of the Duke of Pembroke," Richard continued amiably, and then his voice became lower, and a frown creased his face. "And then—every so often—I would hear something about Amanda. A story about her with some peer out in Shropshire—other stories as well . . ." Richard's voice trailed off.

"But never anything specific?" asked the Earl quietly.

"But never anything specific. And no hint as to the source of these—these unabashed lies. Oh, I fear that I am being no help at all. Mandy did not deserve this, Ainsley. I would I could do more," Richard said, shaking his head.

"All is not lost, Richard. I am going to relate to you some bit of intelligence which I have just acquired. Perhaps—perhaps you may remember something else that may help us make a connection. The whole thing seems fantastic to me, but one never knows. My mother informed me that some four years ago, just prior to his meeting Amanda, my late uncle, Lord Millforte, was meant to have married one Priscilla Claredon, the daughter of Lady Gresham. There had been no betrothal—indeed, the couple had not met— but Arthur had communicated with the family about the possibility of an alliance. Do you know the Marchioness of Gresham, Richard?"

"I have seen her, I believe, though we've not met. One of the Patronesses, is she not?"

"She is. Wields a great deal of power in society. Priscilla is her eldest child and not, unfortunately, a very attractive girl. She is unmarried to this day, and quite on the shelf by now."

"Ah. So the Marchioness would not have taken those dashed hopes kindly," Richard observed.

"No, and I might add that the Marchioness is not the kindest of women. There are those of us who refer to her as the Dragon Lady, I'm afraid," confided the Earl, barely suppressing a grin.

"I have heard the term, Ainsley, and if the picture I have of the lady in my mind is accurate, it is an apt one. Tell me, are there any other Claredon offspring?"

"Yes. There is one son, Roland, who is perhaps four and twenty by now. I've heard naught of him for at least a year now. He was in the service a while back but—" The Earl stopped speaking preemptorily, the corners of his mouth downturned in a grimace. "But he sold out rather—abruptly. Not accounted a very pleasant sort. Fiery temper and very much the gamester. And then there is Eloise. Perhaps Kitty has mentioned her—she is coming out this year as well."

"Yes, she has spoken of Eloise Claredon, now you mention it. Bit of a loose tongue, I believe."

"She is her mother's daughter," said the Earl, a smirk on his face.

"And are you saying that you think it possible that Lady Gresham is responsible—that she is the one who—" Richard began.

"I do not know, Richard, what to think. I tell you this because you have been about town recently, attuned to this matter. Have you met any of the Claredons, heard their names, overheard them talking? Oh, and by the way, there is also the Marquis. One is inclined to forget him, so effaced by his wife is he. Spends his days and most of his nights at White's, I believe. Pleasant enough old fellow, but no match for the Dragon Lady, more's the pity."

"I *have* met him, I believe, Ainsley. Quite often in his cups, poor chap, but seems quite harmless."

"Oh, yes, I do not consider that he would have a part in any of his wife's schemes. But now think—this all may come to naught, but 'tis all we have at the moment."

"Who are the girls, did you say? Eloise and Priscilla?" asked Richard. The Earl nodded. "I have some vague memory, Ainsley, of a conversation involving a 'Priscilla.' I have no idea who was talking, but one woman was addressing the other as Priscilla. I think this was at the Cheswick ball—you know, the one where Kitty and I—well, in any case, there might have been half a dozen Priscillas at that ball."

"Never mind that, Richard," said the Earl, leaning forward in his seat, his hands clasped between his knees. "Can you recall what was said?"

"I don't know. Let me see—I had eased myself behind the curtained arches, and I overheard several conversations. There were two men talking about the new crop of debutantes, I believe. And then there were the two women. I remember that I could see their feet under the curtain, and nothing more. If memory serves me, a mother was talking to her daughter. I do not recall the entire conversation, of course, but I remember thinking at the time that 'twas rather a strange conversation." Richard paused for a moment, his eyes narrowed as he stared straight ahead.

"Go on, Richard," prompted the Earl quietly.

"The older woman addressed her daughter as Priscilla. She said something about a good night's work and that history must not—repeat itself, I think. Although what *that* means—"

"Just repeat the conversation as you remember it, Richard."

"Very well. Something about not allowing history to repeat itself, and the human animal, I think she said, and then a clever person setting the world by its ears. I am afraid that is about all I can recall. I do not think much more was said. Not very promising, I guess," Richard said with a sigh.

The Earl rose from his chair and strolled to the fireplace, his brow deeply furrowed. He leaned one hand on the mantel and stared into the fire. He spoke aloud, but more to himself than to Richard. "Let us suppose, for the moment, that you did, indeed, overhear Lady Gresham in conversation with her eldest daughter. 'A good night's work,' you said. And 'not allowing history to repeat itself.' And 'a clever person.' I daresay, Richard, some of it may be deemed to derive from this very situation. It would take a clever person, after all, to plant such stories, and keep them alive for so long. 'The human animal'—'tis a cynical phrase which might also fit."

"And a cynical person might view it all as a good night's work," added Richard.

"Yes. Very true. But 'history repeating itself'? I own I cannot conceive to what that can possibly refer." The Earl shook his head and walked to Richard's chair. He put his hand on the young man's shoulder.

"I shall take care of this, Richard. Do not trouble yourself. Go off to Surrey in the morning as planned. There is no problem if you need to communicate with me, but I need not tell you, I hope, that there must be no communication with Kitty."

"Of course, Ainsley. I quite understand. And, my lord, I—that is—thank you for taking this task upon yourself," said Richard with feeling.

"Let us hope I can send you good news within a very short while, Richard," replied the Earl, smiling slightly, and thereafter took his leave.

So interested had he been in what Richard had to say that the Earl had very near to forgotten his hunger. But as he climbed into his carriage, directing the driver to White's, he found that he was ravenous indeed. He was also very eager to speak to Ridgeway and knew that he would most likely find his friend there at this hour.

The Earl sauntered through several of the softly lit, plush rooms of his club, crowded now with the cream of the peerage. He found Ridgeway in one of the Card Rooms. Simon seemed glad of the excuse to leave his game, and very shortly the two men were ensconced at a private corner table in the dining room.

"You look calm enough, Charles. Family business taken care of satisfactorily, I hope?" asked Simon with something of a grin as they dined on a light dover sole.

"Now just what do you mean by that, Simon?"

"Just that you dash away on some mysterious family business at the same time that Miss Berenson is said to have taken ill and been packed off to the country. The

311

possibilities are intriguing, indeed."

"Let us hope that no one else is quite so intrigued. But you are not incorrect in assuming the connection. Kitty is back, but, well, it is a very long story, Ridgeway, best told over brandy in my library, if I might prevail upon you to accompany me as soon as this most excellent dinner is over."

It was not until the two had repaired to the Earl's house in Grosvenor Square that he began to relate to Ridgeway the events of the last several days.

Simon was not the least bit surprised to hear that Kitty and her soldier had run off together, having surmised as much from the Earl's abrupt departure from London. But Simon nearly choked on his brandy when his lordship revealed the true identity of Captain Richard Smythe.

"Good God, Charles, do you mean to say you walked right into Millforte Manor without know-ing—"

"I had not the least idea, Simon. How could I? Well, it became immediately clear why the young man had been so secretive, but unfortunately, it was clear to Amanda as well," said the Earl, sitting on the edge of the tufted leather seat which stood at an angle to the fireplace.

"What do you mean?" asked Simon.

"Richard told her about the—unsavory tales. She—she is very angry with me," said his lordship quietly staring into the fire.

"She will come round, Charles."

"She is a very proud woman, and she has misconstrued my—actions. Simon, for the first time in my life I find myself at a complete loss as to how to handle a woman. I would not have thought it possible," confided the Earl, shaking his head and scowling.

"Nor would I, Charles," said his friend smoothly, the corners of his mouth upturned.

The Earl shot Simon a dark look and rose from his chair. He began to pace the room and spoke rapidly. "I now have added cause for needing to resolve the matter of Amanda's—that is—of these unfortunate stories," began the Earl. He went on to fill Simon in as to the status of the relationship between his ward and Amanda's brother, and finished by recounting the two very interesting conversations he had had this very night.

"Well, what think you, Simon? Is it out of the question that the formidable Patroness should be involved in such a thing or is it within the realm of the possible?" asked the Earl finally, sitting once more in his chair.

"I own I am quite taken aback, Charles. I had no idea of the proposed alliance between Millforte and the Claredons. But I do not think you can discount its possibility as a motive behind these stories. What you have, in fact, is precisely what we spoke of before, someone who bears Lady Millforte a grudge. And that bit of conversation—well—it may be reaching, perhaps—but what little you have told me does not in any way contradict my opinion of the Dragon Lady's character," replied Simon.

"Very well, 'tis true the Marchioness might bear Amanda a grudge, but what was to be gained by this very well-executed campaign against her? And what on earth could she mean by not allowing history to repeat itself? Do you suppose Priscilla has another suitor?" asked Charles, for he was truly mystified.

"No, Charles. Have you seen the elder Miss Claredon lately?" retorted Simon, grinning.

"Yes, well, in any case, Simon, another thought has this evening struck me," said the Earl.

"And that is?"

"Ah—more brandy, Simon?"

"No, thank you. What thought is that, Charles?"

"Well, simply that even if we determine to our own satisfaction that the Dragon Lady, or indeed anyone else, is the cause of this infamy, it may be impossible to prove. The nature of rumor is that it is essentially untraceable."

"That is very true, Charles. Then, the answer is that you will not seek to prove it."

The Earl looked questioningly at Simon, who rose from his chair and stood behind it, his elbows resting on the seat back. "Charles," he said, "you needs must ascertain for yourself, beyond a reasonable doubt, that Lady Gresham is your culprit. Then you need only accuse her to her face. Her reaction will establish her guilt or innocence very easily, I should imagine. Of course, if she is innocent, you risk offending her . . ." Simon said this last with a slight smile.

"I'll risk it," said Charles.

"Very well. But, may I ask, even if you establish her guilt, what do you propose to do about it? The damage to Lady Millforte has already been done," ventured Simon.

The Earl was silent for a few minutes. He stood up and walked over to the window and stared out at the black night. At length he turned back and said, "It occurs to me, Simon, that anyone capable of so thoroughly vilifying someone's name ought to be able to clear it just as effectively. Yes, I think I would leave that to her. Once she is aware that I know of her culpability, I would hope that her sense of propriety would guide her to act correctly. But I own that I am not at all comfortable with this conjecture. It does strike me as farfetched. How well do you know the Claredons, Simon?"

"Well, I do not know the girls at all. And the Marchioness I know in the same way you do. I do see the Marquis quite often at White's though. Good fellow. Don't know how he's borne up all these years."

"What about the heir?" asked the Earl.

"Nasty bit of goods, if one listens to his father. The Marquis and young Claredon do not rub along well together at all. Gresham bought him a pair of colors several years ago, in the hope that a taste of war would improve his character. Apparently it did not—Claredon sold out within a year, if memory serves me. Claredon, from what I gather, is a wastrel—a gamester and a womanizer, and Gresham keeps him on a tight string. I should imagine they'd fight about money quite a bit. He is nearly always with his pockets to let when I've seen him in London. Hasn't been in Town for weeks now. There was some talk about trouble with the moneylenders. I would suppose the Marquis paid off his debts and sent him to rusticate for a while. Have you ever met Claredon, Charles?"

"Can't say that I have, Simon, although I have heard talk of him," replied the Earl, thinking that certain things he knew about Claredon and several other sons of peers would not bear repeating in any company, ever. He remembered that unsavory incident eighteen months ago. Claredon was one of the despicable sort who would do anything for money. Fortunately, they were caught before they were able to do any damage to their country. The Earl remembered the pained look on the face of the Duke of Washburne as he had sought Ainsley's advice. The men had been allowed to sell out—only their fathers were told—but the Earl did not know to this day if the right decision had been made.

He sat pensively for a moment, and then said, with an attempt at a light tone, "Tell me, Simon, where am I most likely to find the female Claredons this evening?"

"Today is Wednesday, Charles. When was the last time you made an appearance at Almack's?" asked Simon.

"Oh, damn! I had forgotten it was Wednesday. One loses all track of time when one travels. Very well, if the

315

gossips will talk, so be it."

"By morning the on dits will have it that you are hanging out for a wife," warned Simon, grinning.

"Well, I'm not!" exclaimed the Earl brusquely.

"Ah, of course not, Charles. So you are off to Almack's. You would not think of asking me to go as well now, would you?"

"No, no, to be sure, I would not ask it of you. But, well, Simon, it pains me to ask you to continue in this task, but I have reasons for wanting to resolve this entire matter without delay. It would expedite matters if you would again make the rounds of the clubs tonight. See what you can ferret out about the Claredons. You might concentrate on the heir. A man like that is bound to make enemies, who are only too happy to talk. Perhaps someone knows something. But do not neglect acquaintances of the elder Greshams; one never knows. And, of course, the Marquis himself might, if sufficiently intoxicated, reveal some interesting tidbits about his wife."

"I cannot like this business, Charles, and I would do it for no one else, you must know," said Simon.

"I shall be eternally in your debt, Simon," replied the Earl.

"Yes, well, I own this is not nearly so bad as being asked to go to the Cheswick ball. But I will expect to be invited to the wedding after this, Charles," said Simon amiably.

"What?" exploded the Earl, his brows raised.

"Miss Berenson's wedding. I expect to be invited to Kitty's wedding. You've no objection I hope, Charles?" replied Simon, his eyes a little too innocent, thought the Earl.

"None at all, Simon. Kitty will be honored to have you," said the Earl smoothly, as he and his friend made their way to the door.

Chapter Twenty

After setting his friend down at White's, the Earl continued on to Almack's. He stared out the window of the coach, his face grim. He and Simon might have evolved a plan, but he was beset by doubts. It was sheer fantasy to think that someone of Lady Gresham's standing in society could be capable of such deliberate vilification of character. True, he had never been impressed with the innate goodness of Lady Gresham, and knew her to relish rather malicious gossip. But still, it was a far cry from passing on juicy on dits to actually creating a set of stories designed to destroy someone.

Well, he and Simon would do their work tonight. At the very least he would eliminate Lady Gresham as a possibility. In the morning they would devise their next step. Damn, but this was apt to take a very long time.

The arrival of the Earl of Ainsley within the hallowed portals of Almack's caused quite a fluttering of pulses, as he had feared it would. Despite his reputation with certain ladies of the demimonde, he felt too many pairs of eyes trained on him as he made his way to greet the Patronesses, all of whom extended a very warm greeting.

"Now, Ainsley," bubbled Lady Jersey, "shall I speculate as to the reason for your unprecedented appearance here tonight?"

"No, dear Lady Jersey, I pray you will not," replied his lordship with his most charming smile.

Lady Gresham was most effusive, taking his hand and batting her eyelashes just enough as she said, "Oh, my lord, what a very great pleasure it is to see you here. I was saying to your dear mother, only yesterday, that 'tis a pity we do not see more of you during the Season."

The Earl made some noncommittal reply and would have made good his escape had not the music stopped and Lady Gresham said, "Ah, here comes my dear Eloise. She has been dancing with the Marquis of Fallon. I declare she has not sat out a single dance tonight."

There was nothing he could do but wait for Eloise to be escorted back to her mother, and of course, claim her for the next dance. He sincerely hoped it would not be a waltz. The musicians began a quadrille, and the Earl led Eloise out onto the dance floor. He could feel all eyes on them and knew that tongues would already be wagging, for he had heard himself referred to often enough as a "prize catch" on the Marriage Mart. Another mother might have beamed as her daughter was led away to dance by one of the most eligible though elusive peers in the land. But Lady Gresham seemed to be gloating, as if this were a moment of triumph. He sighed inwardly, not very pleased to be obliging her, and yet knowing that, infrequent as his appearances here were, his claiming Eloise for his first dance was bound to cause comment.

Eloise seemed flushed with pleasure, but a little nervous as they joined the dancers. When they became separated in the movement of the quadrille, he saw her cast openly flirtatious glances toward him, but when the steps of the dance brought them together, she seemed suddenly shy. He could imagine her mother instructing her in the importance of impressing the Earl

318

of Ainsley should he show her any attentions. He tried to put the girl at her ease. "You are looking very lovely tonight, Lady Eloise. By all reports you are accounted quite a success this Season," he said.

"Oh, my lord, you do put me to the blush. But in truth, I have been rather enjoying myself. And, of course, Mama is most pleased. I was so afraid I should disappoint her, for she never got over Priscilla's, well—that is . . ." Her voice trailed off and she looked down at her feet.

A gentleman would have tactfully changed the subject, but the Earl remembered that there was a reason for his presence at Almack's tonight. "Do you mean, Lady Eloise, that your mother has been disappointed over Lady Priscilla's—single state, and has hoped that with you it would be otherwise?" he asked.

"I should not have spoken so, but, well, Mama says Priscilla never really tried, and Mama has been afraid that—that I might not take, and I do so want to please her, for I know she could not bear a repeat of what happened to Priscilla."

Suddenly the Earl felt as though he had been hit between the eyes. He stared at Eloise for a moment before he recovered himself. "You need have no fear on that head, my dear Lady Eloise. You are very charming, and I have no doubt you shall have the Ton at your feet by Season's end," he said, smiling.

He was relieved when the dance ended, and wanted very much to leave. But he could not do so after standing up only with Eloise. He had no wish to give rise to speculation that he had any interest in that quarter. As such he made his way round the room, chatting easily with this group and then that, and dancing with several of the Season's beauties. He led the Incomparable, Lady Isabel Pynchon, out onto the floor, amused at the overt jealousy of several of her court. But he scrupulously avoided the waltz; his next waltz, he told himself, was spoken for.

His lordship made good his exit as soon as he felt he could, and walked out into the night air. He told his driver to follow him; he wished to walk for a bit.

Eloise had been uncharacteristically candid tonight, he was certain. Her mother's hopes had probably made her terrified of his very presence. When she had said Lady Gresham could not bear a repeat of what had happened to Priscilla, he had been stunned. It was part of the answer he sought, but not the whole of it. Having a second daughter accounted a spinster would certainly be history repeating itself, and it might fit nicely with what Richard had told him. But somehow that was not enough. He must think this through logically. Priscilla obviously did not take very well during her first several seasons. Arthur Millforte's tentative offer would have been an unimagined stroke of good fortune, and the disappointment would have been intense. Could the Marchioness have been so angry as to seek vengeance for this unwitting slight? And if she did succeed in discrediting Amanda, would she have kept the on dits warm for so long? And why was it that there seemed to have been a resurgence in the stories these past several months? Why would the Dragon Lady have bothered?

He tried to think of what had happened within the past few months. Amanda was now in mourning, he himself had returned from the Continent, Kitty was making her come-out, along with Eloise and scores of other girls. What did all of that signify? If Lady Gresham was indeed propagating more stories of late, she must have new cause to want Amanda rusticating in Shropshire, branded by the Ton as a scandalous woman. But, he suddenly realized, something very drastic *had* changed recently—Amanda was a widow.

She was once again competition. Competition for whom?

He pictured the Dragon Lady in his mind as he had seen her tonight, fairly dripping charm as he approached. She was so obviously pushing Eloise on him— Good God! he thought. The competition was for himself! Lady Gresham wanted the Earl of Ainsley for her newly launched daughter, and she perceived Amanda, newly widowed, as a threat. He remembered that snippet of conversation about history repeating itself, and Eloise had said tonight that her mother could not bear a repeat of what had happened to her sister. But of course! Lord Millforte had chosen Amanda over her elder daughter, and Lady Gresham was afraid his nephew would choose Amanda over the younger daughter. That would indeed be history repeating itself!

His lordship whistled through his teeth and shook his head. Her plan had been diabolically clever, and completely ruthless, but it was the only thing that made sense. And she had nearly succeeded. He had been fooled like all the rest, though only, he told himself, for a short time. With chagrin he remembered Amanda's face as he had left. Blast it all! He had handled the whole thing wrong from start to finish. Well, he was not finished with Amanda, and the poison-tongued Dragon Lady would not, in the end, emerge the victor.

He turned and hailed his coachman, ordering him to White's as he climbed inside. The Earl wished to speak to Simon without delay. There could be little doubt as to the villain now; it remained only for him to decide how to approach her so that she would comply with what he now wanted.

But Simon was not to be found at White's, and upon inquiry, the Earl learned that he had not more than a half hour before departed for Mrs. Townsend's. The

Earl had no desire to follow his friend there. There was once a time when, perhaps bored with one of his mistresses, he would have been happy to visit Mrs. Townsend's most elegant establishment. But now he found that the idea left him cold.

Sleep evaded him for a long time that night, and when he finally drifted off, he dreamed of green eyes and black hair. The eyes were laughing one moment, but in the next they were stark with fear. The Earl awoke rather early, more anxious than ever to complete the task he had set himself.

"I agree with you, Charles," said Simon as he sat in the Earl's dining room that morning, buttering his second piece of toast. "There can be little doubt now as to how this reprehensible state of affairs came to pass. When will you go to see Lady Gresham?"

"The task is entirely disagreeable, to be sure, Simon. I should not like to delay at all. I mean to pay a morning call today," said the Earl, taking a sip of coffee.

"I would give anything to see the Dragon Lady's face when she realizes she's been found out. She will have the apoplexy, to be sure," grinned Simon.

"Either that or turn on me like a viper. I tell you, I do not relish that task, Simon. But I am persuaded that subtlety is the most desirable means of approaching her. I need not confront her outright, I think, to achieve my end."

"Good luck to you, Charles. In truth, I do not envy you this. Will you take luncheon with me at White's?" asked Simon.

"Thank you, I shall do just that. I shall probably be greatly in need of fortification after my interview with the Marchioness," replied the Earl with a faint smile as

322

he drained his coffee cup.

Gresham House on St. James Square was not a credit to that elegant block of houses. What had once been a stately mansion had been renovated several times until it appeared almost garish in its attempt to dwarf all of the surrounding houses.

Lady Gresham received the Earl in the morning room. "Why Lord Ainsley, what a delightful surprise. I must say you are looking particularly dashing this morning," said the Marchioness, rising from her chair.

"Thank you, Lady Gresham," said the Earl, taking her extended hand for just a moment. She wore a yellow brocade gown that he thought made her skin look positively green. A Dragon Lady, indeed, he thought sardonically.

"You will wish to speak to Eloise, of course," gushed the Dragon Lady sweetly.

Somehow he had not expected this, but of course, to what other purpose would she attribute his visit? "Well, actually, Lady Gresham, I have come to speak with you," he said slowly.

The Marchioness became very flustered indeed. "Well, my dear Lord Ainsley, I must say I had no idea," she said, smiling and casting her eyes down as she adjusted the lace cap on her head, "but, of course, it is to the Marquis that you will wish to speak in that case."

"Lady Gresham, I—" began the Earl, quite bewildered.

"My, but you do make up your mind quickly, my lord. I admire a decisive man. Of course, you have known Eloise for a while now, but after just that one dance last night, well, I truly had no idea . . ." babbled Lady Gresham.

Suddenly enlightenment dawned and the Earl stared

323

at her wide-eyed for a moment, before he was seized by an irrepressible urge to laugh out loud. He choked back the laugh and schooled his face to an impassive mask. "Forgive me, Lady Gresham; I am afraid you do very much mistake the matter. I did not come to speak to you or the Marquis about Eloise. It is another matter entirely which brings me here."

He could see the muscles in Lady Gresham's face tense, and her nostrils flared for a fleeting moment. But she pushed her nose slightly higher into the air as she asked, her tone a bit cooler, "And what is it you have come to discuss, my lord?"

"Would you not care to be seated, Lady Gresham?" asked the Earl amiably.

"Yes, yes, of course," said the Marchioness, and as if suddenly remembering her manners, indicated that he might do the same.

When they had seated themselves on either side of a rather ornate sofa table embellished with gilt carvings of cherubs and flowers, the Marchioness asked formally, "Would you care for some refreshment, my lord?"

"No, thank you, Lady Gresham. I have come to see you on a matter which pains me greatly. I am persuaded that you and only you can help me," said the Earl.

"Indeed, I should be most pleased to be of some service to you, Lord Ainsley," said the large Marchioness, attempting to make herself comfortable in the delicate Chippendale chair that appeared much too small for her.

"Thank you, Lady Gresham. As you know, when my mother's brother, the late Lord Millforte, married some years ago, my mother was distressed at the match. The second Lady Millforte was very, very young and her family unknown to us. But my mother has been even more distressed, over these past several years, at the, shall we say, scandalous on dits which have circulated concerning the second Lady Millforte. I find that I am perturbed as well, for it has very lately come to my attention that these stories are completely unfounded."

"Unfounded? How can that be? I cannot think what you mean, my lord," retorted the Marchioness, her brows raised and her lips pursed.

"I mean, dear Lady Gresham, that someone has very cleverly fabricated the stories about Lady Millforte, at first, I believe, to achieve a kind of vengeance, and later because the continued disgrace of Lady Millforte was perceived as necessary to bring about a certain desired—er—circumstance."

The Earl watched the Marchioness carefully. Her very proper upbringing had probably never stood her in better stead, for her eyes narrowed for but a moment before she schooled her features to a bland expression. "What you say rather strains one's credulity, does it not, my lord? You infer that all of the on dits of the past four years have been created with the deliberate intention of—of—"

"Of discrediting Lady Millforte. Yes, Lady Gresham. And as it concerns my family, and as it affects several people besides Lady Millforte, I wish these stories to cease," stated his lordship quite calmly.

"I understand your concern, Lord Ainsley, but I do not see— I cannot conceive why you have come to me," said the Dragon Lady.

"Can you not, my lady? Ah, well, 'tis really very simple. You see, I *know* who engineered these rumors, and I know *why*. Furthermore, I apprehend fully why they have suddenly increased in intensity these past several months, since I have been in London. I want the stories to cease immediately. And more than that, I want Lady Millforte completely exonerated. You are a clever woman, Lady Gresham, and your consequence is of the first water. I am persuaded that you might accomplish this with little difficulty. I ask you if you would be good enough, Lady Gresham, to take this task upon yourself," said the Earl with a smile on his face that was perhaps belied by a certain firmness of tone.

"Again, my lord, I must ask you to explain yourself. I understand your distress, for surely it cannot be pleasant to have one's family name so—so talked of, but I am afraid I cannot see why *I* should become embroiled in such a—"

"'Tis indeed unfortunate that you do not comprehend, my dear lady. Perhaps I *had* ought to speak with the Marquis. How *is* your husband, Lady Gresham? And how is young Claredon? By the by, have you any idea why your son left the Continent so precipitously? Perhaps you ought to ask your husband; I am certain the Duke of Washburne would have told him. But I have wandered from my purpose, have I not?" the Earl said smoothly. He noted that the Marchioness sat very still in her seat, her face composed, the only evidence of distress a slight trembling of the lower lip.

He went on speaking quietly. "As regards the little favor I have asked of you, Lady Gresham, it is my hope that you will find yourself amenable to helping me. The matter must be taken care of immediately, which I am certain you can appreciate."

When the Marchioness finally spoke, her voice was tightly controlled and her head held high. "I should not care to involve myself in such a task, my lord, but I am persuaded that 'twould be a difficult, if not impossible, task for whosoever should undertake it."

"I think not, Lady Gresham. A few well-chosen words in the right ears should expedite matters. One might invent a disgruntled suitor, one who'd had expectations of marrying Lady Millforte since her childhood, perhaps, and who fabricated the whole thing for revenge. Why, within three days Lady Millforte might be elevated to the position of grieving widow, unjustly maligned for years, and the Ton atwitter with conjecture as to who the infamous suitor might be."

"How very clever of you, Lord Ainsley," said the Marchioness, her voice rather cold as she rose from her chair.

"You flatter me, Lady Gresham," said the Earl, standing as well and favoring the Marchioness with a smile, "but in truth, you are far more imaginative than I. You will send my regards to the Marquis, will you not?"

"I will, my lord. It has been a pleasure to see you," said the Dragon Lady haughtily, as she turned slightly toward the door.

"Thank you for your hospitality, dear Marchioness. Oh, if I may—there are two things more I would have you know," replied the Earl.

"Yes?"

"One is that my mother is unaware of my visit today, and will remain so."

"And the second thing, Lord Ainsley?" said Lady Gresham rather frostily, her hands clutched tightly together in front of what must once have been her waist.

"I shall undoubtedly be obliged to leave London— er—on business within a few days' time. I have a confidential friend here in Town who will keep me informed of all the latest—developments, shall we say. I just wanted you to know that, Lady Gresham."

"How considerate of you, Lord Ainsley. Good day, sir."

"Good day, madam," said the Earl, bowing formally and thinking, as he took his leave, that the Dragon Lady looked spent, as if she had no more fire left.

Ridgeway seemed to delight in the fact that the fire had gone out of the Dragon Lady, as the Earl recounted his interview with Lady Gresham to his friend over luncheon. But his lordship took no pleasure in it, for the interview had been distasteful in the extreme. He declined to relate the details of Roland Claredon's activities on the Continent, but told Ridgeway, whose discretion he trusted without question, enough so that he might, if need be, act in his stead in this matter.

After leaving Ridgeway, the Earl spent the afternoon in his study, attending to personal correspondence. He composed a brief letter to Richard, informing him of developments thus far, and expressing the hope that his exile from London would shortly come to an end. His lordship would have liked very much to have written to Amanda as well, but he doubted that she would read his letter. Besides, what could he possibly say in a letter? No, they must meet face to face and come to terms with one another. Somehow he would have to convince her of his sincerity, convince her that he truly wanted—wanted what? He shook his head as he sat over his desk, for he did not know quite what he wanted. He knew only that no other woman had ever had such an effect on him before, and that the coldness of her parting words had cut him like a dagger.

The Earl methodically went through the pile of papers left on his desk by Jameson, his secretary. As he sifted through bills, notices and documents to sign, he reminded himself that as he was now permanently home from abroad, the time had come to begin taking more of an interest in the management of his estates. If nothing else, Amanda's passionate interest in Millforte had made him realize this. Then, too, he thought, it was time he started thinking about taking his seat in the Lords. He would begin by researching the Corn Laws, a major issue still as agitation for repeal increased.

At this he brought himself up short. Why did he suddenly feel the need to become so—responsible? Not that he had been irresponsible in his wartime activities, but somehow he knew that he'd spent the last ten years of his life in the pursuit of amusement. Lately he had begun to feel that he wanted something more. Would dedication to his land and to politics fill the void he had felt of late? He did not know. He simply did not know.

But one way to find out was to begin working in earnest, and as such he spent the late afternoon closeted with Jameson. The Earl did not emerge from his study until it was time to dress for dinner. He met Ridgeway at White's in anticipation of a much needed evening of diversion. Dinner was superb, the French chef at White's the envy of many a household. Later they made their way through the gaming rooms, but the Earl was restless.

"Perhaps you are in need of a little—softer—companionship than what I can offer you, Charles," suggested Ridgeway.

The Earl looked narrowly at his friend. "Are you going to suggest Mrs. Townsend's again, Simon?" he asked amiably.

"No, as a matter of fact, I had something else in mind. Since you gave up Cecile, you know, speculation has been rife amongst a certain group of—er—ladies as to who would be the next object of your esteem. You have yet to alleviate their curiosity, you know."

"Thank you for your concern, Simon, but I shall pass. I fear I am becoming a very dull companion indeed. Perhaps I ought simply to go home," said the Earl.

"Home? At ten o'clock at night? Come now, at least let me give you a game of chess?"

"Chess?" asked the Earl, and then paused. "I do not think I quite feel up to a game of chess this evening. Forgive me, old friend, but I think I shall just betake myself home."

The Earl saw his friend regarding him curiously, a smile curling his lips. "Very well, Charles. Until tomorrow then. Perhaps you are in need of a good night's sleep."

But a good night's sleep eluded him again. He tossed aside book after book, and drank glass after glass of brandy, trying not to think about why none of his usual pursuits interested him. Why could he think of little else but the pursuit of a tumble of black hair and a pair of fragile sea green eyes? After all, there had been other women before. Why should this one—"Oh, hell and damnation!" he growled, and refilled his brandy goblet.

Chapter Twenty-One

The Earl spent a good part of the next day with Jameson. The lean, quietly efficient secretary could not hide his surprise when the Earl began questioning him in some detail about the farms surrounding Ainsley Court. The Earl pressed him further as to the productivity of the lands and the extent to which fertile ground was being maximized. When Jameson left, the Earl sat very pensively behind his desk for some time. It was time for major changes at Ainsley, he thought. When next he was there, he must make an inspection tour. It was not enough to peruse the facts and figures on paper. He ought not to delay his trip home, but he knew that he was not ready to go just yet. Ainsley could wait; Millforte could not.

At twilight the Earl arrived at his mother's house, for she had invited him to dine, after which he was to escort Kitty and the Dowager to another dreary, over-crowded, glittering ball.

"Charles," began the Dowager as she took a spoonful of the sorbet that followed the salmon mousse, "I have the most amazing bit of intelligence for you. I took tea with the Duchess of Cheswick today, and well—it seems all of London is buzzing with this latest on dit."

"And what, pray tell, might that be, Mother?" asked

the Earl with his usual degree of mockery.

"They are saying, Charles, that all of the talk—the scandalous talk—about Arthur's wife has been false! I find I cannot comprehend it, Charles, but they say that the stories were the work of one man who sought to discredit her. Millicent Enderly said he was a former suitor who had wanted to marry her," said the Dowager.

Kitty had gasped as soon as the Dowager had begun speaking, and had stolen a wide-eyed glance at the Earl. He was pleased to see that she had enough presence of mind to hold her peace, for she kept her eyes down and her attention riveted to her sorbet after that.

"What a curious story," said the Earl, somewhat nonchalantly. "Does anyone actually credit it?"

"Yes, Charles. The Duchess herself affirmed that she has the story on very good authority."

"But Lady Millforte has been talked about for years," the Earl commented.

"Well, it would seem that this man was most devastated indeed by what he perceived as the perfidy of Lady Millforte. His seat is in Yorkshire, I believe it was said, and he has made periodic appearances in London to promulgate these disgraceful stories. A rather terrible revenge, is it not?" asked Lady Ainsley.

"Yes rather, Mother," said the Earl, a smile playing at his lips as he stared ahead at nothing in particular.

"Charles, you have spent a certain amount of time with Lady Millforte. What was your impression of her character?" asked the Dowager.

"Oh, I really could not say, Mother. We—we spent most of our time discussing the business of the estates," replied the Earl, not at all pleased to see Kitty's head pop up as he spoke. She seemed to stifle a giggle and then bent to her food once more.

There was silence for a moment as a footman removed the covers of the next course. When he had departed, Lady Ainsley said, "Really, Charles, I am persuaded that you must have had some personal discourse with her, and some opportunity to observe her behavior."

"Her behavior during the time that I was there was most—exemplary, Mother," he said with some finality, and though his mother looked piercingly at him, he said nothing more.

The Dellethorpe ball was nearly as successful as the Cheswick's had been; there was absolutely no room to breathe, so great a crush was it. The Earl was saved from deadly boredom only by the fact that the ballroom was alive with the latest on dit.

"Is it not beyond anything? They say she was the most devoted of wives," said one turbaned dowager to another as the Earl passed behind a row of chaperones.

"Yes, I know, my dear. But what sort of man would go to so much trouble to take vengeance on a woman?" answered her friend.

"What sort of woman would inspire such vengeance?" asked a third.

The Earl moved on, eventually encountering Thomas Waring just outside the Card Room.

"Ainsley! Good to see you. An interesting evening, is it not?" said Thomas amiably.

"Hello, Thomas. And just what is so interesting about this evening, may I ask?" answered the Earl, smiling.

"Come now. Have you not heard the prattle? There is not a person here who has not heard the story of Lady Millforte and the vengeful suitor. However did you do it, Ainsley?" asked Thomas.

"I assure you, Thomas, I have certainly not contrived this very—interesting—bit of news," said the Earl tranquilly.

"No, of course not, for you are not a gossip. But I suspect that somehow indirectly you are behind this."

"You have a great deal of faith in my abilities, Thomas. And tell me, how is your sister? I have not seen her here tonight," said the Earl, a faint smile on his lips.

"Oh, Anne is here. I believe she is on the dance floor just now. Ah! There she is—over to the right."

"Thomas, is that not Linfield with whom she is dancing?"

"Yes, it is."

"What is he doing in London? When did he get here?"

"Just arrived today, it seems. Rather an unexpected trip, he said. Has a cousin who is a friend of young Stephen Dellethorpe, which is how he came to be here. He—he called at my mother's this afternoon," said Thomas quietly.

"You are concerned, Thomas?" When the young man nodded, he continued. "I do not know his prospects. That you must ascertain for yourself. But I do believe that the Linfield family is an old and respected one in Warwickshire. His sister is Lady Bosley, wife of Sir James Bosley. Linfield himself seems a steady sort, although I do not know him well."

"His prospects are reasonable. I—I had some idea that you disliked him, and I confess I was curious as to why," said Thomas.

The Earl felt himself color slightly. "'Twas nothing, really, Thomas. I was a bit—piqued—that Lady Millforte had received visitors, when she should have been resting. She had been quite ill, you see."

"Ah, yes, I see," said Thomas, in a tone which

indicated that he might see a bit too much.

"Will you join me in the Card Room, Thomas?" asked the Earl by way of changing the subject.

"Thank you, no, Ainsley. Actually I am waiting for Lydia. She went to repair the flounce of her gown, which I am afraid I was clumsy enough to step on," said Thomas, grinning. "But, Ainsley," he went on, "I think perhaps I had ought to warn you—well, that is—you might not care for the Card Room just now."

"And why is that, Thomas?"

"The talk is flying high as to who—er—the vengeful suitor is, and the men are speculating as to when Lady Millforte will next make her appearance in London. I think if you go in there you will find yourself questioned a good deal about her," replied Thomas uncomfortably.

"Go on, Thomas," said the Earl, his brows coming together, for he knew there was more.

"Everyone is very curious about what kind of woman would inspire such vehemence and persistence in a man. And they are taking—wagers, my lord, as to who will succeed in—er—attracting her when she next arrives in London."

The Earl thought Thomas's paraphrase was probably a good deal politer than what was actually said. "Thank you, Thomas. I find I am not much in the mood of a card game at the moment," said his lordship, not at all comfortable with the curious look the young man leveled at him. He was pleased that in the next moment they were joined by a very pretty brunette whom Thomas introduced as his fiancée.

The Earl parted from the happy couple and claimed Kitty for the next dance. He had not cared to dance all evening, but he felt obliged to dance with his ward, and besides, he wished to have a word with her. "And what, may I ask, young lady, did you find so amusing at

335

dinner tonight?" asked the Earl sternly as the steps of the dance brought them together.

"Why, nothing, Cousin Charles. I am certain that you and Lady Millforte had a great many fruitful and—interesting—discussions about the estates, as—as you indicated," said Kitty, her demure tone belied by a certain twinkle in her eye.

"I will thank you to keep your fanciful notions to yourself, miss. Is that clear?" demanded the Earl.

"Why, of course, Cousin," she replied, her eyes sweeping down for a moment.

"Good. Now, tell me, are you enjoying yourself tonight?"

"Yes," Kitty said slowly, "but well—I find myself rather tired already."

"Then you would not mind if we departed early? There is a great deal that I wish to discuss with my mother, Kitty," said the Earl intently.

"Cousin, will you tell her about—"

"Yes, Kitty. I think the time has come to tell her. It will not be easy, despite the latest—er—developments. I should like you to retire as soon as we arrive home so that she and I might be private."

"Yes, of course, Cousin. Does that mean that Richard can—"

"In perhaps a se'nnight or two, Kitty. I have told you that I shall send for him, but you must be patient."

"Oh, thank you, Cousin. I shall be the happiest girl in all of London!" she exclaimed, her face lighting up and her steps suddenly becoming a good deal lighter.

"Kitty, are you *sure* this is what you want? Have you not met any other men who appeal to you?"

"No, Cousin. Has there—has there never been a woman in your life who outshone all the others, one from whom you could not bear to part? One who made you lose all interest in every other woman?" she asked, her eyes regarding him quizzically.

How dare she ask such impertinent questions! And how the hell could he answer her? No, there had never been any such woman. That is, until—until Amanda, dammit! He took a deep breath. It was time he admitted it to himself. Amanda had come into his life and nothing would ever be the same. Nor, he realized, did he want it to be. Yes, it was high time he admitted it to himself, but not, by God, to anyone else!

"Your questions, miss, are impertinent. And you must endeavor to remember that not everyone is possessed of such a romantic nature as you are, my dear Kitty," he said smoothly, and then added, "I believe our dance is coming to an end. Shall we seek out my mother and take our leave?"

The Dowager Countess seated herself on her favorite chair in the exquisitely furnished drawing room. She watched her son as he stood by the fireplace, sipping a glass of wine.

She had been bursting with all of the latest news about the second Lady Millforte as they rode home in the carriage. But Charles had looked very pensive, and remembering his reticence on the subject at dinner, she had held her peace. In fact, now she thought on it, he had been curiously silent about Amanda Millforte since he first returned from Shropshire. He was not given to gossip, of course, but he had been unusually noncommital.

And tonight he had asked to speak with her. Kitty had retired immediately as they arrived home, almost as though it had been prearranged. Yes, the Dowager was very curious indeed, but she waited for her son to seat himself and begin.

"Mother, there is something I must discuss with you.

337

You will forgive me for delaying this long. There were matters to which I had to attend before I spoke with you." She nodded and he went on, leaning forward in his chair. "I must tell you about Kitty's soldier, Mother."

She blanched. Somehow she had expected him to discuss Lady Millforte, not that soldier of fortune who was best off forgotten. "Really, Charles, the affair has quite run its course. Do you not think it better to—"

"No, Mother, I do not," interrupted the Earl firmly. "Please allow me to continue, if you would."

"Yes, of course, Charles."

"The young man called himself Captain Smythe, and did not make himself known to you, because of a family problem which he felt he had to resolve first. I am persuaded you will understand what that problem was when I tell you that he is the brother of—the second Lady Millforte."

Lady Ainsley could feel her eyes nearly pop out of her head. "What?" she exclaimed.

"His name is Richard Talbot. He is Amanda Millforte's brother. He knew that the stories about his sister were untrue, but he also knew that you would never accept him, believing, as did everyone, that they were indeed true."

The Dowager could hardly believe what she was hearing. Suddenly a very uncomfortable thought struck her.

"Charles, this affair with Kitty—it *is* over, is it not?" she asked warily.

His lordship sighed. "Mother, forgive me if I have misled you. I told you Kitty would be guided by me, nothing more."

"What are you saying, Charles?"

"Kitty loves him, Mother. And I am persuaded that he returns her affections. I insisted that they be separated until such time as the Talbot and Millforte names were—cleared."

The Dowager stared at her son for a moment. Since when did he concern himself with love, or consider it a primary ingredient in a marriage? But she merely asked, "Where is Captain—Talbot now?"

"He's at Surrey, Mother."

"Surrey! You extended your hospitality to him?"

"Mother, I have told Kitty that I want her to have one Season. After that, if they are both still of the same mind, I shall countenance a wedding."

The Dowager's hand went to her breast as she felt the palpitations begin anew. But her son did not rush to her side as anyone else might have done, and so she rallied somewhat and said, "No, Charles, surely you cannot be serious? Not when there are so many of the most distinguished men about town vying for her attention. Why, she could have an earl, even a duke, if she set her mind to it. You cannot allow her to throw herself away on a simple soldier."

Charles sighed again and looked intently at his mother. His voice was very gentle as he said, "Mother, Kitty does not want an earl or a duke. She wants Richard Talbot. And from what I have seen, I think they will go on quite well together."

"But Charles, a soldier. A younger son," moaned the Dowager, still not quite able to believe that her son had acquiesced in this match.

"He is selling out, Mother. And he has of late received an inheritance which includes a comfortable income and an estate in Essex. He wants to breed horses."

"I see," said the Dowager, for she did see that argument was useless. "And so," she went on after a moment, "the second Lady Millforte will be Kitty's sister-in-law, as well as mine."

"Er—yes, I suppose she will," replied the Earl, a bit uncomfortably, she thought. Suddenly an idea struck her, and she looked curiously at her son.

"Charles—this story that has just come out about Amanda Millforte—did *you* have anything to do with it?"

"Whatever can you mean, Mother?" asked Charles, his face all innocence.

"I am not certain *what* I mean, my dear son. Only that the timing is rather—fortuitous—shall we say, for Kitty and her young man. Added to that is the fact that you have just been to Millforte. Well, it does rather set one to thinking, you know," said Lady Ainsley, thinking that her very clever son might know a good deal more about this than he cared to say.

"Mother, I have never before known you to be fanciful. Are you feeling quite the thing?" asked her son solicitously.

"I am quite well, thank you," she said curtly, knowing the subject to be closed.

"Good. Now let us get back to Kitty. I have told her that she must be patient, but that I will send for Richard in perhaps a se'nnight or two. I want to be sure there will be no lingering doubts in anyone's mind as regards the Talbot name. I have given him my permission to pay his addresses to Kitty. I know you are disappointed, Mother, but it is my hope that you will allow yourself to become well acquainted with him. I think you will find him a most unexceptionable young man. And, I might add, he has Kitty well under control." He smiled and rose from his chair.

The Dowager Countess knew that she had no choice. Charles was Kitty's guardian, and it was his decision after all. She was most baffled, however. He had given in to Kitty too easily, and there was a softness in his tone when he discussed the young couple that she did not recognize. And then there was the matter of the on dits about Lady Millforte. Just what *did* he know about them? Indeed, she wondered, just what did he know about Lady Millforte herself? She looked quizzically at her only son.

"Tell me, Charles, these stories about Lady Millforte and the disgruntled suitor—why do you suppose they have just now come to the fore?"

"I am sure I cannot say, Mother. But I am indeed pleased at the turn of events. The scandalous rumors about her were quite vicious, and unfounded. Neither she nor her brother deserve to suffer for the petty revenge of an imagined wrong," he said rather earnestly.

"Of course, Charles, I quite see your point," she said, rising and facing her son, not sure she saw anything at all. "Tell me, Charles, is she really so—extraordinary— that a man—a disappointed suitor—would do such a thing?"

He looked at her steadily for a moment before he replied simply, "Yes, Mother, she is." He took his leave but a moment later, and the Dowager found herself staring open-mouthed at the closed door through which he had departed. Charles was simply *not* the same Charles anymore. And just what did it all mean?

The Earl breakfasted with Ridgeway and together the two men sauntered over to White's. He was gratified to note that Lady Millforte was still a favorite topic of conversation. Most seemed to accept the new "evidence" readily, and those who did not were quickly informed that the story had come from an unimpeachable authority, for Lady Gresham and the Duchess of Cheswick had vouched for this unknown source.

"You are to be congratulated, Charles. It would seem that your work is done," said Ridgeway.

"I suppose so. Yet I must remain awhile to see that matters continue satisfactorily. If they do, I shall send for Richard Talbot next week."

"Kitty's soldier?" asked Simon.

"Yes, Kitty's soldier," replied the Earl, smiling.

"And what will you do in the interim, Charles? Somehow I have the feeling that London's standard fare does not at present appeal to you."

"I have begun to turn my attention to my estates, Simon. I am amazed at the amount of detail with which one can become inundated if one chooses to involve oneself."

"Well, good luck to you, old man. I, for one, am content to occupy my time in other ways. Would you care to accompany me to Tattersall's this afternoon? I have my eye on a pair of grays and I should like your opinion."

A time was agreed upon, and the Earl repaired home to do some work. The morning's post had been placed in his study, Jameson having already gone through it and made notations on certain communications. The Earl was in the midst of perusing these when his butler interrupted him.

"Ahem. I beg your pardon, your lordship. There is a special messenger here from Millforte Manor. He claims he has an urgent communication for you," said Elprin.

"Show him in immediately," said the Earl, rising and walking apprehensively to the middle of the room. He recognized the messenger as a footman from Millforte and took the missive from him, fully expecting to see the fine slanted hand he knew to be Amanda's. However, it was not a fine hand, but a rather crude one with straight block letters, that he saw as he looked down at the letter. He glanced sharply at the footman and then quickly broke the seal and read:

Lady Millforte is in great danger. Please come quickly.

Dorothy Havenwick

He frowned deeply and reread the note. His heart raced as he tried to digest the contents. Mrs. Havenwick sending for him? It seemed impossible, and he shuddered as he realized that whatever danger Amanda faced must be grave indeed. But what kind of peril would allow him to arrive in time to be of any help? And why had Mrs. Havenwick written and not Amanda? But, of course, he remembered Amanda's face on that last day. She would not send for him no matter what. Her pride would not allow it, regardless of the gravity of the circumstances.

He looked up at the footman, who was standing nervously and watching him. "Do you know anything about this?" asked the Earl curtly.

"No, my lord," said the footman uncomfortably.

"Who sent you to me?"

"Mrs. Havenwick, your lordship."

"And is Lady Millforte at the manor? And does— does all go on well there?" asked the Earl as impassively as he could, but the footman could only reply that Lady Millforte was indeed at home and that all was well. The Earl handed the footman a coin and dismissed him.

He fought down a sinking feeling in his stomach as he began imagining all manner of perils that might befall Amanda. He strode to the bell cord and pulled furiously. When Elprin appeared, he requested Darby be sent to him. His face was set in a grim line as he sat down at his desk. He did not know what was afoot, but it was clear that he had not a minute to lose. He composed a brief message to his mother, explaining that he had been called away on urgent business, and remarking that he was sure she would receive Richard warmly when he came to call at the Earl's behest. He wrote a second missive to Richard, informing him briefly of the latest developments but bidding him remain at Surrey until the Earl summoned him to London.

Darby entered at this point and his lordship instructed him to pack a small portmanteau for the Earl's immediate departure and to prepare the rest of his things for a prolonged stay at Millforte. He requested that his fastest coach be made ready for departure. The Earl would leave at once but Darby was to follow with his luggage as soon as possible.

He dashed a brief note to Jameson, and then one to Ridgeway, for whom he had the most crucial message. He informed his friend that urgent business carried him to Millforte at once for an unspecified amount of time, and begged that he would see that matters continued in the satisfactory manner in which they had begun. If Simon would keep him posted as to the tenor of the on dits, the Earl would know when to send for the young man. These various communications seen to, he gave instructions to Elprin as to their delivery, and was soon after informed by Darby that the coach was ready. "Have a care, my lord. Do not drive within an inch of your life," said Darby affectionately.

"You sound like my mother," said the Earl, smiling for a moment as he climbed up beside the groom.

The Earl wended his way through the crowded London streets as hurriedly as he dared. He tried not to think of Amanda so that he might concentrate on that task, but once out in the country, his imagination ran rife. He tormented himself with images of highwaymen, memories of the Squire's attack, and various other unspeakable perils. Damn! He should never have left her. She was much too vulnerable, and he would never forgive himself if she was harmed.

The Earl drove his horses and himself much too hard, stopping only when it was impossible to go farther either because the horses were near to collapsing or the roads too precarious to negotiate in the dark. He could not sleep even when he did finally pull up at a posting inn the first night, and he fervently hoped that by some miracle he might spend his next night at Millforte.

This he might very well have done, so frenzied was his pace, had not a broken axle kept him fuming and pacing at the King's Crossing Inn for some two hours on the second afternoon of his travels. He continued on after that, but was obliged to put up for the night at the Black Stallion Inn, where he did his best to ignore the whispers and curious stares of all who wondered at the frequent comings and goings of the Earl of Ainsley.

Although his accommodation was again fairly comfortable, he was haunted by visions of Amanda in the gully, Amanda with the Squire, Amanda, Amanda, as he tossed and turned between the rough sheets. He eventually drifted into a troubled sleep, but awoke just before dawn, his body sweating and his breathing heavy. He had been dreaming again, dreaming of those sea green eyes, looking at him through a veil of terror. He had called to her to come to him, but somehow she could not, or would not, and he did not think he could reach her in time.

He did not try to sleep again, and after a rather simple breakfast, he and his groom took to the road just as the dawn was breaking. And so it was not until midday Monday, on the third day after Mrs. Havenwick's summons had arrived, that a bedraggled, overtired Earl, his entire being a jangle of nerves, strode into the dining room at Millforte to behold Amanda, calmly sitting and partaking of her luncheon.

Chapter Twenty-Two

"Why, Cousin Charles, what—what a surprise. I—I—did not quite expect you yet," Amanda said quietly. The faint smile on her lips was belied by a look in her eyes that was somewhere between astonishment and distress.

She rose and came forward to greet him, extending her hand. Was he imagining it, or did her hand shake just a bit? He took it in his own and smiled at her. "Forgive me for not informing you of my imminent arrival. It seems I have again appeared unannounced on your doorstep. Is—is everything all right, Amanda?" he asked, looking steadily at her. There were dark circles under her eyes that had not been there a se'nnight ago.

She returned his gaze for a moment and then turned away, walking to her place at the table once more. "Yes, of course, everything is quite well, Cousin Charles," she said, looking at the table.

"Amanda—" began the Earl.

"Will you not sit down, Cousin? Will you take luncheon with me?" she interrupted, walking to the bell cord and pulling it before she resumed her seat.

"Yes, yes, thank you." He took the seat opposite her. "Tell me, you—you are well?"

"Yes, Cousin Charles," she said softly, "I am well."

She raised her cup of wine to her lips, and the Earl thought that her manner, rather than being calm, as he had thought upon entering, was somewhat constrained. He watched her carefully as a footman entered and she ordered luncheon to be served to him. Her voice was quiet, almost a whisper, and her tone lacked any animation whatever.

The Earl did not know if her reserve was the result of their previous encounter, on the day he'd found Kitty and Richard here, or if there was some unknown cause of the tightly controlled manner in which she held herself. He was rapidly becoming exasperated, for after his frantic trip here, to be greeted by this evasive facade of calm quite unnerved him. How was he to break through to her? His instincts told him that something was wrong, but would he have thought so had it not been for Mrs. Havenwick's letter?

"By the by, Amanda, where is Mrs. Havenwick?" he inquired when the footman had exited.

"Mrs. Havenwick? Why, she—she's gone to visit her sister, just north of Shrewsbury. Why—"

"Not here? Mrs. Havenwick is not here?" He was suddenly very apprehensive.

"No, Cousin Charles. But I do assure you, the household will run well enough without her for a se'nnight or two," she answered composedly.

"Yes—yes—I do not doubt it, Amanda. But when did she leave—and why—why did she choose to go just at this time?"

"Her sister has been ailing for some time, and so I gave her leave to go. Victor—Victor has gone with her. 'Tis such an adventure for him to go visiting. They left two days ago."

The Earl regarded her intently for a moment, his face, he knew, a picture of jumbled emotions. He suddenly felt quite alarmed. With Mrs. Havenwick gone, and Amanda speaking with such icy formality, how was he to understand what danger lay in wait for her, if indeed any did? And why would Mrs. Havenwick take herself off to a sister who has long been ailing at a time when Amanda was supposedly in imminent danger? That made no sense whatsoever. If there was something dire enough for Mrs. Havenwick to send for him, then surely she too would have stayed, at least until he arrived. Unless—unless Amanda sent her away for some reason. Could Amanda herself be unaware of what peril she faced?

"I see," said the Earl at length. "Is there—is there anything else—changed—since I was last here?"

"In a week's time?" she asked, smiling only slightly. "No, Cousin Charles, but we—we do have a visitor. My—my—father is here," she said in a voice devoid of emotion.

"Your father! When did he get here?" exclaimed the Earl.

"He—he came last night," she uttered softly, and quickly looked down at her food, but not before he'd caught the expression in her eyes. He had seen that glazed look before, whenever her family was mentioned. And behind that look, he knew, was a great deal of pain. If only she would communicate with him the cause of her pain, he might know what to do. As it was, she held herself with an aloof dignity that would not allow him near.

"Where is he now, Amanda?" he asked gently.

She looked up at him without meeting his eyes. "Cousin Charles, you have not touched your food. Are you not hungry?"

"I am fine, Amanda. Where is your father?" he repeated, his voice still gentle.

"He went out riding this morning and has not yet returned," she said in that same expressionless voice.

"This visit—it was rather sudden, was it not? Did he not apprise you of his arrival?" he asked, before he realized that his question pointed out his own failure to do that very thing.

Somehow it would have been a relief had she taken him to task for that failure, but she did not regard it. "A message came—quite some few days ago—saying that he would arrive within a se'nnight. He came late last night after dinner. You will—meet him later this afternoon," she replied quietly.

The Earl's mind raced furiously as he connected the sequence of events. Her father sends a message of his intention to visit. Mrs. Havenwick writes to the Earl to beg his assistance, and before he arrives, she has disappeared with Victor. Did the danger Mrs. Havenwick warned him of have anything to do with Amanda's father, or was Lord Talbot's visit coincidental? Amanda had not been happy at home. That much he knew. But was there more than sadness in her memories of her childhood? Was there fear as well?

Abruptly she rose from the table. "Cousin Charles, I am persuaded that you will want to finish your luncheon and then freshen up after your journey. If—if you will excuse me just now, I—I find I am much in need of rest." Her fists were clenched tightly to the back of her chair as she spoke, and then she turned and began to walk slowly around the table toward the door, her hands grazing the tops of the chair backs.

When she had reached the corner of the table she seemed to trip on one of the chair legs. She stumbled and the Earl was at her side in a flash. He caught her by the elbows and steadied her just as she began straightening up. He looked searchingly at her face and she pulled back, but he did not release her.

"Amanda," he said earnestly. "What is it? Please talk to me."

349

He thought her tone a bit breathless as she replied, "I—I am quite well, Cousin Charles. But—but— perhaps this is not the best—time—for you to be here. I do not mean to be inhospitable, and you must stay the night, of course, but perhaps after that you might— leave Millforte for—for a fortnight or so." She tried to hold herself erect, away from him, but her eyes were pleading.

The Earl did not understand. She seemed deeply perturbed, yet she spurned his help. Not only would she not confide in him, but she would remove him from Millforte if she could. Had he so wounded her pride that she would confront alone whatever difficulty was before her rather than depend on him in any way? But, of course, he knew that that was exactly what she would do. Her pride, if not her fierce sense of independence, would allow her to do nothing else. And had she not several times previously placed herself in danger out of sheer stubbornness?

He still had not released her arms, but his grip slackened as he said gently, "No, Amanda. I am afraid I cannot do that. I shall remain at Millforte."

"I see," she said coolly, pulling her arms away from him. "Then in that case I shall see you at dinner," she continued in a tone that clearly indicated that the interview was over, after which she gracefully moved toward the door.

The Earl watched her retreating form in great consternation. Since when was Amanda in need of rest in the middle of the day? And how could he protect her with no knowledge of what he was protecting her from? And he knew that she would never tell him. Even the formality with which she had treated him when he had first arrived at Millforte was not as distant as her manner now. She seemed numb, as if she had retreated into a world of her own. Was her father the cause of her distress? Could she be afraid of him? But why? And if

350

so, why, upon her father's arrival, did she attempt to be rid of Mrs. Havenwick and himself, two people who might stand between them? It did not seem possible that she would be frightened of her own father, yet she certainly was not overjoyed to see him. Suddenly the Earl remembered his very recent dream of Amanda. He had seen terror in her eyes and he had not known if he would reach her in time. Would he reach her in time now, if indeed she was in danger of some kind?

He would get nowhere standing in the middle of an empty dining room, he thought. He resolved to seek Jeffries out presently; perhaps *he* would know something. Thus determined, his lordship left his luncheon untouched and found the butler coming away from the backstairs that led to the kitchen.

"My lord," said Jeffries, "I did not have the opportunity to welcome you back or to ask if there is anything I might do to make you comfortable."

The Earl smiled to himself, remembering the way he'd deftly bypassed Jeffries in his effort to see Amanda straight away. "Thank you very much, Jeffries. I expect I shall settle in quite easily. Darby should be along later today or tomorrow."

"Ah—then you mean to stay awhile?" asked Jeffries, his face a trifle anxious.

The Earl looked sharply at Jeffries for a moment. It was not like the butler to be inquisitive, nor to betray a trace of emotion on his face. "Yes, I mean to stay awhile, Jeffries. Is there any reason why I should not?" he asked, not unkindly. He thought that the butler breathed a small sigh of relief and his body seemed to bend just a bit.

"No, oh no, my lord. I did not mean—that is—the truth is, my lord, that I am very—happy to see you here," said Jeffries, somewhat flustered for what the Earl thought must be the first time in his life.

"Jeffries," said the Earl, his voice low, "can you tell

351

me what is going on here?"

"Whatever do you mean, my lord?" asked Jeffries, the impassive mask descending onto his face and his head erect once more.

"Jeffries," said the Earl meaningfully, "this is hardly the time to cling to the role of discreet retainer. Something is amiss here. I know it is. I believe Lady Millforte to be in some difficulty. Once before I asked you to enlighten me so that I might be of some use here. I have reason to believe the situation quite grave indeed, and I once again ask your help."

The butler gestured for his lordship to follow him, and they walked silently to the morning room. Jeffries glanced about before ushering the Earl inside and firmly closing the door. Despite these precautions the butler kept his voice low. "It is my impression, my lord, that Lady Millforte is—er—very distressed."

"Yes, I had rather noticed that. Do you have any idea as to why, Jeffries?"

"Why, no, my lord. But, well, it is my opinion that her ladyship has not been quite herself all week."

"Oh?"

"Yes, well, you see, my lord, after you and Lady Millforte's brother and—and the various young people departed last week, I took note of the fact that her ladyship seemed rather—withdrawn."

"I see, Jeffries. We—er—needn't go into that. Tell me what transpired after that. She received a message announcing Lord Talbot's visit, did she not?"

"Yes, my lord," replied Jeffries, the very faintest of smiles grazing his lips. "The letter arrived with the post perhaps two days after you left. Her ladyship came out of the library holding it and handed it to me. She said simply that her father would be coming within a se'nnight and that I should inform the household and make any arrangements. Then she said she was going up to her room and asked me to send Mrs. Havenwick to her."

"I see," said the Earl thoughtfully, walking to the fireplace and resting one hand on the mantel. "And her manner, Jeffries? What can you recall of that?"

"Well, if you'll pardon me, my lord, she had seemed, as I said, rather—er—withdrawn for the several days previous, but now she seemed even more so. She seemed distant. I—I—do not know quite how to put this—as if she was not really aware of me as she spoke," said the butler haltingly, his face quite perturbed.

"You have put it rather well, I think, Jeffries. Do go on," urged the Earl quietly.

"I informed Mrs. Havenwick of the news straight away, and she looked, I would have to say, rather stricken. She went immediately up to her ladyship but I cannot, of course, say what transpired between them."

"Of course, Jeffries. And?" pressed the Earl, a bit amused.

"When Mrs. Havenwick finally came down, I did happen to notice that her eyes were red." Here the Earl regarded him with a hint of a smile, but Jeffries went on. "And then there was a great deal of bustle about the house, and Mrs. Havenwick going about giving instructions to everyone for the next few days, saying she was going to visit her ailing sister near Shrewsbury."

"I see, Jeffries. You are being most helpful. By the by, the letter. Do you have it?"

"No, my lord. I—I put it back on her ladyship's desk. I thought it only proper. It—it is no longer there," said the butler uncomfortably.

"Of course, Jeffries. You acted correctly. Do you recall what it said?"

Jeffries looked taken aback. "My lord, I can assure you that I do not make a habit of—"

"No, I know you do not, Jeffries. But her ladyship gave you the letter, did she not?" When the butler nodded, his lordship went on. "Well then, it was perfectly proper for you to read it. Do you recall its contents?"

"Well, yes, I do recall part of it, because, if you'll pardon me, your lordship, it did seem a strange sort of message. It—it said that he had taken a fancy to see his only daughter after so many years and—expressed condolences on the—the death of Lord Millforte."

"Why did you consider it strange, Jeffries?" asked the Earl, his eyes narrowed.

"Oh, I am sure it is not my place to say, my lord," said Jeffries, his hands clasped behind his back and his usual formality belied only by the concerned look in his eyes.

"Come, Jeffries. Let us not go through all that again," chided the Earl amiably.

"Well, your lordship, the letter gave me the impression that Lord Talbot had only just heard of the master's passing. I did not understand why that should be, nor why he should suddenly come to visit after so many years. And it—if you will forgive me, my lord, it did not seem a very comforting letter from a father to an aggrieved daughter."

"Lord Talbot has never been here before?"

"No, my lord."

"And has Lady Millforte ever mentioned him to you? Or did my late uncle ever say anything?"

"No, my lord. I knew of his existence, and I believe there are several sons, but I know nothing more."

"What else troubled you, Jeffries?"

"There is, my lord, the matter of Lord Victor. He has gone with Mrs. Havenwick. Lady Millforte insisted upon it."

The Earl digested this bit of information. So Amanda had deliberately wanted Victor away. Why? Suddenly, unwittingly, he recalled the nightmare Amanda had had, when he'd given her the laudanum the night after he'd found her in the gully. She had screamed about her father—and then said something about Victor. He could not remember what; he had not remarked it at the time. But she had been frightened for Victor—of that he was sure. He had thought the dream nothing more than the effects of laudanum, but could it have been more? If so, of what was she frightened?

The butler was looking anxiously at him and the Earl collected himself. "Yes? Go on, Jeffries."

"Well, it is not my place to say, but he is Lord Talbot's grandson, and one would think—"

"Yes, I know, Jeffries. 'Tis strange, but I think it best we keep such thoughts between us," said the Earl, shuddering slightly as he remembered Amanda's nightmare. "What happened when Lord Talbot arrived last night, Jeffries?"

"Very little, my lord. He arrived after dinner. Lady Millforte came to greet him in the main hall and then—well—pleaded a headache and retired to her room. Lord Talbot bespoke a bath and a light supper in his room and he, too, retired early."

"I see. And this morning?"

"Lady Millforte took a late breakfast in bed and did not arise until her father had gone out." The butler said this last uncomfortably and the men exchanged anxious glances. The Earl knew that Jeffries was very well aware that his mistress did not, as a rule, plead headaches, nor take late breakfasts in bed.

His lordship regarded Jeffries intently for a moment before making a decision. He could not do this alone, not without knowing precisely what it was he had to do. "Jeffries," he said, "what I would say to you must be held in the strictest confidence. I know I can trust your discretion to the utmost." Jeffries came forward and stood before the Earl, hands at his sides, head erect.

"Are you aware, Jeffries, that Mrs. Havenwick sent

for me?" Jeffries's eyes widened and the Earl continued. "I was as surprised as you are. She sent a message saying only that Lady Millforte was in danger. I came straight away." The butler said nothing but his eyes were narrowed. "Do you have any idea what she might have meant, Jeffries? Did she say anything to you before she left?"

"No, my lord. And I cannot say that I have had reason to believe Lady Millforte to be facing any particular danger. There was, of course, the little matter we spoke of before you left Millforte, but he has made no attempt to gain entry here."

"No, I did not suppose it would be that. I confess myself perplexed, Jeffries, but very uneasy for all that. We shall both have to keep very alert. Her ladyship has retired, I believe for the afternoon. I shall go now to divest myself of my travel dirt. Pray inform me if Lord Talbot arrives back at the house, for I should like to be present when she and her father next meet."

"Very good, my lord, it shall be done. I shall aid you in any way I can."

"Thank you, Jeffries. Let us hope we are all of us, including Mrs. Havenwick, merely being fanciful."

"Yes, my lord. Oh, my lord, if I may say—one thing more. Perhaps it will cheer you a bit. We have not had any—er—violets in the past week," said Jeffries, his lips curling slightly into a smile.

"Thank you, Jeffries. I had a feeling there mightn't be," replied the Earl, smiling for the first time.

After a most welcome bath and a change of clothes, the Earl was informed that Lord Talbot had come in from his ride and was presently partaking of a late luncheon. As such, his lordship ventured down to the family dining room, where he found Amanda's father sitting at the head of the table.

356

The Earl wore what he considered easy afternoon dress for the country—britches rather than pantaloons, a brown coat cut very simply, neckcloth casually arranged. Still, he knew he cut a striking figure, and apparently Lord Talbot thought so as well, for the latter rose immediately when the Earl entered the room, seemingly quite impressed.

The Earl moved forward into the room, studying Amanda's father as he did so. He was a tall man, broad and husky. There were tiny red lines near his eyes and running across the bridge of his nose. His face was a bit puffy, but even so, one might still have called him a good-looking man. In fact, the Earl imagined that as a young man he must have been quite handsome. As he approached the table, the Earl extended his hand and said, "Lord Talbot, I presume?"

The older man's eyelids flickered for a moment as he replied, shaking the Earl's hand, "Why, yes, and you—"

"Charles Ainsley, sir. I am pleased to meet you."

"Ah, yes, the Earl. The servants have been whispering that you had come." Lord Talbot flashed a very engaging smile. "Old Millforte's nephew, are you not?"

"Yes, I am," replied the Earl.

"Come for a visit, have you?"

"Well, yes. Actually, Lady Millforte and I have some business to take care of with regard to the estates. I have been named guardian of the heir and the estates, along with Lady Millforte, you must know."

"I see," said Amanda's father, his brows arching just a little. "Care to join me, Ainsley?" When the two had seated themselves, he went on. "Glass of wine? Excellent claret Millforte kept. Don't know why Manda keeps it hidden and barred up in the cellar. Had to go and fetch it myself."

The Earl was not aware that any wine was kept hidden at Millforte, but he kept his face impassive as he said, "Yes, I will, thank you." Lord Talbot began to rise but the Earl forestalled him. "Pray be seated. I shall take a glass from the sideboard." Having secured a wineglass, the Earl sat down once more, noting that the bottle of wine in front of Lord Talbot was three-quarters empty. He wondered if the man had indeed imbibed so much of it over luncheon.

As Amanda's father filled the Earl's glass and replenished his own, the Earl tried to recollect what he knew about him. Very little, it seemed. He held a minor barony in Lincolnshire and had married a Spanish woman, who was reputed to have acted on the stage, though her family was old and respected. The Earl found himself wondering how that marriage had fared. Would the Talbot family have accepted a Spanish actress? He thought not. He looked closely at Talbot's coat. It fit him well enough, but it was not the work of a first-quality tailor, and it was frayed about the collar. It would seem that the barony had not proved itself entirely prosperous.

The Earl was recalled from his speculations as Talbot said, "I gather from the servants that you have been here before, Ainsley?"

The Earl took a sip of the claret before replying, "Yes, as I said, Lady Millforte and I have a great deal to accomplish with regard to the estates. I was here several weeks ago and then was recalled to London."

"I see." The Baron drained his glass and filled it again. "My daughter is very beautiful, is she not?" he asked, his eyes narrowing a bit.

The Earl wondered at such a question, but nevertheless replied, "Why, yes. Quite beautiful, Talbot."

The Baron said nothing for several moments but sipped his wine. Then he ventured, "Fertile green country here. I rode out this morning. Fine horseflesh in the stables, too. Do you not agree?"

"Er, yes," replied the Earl, upon which followed a

rather prosaic discussion of horseflesh.

When the claret had disappeared, Talbot excused himself, pleading a need to rest after the morning's excursions. The Earl was left to ruminate upon Amanda's father, who had not mentioned his grandson, nor the reason for his absence from Millforte until now, but who appeared, despite all, a rather amiable, if dull, older gentleman, perhaps a bit too devoted to his claret.

Neither Amanda nor the Baron appeared again until dinner. The Earl noticed that Amanda had chosen to wear a rather demure black silk evening dress cut high across the bosom. She sat at her usual place at the end of the long table and the Baron at the other; the Earl was placed between them. Amanda seemed very pale, and when she had greeted him, her hand was limp and cold.

The conversation at dinner seemed almost a continuation of the Earl's previous discussion with Lord Talbot, for Amanda said very little. The Baron exclaimed once again over the fine horses to be found in the Millforte stables and went on to expound about some of the "superior" equestrian specimens that had passed through his own stables over the years. He questioned the Earl as to whether he enjoyed a good horse race as much as the Baron, and about his preferences in the gaming room, faro being one of the Baron's favorites.

The Earl answered him politely, even amiably, but surreptitiously stole glances at Amanda when the Baron was preoccupied with his food or the new bottle of wine he had ordered opened. Amanda ate very little, he noticed, but made a great show of concentrating on her food. Rarely did she raise her eyes from her plate, and she made no attempt at conversation.

Lord Talbot, finding that the Earl was not much of a gamester, changed the subject. He began to discuss the farms attached to his estate in Lincolnshire, and at length, he addressed Amanda. "Amanda, you have been very quiet. Tell me, my dear, how do you manage this large household and the estates, now that your husband is—no longer here?" he asked in a strong voice, the tone of which jarred the Earl because it sounded almost like a challenge.

Amanda lifted her head as she replied quietly, "I manage well enough, Father. The staff is quite diligent and devoted to me."

"And what kind of business have you and the Earl been discussing? I understand he has been here before," inquired the Baron with what the Earl perceived as a trace of harshness.

The Earl thought Amanda went a shade paler and she answered in a small voice, "I have been acquainting Lord Ainsley with the economy of Millforte, Father. We have discussed ways of—of increasing the productivity of the land."

"I see. And do you find things running smoothly, Ainsley, or will you be making changes? Looks to me like the coffers are quite full here," said Talbot, his eyes narrowing.

The Earl did not know how to reply. The Baron's questions were making him uncomfortable, but he could not say why. He caught Amanda's eyes for a moment. They held a pleading look, and he remembered her formal reference to him as Lord Ainsley. He answered as noncommittally as he could. "The affairs of Millforte appear to be quite in order, Talbot. Lady Millforte and I have met with the man-of-affairs and have been reviewing figures pertaining to the farms as well as the revenues from wool and mutton."

Amanda seemed to breathe an almost imperceptible sigh of relief at that, and her father could think of no reply. He drained a third glass of wine and, when dessert was brought, set himself to it quite diligently.

At length Amanda rose. "Father, Lord Ainsley, I am persuaded you will want to take your brandy now, will you not?"

The Earl blanched inwardly at her formal term of address, but was careful to keep his face impassive. He would gladly have forgone the traditional male prerogative of brandy after dinner, but Lord Talbot insisted upon it, and Amanda, pleading a headache, went up to bed. The Earl watched Lord Talbot down a good deal of brandy, and after repeated suggestions that the Baron might want to retire for the night, the Baron did in fact rise and declare his intention of doing just that. His speech was somewhat slurred by this time, but he seemed to have little difficulty keeping his powerful body steady as he made his way up the great staircase.

The Earl followed closely behind, and walked the older man to his room, which was at the opposite end of the long third floor corridor from his own. Amanda's bedchamber was somewhere between their two rooms, and as he passed her closed door on the way to his own room, he found himself hoping that she would sleep soundly. She had looked as if she had not slept well in a very long time.

Upon entering his own room he reflected that the evening had been without incident, but he was left with an inexplicable uneasiness. Perhaps it was that the relationship between Amanda and her father had seemed so distant. It struck him forcibly that while Amanda herself was such a devoted parent, her relationship with her father was most unnatural. The Earl was very perturbed indeed, and it was only the fatigue he felt after his three-day journey that enabled him to sleep at all.

Chapter Twenty-Three

The Earl was running through the grass toward Amanda, but she backed away from him, fear in her eyes. "No, no! 'Tis not true! No!" she screamed before she turned and ran.

Her screams jarred the Earl into wakefulness. He sat upright in bed, but the house was silent. The night was well advanced, for the fire seemed to have died out long since and the moonlight streamed in through the windows.

The Earl had the eerie sensation of not being quite sure whether those screams had been real or part of his dream. The uneasiness of this past evening began to creep over him once more, and he found that he was not the least bit sleepy any longer. He stilled his breathing to listen for any untoward sounds in the house, but the walls, after all, were very thick, and he heard nothing. It would not do any harm, he thought, to take a walk down the corridor, just to assure himself that all was well.

As such he rose from his bed, drew on his dressing gown and slippers, and made his way to the corridor. Moonlight streamed in through several windows as he walked slowly and silently toward Amanda's room. He drew his dressing gown more tightly around him; he was not sure whether it was the cold or some sense of foreboding, perhaps stemming from his disconcerting dream, that made him shiver.

He did not hear a sound until he was about three doors away from Amanda's room. He stopped short as soon as he heard the noise, for he could not at first discern what it was, nor where it came from. Footsteps—a scuffling along the floor. A thud—perhaps a table had fallen. The Earl advanced forward noiselessly, his ears alert, his whole body tensed as he tried to fathom the source of the noises.

He heard a sharp crack, and then another and another, but it was not until he was some five yards from Amanda's door that he heard the voice.

"Whore! I always knew you were a whore! All those stories these many years—I wondered. Yes, I wondered. But now I know!" growled the Baron, his words slurred slightly but his voice strong for all that.

For a moment the Earl felt frozen to his spot, so menacing was the Baron's tone. Then he heard another crack, and without thinking about what he was doing, he ran toward the door.

"How long, Amanda? How long have you been whoring with Ainsley?" he heard the Baron shout, and then came the whistling of something moving through the air; then the sound of another crack.

The Earl's heart was pounding fiercely with some unnamed dread as he lunged for the door and thrust it open. In the moonlight he saw the Baron bring his riding crop down with brutal force. It was too dark to see its target, but he knew it anyway. He heard a muffled whimper as he grabbed the Baron from behind, pinioning his arms to his sides.

"What the—who the hell—get out of here!" yelled Amanda's father as he struggled violently. The Earl braced the Baron against his knee and shoved him to the right, away from where he thought Amanda must be.

The Baron spun onto the floor in the middle of the

room, his fall cushioned by the carpet. The Earl stood over him as he staggered to his feet, the riding crop still clutched in his right hand. "You have no right, Ainsley. She's *my* daughter and I will do with her what I will. Now, get out of my way!" shouted the Baron, his face contorted with fury as he tried to push the Earl out of his path.

But the Earl grabbed the Baron's wrist with both of his hands and twisted it down until the Baron's grip slackened and the crop fell to the floor. "Damn you!" shouted Lord Talbot as he jerked his wrist free and rubbed it for a moment.

Then he lunged to retrieve the whip, whereupon the Earl struck him with the full force of his right fist, sending him sprawling again to the floor.

The Baron lifted himself up on his elbows and tried to rise, snarling. "How dare you interfere, Ainsley! How dare you! You, who put your filthy hands on my daughter!"

The Earl was on him in a moment, pushing him back to the floor. He seized the Baron by his throat and shook him fiercely. "If you ever touch her again, I'll kill you, Talbot! Do you hear me—father or no, I swear I'll kill you!" the Earl raged, the veins throbbing at his temples as he shook the Baron brutally. The Baron began to choke and the Earl slackened his grip, letting Talbot's head fall to the floor. The Earl stood up and commanded, his voice filled with disgust, "Get up, Talbot."

For a moment Amanda's father lay on the floor, his breathing heavy, one hand massaging his throat. In that moment, the Earl's attention was caught by the sound of hurried footsteps in the corridor, coming from the direction of his own room. Damn! he thought. It would be too much to hope that no one had heard the fracas. Come to think of it, where the hell was Amanda's maid? Surely if she was asleep in the dressing room, she would have been awakened.

In a matter of seconds Darby appeared in the doorway. "Oh, it's you, thank God," said the Earl. "You'd better come in." As Darby entered the room, the Earl repeated in a cold voice, "Get up, Talbot."

Darby looked questioningly at the Earl, but the latter concentrated only on Amanda's father. As Lord Talbot struggled to rise, the Earl caught one of his arms, helped to pull him up, and then twisted it behind his back. He spun the Baron toward Darby, who grabbed the Baron's free arm. "Take him to his room, Darby. Lock the door and keep watch until I get there," said the Earl, helping Darby yank the Baron to the door.

Once in the doorway, the Earl let go Lord Talbot's arm and Darby moved to grasp it. The Baron tried to wrest himself free but Darby held him firmly. "I won't forget this, Ainsley," spat the Baron, but the Earl ignored him, speaking instead to his valet.

"Bring some brandy here as soon as you can, Darby," he said grimly, his eyes moving toward the silent shadows where he knew Amanda must be.

"Yes, my lord," was all Darby said as he led the Baron away.

The Earl closed the door behind them and advanced into the room. Now he became aware of soft muffled sobs coming from the right side of the room. He still could not see Amanda. She had not moved from the shadows, but he knew by the barely audible sobs where she was. He walked to her and bent down. He could see that she was crouched on her knees, next to an overturned table. Her head was down, protected by her arms.

"Amanda," he whispered.

"Go away," she said in a choked voice.

"No, Amanda, I will not go away," he said gently, and put his hands around her shoulders to lift her.

"Ahh!" she cried out in pain.

As he dropped his hands from her arms he realized she was bleeding. Damn! He needed to see where she was injured. He walked quickly to the bedside table, upon which sat a candelabrum. It had several good tapers in it, which he lit immediately. Then he righted the small table next Amanda and set the candelabrum upon it.

"Good Lord!" he gasped as he dropped to the floor beside Amanda. Her arms looked black and blue in places, and they were bloody with raw welts. On her back the blood came through her white lawn nightgown, torn jaggedly wherever the riding crop had savagely cut her. He gently placed his hands under her arms, carefully avoiding any of the bruises. He tried to lift her but she resisted. She raised her head slightly, so that all he could see were her wet eyes, and she whispered, "Please go away. I cannot bear to have you here. Don't you understand?"

"Yes, I understand," he replied as he pulled her up towards him and then, standing, scooped her into his arms. "But you shall have to learn to bear with me, my dear, for I shan't leave you alone."

She turned her face into his chest, so that he could not see her, and she tried to stifle her cries. He carried her to the bed and sat down, cradling her in his arms. He held her very tightly against him and began rocking her gently. He felt the convulsive shudders as the sobs began again, and she tried to choke them back.

"Let it come, Amanda. 'Tis good for you to cry," he said softly, still rocking her, and finally, after several moments, he felt her body relax, and the tears came. Her whole body shook, and she cried deeply, the pent-up cries of a lifetime, he thought.

He cringed when he remembered her father's vile words, and then he recalled her hysterical outburst the day Kitty and Richard had come. "I'm a whore, is that not what you think?" she had cried. A woman with so much pride, so much dignity. How often before her marriage had this happened, and how had she managed to survive at all? He felt more ashamed than he ever had in his life for his part in her misery, for ever doubting her at all. And if not for their terrible argument that day, would she have confided in him or would she have insisted on facing her nemesis alone? Somehow he knew that she would have done the same thing. That very pride that could almost destroy her was also her greatest strength. How could he make her see that it was all right to share her burdens?

He did not know how long he held her; perhaps five minutes, perhaps a quarter of an hour, but his dressing gown and nightshirt were wet with her tears as he stroked her hair and rocked her gently. At length her body stilled itself and she choked back the last of her sobs. She lay limp in his arms. He held her a little away from him and looked at her face for the first time. It was streaked with her tears and her hair streamed forward wildly, but the clear white skin was smooth and unharmed. He remembered the crouching position he had found her in, face bent into her knees, arms covering her head. She had known instinctively to protect her face. God! How many times had she been through this before?

"Amanda," he whispered softly, but she was silent and would not meet his eyes.

He lifted her from his lap and, standing, gently placed her upon the bed. Then he retrieved the candelabrum and replaced it on the bedside table. He looked down at her, curled up on her side, the blood beginning to dry but still visible even through the nightgown, and his heart was torn apart. He felt an overwhelming wave of emotions—fury at the man who had done this, a fury that made him regret he had not killed him right then—fury, and at the same time, a deep protectiveness for the proud, beautiful woman with the fragile eyes.

The Earl went to the washstand. He found water in the basin and a few pieces of clean linen, but he would need more. He brought the basin and linen to the bedside table and sat down next to Amanda. He took her hand and said, "Amanda, I will need to bathe those cuts. Where will I find more linen?"

"No, Charles, please go," she pleaded. "I shall be right."

"No, my dear. The time for that is past. You'll not be rid of me so easily. Now where is the linen?" he asked, smiling down at her.

She turned her head slightly and looked at him from the corner of her eye. "In the dressing room. I believe Bessie keeps some in the bottom drawer of the cupboard."

"Where is Bessie, Amanda? Does she not sleep in the dressing room?"

"Well, yes, she—often does—but I—I sent her to sleep with the housemaids upstairs," she said quietly.

"Why, Amanda?" he asked, tightening the grip on her hand.

"Sometimes when he—when he'd finished with me—my—my father used to—to beat my maids," she rasped, and turned her face down into the coverlet.

"And so you sent her away, just as you sent Victor away. Everyone but yourself. You protect everyone but yourself, Amanda. Why?" he whispered, stroking her hand with his thumb. She did not answer, as he had known she would not, and he rose, taking the candelabrum, and went to the dressing room.

He found the linen easily, and it struck him that he would have to remove her nightgown in order to tend the bruises on her back. Better not to ask her where she kept her nightgowns—the mere suggestion would infuriate her. As such, he began rummaging through several drawers of the cupboard, too upset for his mind to indulge in any fantasies as he beheld the rows of female underthings. He did not find any nightgowns, however, and then he realized that perhaps they were hanging up. He opened the large doors of the hanging cupboard, which took up one whole wall of the room, and beheld an array of gowns—taffetas, silks, ball gowns, morning dresses, the gamut. Damn! he thought, annoyed that he was wasting time. He held the candelabrum up to the cupboard and walked to the far end. Here, finally, were rows of fine lace and satin dressing gowns, and delicate nightgowns. He quickly selected a long-sleeve one that did not seem to have too many buttons—he did not want to give Amanda much time to object to what he was doing.

The Earl sat once more upon the bed. Amanda had not moved. The nightgown she was wearing had tiny puffed sleeves of lace and her arms had been exposed. Only one arm was visible as she now lay on her side, and he began very gently to bathe the raw welts. She flinched as the cool water touched her, but she did not utter a sound. When he had finished, he patted the wounds with a dry cloth and then, taking both her hands, gently lifted her up, twisting her a bit so that he could reach her left arm. She was sitting up now, facing him, her feet tucked under her. She would not look up at him, but she did not try to stop him as he cleansed her other arm.

As he dabbed her arms gently with a dry cloth, he heard a knock at the door. He went and opened it just a tad to assure himself that it was Darby. He slipped outside the room and closed the door partially behind him, then took the tray of brandy from Darby. "The Baron?" he asked quietly, and Darby held up a key.

"I have taken care of him, my lord," said the valet. His eyes traveled to the Earl's nightclothes, by now wet and stained with blood.

The Earl followed his gaze and said, "Keep watch over the Baron. See that he remains quiet. I shall join you as soon as I am able. And Darby, this—this entire affair is not to be spoken of."

In the dim light the Earl could see that the valet's face showed concern, but he merely said, "Of course, my lord. And if I may be of assistance in any other way—"

"No, Darby, I—oh, there is one thing," said the Earl, a thought just occurring to him. "That excellent salve you always carry . . ."

Darby nodded and disappeared, and the Earl went back into the room, shutting the door behind him.

He placed the tray of brandy on the table nearest the door and, pouring a glass, carried it to Amanda. "Drink this, my dear," he said gently, sitting next to her, but she made no move to take the glass from him. "It will ease the pain," he urged, lifting the glass to her lips, and her hand closed around his as she took a sip. She choked slightly, but swallowed several more large gulps before she pushed the glass away.

He placed the glass on the bedside table next to the candelabrum and his hand went to her back. He had left it for last, knowing that she would not take kindly to what he was about to do. But before he could begin, there came another knock. He went to retrieve the small jar of salve from his valet, then closed the door firmly and came back to the bed.

"This is a very soothing ointment, Amanda. It will help the wounds to heal," he said, and she nodded silently.

Ever so gently, he smoothed the cool salve over the cuts on her arms. Other than a tightening of her muscles when he began, she made no demur. He put the jar on the table when he'd done and turned his attention to her back. He tried to pull the torn nightgown away from her skin, but as he had feared, the blood was caked dry in several places and the fabric of her nightgown was stuck to her.

"Amanda, the blood is caked dry. I must remove the nightgown or the cuts will never heal," he said softly.

She looked up at him with lost eyes. "No," she whispered. "You have done enough."

"Would you prefer I go to get Bessie? I shall if you wish it. As it is now, no one knows of this but me. Darby is seeing to your father, but he did not see into the room, and he will never say a word of this night to anyone. You must be cared for, Amanda. Shall I go for Bessie?" he asked gently.

She looked down and shook her head.

He put his fingertip under her chin and lifted her head. "Are you hurt anywhere else, my dear? Your chest, your legs? Tell me the truth, Amanda," he insisted. He had seen blood only on her back, and though he thought her crouching position most likely would have shielded her, he wanted to be sure.

"I think he hit me—here—" she said faintly, pointing to her right thigh, which, hidden as it was from the candlelight, he could not see.

He nodded and stroked her brow for a moment. "Turn around," he said, and assisted her to turn so that her back was to him.

He thought to lift the nightgown over her head and remove it, but then thought better of it. "I am going to tear the gown," he said, knowing that at least this way she would be partially covered. When she nodded, he began wrenching the tattered gown from the neck down, but she cried out and he saw that the lawn was still clinging to the cuts in several places.

He stopped tugging at the nightgown and began to moisten the dried welts through the fabric. It was some time before he was able to lift the lawn away from her, and he tore the gown so that it gaped open the length of her back. She shivered slightly, though the room was still fairly warm, for a small fire burned in the grate.

She had probably kept it burning; he wondered whether she had slept at all tonight.

The Earl gritted his teeth at the sight of her beautiful back, the white skin marred and bloodied by the savage force of a riding crop and a demented man who dared call himself her father. For a moment his eyes went to the jagged scar just beneath her shoulder, the scar he'd seen that day in the hut. A carriage accident, she'd said, and he'd known she was lying. But *this!* This horror he would never have guessed. Grimly, he bathed the broken skin again, on her shoulders and down her back, careful to remove whatever bits of fuzz from the gown he could see.

He patted her dry and began to apply the salve over the wounds. She was shivering again and he cursed inwardly, hurrying his task. "We must wait a few moments for it to dry. Then I shall give you a fresh gown," he said hoarsely when he finished.

Then he went to stoke the fire. He fanned it with the bellows and watched several flames shoot up. He added a log and the fire blazed.

When the Earl went back to Amanda he saw that she had turned around so that he could not see her exposed back. He smiled and handed her the fresh nightgown that he had placed at the far end of the bed. "Can you manage this by yourself?" he asked.

She nodded and he walked to the far window and turned his back. After several minutes she said, "'Tis all right, now," in a tiny voice.

He came to the bedside and removed the torn nightgown. She was still sitting with her legs tucked under her. "I must see to the leg, now. You must sit with your legs extended in front of you," he said quietly, carefully avoiding the use of the word *thigh*. This was going to be difficult enough as it was.

"No," she said, her voice stronger for the first time. "Please leave me now. You—you have done enough. I shall be fine."

"Amanda!" he said with a harshness he did not feel.

She sighed and slowly brought her legs out from under her torso. "Move over a bit," he said, so that, from his perch on the left side of the bed, he could tend her right thigh.

He lifted the nightgown up over her leg until the raw wound was revealed. He was careful not to expose any more of her fine white skin than he had to. Her head was bent and he could not see her face, but he could imagine her blushing. The crop had cut a long welt along the length of the thigh, but it did not appear to be as deep as the other wounds. He repeated the cleansing process and lowered the gown over her legs as soon as he could.

Then he lifted her chin with his finger and looked down at her face. Her eyes held that same mixture of fear and trust he had seen that day in the crofter's hut. "I'm sorry," he said, his voice low, "but it had to be done." He brushed several strands of hair from her face. "You must sleep now, Amanda. I shall give you some laudanum to ease the pain." She had not cried out, but he knew the pain had to be severe, despite the brandy he had given her.

He was surprised therefore when she shook her head. "Please—I do not wish to sleep yet. And the laudanum—it—it makes the nightmares worse."

He remembered the dream she'd had under the effects of laudanum and did not press the issue. "Then you must drink some more of the brandy." He lifted the glass and put it to her lips. She took it from him and downed the remainder of the brandy. The Earl replaced the glass on the table and then said gently, "Come, let me make you comfortable. You must rest, and sleep will come in time."

He stood and carefully swept the comforter from under her. She allowed him to help her to lie down on her side, and he saw her grimace as her body moved, but she said nothing. He gently covered her with the comforter before sitting down beside her once again. Her body seemed tense, and her hand smoothed the comforter nervously.

The Earl took her hand in his and began to stroke it softly with his other hand. "Relax," he said. "You need to rest."

"You—you needn't stay here, Charles. I shall be right now, and I am persuaded that you also must need to rest," she murmured, looking up at him. She made no attempt to retrieve her hand, and he realized with a mixture of surprise and pleasure that, for the first time, she did not want him to leave. Her face looked very troubled, still fearful.

He smiled at her. "I shall let you know when I am tired. But I do think you should sleep, Amanda."

"I—I—was always afraid to sleep—afterwards," she said quietly.

The Earl momentarily tightened his grip on her hand. "How long—how long has he been doing this to you, Amanda?" he asked hoarsely, afraid of the answer.

"I have not seen him since—since my marriage to Arthur," she replied in a hushed voice.

"I know that. And before your marriage? Was it always like this?" he pressed.

She sighed and turned her head away. Her hand still rested in his. "No. It—it started when I was twelve years old."

"When your mother died?" he asked gently.

"Yes," she said, her voice a whisper. "When my mother died."

"Tell me about your mother, Amanda. How did she die?"

"No." She turned back to him, her eyes pleading. "Do not ask that of me. Please—go now, Charles." She pulled her hand from his and covered her face.

"Amanda," he commanded softly. "Look at me." When she uncovered her face, he took her hand once more. "It is best to speak of it, Amanda. You are tortured by your memories. It is time you let them come out. Then perhaps, they will leave you in peace." He looked into her eyes and smiled reassuringly.

"I cannot speak of it," she said, her voice tremulous, and suddenly he recalled that long ago day when they had toured the estates together.

"Amanda," he said, "you once said that your mother's death was not—an accident. How did she die, Amanda?"

"He was drunk," she rasped. "He—he—pushed her—down the stairs." As soon as the words were out, her eyes widened in anguish, and wrenching her hand from his, she buried her head in the pillow.

She began to cry softly, and the Earl cursed under his breath, holding his head in his hands. My God, he thought, 'twas no wonder she could never speak of it. But he knew that it was better that she had. Perhaps later she would tell him more, but now she must rest. He began to stroke her hair tenderly. "'Tis all right. You are safe, now, my dear," he whispered, and then added, "Your—father will be leaving here tonight, Amanda. Sleep now. You are safe. Do you understand?"

Slowly the tears subsided and she turned her head slightly to him and nodded. He brushed several strands of hair from her face and ran his finger down her cheek for a moment. He reached for her hand and held it until, finally, she fell asleep.

The Earl found Darby in the corridor outside Lord Talbot's bedchamber. The two men entered the room together. The Baron had been seated on the bed and stood as soon as they entered.

"You have one hour to get out of here, Talbot," said the Earl coldly. "I meant what I said. If you ever touch her again, I'll kill you. And do not ever set foot on Millforte again, nor come near your daughter, no matter where she is. Do I make myself clear?"

The Baron's face was flushed with anger. He advanced menacingly toward the Earl, but Darby darted behind him and grabbed his arms. "You have no right," growled the Baron. "She is *my* daughter and—"

"I have jurisdiction over Millforte, and I am not without influence in this county, nor in London. Do not push me, Talbot. Were you anyone but her father you would not have breath left in you with which to speak," retorted the Earl with contempt. "Now start getting dressed," he continued as he looked at the Baron's disheveled evening clothes.

The Earl instructed Darby to summon the Baron's valet, and he glared at Talbot as the latter slowly began to divest himself of his coat and neckcloth. Darby returned but moments later with the sleepy-eyed manservant.

"Your master finds it necessary to depart from Millforte straight away. You will assist him to dress and pack his things so that you may be gone within the hour," said the Earl authoritatively.

The Baron's valet, a rather slight man, looked curiously at his master but said nothing. Talbot glowered fiercely as the valet began to undress him.

The Earl whispered some final instructions to Darby and then turned to the Baron. "The household is asleep, Talbot. I trust you will leave quietly, and with dignity," he said, and then he strode from the room.

When he returned to Amanda's room he was pleased that she was still asleep. He retired to the dressing room, but though the bed was comfortable enough, he could not sleep. His mind relived over and over the ghastly scene upon which he had burst, and he could not stop thinking of the extraordinary revelation Amanda had made. What a terrible burden to have carried that knowledge within her so long. He wondered if anyone else knew.

He had lain awake for what seemed a very long time when he heard movement in the bedchamber. He rose quickly, and as he opened the door between the two rooms, he beheld Amanda, standing at the window. He rushed to her. "Amanda," he said gently, "come back to bed." She shook her head and he asked, "Are you in a great deal of pain?"

"'Tis not—the pain, Charles. I cannot sleep. My head is full—of—of all the memories," she replied, her voice barely audible.

"Come," he said, and gently took her by the elbow to lead her back to the bed.

She did not protest, but when he tried to help her lie down she said, "Please, I—I would rather sit up awhile."

"Will you be comfortable—with your back?"

"I shall be fine propped with some pillows, I think. I'll not be putting my weight on my back, after all."

He eased her to a sitting position and, propping the pillows for her, helped her to move back against them. He covered her with the comforter and then sat down beside her on the bed.

She looked down at the hands in her lap. He covered them with one of his. "Amanda," he said tenderly, "you have been tortured long enough by your memories. Speak to me, Amanda. It is best. The time has come, my dear."

She lifted her head and stared at him, her fragile eyes filled with anguish. Then she swallowed hard and began speaking in a soft voice, turning her head away from him as she did so.

"My mother was very beautiful. She was possessed

of an inborn grace and a deep sense of dignity. She came from an old aristocratic Spanish family, much renowned for their abilities as actors. The family fortune had long since been run aground, and for generations several members of the family had taken to the stage. My mother was a very well-beloved actress in her day. She and her brothers acted in the same company, and they chaperoned her wherever she went. I do not think she ever looked at another man before— before she met my—my father."

Amanda turned her head back to the Earl. He squeezed her hand. "Go on, Amanda."

"When I was a little girl, my mother used to tell me about how they had met. He had come to the theater one night. My mother was acting the part of Ophelia in *Hamlet*, and he fell in love with her on first sight. I am persuaded that she loved him as well. I can still remember the look in her eyes when she would speak of him, for I think they were very happy in those early years. Then, when I was perhaps six or seven years old, it began to change. My father began to drink a great deal, and my mother looked sad and frightened much of the time. There was much that I did not understand then—that I found out later. The Talbots had never forgiven him for marrying my mother, and he was cut out of his father's will. He got the estate, of course, for that was entailed. But he received nothing else, and there was never enough money to keep the estate up, especially since he was an inveterate gamester.

"I do not know when I became aware that he—he beat my mother, but somehow, I knew. Sometimes I would creep downstairs to the corridor around the corner from their rooms, and I would hear him screaming at her. 'Whore' he would call her. 'All actresses are whores. You have been the ruin of me.' I did not know what the word meant at the time, but I knew he was beating her. Then we children would be

378

told that Mama was ill, and she would keep to her room for days. I do not think the others knew, but I did. I never said a word to anyone, of course, but when I was perhaps ten years old I asked her why she did not run away so that Father could not hurt her anymore. She was devastated that I knew. She told me that Father sometimes drank too much and then did things that he did not mean, but that truly he loved her. And she said that if she left she would not be able to take us with her, and she loved us above all else. I remember I cried all night, thinking that if not for us Mama could run away."

Amanda stopped for a moment, her eyes suddenly moist. Her words were coming rapidly now, as if, once she had started, the words spilled out in a flow that could not be checked. She brushed away a tear and continued, her voice now a haunted whisper.

"I was twelve years old when she died. I heard noises one night and crept from my bed, as I had done so often before. I saw them on the staircase. I could see that my father was drunk. He was hitting her and she tried to struggle from his grasp. He—he—pushed her and she—tumbled—down the stairs. She didn't move when she reached the bottom. She just stayed there; she had broken her neck. I—I never told anyone. I was afraid he would kill *me* if he ever found out I knew. So I— crept back to bed and cried all night. I cried every night for at least a year after that. I've never told anyone— not anyone at all—until—until now."

Tears rolled down her cheeks now, and she did not try to check them. He drew out his own handkerchief and dabbed her eyes. "I am sorry, Amanda. I am so sorry," he uttered very softly.

She took the handkerchief from him and spoke again. This time her voice was bitter. "She was gone but a few months when he began to—to beat me. He called me 'whore'—I still did not know what it meant. He did it often. Once a month at least, I suppose, and always when he had drunk too much. But he was never beyond sensibility. I always believed he knew what he was doing. By then Mrs. Havenwick had come, and she took care of me."

"And your brothers? Did they know what was happening?"

"My older brothers must have known, but they did nothing. They are both my father all over again. William, the eldest, used to seduce the housemaids and beat them up until my father made him stop because we could not keep a maid above six months. Giles married several years back, but I have heard that his wife ran away from him. But Richard," she said, her face softening, "Richard knew, and he, several times, when he was a mere boy, perhaps thirteen, tried to make my father stop. He received a severe flogging each time for his pains, and I bade him cease trying. It made no sense for us both to suffer. But he stayed by my side whenever he could, as if it were his mission in life to protect me from the world, even if he could not protect me from my father. When I married, he came to stay with me for a while, and then Arthur bought him his colors."

"I understand how Richard must have felt. I would I could have spared you this tonight. Why did you not let me?" the Earl said earnestly.

For several moments Amanda did not answer. When she did speak, her head was down, her voice a barely audible whisper. "Charles, don't you understand? My mother—for all she suffered—kept her dignity. Always. I have—I have lost mine."

"No, you have not. Oh, my dear, dear Amanda, you have not lost your dignity. It is no shame to share your burdens. Don't you understand that?" he asked, taking both her hands in his.

She lifted her wet eyes to his and said hoarsely, "I do

not know, Charles. I have carried my pain and my grief within me for so long."

"It is time it came out, my dear. Now, I think you should sleep. Come, let me help you," he said soothingly, rising from the bed and helping her to lie down on her side.

"Charles," she said, "you will—"

He took her hand once again. "I shall remain in the dressing room. If you are in pain, my dear, you must call me. Or if—if you are troubled by your dreams."

"Thank you, Charles," she murmured. "But—but—" she said, picking her head up from the pillow, "the servants. What will the servants say in the morning?"

"It will not be the first time, Amanda. We will have to invent some story to explain your—indisposition—in any case, and we shall simply say that I cared for you, no one else being about. You have an amazing ability to remember the proprieties in any situation. Now go to sleep!" he reprimanded gently.

"Yes, Charles," she said demurely, and squeezed his hand.

Despite the horror of the evening he could not help a small surge of joy as her hand closed on his. The candles were flickering down into their sockets, and he stood there for several moments, watching her beautiful face, now in repose as her eyes closed. Her grip slackened and he placed her hand upon the mattress. He bent over her and kissed her brow. "Good night, my dear Amanda," he whispered, before he repaired to the dressing room, where sleep finally came to him.

Chapter Twenty-Four

The Earl awakened early, happily enough, and was able to wend his way to his own room without anyone the wiser. Darby did not utter a word as he helped him remove his crumpled, bloodstained nightclothes. Once dressed, the Earl summoned her ladyship's maid. He told her, in the presence of Darby, that her ladyship had risen during the night to investigate strange noises about the house. She must have tripped, for she fell down the stairs. The Earl heard the noise of her tumble and went to her, carrying her back upstairs. Her ladyship was in a great deal of pain and would not rise today. Bessie was to be reinstalled in the dressing room, but for now she would await her ladyship's summons before bringing her breakfast.

The Earl cut short the maid's wailing that she had not been there to help her mistress and sent her scurrying away. He was pleased, though, for he thought his explanation would account nicely for any strange sounds overheard by the servants in the middle of the night, as well as Amanda's indisposition and any involuntary grimace of pain that might escape her. It remained only to find some explanation for the Baron's abrupt departure last night.

He took his cue from Darby, who had indicated to the stableboy, whom he roused to make ready the

Baron's carriage, that the Baron sometimes did strange things when he was in his cups. That story would do well enough, the Earl thought, and directed Darby to see that it filtered through the house.

The Earl made his way back to Amanda's room. He espied the riding crop lying on the floor and placed it near the door, so to remove it on his way out. Then he sat waiting for Amanda to awaken. She would need to know what had supposedly happened last night as well as anyone. He watched her for a long time, thinking that she slept very peacefully, perhaps for the first time in many days. She lay curled on her side, one hand beneath her cheek.

At length she opened her eyes, and as they fell upon the Earl, they widened in momentary surprise. But when she tried to sit up, she gasped as the pain overtook her, and then she seemed to remember. "He is gone?" she asked quietly.

"Yes, he is gone," he said, coming to stand by the side of the bed. "He will never come again, Amanda. You need have no fear of that."

She closed her eyes for a moment and nodded slowly. Then he quietly recounted what the servants had been told about her "fall" down the stairs and the Baron's abrupt departure. A look of such relief washed over the fragile sea green eyes that it wrenched his heart. God, what must her life have been like before her marriage?

"Thank you, Charles," she said, and he had to restrain the impulse to gather her in his arms.

"Shall I help you sit up, Amanda?" he finally asked.

"No, no thank you. I shall manage quite well," she replied firmly.

"You are the most incorrigible woman I have ever met, Amanda Millforte," he retorted, smiling. "Well, go ahead. Let me see you try."

Amanda was furious. Did he not see that she was trying to retain a small shred of her dignity? How did he contrive to turn everything around so that she felt like a foolish child?

She anchored herself with her left elbow and her right hand, and tried to pull herself to a sitting position. But her arms felt weak and her back burned as it rubbed against the bedclothes. She sank back into the pillows and glared at him. "Pray do not stand there looking so damned superior!" she shouted, and the Earl laughed as he bent over to help her.

The minute he touched her she remembered the way he had cared for her the night before. She wished him gone from the room. "Charles," she said as casually as she could, "perhaps you could have Bessie sent to me."

"But, of course, my dear," he said amiably. "And by the by, shall I recall Mrs. Havenwick as well? I am persuaded that you would prefer her care to mine."

She was piqued at his ungentlemanly reference to what had transpired the night before, and to her dismay found that she was blushing again. "Yes, Charles, do send for her. Straight away, if you would," she said sharply.

"Fine. I shall come to visit with you after breakfast. I trust that *this* time at least you will stay in bed where you belong, will you not?"

How dare he take such a superior tone with her! It was only a niggling feeling that she had reason to be grateful to him that kept her from throwing him out of the house. "I shall wish to rest after breakfast, Charles. You may come in time for luncheon," she said haughtily, by way of dismissal.

He raised one eyebrow and regarded her curiously for a moment. Then he smiled warmly and, bowing ever so slightly, left the room.

She was much relieved when he did, such a tumble of

emotions did she feel. The humiliation of last night overwhelmed her. She had lived for months with the fear of her father coming to Millforte. But the horror of her degradation at his hands was made all the worse by the fact that Charles had been there. Charles. Even now she covered her face with her hands at the memory of what he had seen and done last night. She remembered him picking her up, holding her while she cried, bathing the blood away. It would have been better to bear it alone than to have had him see her like that.

But even as she thought that, her practical sense took over. If not for Charles, how long would she have stayed on the floor? And who would have found her there? Or if she had managed to crawl to bed, who would have found her, sprawled across it, gown bloody? Bessie? One of the other maids? How long before the entire household knew? No one would say a word to her, but there would always be the knowing whispers, and the pity. She had been through that before. And worst of all, her practical sense told her, if not for the Earl, her father would still be here, waiting for another opportunity. She did not know how long Charles could stay here to protect her, but at least for now, she was safe. She sighed, knowing that by all rights she ought to be very grateful to the Earl. But she was not much more comfortable with that than the feeling of humiliation.

And now that she thought on it, what was he doing here at all events? It would have to be coincidence that he had appeared just at this time. Oh, she could imagine *why* he had returned. He had said he would, to have a long talk, no doubt to set her straight on the matter of a governess for Victor and to thwart her efforts to improve the land. Yes, she knew why he was back, and yet, 'twas strange that he had come just then. She must remember to ask him about it when next she saw him.

Presently, Bessie knocked softly and entered the room, bringing a cup of chocolate with her. Amanda dismissed her, bidding her return in half an hour to help her complete her toilette.

As she savored the sweet drink, Amanda thought of her last meeting with Charles, that awful day when Richard had come. She had been so happy to see Richard. Even when he'd told her who Kitty was and she'd known they would have to face the Earl's wrath, she had thought that perhaps she could bring Charles around. And then the blow had fallen. Richard had told her about the terrible gossip. She had been stunned, devastated. Richard had been beside himself. "I'm sorry, Mandy. I did not know you would be so distressed," he had said. How could she tell him she did not care a whit for what the London tabbies said about her? That it was only one man's opinion that mattered?

She remembered so well that day in the hut, and even the day after. "Stop pretending nothing happened between us," Charles had said. She remembered their waltz about her room. Oh, how she had wanted to trust him! But always, some instinct warned her and she had held back. She could not reconcile his seeming sincerity with the insolence she remembered from their first days together, especially that night in the library. Only when Richard came did it all become clear. She had been right to hold her emotions in check. The Earl had been toying with her all along, had heard those dreadful stories and believed them.

And yet, he had not seduced her in the crofter's hut, when he had had ample opportunity, and he had tried very hard to reconcile with her the day of Richard's visit. How torn apart she had felt then—she had not been able to help feeling some affection for him as he swallowed his pride and agreed to countenance a match between Kitty and Richard. At the same time, she had been chagrined that she had come so close to losing her heart to a calculating man who had no respect for her.

After they had all gone, she had tried to convince herself that Charles would not come back and that it was best that way. She told herself in the days that followed that the emptiness she felt would soon dissipate, but she knew by then that her heart had played her false. She had tried so hard to resist that devastating smile and the entreaty in those slate blue eyes, but in the end she had lost. Lost her heart and her soul to a man who thought she was every man's mistress. Fool! she had railed, and she'd cried in her bed at night.

And now, what was she to think now? The way he looked at her, spoke to her. And the way he had taken care of her so tenderly. Oh God, whatever did he want of her?

She was not at all sorry when Bessie interrupted her ruminations a while later. She did not allow the maid to change her nightgown, but bade Bessie comb her hair and help her to wash. Bessie brought her a lovely ivory satin bedjacket, and she stifled a gasp as she twisted into it.

She tried very hard to occupy her mind with the business of the estates as she consumed her breakfast, but her thoughts kept returning to Charles. Damn! How was she to face him in the next few days? It was too humiliating, and at the same time, she found his closeness most disconcerting. And this time she could not escape her bedchamber, not for at least a day. Movement was too painful and it was possible for the wounds to reopen if one jerked suddenly or bumped into something.

And so it was a rather agitated Amanda who greeted

the Earl as he entered her room just at lunchtime, followed by a footman bearing the massive chessboard, and two of the upstairs maids carrying bountiful lunch trays.

The Earl watched Amanda carefully as she nibbled a piece of cheese and sipped her wine. She had little appetite and was clearly nervous. He wanted to put her at ease, but it was hard to find a topic of conversation that was not uncomfortable. At length he said, "Do you have much pain, Amanda?"

"'Tis all right if—if I do not move about too much," she said quietly.

"I have sent for Mrs. Havenwick. She may not come until tomorrow. Amanda, will you be all right until she comes?" He kept his tone soft and solicitous, but still she blushed deeply. He was sure she would prefer he not make reference to that and quite a few other things, but dammit, they had got to clear the air between them.

"Yes, I—I shall be fine," she murmured, looking down.

"And did you sleep well, my dear?"

"I slept well, Charles, thank you. And tell me, what will you be doing now that you have returned?" she asked with a brittle lightness in a desperate attempt to change the subject.

"As I said before, Amanda, there is much that I left—unfinished," he said smoothly. He began nonchalantly to cut and eat some of his cold meat, watching her with a half-smile.

She seemed at a loss for words for a few moments, and then she rallied, attempting to muster some of her old strength. "I see. Yes, I do seem to remember some unfinished business. But if I recall, most of it was *my* business, and not yours."

The Earl smiled to himself. So it was confrontation she wanted. It would give her the security of not having to discuss last night. Very well. He would oblige her for a while. He favored her with a smirk and said mockingly, "There was the matter of Victor's governess. I believe that is very much my business. I have a paper from the solicitors to prove it, you know."

Amanda's eyes flashed as she replied, "The very idea of a governess for Victor is pure fustian, and well you know it. And if you did not think so yourself then surely you would not—" She checked herself just short of blurting that he had not mailed the advertisement. Well, she was no fool. Let him go on thinking that it had been sent. He would spend a long time awaiting a reply.

The Earl looked curiously at her, wondering if she was about to remind him that he had neglected to send that advertisement to the *Gazette*. He had not realized it until several days afterward, and had been annoyed with himself, but now he found that he was in no great hurry to send it. He had enough problems here without engaging in violent arguments with Amanda if he began to interview prospective governesses. Somehow he thought the entire issue could wait a few weeks' time. A great deal could happen in a few weeks, after all.

If Amanda had indeed been about to remind him of his lapse, she thought better of it, and merely sipped her wine. "Ah—you were saying, Amanda?" he asked with an amused grin.

"I was simply reiterating the fact that Victor does not need a governess. And since you are so concerned with the business at Millforte, it may interest you to know that Lord Windham has been kind enough to share with me some of his figures for projected costs of his reclamation project. Higgins went to see him last week. There is the purchase of machinery required, of course, but even you will own . . ." Amanda went on in this vein for some time, seeming to forget her distress as she

389

became caught up in her plans. "'Tis the course of the future, Charles. Surely you must see that," she concluded earnestly.

He did not at all believe that such projects were the course of the future, and it struck him that English lands had provided for their landlords quite well just as they were for generations. He had no wish to tamper with nature. He also had no wish to engage in a full-scale argument about it at the moment. There were so many more important issues between them—his trip to London, for one, and what had transpired the preceding night. Somehow he knew that when they had reached some level of understanding between them, he could bring her round on these other issues.

"I have already made my feelings on the matter quite clear, I believe," he said amiably, and before she could protest, he deftly changed the subject. "You know, Amanda, you have not asked me about Richard and Kitty. I am persuaded that you must be concerned with how they fare." He pushed back the table that held his lunch tray and reclined a bit in his velvet chair next to the bed.

"Yes, of course, I am concerned about them. There has been—so much on my mind of late, that I—" she said uncomfortably.

"I know that, my dear. But you will be happy to know that Richard is presently enjoying himself with my horses at my estate in Surrey. Kitty is quite behaving herself in London, although a bit anxious for me to send Richard to her. I—er—suggested he rusticate at Surrey until I had resolved the very delicate problem in London. Richard Smythe is simply too havey-cavey a fellow to be allowed to walk about London streets, you must know," he said with a smile. But behind the smile there was the anxiety of knowing that he had broached a tender subject. She drained her

390

wine goblet and pushed her tray from her. He removed it to the floor and awaited her reply.

"You have been very kind to Richard. I cannot tell you how grateful I am. I do not think you will have cause to regret it. Richard has a sweet nature, but he is strong. I am persuaded that he and Kitty will go on well together."

"I do not doubt of it, Amanda. He is well able to curb her more capricious tendencies, and he seems quite devoted to her. Amanda," he said, deciding to confront the issue directly, "are you not concerned with how *I* fared in London? I went with a very specific mission, you must recall." He sat up straight in his chair.

The muscles in her face seemed to tense and she turned her head to the side. She had retained her linen serviette and twisted it nervously in her hands. Then she turned back to him and said lightly, "Kitty is a charming girl, Charles. I shall be most happy to call her my sister. And I did so enjoy meeting her little friend, Anne. And even Anne's brother was quite—"

"Amanda," he interrupted, moving his chair closer to the bed, placing his hand over both of hers, "that is the second time in less than half an hour that you have sought to divert the topic of conversation from one that was in some way uncomfortable. I had not thought you such a coward."

"I am *not* a coward, Charles!" she exclaimed indignantly. "I have been through a great deal and I— and I—oh damn and blast it all, Charles, if you were any kind of a gentleman you—" She seemed quite exasperated, and he grinned rakishly at her, his hand holding hers quite firmly.

"If you were any kind of a lady, Amanda, you would not use such explosive language. Really, my dear, you do quite shock me," he said with mock severity.

"Fustian! I do not shock you in the least. And now I

think on't Charles, just why did you choose to come at this very time? I know *why* you have come—you needs must harass me and seek to prove your superiority in matters concerning Victor and the estates. But why now? Surely your—business—in London could not have been completed," she declared, her eyes sparkling and her brows raised in an attempt at hauteur.

The Earl hesitated for a moment, regarding her closely. Then he made a decision and said quietly, "Mrs. Havenwick sent for me."

"What?" exclaimed Amanda, pulling both hands from his, her eyes wide.

"Mrs. Havenwick sent for me," he repeated simply.

"Yes, I know, you've said that. But why? Whatever—"

"Mrs. Havenwick sent a message saying that you were—in danger," he replied.

She was silent for a moment, and she swallowed hard. "And you—you came?" she whispered, almost disbelieving.

Good God! he thought. Did she trust him so little that she could imagine he would ignore such a summons? "Yes, I came," he responded softly, his eyes boring into hers.

She searched his face with troubled eyes for several moments. Then she looked down and murmured, "I must tell you that I—that I am truly—grateful—that you did come here, Charles." Slowly, she raised her eyes again.

God, how he longed to take this woman in his arms! She was so vulnerable, and she looked so devastatingly beautiful in her ivory satin bedjacket, her lustrous hair pulled back softly from her face. He rose and sat next to her on the bed, taking her hand again.

"Amanda, that is the second time in less than half an hour that you have expressed gratitude toward me. I do not wish you to be grateful to me. I wish you to be—happy to see me. There is a difference, you know," he said intently, his eyes holding hers.

She caught her breath and turned her head from side to side, as if looking for some means of escape. He knew he should not press her further just now; there was time enough later. Yet he did not release her hand, nor move from the bed. "Amanda," he said in a low voice, moving his face toward hers, "are you not at all happy to see me?"

Her color rose as she said somewhat breathlessly, trying to inch away from him. "Charles, I—I think it highly improper for you to be here."

He tightened the hand that held hers, and moved yet closer to her, as he whispered, "I have never agreed with you on that particular point, Amanda, but I do now." Her brows flew up in astonishment, but he gave her no time to reply.

He brought his lips to hers gently at first, and then his free hand caught her behind the neck and he pressed her to him. She kept herself stiff for a moment, and then she tilted her head and returned his kiss. He held her carefully, so as not to hurt her back, but he kissed her hungrily. He let go her hand and began to caress her throat, his fingers seeking the top buttons of her bedjacket. He felt her hand steal to the back of his neck, and suddenly he stopped, somehow pulling away from her, his breathing ragged. My God, what was he doing? The crofter's hut was one thing, but here, in her bed—a sickbed, for God's sake! He was compromising her, taking advantage of her. Whatever could have possessed him?

Amanda's face was pink and her eyes downcast. He stood up rather unsteadily from the bed. "Amanda, I—ah—I think I should leave now, my dear. I shall return—perhaps at tea time, and we can—play chess," he stammered, and then bowed somewhat formally and took his leave.

She stared at the door long after he had gone. How had she allowed this to happen? How could she ever have faced him, talked to him, after last night? She had tried to retain a shred of her pride, and he had called her coward. He had *made* her face him. What was he trying to do to her? He was twisting her inside out, and this last had been the worst of all. Surely if he had any respect for her he would not have taken advantage of her in such a manner.

And why could she not resist him? Why did she allow this man near her? But even as she wondered she knew.

God forgive me, she thought. Arthur was gone less than a year and it was another man who filled her heart and her thoughts. Charles had once mockingly referred to her as Guinevere. How right he had been, for already she had betrayed Arthur in her heart, betrayed him with the man he himself had brought to Millforte.

Chapter Twenty-Five

The Earl's head was spinning after his encounter with Amanda. What he needed was fresh air, he decided, and made his way down the great staircase. When he reached the main hall, Jeffries informed him that the Vicar and Mrs. Trumwell had come to call, inquiring as to how her ladyship fared. The Earl blinked for a moment in disbelief; he would never grow accustomed to the rapidity with which news traveled in the country. And he was even more abashed by the intelligence that Miss Lavinia Prescott at that very moment awaited him in the Green Salon. He sighed deeply, musing that the servants' grapevine in the great country houses could quite put Lady Gresham and all of her machinations to shame.

"Miss Prescott," said the Earl, striding into the Green Salon, "what a very great pleasure to see you."

She stood to greet him, extending her hand. There was a decided glint in her eye as she said, "I doubt it. Do not gammon me, my lord. I should imagine you are exhausted, not to mention fraught with worry, and the very last thing you wish is to sit here entertaining your overly inquisitive neighbors. But do not trouble yourself, for I shall remain only a minute." So saying, that very singular lady took a seat and actually indicated that the Earl might do the same.

Lord Ainsley, too amused to be at all put out, obeyed.

To his amazement, and true to her word, Lavinia Prescott took her leave in short order. She inquired after Amanda's injuries, expressing the concern of Windham and her sister as well. And she conveyed Windham's invitation that the Earl visit at any time. In truth, it would have been a pleasant visit had she not concluded on a most odd note.

"I do worry so about her. I own I could hardly credit it when word reached me this morning that Amanda had had yet *another* accident. It leads one to conclude that she is in need of some kind of permanent— protection, would you not agree, my lord?" she asked, her head cocked to one side, with a hint of mischief in her eyes that made the Earl most uneasy. Just what the devil was that devious mind intimating?

He was most relieved when she left, and more in need of fresh air than ever. He would ride, he thought. He had got to get away from this house, and a brisk gallop over the hills would be just the thing. He welcomed the solitude as he rode out into the countryside, but he could not force Lavinia Prescott from his mind. He had not liked her tone at all. "Yet *another* accident" indeed! And as to protection—was he not doing his level best already? Damn her for a meddlesome female! How dare she speak so to him!

He remembered the machinations she had stirred up the day of that most unusual luncheon at Millforte. She had been matchmaking and— Suddenly the Earl pulled the reins and slowed his horse. And that was exactly what she'd been doing now. Matchmaking! He laughed aloud at his own blind stupidity. "Permanent protection" indeed! Any fool would have known to what she referred, any but the fool who did not want to face it.

He pulled his horse to a complete stop under a large oak tree and dismounted. He tethered the horse to a low branch and stood with his back to the tree, his foot resting on a rock protruding from the ground. He gazed ahead at Millforte Manor and thought of Amanda.

He had wanted her in his bed since first he'd met her, and he still did. Now more than ever. But how much more he wanted from her now! He wanted her at his breakfast table, at his dinner parties. He wanted her as the mistress of Ainsley Court, and the mother of his children. He wanted to care for her, protect her. He wanted her by the fireside in the evenings. In short, Charles Ainsley, he told himself, what you want is to marry the second Lady Millforte.

He shivered even as the sun filtered through the branches of the tree. Marriage! Somehow that was something one did *someday;* one had a responsibility, after all. But it was not something one contemplated for the present. He smiled to himself. How long had he scrupulously avoided thinking of marriage with regard to Amanda? That day in the crofter's hut, he had found, to his surprise, that he would not seduce her, yet he had not considered marriage. Nor had he done so at any time afterward. Indeed, he had never allowed his mind to come to any logical conclusion about Amanda. He had followed his heart, and had known only that he could not bear to part from her.

Had he known for some time, without realizing it, that he wanted Amanda for his wife? Was that the real reason he had been so determined to ferret out the source of the disastrous stories? But no, he had known for a very long time that the rumors were false, and he thought now that he would be willing to face all of the slammed doors in London if he could but have Amanda to wife.

But those rumors reminded him of all that was unresolved between them. She would probably be very angry about what he'd done in London. And on top of that had come last night's debacle. Her pride had suffered mercilessly. She had been uncomfortable with him this morning, and his ill-timed kiss had probably not helped any. Damn! It was the first time he could remember feeling out of control with a woman. It was a sobering thought, and he knew he had got to make his visits to her bedchamber rather briefer.

For somehow she must come to trust him. She never really had, and part of that was his own fault. But he did not doubt that her affections were engaged. She was as passionate as he, and had shown on more than one occasion that she was not indifferent to him. Her pride might make her obstinate, but once he had made her an offer— Yes, he thought, it was merely a matter of choosing his moment well.

He took a deep breath of fresh spring air. He felt quite ready to return to the manor; the ride had, indeed, cleared his head. In fact, his head felt clear for the first time in weeks. But if he returned, he would undoubtedly find some pretext for visiting Amanda again. No. Better to keep riding. Perhaps he would go to Windham. It might behoove him to learn a bit more about marshland drainage from the Viscount. Amanda needn't know what it was that they had talked about, after all.

Windham was indeed pleased to see him and invited the Earl into his comfortable library. They exchanged pleasantries for a bit, and Windham expressed his chagrin at the accident that had befallen Lady Millforte, coming so soon after several others. The Earl was very happy, after that, to let conversation drift to farming and Windham's proposed marshland drainage.

"Lady Millforte's man-of-affairs, Higgins—I believe?" began Windham, and at the Earl's nod continued. "Higgins was here and I showed him the figures for initial costs against likely revenues the first two years after completion of the project. I have hopes of recouping my initial investment within two years. Have you had the opportunity to peruse the figures, Ainsley?" asked Windham amiably.

The Earl replied in the negative and Windham showed him a few summary figures. As the Earl scanned the sheet, Windham said, "Lady Millforte seems very excited by the idea. You, I gather, are a bit hesitant."

The Earl colored slightly but, realizing that Windham considered nothing amiss in this disagreement, went on more comfortably. "You must understand, Windham, that Millforte has been quite prosperous up until now. The reclamation project is costly, time-consuming, and not without risk. I am not convinced that it is the wisest course for Millforte."

"I understand your reservations, Ainsley. I have had similar ones myself. But I am persuaded that this is not unlike crop rotation; it is a matter of maximum utilization of land."

"Crop rotation, of course, we have utilized on the Ainsley lands for years. But we are speaking now of a venture of another sort. Not all marshland is arable."

"To be sure, Ainsley. Indeed, I would not attempt such an endeavor in the more northern regions, where the marshes are deeper and very likely not reclaimable, but here I believe it is a worthwhile undertaking. There are many people who go hungry hereabouts in a bad year. I hope to alleviate some of that as well as augment the estate coffers."

The Earl studied the pleasant-faced man before him. The better acquainted they became, the better he liked this amiable, steadfast man. He was a man who had the rank and means to live quite well in London, and to move in the highest circles. Yet he seemed to derive complete contentment from his rural occupations.

After some time Lady Windham, wearing a simple blue muslin dress, her hair a bit tousled, interrupted him and bade the Earl take tea with them. He was struck anew by the easy affection in which Lord and Lady Windham held each other, and he found himself warming to the Viscount and his wife.

When he was about to take his leave, Windham walked with him to retrieve his horse from the stable. "Ainsley," said Windham, "I had thought to put this suggestion to you and Lady Millforte together. But as she is, unfortunately, indisposed, and as I am rather eager to begin, perhaps you might convey the matter to her. Should you both be so inclined as to consider a reclamation project for Millforte, well, it struck me as not unreasonable for us to contemplate the joint purchase of at least some of the machinery. The distance is not so great between our lands, I am persuaded, and clearly a major cost reduction would result for both estates. We might even consider the feasibility of those new steam pumps, you know. Perhaps you would care to think on't, and to broach the idea to Lady Millforte within a few days' time?"

The Earl looked directly at Windham, and then turned to let his eyes survey the lush green fields stretching out beyond Windham House. He had known, as he'd listened to Windham throughout the afternoon, that what the man said did indeed make sense. And if he was totally honest with himself, he would have to admit that Amanda had said much the same things to him several times over. True, he had now seen more clearly delineated figures than he had before. But still, the fact remained, he admitted ruefully, that he had not rationally considered the matter when Amanda had discussed it. Perhaps, he thought, that was because he had never before been called upon to respond to a woman rationally. Most women of his acquaintance did not seem to expect it. But Amanda did.

Windham cleared his throat and recalled the Earl to himself. "Forgive me, Windham, my mind meanders. I have no doubt that Lady Millforte would applaud your scheme. And I find that I myself am hard put to decline your offer. Windham, I think we may consider ourselves associates in what I pray will be a mutually beneficial venture." He extended his hand to Windham, and the latter shook it warmly, inviting the Earl and Amanda to take dinner at Windham House within the next se'nnight.

The Earl gladly assented, and as he rode the wind back to Millforte, he speculated as to the best time to relay the news to Amanda. He would enjoy telling her, to be sure, but he must do it in just the right way. She must not take this to mean that he would readily acquiesce in any other schemes of hers. This one happened to make sense; others might not. Heaven knew that harebrained scheme for the Low Cottages did not.

He sighed, thinking that the matter of the Low Cottages would come to a head between them soon enough. He would rather that particular—discussion —take place after they were married. And as he thought on the subject of matrimony, he thought that he should like to marry Amanda as soon as possible, for more reasons than one. Not the least was the fact that once he had made his intentions known to her, his continued presence at Millforte went perhaps beyond the bounds of propriety. What had seemed perfectly proper and sensible to him a short time before was beginning to seem highly improper indeed. Paradoxically, the fact was that he could not leave Millforte, because he feared for Amanda's safety. Furthermore, he had waited for Amanda about as long as any man should have to wait for a woman, and would she but admit it to herself, Amanda would feel the same way!

It was clear to him that once she had accepted his offer, they must marry as soon as possible. He had no intention of waiting for banns to be posted, nor did he care to hear from his mother, nor anyone else for that matter, when their engagement was announced. Amanda would be most chagrined, he was sure, by any to-do whatever, and he would much prefer presenting her to the world as his wife, rather than as his fiancée.

No, the only thing for it was to obtain a special license; he was certain Amanda would wish to be married quickly by the Vicar, particularly given her state of half-mourning. As his horse cantered over the gentle hills, the Earl pondered the problem of where to obtain a special license. He needs must apply to someone he knew, of course, someone whose discretion was unquestioned. Amanda had not yet accepted him, after all. There was always the chance—but no, that simply was not possible.

There were several men in London who would be more than happy to oblige him, but he could not leave Millforte. Surely in all of Shropshire there must be—But, of course. Coninghill was the county magistrate. His seat was just south of Shrewsbury. According to what the local magistrate had said, he ought to be in residence now. The Earl would ride over in the morning; with any luck he might return after luncheon.

As such, the Earl's spirit was rather buoyant as he mounted the great staircase once back at Millforte. He knocked softly on Amanda's door. He had expected a muffled reply from the bed, and therefore was somewhat surprised when, in response to his knock, Bessie opened the door and stepped out.

The maid looked down at her feet and spoke quietly, if somewhat nervously. "Beggin' your pardon, your lordship, but my lady is resting just now and she—she bade me give her excuses."

The Earl would have applauded this, thinking it about time Amanda did rest, except that the maid seemed decidedly uncomfortable.

"Bessie," he began sternly.

"Yes, my lord," mumbled the girl.

"Look up," he commanded. When she complied he said, "Is your mistress in bed?"

"No, my lord."

"Has she been resting since the morning?"

"Yes, my lord," the maid said slowly, her eyes darting from place to place. Clearly, she was hiding something.

"Bessie, is your mistress ill, or in great pain? Shall I send for the doctor?" he asked, his eyes looking intently at her.

"N—no, my lord. I—I am sure 'tis just rest she needs," replied the maid as if she was at her wit's end.

The Earl thought it very likely that Amanda was simply trying to avoid seeing him. "Very well, Bessie. Tell your mistress that I shall take dinner with her."

The maid looked clearly distraught now. "But—but—beggin' your lordship's pardon, my lady said she did not think she would care for company for dinner. She—she is not feeling herself just yet, my lord, and she wishes to rest until—until tomorrow." Bessie sighed with relief when she finished her little speech. It was so obvious that she was lying that the Earl almost laughed aloud.

So, Amanda meant to keep him from her bedchamber. She had been through a great deal recently, and this morning's rather intimate encounter, so ill-advised on his part, had probably only served to make her more uncomfortable. Well, he would give her time to collect herself. But tomorrow morning, they would talk. Enough was enough, after all.

After a solitary dinner, the Earl was relieved when Mrs. Havenwick arrived with Victor. He laughed to himself, thinking it ironic indeed that he should actually welcome the arrival of the formidable housekeeper. But Amanda needed to be cared for, and from Mrs. Havenwick he would at least receive a more accurate gauge of her condition and emotional state than would be forthcoming from that dithering maid of hers.

Mrs. Havenwick settled Victor with Nurse, she and the Earl having agreed that it would be better if he was not to see his mother until morning. Then she presented herself in the library, and the Earl briefly related the events of the night before. He omitted everything that Amanda had told him about her childhood—he did not know how much Mrs. Havenwick knew and had no wish to betray Amanda's confidence. Mrs. Havenwick looked grim indeed.

"'Twas just as I feared," she whispered.

"Thank you for sending for me, Mrs. Havenwick," said the Earl. "I only would I had been able to prevent his coming near her at all. But she—she did not seem to welcome my protection."

Mrs. Havenwick eyed him steadily. "She is very proud, my lord. But I am very grateful to you for coming. 'Twould have been much worse, you know, if you had not been here. I was beside myself when the Baron sent word of his arrival, and then, what with her ladyship sending me away—truly I had nowhere else to turn and I—well, I did think it were a good chance you would come, my lord, if you will forgive a bit of presumption," she said, gazing at him knowingly.

It seemed to the Earl that several people had been presuming a bit too much about him lately—Kitty and Lavinia Prescott sprang immediately to mind. In other circumstances he would have taken exception to such presumption, but he was very grateful to Mrs. Havenwick and so held his peace.

He bade the housekeeper go up immediately to care for her ladyship, and to report to him thereafter. When the housekeeper returned sometime later, it was to relate that her ladyship seemed to be healing well. She added, somewhat sheepishly, if indeed such a forbidding woman could ever be called sheepish, that her ladyship did not wish for company for the remainder of the evening. "The rest will do her good, my lord. Do but give her time."

The Earl sighed and nodded. Well, he was a man of great patience. And so he would be—until tomorrow.

It was therefore not a very patient Earl who presented himself at Amanda's door early the next morning. He was met in the hallway by Mrs. Havenwick, who looked rather chagrined and was very loath to tell him that her ladyship would breakfast alone and did not wish to be disturbed.

The Earl was most annoyed, to be sure, and thought momentarily of ordering the housekeeper aside and bursting into the room. He had done it often enough in the past, he knew. But this time he thought better of it. "If you will await me here, Mrs. Havenwick," he said calmly, "I shall return in but a minute with a communication for her ladyship."

Which, not three minutes later, is exactly what he did, rather smugly handing a note to Mrs. Havenwick and then taking himself back down the stairs. He was met in the main hall by Jeffries, bearing a letter on a silver salver.

"Thank you," said the Earl. "And would you please send word to the stables to have my horse put to? I shall ride out presently."

The Earl took the letter and walked to the library. It was from Ridgeway, and the Earl chuckled as he read his friend's accounts of overheard conversations regarding the second Lady Millforte and the disgruntled suitor. It seemed that all was well, and he composed a brief reply to Ridgeway, bidding him carry on, and begging his forgiveness if the Earl reneged on his promise to join him at his hunting lodge shortly. He then wrote to Richard, informing him exactly when he might leave for London, and to his mother, apprising her of Richard's imminent arrival and asking her once again to receive Richard kindly.

He sealed and franked the letters, and bade Jeffries dispatch them. This bit of business seen to, he took himself off to the stables, for he was most anxious to visit the Coninghill family seat.

Amanda waited for Mrs. Havenwick to depart before opening the Earl's missive. It contained but one word, centered on the page in Charles's bold scrawl.

"Coward!" was all it said.

Damn you, Charles Ainsley! she thought. I am *not* a coward!

No, she was most definitely not a coward. It was not as though she were afraid to face him. It was just that she simply refused to discuss the deplorable London on dits, which topic she knew he would broach. And whatever had possessed her, that dreadful night, to reveal so much of her past to him? Why did he have that effect on her? And if she would be totally honest with herself, it was that very effect that made it encumbent upon her to keep him from her room. She did not understand what happened to her in his arms. She became shameless—a woman incapable of loyalty to the husband who had saved her from the nightmare that had been her life.

Poor, dear, misguided Arthur. Could he not have foreseen that such a thing might happen and so stipulated that the Earl should not begin his guardianship for several years? Whatever could have possessed him to place her in such an untenable position as she now found herself?

No, she was not a coward. But neither was she going to betray Arthur. Perhaps if she kept to her room, and succeeded in keeping the Earl out, he would give up and go back to London. But even as she thought this, she knew that his departure would leave her with an unbearable emptiness.

The Earl returned sometime after luncheon, feeling rather elated after the success of his trip to Shrewsbury. He had enjoyed renewing the acquaintance of his old school friend. Coninghill had been only too happy to oblige him in the little matter of business upon which he had come, and had expressed the hope that Ainsley and his new bride might visit with the Coninghills in the near future.

How he was ever to make a bride of Amanda he was not quite certain at this point, but bride she would be before the week was out. It struck him as absurdly ironic that young women had been falling at his feet for years, all but begging for the privilege of marrying him, while this exasperating, headstrong, proud woman he would take to wife refused even to speak to him. It was outside of enough—indeed, whoever would have believed it?

After delivering his horse to the stables, he lingered about the back of the house and sauntered toward the rear gardens. He was lost in thought, wondering whether his little note to Amanda would have made any dent in the armor in which she seemed determined to hide herself.

He had not realized that he had already come within the formal gardens, but as he advanced along one of the paths he became aware of a strange sound coming from the center of the gardens. He thought the sound came from above him, perhaps from one of the trees, but it did not sound like the call of a bird. As he advanced closer he realized that what he heard was more like a whimper, a muffled sob perhaps. But up in a tree? Oh, my God! he thought, and bounded into the center courtyard.

As he came near to the ancient oak tree, he looked up. There, on one of the highest horizontal branches, was Victor, stretched out on his belly, his little arms encircling the branch and his feet dangling on either side.

"Do not look down, Victor," shouted the Earl. "I am coming for you. Hold on, Victor, and do not move." With that the Earl wrestled out of his perfectly fitted coat, flung it to the ground, and pulled himself up into the tree.

"I cannot hold anymore, Cousin. I cannot," wailed the child.

"Do not try to talk, Victor," called the Earl somewhat breathlessly as he wedged his left foot between two branches and heaved himself yet higher into the tree. "I shall be there in a trice."

In truth it took him more than a trice to reach the child, for the tree was tall and not all the branches did he deem sturdy enough to support his weight. He thanked God that he was in his riding clothes, which afforded more room than any others. He would have thought the task nary impossible in his tight-fitting pantaloons. As it was he wondered how Amanda had ever contrived to do such a thing in skirts.

When he finally reached a position just under the branch where Victor was perched, he said, "Now, Victor, I am going to put my hand on you, in this way, and I want you to slide backwards, closer to me."

"I cannot, Cousin," sobbed the child.

"Yes, you can, Victor. I am holding you. Just move your arms—pretend you are pulling back on your horse's reins. There you are. Now I want you to let go this hand," directed the Earl, stretching to touch the boy's right hand, "and roll toward me. You grab my neck and I shall catch you."

The Earl spoke a good deal more confidently than he

felt, and somehow, miraculously, Victor was in his arms within moments. The little boy clutched convulsively at his neck with his two little arms as he sobbed into his collar.

At that point the Earl made the mistake of looking down. He gulped, for they must easily have been some thirty feet from the ground. He had no idea how to proceed from here, and wondered again how the hell Amanda had managed this, skirts or no, and with a child a good deal heavier than Victor.

He instructed Victor to hold him tightly, and to wrap his legs around the Earl's waist. He then began to ease his way back along one branch and then another, praying that each one in turn would hold them. He felt his legs being scratched beneath his britches, and knew that his boots were being ravaged beyond repair. But he cared for nothing at that moment but the little heart beating so quickly next to his, and he barely took note the two times he heard the sound of his britches being torn by the rough bark of the tree.

He jumped the last few feet, clutching Victor protectively, and when at last he set the boy down and stood up, the child grasped him around the legs. Victor did not say a word, but squeezed his legs and sniffed as if to control his crying. The Earl took his hand and silently led him to the house.

When they reached the main hall Victor seemed to rally, for his face brightened and he tugged at the Earl's hand. "Come, Cousin. We must tell Mama *all* about it!"

As the little boy eagerly pulled him along, the Earl felt a reluctant smile curl his lips. So, it had taken a three-year-old child to gain him entry into Amanda's room. Well, so be it, he mused, and followed Victor willingly.

Chapter Twenty-Six

Amanda's eyes widened in astonishment as Victor, the Earl in tow, burst into her room. She had been standing at the window near her bed and he thought she looked beautiful in a gown of pale lavender silk. How he had missed her, even for this short time!

Victor let go the Earl's hand and danced over to his mother. "Mama! Mama! He saved me! Cousin Charles saved me! He climbed all the way up to get me!"

Amanda tilted her head and looked inquiringly at the Earl before looking down at her son. "Whatever can you mean, Victor?" she asked.

"I climbed the tree, Mama. I only meant to sit on Zeus, but then I went a little higher, and a little higher, to see if I could find a better horse. It was easy to climb, Mama, and then I got to the top. As high as the birds go, but—but—I could not get down," Victor ended with his eyes narrowed in fear and a sob rising in his throat.

Amanda looked up at the Earl, a look of consternation on her face even as her eyes were questioning, as if awaiting the Earl's corroboration of Victor's story.

The Earl nodded, a flicker of a smile on his face, as he advanced into the center of the room. Victor tugged at his mother's skirts to gain her attention before continuing his recital. "I stayed up there a long time,

410

Mama. I called but no one came. I thought I was going to fall, Mama. Then I would be bleeding and break my bones."

"Oh, Victor, my poor Victor," said Amanda, bending and hugging the child for a moment. "And then what happened?"

"Then Cousin Charles came. He told me not to move, and he climbed all the way to get me."

Amanda straightened up and faced the Earl. He saw a gleam in her eye such as he had not seen since she had found out about the London gossip. She raised her brows imperiously. "Cousin Charles climbed a tree?" she drawled. "But I am persuaded that Cousin Charles would *never* climb a tree."

"But he did, Mama, he did! And he carried me down. Look Mama, he even took off his coat to come and get me!"

"Indeed," said Amanda, her eyes going from her son to the Earl, who stood before her in his shirtsleeves, the coat, he realized, still on the garden floor. "I cannot credit it, Charles. Have you no concern for your own consequence? And where is your sense of propriety— removing your coat in broad daylight, and worse, appearing in the house in your shirtsleeves! And I do believe you have torn your britches! I own I am quite shocked, Charles, at such unbecoming behavior!" she scolded, trying to keep her expression sober.

The Earl grinned devilishly at her, advancing several steps closer. He would have spoken, but that Victor appointed himself his defender. "Please do not scold Cousin Charles, Mama. He brought me down. Truly he did not mean to do anything wrong."

Amanda smiled down at the troubled little boy. "Very well, Victor, I won't scold, for indeed, I am very happy that he took you down." Amanda walked to the bell cord and pulled it before returning to Victor and bending down. "Now Victor, you must promise me that you'll not climb trees anymore. Not even to ride upon Zeus. 'Tis very dangerous, Victor. I do not want you to be bleeding and have broken bones. When you are much, much older we may discuss it again. But for now, no more trees. Do you promise, Victor?"

"Yes, Mama," said the boy very seriously. Amanda hugged her son, and in the next moment Mrs. Havenwick appeared. Amanda instructed her to take Victor to Nurse and to request that Nurse come to see her after dinner, for she would speak with her.

Victor took Mrs. Havenwick's hand and allowed himself to be led from the room, but not before he had once more grasped the tall Earl around his legs in the most fervent hug his little arms could manage.

When they had gone, Amanda turned concerned eyes to the Earl. "What really happened, Charles? Was he so very high up?" she asked quietly.

"Yes, he was," said the Earl bluntly.

Amanda turned very pale and she closed her eyes for a moment. "I did not quite believe him. Thank God you were there," she whispered, and then after a moment added, a sigh in her voice, "I suppose you are going to read me another lecture on Victor's need for a governess."

"No, I shan't, Amanda. The danger is as apparent to you as to me. I am persuaded that you will see that such incidents do not recur," he replied, smiling and taking a step closer to her.

"Charles, I—I am truly grateful to you. The gravity of the circumstance is such that I can hardly bear to think on it. And if you had not been there, Charles, I—"

"But I *was* there, Amanda. Do not torture yourself. He will not attempt such a thing again—he was duly frightened, I do assure you. And you know, Amanda, you have been entirely too grateful to me of late. I have already told you that I do not want your gratitude," he said, moving still closer.

Amanda took a step backward, and found herself flush against the wall next to the window. "Well then, what—what *do* you want, Charles?" she asked, somewhat distractedly, but then added, "No—I—pray do not—do not regard that question, Charles. I—"

"Why? Why shall I disregard that question, Amanda?" he asked, his voice very low, his eyes warm as he moved toward her until he stood not a foot away. "Could it be that you are afraid of the answer?"

"Please, Charles, I—" she began softly.

"I shall answer by telling you I want first for you to stop avoiding me, Amanda."

"Avoiding you? Whatever can you mean, Charles?"

"'Tis more than four and twenty hours, Amanda, since I have last seen you. That, I do assure you, was not by my design."

"I—I needed my rest, Charles," said Amanda, her eyes downcast.

"Can you not invent a Banbury tale with which you can look me in the eye, my dear?" he said smoothly.

Amanda colored slightly and he took her hands in his. "Amanda," he uttered, his voice low and caressing. She found her eyes lifting to meet his against her will. "Will you dine with me this evening?" he asked.

"Yes, Charles," she replied softly, and then suddenly recalling herself, added, "in—in the dining room."

He smiled that very devastating smile of his. "Very well, Amanda, since you are so well rested, I will own that perhaps you are ready for a trip below stairs. I shall escort you myself. Until dinner, then, my dear," he agreed, then raised one of her hands to his lips in a kiss that was much too lingering for her peace of mind.

After leaving Amanda, the Earl went to the gardens

to retrieve his coat. He did not send Darby, as he was certain that the poor man would have the apoplexy should he come upon his lordship's finely tailored woolen coat crumpled in a flower bed beneath the ancient oak tree. And he did not send a footman lest he or anyone else somehow glimpse the contents of the envelope resting safely in the inside left pocket.

As it was, Darby turned pale as he beheld his lordship in his shirtsleeves, muddy coat hung carelessly over one arm. He uttered his accustomed sigh of dismay at the sight of the once flawless brown Hessians which Darby had just this morning polished to perfection, now scratched and torn beyond hope. But the realization that his master's britches were indeed torn was too much for the good valet. "My lord, I must say, well, do forgive me, but not since you were a little boy have you come to be quite so—quite so—well—I do not know just *what* to say, my lord."

"Well, Darby," said his lordship, grinning, "that is undoubtedly because it is not since I was a boy that I have climbed some thirty feet into the highest boughs of an oak tree."

Poor Darby could not vouchsafe any reply at all, and the Earl felt truly sorry for him, for he would hardly be able to hold his head up in the servants' quarters when it became known that his master had been occupying himself that afternoon in climbing trees.

As if in reparation, the Earl permitted Darby to fuss about his evening's attire as much as he wished. No less than four white cravats were discarded before Darby considered that he had arranged one to do justice to the Earl of Ainsley. When Darby finally stepped back with a self-satisfied nod, the Earl glanced briefly at the results in the looking glass. Somewhat reluctantly, the Earl admitted to his valet that the extra care he had taken manifested itself. He wore an elegant coat of charcoal gray superfine, one of Weston's finest achievements, he thought. The many intricate folds of his cravat were accentuated by a small sapphire stickpin, and his dark brown hair framed his face in a most distinguished way.

Amanda seemed to eye him appreciatively when he presented himself at her door to escort her to dinner. She herself wore a black crepe evening dress, trimmed across the low-cut neckline with pale lavender rosebuds of satin. She moved very stiffly as they descended the stairs—whether because of her injuries or out of a desire to maintain her distance from him he could not know.

Dinner was superb. Cook had outdone herself with a stuffed goose with currant jelly, which served as a prelude to the roast loin of pork. For once the Earl had arranged to sit adjacent to Amanda, rather than at the far end of the table. No one seemed to take it amiss, the servants being even more discreet than usual in removing the various covers and then rapidly disappearing. Amanda had glanced his way for a mere second upon seeing the table arrangement, but chose to ignore it.

Conversation began on an amiable, if innocuous, note. They discussed how each had spent the day, the Earl carefully omitting the gist of his conversation with Windham and his trip to Shrewsbury. Amanda expressed the hope that the Earl had not injured himself recovering Victor. When at last he felt that the pleasantries had exhausted themselves, the Earl took a long sip of his wine and asked, "And did you receive my note this morning, Amanda?"

"Yes, Charles, I did. Surely you did not expect me to dignify it with a reply?"

"The idea had crossed my mind, I must own," retorted the Earl, smiling.

415

"I am not a coward, Charles. Indeed, 'tis naught to do with cowardice. I simply needed—need—time," she said calmly.

"Time for what?"

"Time to think . . . to heal. Physical wounds heal quickly. There are others—Charles, I simply cannot discuss these things with you. Do you not understand? And you must not—you must not look at me in that way, Charles," said Amanda in some desperation as the Earl looked at her with altogether too much warmth.

"'Tis not time to heal that you wish for, Amanda, but time to push it all from your mind. But 'tis never really forgotten, is it? No, for I have seen that haunted look in your eyes often enough to know. You are running away from it, Amanda. And that is called cowardice. And you cannot face me because I know, because I have seen and heard. And *that* is called cowardice," he insisted, putting his fork down, his slate blue eyes looking intently at her.

"No, Charles, no! I will not listen to this! You have no right to address me thus," she cried in anguish, rising abruptly from her seat.

"Sit down, Amanda," he commanded. "You shall not make a scene. And you shall not run away." When she complied, he continued more softly. "I cannot sit by and allow you to torture yourself with some misguided sense of pride. You have no reason to feel such mortification, Amanda. You have done nothing wrong. Your father has, but not you."

"Charles, please!" she pleaded, turning away from him. Oh God, what did he want of her? What was he doing to her?

"Amanda—will you turn away from me because of what I have seen and heard? Are you perhaps afraid that your esteem in my eyes has been lowered? Could it be that you think me as addlepated as all that?"

She turned back to face him. How did he always contrive to twist her words and make her appear foolish? "No, Charles. Of course, I—I do not think that of you. 'Tis just that I—I spoke to you of matters which I have never told—anyone," she said in a barely audible whisper.

"I am glad, Amanda. And there are many things I would say to you, which I have told no one, if you would but grant me the time," he said very gently, his eyes smiling.

She colored and felt tears spring to her eyes. He leaned over and squeezed her hand. "It is as I said, my dear. A shared burden carries half its own weight. Can you not understand that?"

"I—Charles, if you have finished your dinner, could we not adjourn to the Green Salon for coffee?" she asked rather breathlessly.

"But of course, my dear. Allow me to assist you," he replied smoothly, rising and pulling back her chair.

The Green Salon appeared stately in the muted light of the candles flickering in the brass sconces along the walls. A fire burned in the grate, so that the room was pleasingly warm. When the coffee had been served, the Earl seated himself in one of the green damask wing chairs adjacent to the sofa upon which Amanda now sat.

"As you have asserted several times most emphatically that you are *not* a coward, Amanda, I am persuaded that you will allow me to tell you that my London endeavor has been most successful," began the Earl. "It is my hope that Richard will be able to call upon Kitty within a se'nnight. And I am persuaded that you, my dear, will find a very warm reception awaiting you when next you venture to the metropolis."

"I have no desire to go to London, Charles," she said coolly. "Nor do I care to hear about—about your most recent visit."

"Running away again, Amanda?" he asked pointedly, placing his coffee cup onto the silver serving tray.

"I am *not* running away, Charles! The subject is most—distasteful to me. It—oh, dammit, Charles—I have told you before that I find the entire matter humiliating in the extreme. Why do you—"

"And again I tell you, Amanda, that you torture yourself with some misguided sense of pride. *You* have not the cause to feel humiliated, my dear, for you have done nothing wrong. If you will but permit me, I shall tell you who *has* in this case. I think you may be amused."

"Amused? I should think not, Charles. And I do assure you, I shall hear none of it. You chose to believe those rumors, and you chose to go flying to London to 'avenge' my good name. Well, I have never doubted my honor, and I shall not be fool enough to listen to this—this account of—of tale-bearing in London!" exclaimed Amanda, her eyes flashing in anger.

"I shan't apologize again for having believed those stories at the outset, Amanda. But that my—feelings—changed from the first I met you, I should not have to reassert. Or do you credit me with so little intelligence and so little understanding that you are certain I could not, upon coming to know you as I did, really see what kind of woman you are?" he said intently, leaning forward in his chair.

"It is maddening, Charles," countered Amanda, rising from the sofa and walking to the window, "simply maddening the way you constantly contrive to twist my words to make me appear so foolish!"

The Earl watched her move gracefully in her soft black evening dress until she stood at the window, her figure silhouetted by the moonlight. Then he rose and strode to her. "But you *are* being foolish, my dear.

Pride can be carried just so far, you know," he said, his lips curling in amusement.

"Oh, do not let us begin discussing pride, my dear Charles, lest I be compelled to read you quite a lecture on your own!" she exclaimed.

"Are you intimating, madam, that *I* have an excess of pride? Truly, you do malign me, Amanda. A man who tears his britches climbing thirty feet into a tree can hardly be accused of having an excess of pride!" said the Earl mockingly.

"No—well, in truth, I own I am quite sensible of the fact that you acted most—heroically, without regard to your own safety—or consequence," she admitted softly, her eyes lowered.

The Earl took a step closer to her and, taking her hands, said, "Let us say that I acted—sensibly, rather than heroically, shall we, my dear? Indeed, when I realized where Victor was, I could not have acted otherwise, could I?"

Amanda looked up at him and regarded him with narrowed eyes. Was this really the same man who had railed at her for climbing a tree to save the life of little Jimmy? How little she had known him then.

As if reading her thoughts, the Earl said, his voice caressing, "We must all, at some time, come to terms with our very aristocratic pride, mustn't we, Amanda?"

The Earl drew her closer to him and she found herself whispering, "Yes, Charles, I—I suppose we must."

"Amanda," he said, "are you feeling well enough to fulfill a promise that you made to me?"

"A promise?"

"Yes. You promised me another waltz. Have you forgotten?"

"No, I—that is—I shall be happy to dance with you, Charles." Oh, why had she said that? It was a mistake,

419

and yet, how could she not?

"Come then, my dear, do you recall the step? Yes, we begin thus, and thus," instructed the Earl, as he led her into the steps of the dance. He held her gently, lest she feel any pain from her injuries, but she seemed fine.

When they had gone once about the room, he pulled her closer, and her head came to rest upon his chest. "You do this very well, you know, Amanda. You will be the toast of London when next you make an appearance," he said lightly.

"Charles, you know very well I have no intention of making an appearance in London," she replied, picking her head up and looking him in the eye.

He advanced their pace a bit. "You will so disappoint the Ton, my dear. Do you know that all of London is agog with curiosity about you? The on dit circulating now has it that the scandalous stories about you were the work of a rejected suitor."

"Oh, no, Charles, you didn't!" she said, her mouth partially open, her eyes wide in disbelief.

"I? Plant such a faradiddle? Why, of course not. I do not gossip, Amanda. But I did have a little talk with a certain Dragon Lady—"

"The Dragon Lady? Lady—what was her name? Gresham? The Patroness? What had she to do with this?"

"Ah—so, I have piqued your curiosity at last, Amanda. I have worked very hard, my dear, so that your brother can marry my ward. But you, of course, have no interest in Lady Gresham, or London, or the disgruntled suitor who sought revenge."

"Very well, Charles. You have piqued my curiosity. Now will you please tell me what in the name of heaven all this is about? Tell me once, and then pray do not ever mention the subject again!" she said, a glint in her eye.

And so the Earl told her, in his most melodramatic tones, the story of the Dragon Lady and her two daughters, and exactly how Amanda, who had spent no more than a few short weeks in London in her entire life, had been, and still was, a favorite topic of drawing room conversation in London.

Amanda, to his immense relief, seemed relaxed in his arms, and though she was not exactly amused, neither was she horrified. "You are very clever, sir," she said at last.

"You are surprised, madam?" he countered.

"No, that is not at all what I meant. I—"

"At all events, my dear, I have another surprise for you. I visited Windham House today, as I told you. Windham and I spoke about his reclamation project. He suggested that we might be interested in purchasing the necessary equipment jointly with him. It seemed a sensible idea and so I accepted his proposal."

"You did what?" exclaimed Amanda, pushing away from him and terminating the dance, her eyes wide with fury.

"I agreed to share the cost of the machinery with him. I thought you would be pleased, Amanda. We shall drain the marshlands here at Millforte, after all. That is what you wanted, is it not?" he said, rather bewildered.

"I own that is much beside the point, Charles!" she snapped angrily. "You and Windham have conspired, without my knowledge, in a—"

"Amanda! We did no such thing!" said the Earl emphatically. "Windham happened to mention the matter and I agreed only because I knew your mind. Windham, I do assure you, has a great deal of respect for your judgment and capabilities. In truth, he said that he had meant to speak with us both simultaneously, but as you were indisposed and he eager to

421

embark on his drainage work, he bade me convey his offer. He invited us both to dinner next week to discuss the matter further. Indeed, I thought it most reasonable of him, and you, my dear, are being most *un*reasonable. You shall have exactly what you wanted. What cause then to fly into such a passion?"

Amanda eyed him narrowly for a moment before saying smoothly, "Well, I suppose I *shall* have what I wanted. I own I shall be most especially pleased to see the Low Cottages come down."

"The Low Cottages? I said nothing about the Low Cottages!" exploded the Earl.

"But they are a part of the marshlands. Surely—"

"The Low Cottages are another matter entirely, and well you know it! We shall discuss them at a later time," said the Earl, his brow furrowed.

"But—" began Amanda.

"Amanda!" shouted the Earl, and then extending his hand, said gently, "Dance with me."

She hesitated only a moment before taking his hand. He held her very close, and they began to dance more slowly than before. She relaxed against him, her head once more against his chest. He kissed the top of her head and then bent to kiss her ear.

He did not know how long they danced, moving ever so slowly, their bodies swaying together in perfect harmony. At one point he heard the door handle turn and from under half-closed eyelids saw Jeffries's stately form outlined in the doorway. The butler looked amazed for a moment and then smiled and silently withdrew. Amanda, happily enough, had not seemed to notice, and their dance continued uninterrupted.

Several times the Earl whispered her name into her ear, and she sighed contentedly. The candles eventually guttered in their sockets, yet neither had seemed to tire. The Earl had not meant to say what next he did, but there was little left to argue about, excepting those damned Low Cottages, and it seemed the most logical thing to do.

"Marry me, Amanda," he whispered into her ear as he held her tightly.

"Hmm?" asked Amanda dreamily, as if she had not heard.

"Marry me, Amanda," he said again.

Suddenly her head came up and she stopped dancing. There was a look of dismay in her eyes as she shook her head and whispered, "No, Charles. Do not ask me that." She tried to back away but he held her close to him.

"What do you mean, 'Do not ask you that'? Why not?" he demanded, his eyes narrowed.

"Because—because I cannot—marry you," she said quietly.

The Earl could not believe his ears. He did not understand this at all. "What do you mean, 'You cannot marry me'? Why can you not marry me, Amanda?"

"Please, Charles, do not ask me to explain. I cannot speak of it. I would it were otherwise, Charles, but indeed, I cannot marry you."

This could not be happening! The Earl felt as if he were having a nightmare. She was refusing him, yet he was completely confused, for despite Amanda's words, there was deep anguish in her eyes. And he knew she was not indifferent to him—her warm body against his all evening could tell him that, if nothing else did. What kind of terrible game was she playing?

"Amanda, you are not—still distressed over the nonsense in London—or—or anything else that happened between us?" he asked hesitantly.

"No, Charles. I am not so foolish as that. Please, let me go, Charles. It is no use, I tell you," she pleaded, trying to twist away from him.

"No, Amanda. I will not let you go," he said huskily bending to kiss her.

Amanda felt a sob rise in her throat. Oh, God. She wanted this man so much—to share his life, his bed everything. But if she gave in, she would never be able to live with herself. She would be tortured by guilt. She had to say something to make him back away, or she would be lost.

She pushed her head back and turned cold eyes to him, saying coolly, "No, Charles. I know that you are unaccustomed to being—refused in any way. And I am indeed sorry if I led you to believe that I—that is Charles—I—I cannot—marry you." With that she broke from his arms and backed away from him.

He was shattered. He had never felt more bereft confused, devasted. "Is—is that your final word Amanda?"

She nodded her head, and he thought her eyes were moist, but she said quietly, "I must go now," and silently walked from the room.

He stared at the closed door for a very long time unable to move, before he finally staggered up the great staircase to his room.

Chapter Twenty-Seven

The Earl spent a tortured, sleepless night. He arose rly and splashed cold water from the wash basin onto s face. One glance into the looking glass told him that e looked as haggard as he felt. He was distraught, to e sure, but he was also quite shaken. How could he ave been so mistaken in his assessment of her feelings? hat had gone wrong? He did not understand nything anymore; he knew only that he had no choice ut to leave Millforte straight away. Any business he ad to take care of with regard to the estates could be one by correspondence. It would simply be unbearle to remain here another day.

As such, when his valet appeared presently, he rdered him to organize his luggage, as he intended to ave Millforte before noon that very day. "Leaving, y lord? Leaving Millforte?" asked Darby, surprise in s voice.

"Yes, dammit. Is that so difficult to understand?" apped the Earl.

"No, my lord, of course not," answered the valet uickly. "Er—beggin' your pardon, but does your rdship mean to return soon?"

"No, dammit, I do not mean to return! Now, *if* you ave no further questions, Darby, I suggest you go own to see about my breakfast! I should like to

breakfast here in my room within the next half ho[...]
Are there any further questions, Darby?" barked [...]
Earl, in reply to which a red-faced Darby bowed a[...]
hurried from the room.

After breakfast the Earl, dressed in his travel[...]
clothes, made his way to the stables. He would not [...]
Amanda this morning, for he knew that there [...]
nothing else to say. But he felt the need to see the Vi[...]
before departing, for he feared for Amanda's safe[...]

He found the Vicar in his comfortable book-li[...]
study. "Ainsley, so good to see you! And how fa[...]
Amanda? Is she up to receiving visitors?" asked [...]
Vicar, rising from his chair and coming toward [...]
Earl.

"Amanda—does very well, I think," replied the E[...]
his tone flat. He took the comfortable leather chair [...]
Vicar indicated.

"Ainsley," said the Vicar earnestly, sitting acr[...]
from the Earl. "What is wrong? You do not look at [...]
well."

"I came to—to say good-bye, Trumwell. I am leav[...]
Millforte today," said the Earl impassively.

"Leaving? Are you called away again? When do y[...]
plan to return?"

"No, I have not been called away, and I—I have [...]
plans to return."

Trumwell's mouth fell partially open and his f[...]
looked distressed. "But I—I do not understa[...]
Ainsley," he said, his eyes searching the younger ma[...]
face.

"I beg your pardon, Trumwell?" asked the E[...]
mystified at Trumwell's curious reaction.

"Well—I—that is—I had actually expected you [...]
remain awhile."

"Oh? Why is that? My visit initially was to have be[...]
quite a bit shorter."

"Well, it—oh, dear. I suppose I had no right to say anything. Forgive me, Ainsley; I did not mean to meddle," said the Vicar uncomfortably.

"Trumwell, in truth, I have not the least notion of what you are talking about. Pray do speak plainly."

"Very well, Ainsley, perhaps I shall. But may I first procure for you some refreshment? You look as though you could do with some brandy."

"Nothing, please. Pray go on."

"Well, Ainsley, I had rather thought, as did Sally, and some others, actually, that you had—er—developed something of an affection for Amanda," said the Vicar, looking acutely embarrassed.

The Earl's brows came together and he stared intently at Trumwell for several moments. At length he sighed and said quietly, "I shan't deny it to you, Trumwell, although I own I am rather taken aback that not only you, but others—Trumwell, is it—so very obvious, then?"

"Let us just say that in these country villages, people do tend to be rather—observant."

"So I have noticed," remarked the Earl dryly.

"I do not mean to pry, Ainsley. If you would prefer not to discuss it—'tis just that I—that is—you do not appear particularly—happy at the moment, and I—"

"Trumwell, I own I have not slept at all. Pray, go on."

"Very well. I confess myself mystified by your departure, because it is equally obvious to me that Amanda's affections are most strongly engaged, and so—"

"But I fear you much mistake the matter, Trumwell," interrupted the Earl quietly.

"What are you saying?" said the Vicar, leaning forward in his seat.

"I, too, had thought—but—well, she has made it

plain that such is not the case." The Earl's face w
tense, his mouth barely moving as he spoke.

"But that is impossible! I cannot believe that s
would deny a feeling which is so plainly there. Forgi
me for saying this, Ainsley, but 'tis not just I who a
aware of the—affection—in which she holds you. O
need only watch her eyes light up whenever your nan
is mentioned," responded the Vicar.

"Nevertheless, I have made her an offer and been
refused," said Charles with much difficulty.

The Vicar eyed him narrowly. "Do you love he
Ainsley?"

"Yes, very much," said the Earl softly, rubbing l
brow with his hand.

"Have you told her that?"

"Trumwell, I have made her an offer. What furth
indication does she need?" asked the Earl, rising fro
his chair and beginning to pace the room.

"Oh, come now, Ainsley. Since when is lo
considered a prerequisite for marriage, particularly
men and women of your rank and station? So, you d
not tell her that you love her. And I assume she did ne
then, deny her feelings for you?" asked the Vicar, t
seeming impatience in his voice belied by the slig
smile curling his lips.

"Not in so many words, no," answered the Ea
suddenly feeling like a schoolboy being instructed
his tutor.

"I am persuaded, Ainsley, that for all of yo
sophistication, you know frightfully little abo
women. My dear Sally taught me something when
was but a callow young man. And that is that thou
there are many reasons why men and women marr
yet there is only one that brings them happiness. I ha
since seen enough to know that few people are
blessed. But to have such a mutual affection and

428

llow it to slip away—"

"Trumwell, she made it abundantly clear that my suit was—distasteful to her."

"And you walked away like a young boy rejected by the first woman he made up to? You accepted defeat where no statement of affection was yet made? Is this the dashing, debonair Earl that all England talks about, the one who for ten-odd years has squired the most elegant ladies of the land? You must forgive me, Ainsley, but I had not thought you such a coward."

At this last the Earl started. "I am no coward, sir," he said somewhat angrily, taking a stance at the fireplace. Then he added, hesitantly, "'Tis true that I made no mention of—of love, but she did not give me the opportunity to do so. The moment I mentioned marriage, she backed away from me, saying she could not marry me, nor tell me why."

"If that is the case, Ainsley, then something is sorely troubling her. My conjecture is that she is as distressed as you are at the moment," said Trumwell quietly.

"But then why in heaven's name will she not speak to me? What is she afraid of? What can possibly be standing in her way?" asked the Earl, much exasperated.

"I own I do not know, Ainsley, but I am persuaded that you know her better than I do by this time," said the Vicar.

The Earl felt himself color unaccountably, and the Vicar smiled faintly before he rose and walked to the sideboard, which contained a decanter of brandy and several glasses. He poured two glasses and walked over to the Earl, handing him one. "Here. You need it," he said.

The Earl took a large swig of the drink and Trumwell, facing him at the fireplace, continued. "I do recall Arthur saying that she had told him on several

occasions that she would not marry again. I know tha
disturbed him very much."

"Now that I think on it, she once mentioned that t
me. When we first met. She had such a haunted loo
about her—as if she was afraid of something," reflecte
the Earl.

"What do you suppose that might be?"

"I don't know," began the Earl. "It cannot be that sh
is—afraid of men. That is—it has not seemed that she i
frightened in any way of me. And she has, of course
already been married. It is not as though—"

"No, no, of course. I do not think she was ever afrai
of men in the way that young girls sometimes are. Bu
Arthur made occasional references to her childhood
He never said anything specific, but I gathered that he
father was rather—cruel. It is often the case that
young girl assumes that all men, or most, are like he
father," the Vicar replied.

"But she is no longer a young girl. Surely she canno
think that I—" said the Earl, much distressed as h
thought of the Baron.

"No, I should think not. I merely repeat what Arthu
said. He spoke to me often, in the last year of his life, o
his wish for Amanda to remarry. He said he wanted t
include some provision in his will to encourage that. H
loved her very much. He was very kind to her, knowing
somehow that that was what she most needed from
him. But a woman needs more than kindness, and h
knew that, too," said Trumwell, placing his glass o
brandy on the mantel.

"Did she love him?" asked the Earl, quietly.

"Yes, she loved him. She was a loyal wife, and he
gentle husband. But she never looked at him the way
have seen her look at you. And her face never flushed a
the sound of his name, if that is what you wanted t
know," the Vicar answered, a soft smile on his face.

The Earl felt himself color again, and found that he was rather relieved by the Vicar's disclosures. He walked back to his chair and sat down. "Why do you suppose Arthur named me as he did, joint guardian with Amanda of Victor and the estates? I can understand that Victor might need a male guardian, but probably not until he is older. And the estates—well—she can manage them as well as any man. Surely he knew that."

"Yes, he did." The Vicar went to stand in front of the window.

"Well, then? Have you any idea?"

"Oh, yes, I have an idea, although Arthur never said so in so many words," replied the Vicar.

"Yes?"

"Arthur spoke of you to me a number of times. He followed your career. Even some of your—er—romantic attachments. He remembered you with a great deal of affection. He had seen you on and off until you came of age, I gathered."

"Yes, somehow after that our paths crossed rarely," the Earl recalled.

"Arthur was much distressed over the estrangement between your families. But, if you will forgive me, he attributed it for the most part to his sister. He had a great deal of respect for you, and he did not wish to leave Amanda without any—man to turn to, if need be. Had he not named you as he did, the two of you might very well never have met."

"What are you saying, Trumwell?"

The Vicar sat down again and faced the Earl, looking him squarely in the eye. "It is purely conjecture, Ainsley. Arthur intimated certain things, 'tis true, but—"

"Nevertheless, you are saying that Arthur may have desired circumstances to—"

431

"I am saying that he thought it a distinct possibility," replied the Vicar.

The Earl was pensive for a moment, and then said, "That seems rather farfetched, does it not, Trumwell?"

"In many ways he was like a father to her. It is not unusual for fathers to choose, by virtue of a provision in their wills, a husband for their daughters. Arthur did not choose; he merely—set the stage, shall we say."

The Vicar's last statement brought the Earl up short. He recalled that when he'd first met Amanda, he'd thought she was enacting some role in a script she herself had written. How ironic that instead they had both been players in a drama of Arthur's design. He was not at all sure he cared to enact someone else's script, but nevertheless, he grudgingly admitted to himself, Arthur had been a good judge of character.

He smiled slightly at the Vicar and stood up. "If that is the case, Trumwell, then I am persuaded that the final act is yet to be played," he said smoothly, moving to shake the Vicar's hand. Trumwell rose, a warm smile on his face.

"Will you be here later today, Trumwell?" the Earl asked, somewhat abruptly.

"Why, yes, of course," said the Vicar, his eyes curious.

"Good. I shall be returning," stated the Earl emphatically, as he turned and strode from the room.

The Earl felt immensely relieved, even lighthearted, as he rode home from the vicarage. But at the same time, he began to feel rather angry at Amanda. How dare she put him through a night of hell such as he had never known before! And for what? He would learn the reason, straight away, even did he have to wring her neck to do it!

As he galloped to the front entrance of Millforte, he beheld Darby supervising the strapping of several of

432

his portmanteaux onto his carriage. He dismounted and handed his reins to one of his grooms standing about. "Take that luggage down, Darby," he commanded, his brows knit together.

"But, my lord, did you not say—"

"Darby, have my luggage put back upstairs where it belongs. Is that clear?"

"Yes, sir," said the valet, and the Earl turned to see Jeffries, standing in the open doorway. The butler's brows shot up for one moment, and then he favored the Earl with a very un-Jeffries-like grin before following him into the hallway.

The Earl yanked off his hat and gloves and tossed them onto the trestle table. "Where is she, Jeffries?" he asked menacingly.

"In the Green Salon, my lord," said the butler, his countenance returned to its usual impassivity.

"Good. See that we are not disturbed!" the Earl barked, and dashed up the stairs, taking two at a time.

She was sitting, very still, in one of the green damask wing chairs as he quietly entered the room. He could see the profile of her face as she stared at the fireplace. He did not think she had heard him, for she did not move, but then she said, her voice very flat and low, "What is it, Jeffries?"

"I beg your pardon, madam!" said the Earl forcefully, striding toward her.

"Oh! Charles," she gasped, turning red eyes up to him as he stood before her. She was wearing the same black dress that he had first seen her in. The Belgian lace at the neck and cuffs, as before, accentuated the look of dignity she always bore. Her hands were folded in her lap, a handkerchief clasped between them.

Presently she turned her head back to stare at the fire. "I had thought you would be gone," she said without expression.

433

"Is that what you want, Amanda?" he asked earnestly.

She rose and walked to the fireplace, her back to him. "Have you forgotten something, Charles?" she said, almost nonchalantly.

"Yes, Amanda, I have." He moved to stand directly behind her. "I have forgotten," he began gently, putting his hands on her shoulders and turning her to face him, "I have forgotten to tell you that I—I love you very much, and I—I find that I cannot bear the thought of living my life without you." His voice was tender and his warm eyes searched her face, his hands still on her shoulders.

Her eyes filled with moisture and she shook her head. "Oh, Charles," she whispered, twisting away from him and turning her back.

The Earl was beside himself. What more did she want? "What is it, Amanda?" he asked softly.

She wrapped her arms about herself and shook her head. "You should have gone, Charles."

He could not take much more of this. This time he put his hands roughly upon her shoulders and twirled her round. "Dammit, Amanda, I'll not leave here until you look me in the eye and tell me that you do not in any way return my—my regard!" he fairly shouted.

"Please, Charles," she said pleadingly, tears beginning to roll down her cheeks even as she turned her head aside.

He grabbed her arms by the elbows and shook her. "Look at me! Look at me and say it, Amanda!"

The tears streamed unheeded down her face as she looked up at him. "Charles, you do not know what you are doing. I cannot—I cannot marry you," she said, almost sobbing.

"That is not what I asked you, Amanda," he said huskily, pulling her closer. "I want to hear you say it, Amanda!"

"I—I—cannot," she sobbed, and in that moment he crushed her to him and enfolded her in his arms. There was nothing gentle about his kiss. It was fierce, even angry, with all of his passion unleashed. He kissed her long and hard, tasting the salt of her tears.

She did not try to resist. Her hands moved to hold him tightly about the back of his neck, pressing his face to hers. Her body molded to his and she kissed him with an intensity to match his own. Yet the tears came unchecked, as if she was releasing, simultaneously, the pent-up passion and emotion of all the past weeks.

He pulled at the pins in her hair until the thick locks cascaded down her back. He wound his fingers through her hair, and he kissed her neck, her eyes, her chin. Amanda moaned softly and he sought her lips again.

It was some time before the Earl picked his head up just enough to say, in a voice heavy with passion, "Now, I wish to know, Amanda, why you persist in this nonsense about not marrying me. I warn you, I shan't release you until you tell me."

"Oh, Charles, I cannot deny my feelings, 'tis true, but I—I would be consumed with guilt should we marry. You see, I feel so disloyal," she said in a barely audible whisper.

"Disloyal? To whom?" asked the Earl, mystified, as he loosened his hold upon her somewhat.

"How very right you were, Charles, that day we toured the estates. Arthur was so good to me and I—I—am just like Guinevere."

"Guinevere? What are you talking about, Amanda?" asked the Earl, momentarily dropping his arms.

"Do you not recall when you likened me to Guinevere? Do you not see, Charles? You are Lancelot, brought here by Arthur himself, and we've—we've—"

"We've what, Amanda? Come to love one another?

435

And that is disloyalty to Arthur?"

She nodded through the fresh tears that had begun to fall. The Earl closed his eyes with an inward sigh of relief. It was inconceivable that one ill-chosen and long-forgotten remark had almost cost them both a lifetime of happiness. He smiled warmly and took her in his arms again.

"My dearest, I am persuaded that you have failed to see a rather basic flaw in your rather interesting analogy. Arthur Millforte is *dead,*" he said emphatically.

"Oh, Charles, but I am yet in mourning," Amanda said, looking up at him through still-moist eyes.

"You are in half-mourning, my love. Do you not think that Arthur would have wished you to marry again?"

"Yes, he—he spoke of it many times."

"Well, then?"

"But not—not so soon, Charles. And his own nephew! Why 'tis practically—incest!"

"You have been reading too many Greek tragedies, Amanda. It is no such thing, as you know full well. My remark, that long-ago day, for it does seem a very long time ago, was unkind to say the least. I pray you will put it from your mind. No one questions your love or your loyalty to Arthur. But you are a young woman and you must live your own life now."

"I know that, Charles, but—"

"Amanda, Arthur was not, if I recall, in any way a fool. Do you not think he—knew what he was doing?"

Amanda tilted her head and looked at him with narrowed eyes. "Whatever do you mean, Charles? You cannot think that he—that he intended—"

"You must own that 'tis a possibility. You certainly did not need me to run the estates for you," replied Charles, grinning.

Amanda disengaged herself from his arms and sat down upon the sofa. "No, and I confess that I was rather mystified as to why he—that is, I have not thought about it of late, but at the beginning, I wondered why Arthur—" She stopped, suddenly rising, and went on. "Charles, he once said he would make some provision in his will to ensure my protection from—from my father. You do not suppose—oh, but 'tis hardly credible . . ."

"But not impossible, Amanda," said the Earl, coming toward her.

"No, I suppose not," agreed Amanda.

The Earl took both of her hands in his. "Last night I asked you a question to which I received a most unsatisfactory answer. I ask it again. Will you marry me, Amanda?" he said, his eyes smiling and his voice strong and confident.

Amanda looked up into his eyes and searched his face. Was he right? Would Arthur really have approved, perhaps anticipated this?

She gently pulled her hands from his and walked to the large window overlooking the front drive. She stared out without seeing. Charles was right, she told herself. Arthur was gone and she must live her own life. She had been a good wife to Arthur and now it was time to move on. Suddenly her eyes focused on the scene below her. The Earl's carriage was being unloaded, his portmanteaux carried back into the house. Charles must have ordered it done before he came in to see her. So sure of himself, was he?

She turned to face the Earl, who was watching her bemusedly. There was a gleam in her eye as she spoke. "Well, Charles," she said slowly, beginning to pin her disheveled hair back into place, "there are several, shall we say, impediments to our marriage."

"Such as?" he asked, much amused as he sauntered

toward her.

"Such as your mother. I am persuaded that she will like me even less as a daughter-in-law than she did as a sister-in-law."

"My mother has been afraid of but two things in her life. One was my father's temper. The other is mine. Are there any other impediments, my dear?" he asked, very close to her now.

"Well, yes. There is the matter of Millforte. You will wish us to spend most of our time at Ainsley Court, which I well understand. But I cannot totally forsake Millforte, you know," she said.

"Nor should I wish you to. I fully understand, and admire, your commitment to Millforte. I own I myself have grown quite fond of it, and of the people here. I am determined that we must spend several months here every year. I think it important for Victor as well. I would not wish him to be a stranger to his own land. And this way you can watch the progress of your blasted marshlands," said the Earl amiably.

"I should like that very much, Charles," replied Amanda, placing her hands on the lapels of his coat. "I am truly happy you have decided that we may drain the marshes, and I am persuaded that now you will not contemplate felling the beautiful orchards."

"Very well, my dear, we shall leave the orchards just as they are," he conceded, grasping the lovely white hands resting on his chest.

"And now, Charles," she continued, "there is just one thing more."

"Yes, my love?"

"It would be such a simple matter, as part of the reclamation work, to tear down the—"

"No, Amanda," he said strongly, tightening his hands on hers.

"But Charles, how can we allow people to live in

misery when we have the power to change things? Truly, it cannot be that costly. And with the increased revenues we may hope to see as a result of the drainage project, why, it shall hardly set us back. Charles, do you not—"

"Amanda, I am proposing marriage and you are conducting a business discussion. Is this the way it is always to be in our more—tender moments?" he asked in mock anger. Amanda colored and let her body sway to his.

"No, of course not, Charles. 'Tis just—"

"Oh, very well, Amanda, we shall tear down your infernal Low Cottages! But do you remember this. Millforte may belong to your son, but you are not to make any major decisions or changes without my prior knowledge and approval. Is that clear?" he said as sternly as he could with Amanda's body pressed against his.

"Yes, Charles," she said demurely. "And Charles?"

"Yes, my love?"

"If we have a son," she asked softly, her eyes downcast, "Ainsley Court will go to him, is that not correct?"

"Yes, of course, Amanda," he replied, smiling as she looked up at him.

"Well then, Ainsley will belong to your son, but you must not make any major decisions or changes without my prior knowledge and approval. Is that clear?"

"Why you incorrigible, managing female! 'Tis not the same thing at all, and well you know it."

Amanda pulled away from him, saying, "I see. Then you, of course, shall be involved with Millforte but Ainsley shall be your province solely."

"I did not say that," he said, suddenly annoyed.

"But you implied it. What shall be my province at Ainsley? To decide the color of the draperies? To prepare the dinner menus? I shall expect to do those, naturally, but I own I am used to a good deal more stimulation than that!" she exclaimed, those beautiful sea green eyes flashing.

"Very well, my dear. I shall go through every blasted ledger with you, at Ainsley and Surrey and every one of my—*our* homes, and make you sit through endless meetings with agents and bailiffs and secretaries. However," he said, his voice suddenly low as he took her hands, "I must confess that I was hoping to—stimulate you—in quite another way. And I am still awaiting an answer to my question."

Her color was high as she said calmly, "I shall be honored to marry you, Charles."

He traced his fingers down the side of her face and over her mouth. Then he kissed her very gently on the lips. "I shall make you very happy, Amanda," he whispered.

"Oh, Charles," she said softly. "I—I love you so much. Six months shall seem an eternity."

"Six months?" He blinked in surprise, stepping back.

"Well, not quite six months, but until the year is up. We cannot marry while I am in mourning. I would it were otherwise," she said, turning to look out the window again.

He began to pace the floor. Six months? How was he to talk her out of that?

"Six months! Amanda, if you think I—" he began rather forcefully, but checked himself, took a deep breath, and said in quite another tone, "Very well, Amanda." He came toward her and put his hands on her shoulders, her back to him. He moved very close and whispered into her ear. "You are right. 'Tis the only appropriate thing to do."

He slid his hands slowly up and down her arms and kissed the back of her neck. "I can wait if you can,

Amanda," he whispered, and then proceeded to nudge away her hair and gently nibble at her ear.

Amanda said nothing, but he felt her body sway. Finally, she said in a rather hoarse voice, "There is no other way, is there?"

He turned her round to face him, still holding her. "My dear, you have had three spurious, shall we say, accidents inside of a very short space of time. There is no one in all the county who would question your need for protection, nor will there be anyone the least bit surprised that you are marrying *me*."

"There won't?" She stepped back and out of the circle of his arms.

"Er—no," he said, smiling warmly. "It would seem that everyone but us has been expecting it for some time now."

"Who told you that?" she asked quietly, walking to the sofa and sitting down.

"Trumwell. I'm sorry, my dear, but apparently, well—I believe we are quite the last to know." He sat down next to her.

"Oh," she said, as if trying to digest this information. "Well, then, I suppose we must post the banns. How long will it take?"

"The whole process? Several weeks at least. Unless, well, unless one has a special license," he said softly, taking her hand in his.

"And how does one go about obtaining one?" she asked, swallowing hard as he put her hand to his mouth and kissed the palm and then each finger, slowly.

"One must have very powerful friends," he said, pulling her to him so that her head rested on his chest. He held her with one hand and stroked the top of her head with the other.

After several minutes she said, "And then how long does it take?"

"Oh, under an hour," he murmured, still holding he

"An hour!" She sat upright and looked him square
in the eye. "Why, Charles, I do believe you have g
one with you at this very moment!" she exclaime
jumping up from the sofa.

He grinned rakishly and stood also. She was furiou
How long ago had he procured that license? Sh
thought of the carriage being unloaded, of the clothin
probably all neatly in place again by now. For som
reason she remembered, too, his agreement wit
Windham to purchase equipment for the marshland
How dare he take so much for granted!

"Why you arrogant, overbearing, presumptuous—
so sure of yourself, were you?" She grabbed a velve
pillow from the sofa to throw at him, but he caught he
arm and twisted the pillow away. She struggled and h
pushed her down onto the sofa, falling right on top o
her, her hands pinioned at her sides.

"If ever I were too sure of myself," he said in a husk
voice, "the hell you put me through last night has cure
me. Now, if you do not stop these silly tantrums, I sha
make a wedding ceremony quite irrelevant! Now, ther
do we wait six months or do we make use of the l
cense resting at this very moment in my coat pocket?

"The license," came a weak voice.

He kissed her brow and picked himself up. He hel
out his hand to her and helped her to stand. She looke
delightfully disarrayed.

"I believe the Vicar awaits us, my dear."

"What—now?" she said, seemingly amazed as sh
smoothed her skirts.

"Must we go through all this again? Yes, 'now'! D
you know of a better time?" he exclaimed, exasperate

"No, I—I suppose not. But—but—just like that?"

"Just like that. Do you wish to have anyon
accompany us—Mrs. Havenwick, perhaps, or sha

we—surprise them all?" he suggested, grinning mischievously.

"You would like that, wouldn't you, Charles?" she said, smiling.

"Everyone has seemed so—sure of us. I have endured a good many all too knowing glances of late. I should rather enjoy presenting them all with a fait accompli. What say you, Amanda?"

"Yes, let's. But I do need to change my dress. I cannot very well get married in black. And my hair!" she said, hastily trying to pin some of the wayward curls back into place.

"Here, let me help you," he said, moving behind her and helping her to pin the locks back into some semblance of order. "We cannot very well have you running through the corridors looking like—like we've been doing what we've been doing, now can we?" he whispered.

Then he kissed the back of her neck and, turning her round, said sternly, "I give you twenty minutes, madam. Not a moment longer."

She was blushing furiously as she whispered, "Yes, Charles," and hurried from the room.

Chapter Twenty-Eight

Charles smoothed his own hair and coat before leaving the room. He went in search of Jeffries, for he wished the carriage brought round, and he had other instructions besides for the good butler.

It was just under twenty minutes when Amanda met him in the main hall. She wore a sarcenet dress of deep mauve, with ivory lace, the color of her skin, covering most of the bodice. On her head was a lovely small brimmed hat in the same mauve fabric, a plume of ivory ostrich feathers draping gracefully down to her right shoulder. She looked elegant and enticing all at once, and his blood raced as he escorted her to the waiting carriage.

The Vicar was not at all surprised to see them, and had apparently already enlisted his wife and Annie, the Trumwell maid, as witnesses. Sally Trumwell blew her nose several times into a handkerchief as the marriage vows were exchanged, but Amanda was dry-eyed and radiant.

The Trumwells drank their health when the ceremony was over, and it was but a short time later that they were once again approaching the circular drive at Millforte.

The Earl drove the carriage round to the back of the house, and stabled the horses himself. Amanda stared at him curiously but he said nothing. He walked her to the front of the house and escorted her inside. She looked about her for a moment, as if searching for someone. He drew an envelope from his coat pocket and placed it on the trestle table. Then he removed his hat and gloves. Amanda began to walk toward the back of the house.

"Where are you going, Amanda?" he asked.

"Why, to find Mrs. Havenwick. To procure some luncheon. Are you not hungry?"

"Come here, Amanda," he commanded. When she complied, he put his arms around her.

"I am very hungry, my dear," he said huskily, "but luncheon can wait."

She blushed and whispered, "Please Charles, not here."

"Oh, definitely not here," he said, grinning, and disengaging his arms, took her hand and led her up the great staircase.

He led her into her room and closed the door behind them. She walked to the center of the room and turned to face him. "Charles, what can you be thinking?" she asked, rather incredulous.

"Exactly what it is logical to be thinking at a time like this," he said smoothly, moving toward her.

"But Charles, 'tis the middle of the day," she protested, taking a step backward.

"I am aware of the time, Amanda," he said dryly, advancing closer to her.

"But Charles, the servants!" she exclaimed.

"What servants? Have you seen any servants?" He grinned and took another step toward her.

She moved backwards again, until her back came almost to the wall. "No, no I haven't, now I think on it. The stables were empty, and Jeffries—Charles, where is everyone? Victor, Mrs. Havenwick—'tis very quiet here. Where can they all be?"

He strode to her, saying nonchalantly, "I own I cannot say for certain, but I do believe they have all gone on a picnic."

"A picnic?"

"Yes, a picnic," he said slowly, untying her bonnet and tossing it onto a nearby table. "You know, with baskets of fruit and cheese and—"

"Yes. I *know* what a picnic is, Charles. But why— why have they—gone on a picnic?" she asked somewhat hesitantly as the Earl began to pull the pins from her hair.

"I am sure I could not say, Amanda."

"Are they—all gone, Charles?" she asked softly.

"All, Amanda," he said, pulling the last few pins and watching her hair tumble down her back.

"You—you arranged this, did you not, Charles?" she asked nervously.

"I? Whatever gave you that idea?" he countered, his tone ingenuous as he took one of her hands and began kissing each finger, slowly.

"We are all—alone—then, are we not?" she breathed, her face flushed.

"Quite alone, my love. This is our wedding day. How much company do you want?"

"None, of course. I did not mean, that is—" she stammered, her face very red by now.

"Amanda," he interrupted, kissing the palm of one hand and then beginning on the other, "would you like to go to Spain for our wedding trip?"

"Oh, Charles, I should like that above all things!" she exclaimed. "But—but does it not hold—unpleasant memories for you?" she continued hesitantly.

He smiled, touched by her concern. "We shall make new memories, Amanda," he said, and kissed her eyes and her chin. He put his arms around her and pushed er to the wall with his body.

"Charles, the servants—what will they—think when they—return? We shall cause a scandal," she said rather breathlessly as he began to kiss her neck and her earlobe.

"They will think what they damned well please," he mumbled, adding, "and besides, I left the marriage papers on the front trestle table."

"You did what? Charles, how could you—"

"You would prefer the scandal?" he blurted, picking his head up, somewhat perplexed.

"No. I—that is—"

"Amanda," he breathed, running his hands softly down her sides, "I am beginning to think I've married a magpie."

"Oh no,Charles, but—there is one thing more."

"Yes?" His hands began to explore her body.

"Well, the village is still in mourning. We cannot hold a full celebration. But must we not at least—hold —dinner—for the servants? It is customary, is it not?" he asked, even as she swayed beneath his touch.

"They are having their celebration now."

"But they do not know—what—it is for," she said, her voice growing husky.

"They'll figure it out," he muttered, and then his mouth sought her lips. He pressed her against the wall as he kissed her, his mouth demanding, his hands seeming to sear the fabric of her dress. She put her arms about his shoulders and he felt her quiver against him.

At length he moved her slightly away from the wall in order to reach the buttons at the nape of her neck. He kissed her neck and her hair as he fumbled with the buttons.

"Amanda," he said, his voice heavy, "you will immediately replenish your wardrobe with dresses, and nightgowns, of no more than three buttons each! Is that clear?"

"Quite clear, Charles," she whispered, her face pin
as her hands stole to his chest to unbutton his coa
When she had succeeded, she put her hands inside th
coat and around his back.

He kissed her again on the lips, his mouth searchin
hers hungrily, and he felt her knees weaken as she fe
toward him. Suddenly he pulled away from her an
said nonchalantly, "You are quite right, Amanda. W
must immediately go down and see about a weddin
dinner for the servants. 'Twould not be seemly—"

"Charles!" she fairly shouted, quite horrified.

He grinned rakishly, saying, "Just wanted to be sur
of you, Countess. Just wanted to be sure."

Then he picked her up and carried her to the bed

"Countess?" she echoed, when he'd placed her gentl
upon the coverlet. "I had not thought of it; I suppose
am a Countess, am I not?" She smiled up at him
winding her arms around his neck.

He thought of the dozens of eager young wome
over the last ten years who, hardly caring for him at a
had fallen at his feet for the privilege of having that titl
bestowed upon them. And here was this woman, hi
bride, who had never even realized—had not eve
cared—that the title came with the man.

"Yes, you are my Countess," he whispered, an
thought he was the happiest man in all England as h
bent to make her his wife.